Donovan's Brides

by

Pepper Durcholz

The Wild Rose Press, Inc.
PO Box 708
Adams Basin, NY 14410-0708
Visit us at www.thewildrosepress.com

Publishing History
First Edition, 2025
Trade Paperback ISBN 978-1-5092-6233-5
Digital ISBN 978-1-5092-6234-2

Published in the United States of America

Dedication

I want to dedicate this book to the members of Word Wranglers Workshop without whose help and urging, Donovan's Brides might still be under the bed, so to speak. Thank you so much.

Prologue

Pineville, Missouri—January 1868

Millie Watts took hold of Reverend Potter's hand as she climbed down from the buggy. Tucking a wisp of blonde hair beneath her black mourning hat, she looked at the lovely little cottage she'd shared with her aunt for the last three years. The crisp breeze gently swayed the porch swing. The roses planted on each side of the front steps would bloom in a couple of months. Everything was as she'd left it this morning. Yet, without Aunt Lavinia, nothing would ever be the same again.

She brushed a tear away before turning to Reverend Potter. "Would you please greet the neighbors and give me a few minutes before bringing them in?"

"Certainly, Miss Millie, you go right ahead."

She walked slowly up the steps. Millie had always known this house would be hers someday, but she hadn't expected it to be so soon. Inside, she caught a glimpse of a sampler on the far wall. Red and blue letters lovingly stitched by Aunt Lavinia proclaimed *Home is Where the Heart Is.*

She shut the door and, leaning against it, closed her eyes, trying to absorb all the love she'd known these last years.

Something wasn't right. The odor of liquor permeated the air.

An all-too-familiar voice shattered what little peace remained. "Didja git the ol' biddy planted?"

Millie's eyes flew open. She glared at the man slouched on the pink brocade loveseat, his dirty boots propped on the newly covered tapestry stool. He guzzled whiskey straight from Aunt Lavinia's square cut-glass decanter.

"Pa! What are you doing here?"

He took another loud gulp from the decanter, then wiped his mouth with his sleeve. "What's it look like I'm doin'? With the ol' crone gone, this place's all mine."

Millie drew herself up to her full five feet five inches. "It most certainly is not! It's mine." She stepped closer, jerked up his feet by the pant legs and slid an old newspaper beneath them. Aunt Lavinia had called Pa trash and wouldn't even allow him in the yard, much less inside the house. She must be turning over in her grave.

"Well, it's all the same," he said. "You're my lovin' daughter. What kind of pa would I be iffin I didn't move in and pur-tect ya from all them saddle tramps out there wantin' your inheritance?" He took another swig. "Not that anyone'd want a skinny bitch like you."

Rolling her eyes heavenward, Millie returned to the fireplace. Her hands shook as she added another log to the fire. He was the one after her inheritance, but it was no use talking to Pa when he was like this. He could be dangerous when drunk. After he passed out, she'd find someone to carry him to his shack at the edge of town.

He belched loudly and Millie shuddered. She stared in horror as the empty decanter tumbled from his hand onto the loveseat and rolled toward the edge. She snatched it up before it hit the floor and hugged it to her breast. Thank goodness it hadn't broken. Was nothing sacred to the man? Aunt Lavinia had given this decanter set to Uncle James shortly before his death. Millie placed it gently back on the table.

Pa stretched. "Soon's those nosey ol' biddies and their hen-pecked husbands leave, git Lavinia's junk outta the front bedroom. I'm movin' in there."

Millie whirled to face him. "You'll do no such thing. If you stay here at all, you'll take the room off the kitchen."

"Off the kitchen?" he growled. "That's the servant's room."

"It...it has a private entrance."

He glared at her. "I ain't goin' in and outta no back doors. I'm takin' the front room."

"No, you aren't. This is my place now. I don't want you here at all."

He jumped up from the loveseat and, before she could blink, was across the room and slapping her across the cheek. "Don't sass me, girl!"

She staggered backward against the hearth. He reared back to strike her again. Millie grabbed the poker and raised it threateningly. "If you ever hit me again, so help me, I'll kill you!" He had beaten and abused Ma for years, until the day she died. But he certainly wouldn't beat her. If nothing else, Aunt Lavinia and Uncle James had taught her she didn't have to put up with that. Still, she shook all over as she tightened her grip on the poker. "I'll...I'll do it, so help me, Pa."

At the squeak of the front door hinges, Pa jerked around. Reverend Potter stuck his head inside, glared at the man threatening Millie, and then stepped boldly into the room. Without taking his gaze from the man, he spoke to her. "Miss Millie, the neighbors are here. Is it all right for us to come in now?"

Millie nearly swooned with relief when her pa dropped his hand and, without a word, shoved past the reverend and left the house.

Chapter One

Millie sat on the hard wooden bench fanning herself as she watched people congregating around the train station. The little sign saying *Independence, Missouri Train Depot* creaked lazily above the platform. The wind filled the air with dust and the overpowering smell of horses, but couldn't manage a simple cooling breeze.

She looked nervously from one corner of the platform to the other. Don't be such a ninny, she chided herself. Pa wasn't going to jump out and grab her. She'd be long gone before he found out where she was, if he ever did.

She leaned her head back against the wall, closed her eyes, and indulged in a small satisfied smile. She still couldn't believe she'd actually left like she had.

Much to Millie's surprise, Aunt Lavinia had sold all her properties, including the house. Millie was left very well off financially, but homeless. If she stayed in Pineville, Pa would take all the money. Aunt Lavinia must have known how sick she was, to have made these arrangements. Millie opened the circular she'd been fanning herself with and read it for the hundredth time.

BRIDES WANTED
For Meandering Valley, Montana Territory.
Hard-working Christian men looking for Christian women of marriageable age for wives.
All expenses paid.

*Women must be eighteen years old or older,
healthy, and willing to work beside the men
to make homes and raise families.*

She refolded the circular, then idly watched each man on the platform. Blake Donovan, the wagon master, must be here somewhere. Mr. Harkins, her aunt's lawyer, said Mr. Donovan would meet a Mrs. Hogan and about a dozen or so prospective brides coming in on the morning train. Three men standing to her left drew her attention.

The older man wore a dress suit and had dark gray hair around his balding pate. The second wore soft-looking Indian boots, a beaded knife scabbard on one hip and a handgun on the other. Though he had a white man's haircut, he wore a leather headband.

The third man looked about the same age as the Indian, maybe twenty-five or so, but stood a little taller. He was dressed like any other cowboy, except that his beaded knife scabbard matched the Indian's. His clean-shaven, rugged features, broad shoulders and narrow hips would make him stand out in any crowd. He looked competent. Most definitely like someone she'd hire, if she owned a ranch.

The Indian said something, and they all laughed. The cowboy's eyes twinkled. He had dimples! Millie's stomach fluttered. She looked away, not that she cared, of course. All men were trouble. The only thing she didn't like about this whole move to Montana was the idea of a husband at the other end, but she'd worry about that later. Right now, getting on the wagon train was her immediate goal.

She let her gaze move on, but quickly turned back as bits of their conversation drifted her way.

"My sister-in-law's one gutsy female," said the older man. "I don't know many men who'd travel across country with two dozen single women in tow, much less a woman."

Two dozen women? Surely there couldn't be more than one group like that. She swallowed and clasped her hands together to stop their shaking. One of these men must be Mr. Donovan, but which one? She'd laughed when Mr. Harkins said she could recognize him by the wide white streak in the middle of his dark brown hair. She'd pictured a skunk in western boots.

A train whistle sounded, and as everyone began gathering their things. Millie stood so she could see over the crowd. The cowboy removed his hat, exposing a white streak slightly off center on the right side of his head. "Well, I'll be," she muttered. "He certainly does look like a skunk." She tried to work her way toward him. However, the press of the crowd carried her in the opposite direction.

****

The train belched black smoke and jerked to a stop at the Independence station. Hannah Hogan groaned as she raised her ample figure off the train's seat and shook the wrinkles out of her brown skirt. Her muscles throbbed, and her head ached. One would think, with all her natural padding, that seat wouldn't feel so hard. But being cooped up in a train car for three days with a dozen chattering young women would give anyone a headache. She slowly worked the kinks out of her legs.

Someone dislodged a valise from the overhead rack. It knocked her hat askew and pulled her graying brown hair loose. "I must have been crazy to let my husband talk me into this," she muttered as she pinned her hair back in place, then re-settled her hat. She was responsible for these twenty-four women and at least as many more already waiting at her brother-in-law's ranch. When her husband wrote asking her to join him in Montana and to bring fifty prospective brides for the other men in the valley, she should have said no.

As she stepped off the train, Blake Donovan reached out to help her. "Good morning, Miss Hannah. I hope you had a good trip."

"Good? Blake Donovan, if I weren't a lady, I'd tell you exactly—"

"Hannah, it's about time." A smiling, slightly bald man of about forty shouldered his way to her side. "Aggie and the kids can't wait to see you."

"Jim!" She threw her arms around his neck. "It's so good to finally get here. I can't wait to see Aggie and those two little darlings of yours."

Jim Hogan led her toward the far side of the depot as Blake Donovan helped the other young women from the train. "Good morning, ladies. If you'll show me which bags are yours, then follow Miss Hannah, I'll see to your baggage," he said as he helped the last young lady down the steps.

He turned to look for the conductor, but bumped into a woman who stood so close she was almost in his hip pocket. He grabbed her upper arms while they both struggled to keep their balance.

As soon as he'd steadied her, he released her arms and stepped back. "Are you all right, miss?"

She nodded, jiggling the little black hat perched haphazardly on her head. "Are…" Taking a deep breath, she started again. "Are you Mr. Donovan?"

He shoved his hat back on his head. "Yes, ma'am."

"I came to join your wagon train—"

Blake inhaled sharply. "I'm sorry, miss, but we have everyone we can take."

The top of her blonde head barely reached his shoulder. Her eyes were the color of new pine needles. With a little more flesh on her, no, a lot more, she would be a nice-looking woman. Lord, he'd never seen such a skinny female. A good wind could blow her off her feet. He shook his head.

"Please, Mr. Donovan, you don't understand."

"Look, Miss—"

"Missus, Mrs. Millicent Watts. I'm a widow," she hastened to add.

He readjusted his hat. "Mrs. Watts, this is no pleasure trip. We'll travel for several months under very difficult circumstances, with no guarantee that everyone will make it."

He reached past her for some of the ladies' luggage that sat by the steps. His conscience stabbed at him a couple of times, but he saw no reason to let her go on hoping. She wouldn't last the first fifty miles. Too bad. She wasn't a bad-looking woman, but he'd purposely selected women on the hefty side, knowing they'd be skin and bones by the time they reached Montana. This girl was practically a skeleton already.

She stepped in front of him. "I know I don't look it, Mr. Donovan, but I'm strong and a hard worker, and Mr. Harkins said…"

Blake was about to refuse again, but a commotion at the other end of the platform drew his attention. A stocky, gray-haired man in dusty dungarees seemed to have taken an unwanted fancy to one of Miss Hannah's ladies.

"What in hell?" Blake excused himself and hurried to intercept the angry man.

"No! I won't go," the red-haired woman cried.

"Yes, you will. Jest wait 'til I git ya back home, gal. Your backside'll be smartin' fer a month!"

Blake stopped a few steps away from the two. "Hold it, Mister. This girl is promised. You'll have to look elsewhere."

The man stopped before Blake. He held onto the girl's arm and clenched his other hand into a fist. "Yeah? Sez who?"

Blake jammed his fists onto his hips. "Sez me. I'm in charge of these young ladies."

The man leaned close to Blake's face and tapped him on the chest with his finger. "Do tell? Well, this *young lady* is my daughter, and I'll have the law on ye fer stealin' her off!"

Blake slapped the man's hand away. "Hold on. Daughter or not, she's old enough to decide for herself."

The man tightened his hold on the struggling girl and glared at Blake. "Mister, fourteen ain't hardly old enough to decide to go to the privy."

"Fourteen!" Blake glared at the girl. "Is that right, Miss? Are you only fourteen?"

The girl stared at her feet and nodded. "Yes, sir."

"Hell, a blind man could tell she's jest a young'un," her father growled.

Blake looked hard at the girl. She had a baby face, but there was nothing babyish about the rest of her. He ran his hand over his face. It had never occurred to him to watch for children trying to get husbands. He still didn't think she looked that young.

The man stalked away with his sobbing daughter in

tow. "I ruint three good horses gittin' here, gal. Jest wait 'til we get ta home."

Swearing under his breath, Blake pulled his hat low on his head and glared at each of the women who had gathered around. Some had the bodies of women and faces of children and others the reverse. "All right, ladies, I'm giving you a chance to clear the air. Is there anything else I should know? I don't like surprises."

The prospective brides looked from one to another, but no one offered any further comments. Blake shook his head. When he turned to retrieve his gear, his nose hit the flower sticking up from Millicent Watts' silly little hat. She stood so close he should have felt her breath on the back of his neck. Damn it, he hated surprises—and being crowded.

Blake stepped back, stumbled over a piece of luggage and staggered, wildly grabbing for something to break his fall. His arm wrapped around a soft body as he fell backward. "Oof!"

He was wedged between two large crates and covered with…his eyes flew open…Millicent Watts. Her forehead rested against his chin, her body stretched full length upon his. Her knee was between his legs, exactly where no woman's knee should be, at least not in broad daylight, on a public train platform. When she tried to get up, her knee pressed against his groin.

Blake gasped as pain shot through him like a knife. Perspiration beaded his brow. He grasped her shoulders and held her tightly against his chest. "Dammit, woman, would you hold still?" he demanded through gritted teeth.

Millie's face burned as she averted her eyes. *Good Lord, not only have I turned into a clumsy ninny, but I'm lying on top of a man, in public.* Mr. Donovan's anger was evident and so was something else. She felt his body quickening beneath her. Before she could move again, two strong hands lifted her by the waist and set her on her feet.

Donovan scrambled to get up. "Sorry, ma'am, but you still aren't going."

Millie turned away, cheeks burning. She adjusted her hat, then looked at the man who had lifted her off Donovan. He was a stout older man with a graying, tobacco-stained beard. She smiled and tried to swallow her embarrassment. "Thank you, sir."

He tipped his hat. "Ye're welcome, Missy. The name's Oats, Ezra Oats." He turned and, while chuckling, extended a hand to Donovan. "Guess you're Donovan. Jim Hogan sent me. Said ya'd be the only dang fool herding a passel of she-males." He spit a stream of tobacco juice across the platform, and grinned. "I know being around all them wimmen can git to a man, but, honestly, young feller..." He lowered his voice. "Don'cha reckon ya could find a more pri-vate place?"

"Very funny," Blake grumbled as he retrieved his hat. Thanks to that Watts woman, he was already out of sorts. The last thing he needed was wisecracking from this tobacco-spitting old codger. "Did you bring transportation, or did you plan to float us out to Hogan's on hot air?"

"Touchy, ain't we?" Ezra snickered and picked up several pieces of luggage. "Wagon's over yonder." He led the way toward the east side of the depot.

Millie almost ran to keep up with them. "Mr. Donovan, Mr. Harkins said I could go, and I am going even if I have to follow you to do it, so you might as well accept it." He didn't respond, just kept walking. Millie hurried past him, whirled, and abruptly stopped between him and a wagon.

Blake stopped dead in his tracks, dropped a valise, then thumbed his hat back, shaking his head. "Look, lady, I don't know who this Harkins is, but you *are not* going. We purposefully chose stout women because this trip will be hard. By the time we arrive in Montana territory, those who survive will be skin and bones. You wouldn't have a chance. There's nothing for you to fall back on." He moved his hand up and down, indicating her slight figure. "The first time a breeze came up, we'd have to tie you to a wagon wheel to keep you from flying across the prairie like a kite."

She drew herself up and planted her fists on her hips. "Mister, I've been thin all my life. None of these women will ever go through half of what I've been through in my nineteen years, and I'm still alive. And I'll still be alive when we reach Montana territory. If the wind bothers you so much, I'll put rocks in my pockets."

He picked up the valises, brushed past her, and tossed both bags into the wagon. "No. Absolutely not! I don't enjoy burying women!" They glared at each other. There was no way this woman was going anywhere on his wagon train.

Ezra took Blake by the arm. "'Scuse us a minute, Missy."

He pulled the wagon master to one side. "Shoutin' at her ain't gonna do no good. That she-male done made up her mind, and you ain't gonna ar-gy her out of it."

Hannah Hogan joined them. "What's the trouble, Mr. Donovan?"

Thank goodness. Maybe Miss Hannah could talk

some sense into that crazy female. "That woman over there, the thin one, seems to think we're going on a picnic. She insists she's coming with us."

Hannah glanced at the young woman, then squeezed Blake's arm. "I'll have a talk with her." She drew her skirts close and carefully moved through the crates and luggage to the girl. "Hello. I'm Hannah Hogan."

"How do you do. I'm Millicent Watts from Pineville, Missouri. Our lawyer, Mr. Harkins, made the arrangements for me to be on this wagon train, but Mr. Donovan won't listen to me."

"Watts?" Hannah repeated thoughtfully. "I talked to a lawyer named Harkins a few weeks ago. He had a young woman named Watts that he wanted to get on our wagon train. If I remember correctly, he was trying to help the niece of a very ill friend. The woman was dying and wanted to make sure her niece was cared for." She looked thoughtfully at Millie. "You're the girl?" When Millie nodded, Hannah sighed. "Are you certain you want to do this?"

Millie nodded. "Yes, ma'am. I really don't have anyplace else to go."

Hannah exhaled again. "All right, I'll speak to Mr. Donovan for you." She walked slowly back to the wagon. He wasn't going to like this one little bit, but anyone who'd stand up to Blake Donovan, like this girl did, had grit. She'd be an asset to the town they were starting, if she survived the trip.

Blake stopped loading the wagon. "Well, did you put her straight, Miss Hannah?"

Hannah cleared her throat. "Not exactly. It—"

"What do you mean, 'Not exactly'? You did tell her no, didn't you?"

"I…tried, but it seems I made arrangements through her lawyer several weeks ago for her to go with us."

"What?" he fairly shouted. "You couldn't have. We agreed. *No thin women.* She won't make it across Kansas. There's so little meat on her, no self-respecting buzzard would even waste his time picking at her bones." He leaned toward Miss Hannah and lowered his voice. "She can't go," he repeated through clenched teeth.

Miss Hannah sighed. "I agree with you, but surely two weeks on Jim's place will change her mind."

Ezra scratched his bearded chin. "Shore, by the time we get them greenhorns teached and trail ready, we'll scare off more'n one, and I'm abettin' Missy there'll be one of 'em."

Blake rested his arms against the wagon side. He counted to ten, then glanced sideways toward Millicent, who had moved up almost to within earshot. Her expectant expression irritated him. Hell, everything about her irritated him.

Maybe Oats was right. If he couldn't talk her out of it, he could sure as hell work her out of it. Blake rested his head on his arm for a moment. He slowly wiped his forehead on his shirtsleeve. Finally, he straightened and faced her. "All right, you win. Get in the wagon."

"Thank you, Mr. Donovan, thank you." She turned and hurried down the street. "You won't be sorry, I promise," she called over her shoulder, then stepped on the hem of her skirt and stumbled briefly.

"The hell I won't," he muttered. He was sorry already.

"Where do you think you're going?" he yelled irritably.

"To get my wagon," she called back.

"To get your wagon." Blake muttered an oath. On the other hand, maybe she'd get lost.

Blake helped two young women into one of the three waiting wagons before climbing up beside Ezra and wondering again how he'd let himself be talked into this madness.

Chapter Two

They'd been traveling about an hour when the conversation behind him began to register.

"I can't wait to get there," he heard one woman say.

"All I want is a hot bath and a featherbed."

"I could sleep for a month," a third said with a sigh.

Blake shuddered. He was a cow man, not a sheep herder. That's what these women were, sheep, and he was beginning to feel like a Judas goat.

The wagons were lined with straw and a thick quilt for the girls' comfort. Someone at the ranch had erected a pole at each corner and stretched muslin across the top to afford a measure of shade. Despite this extra effort, by the time they'd been on the road two hours, the girls were grumbling.

"How much longer before we reach Montana, Mr. Donovan?"

Blake turned to glare at the woman, then groaned. Their belongings were squeezed in between them without any thought to comfort. No wonder they complained. He'd been so angry with Millicent Watts he hadn't noticed how cramped they were. Blake grimaced. "About three or four months, ma'am." Turning back around, he stared straight ahead and muttered under his breath, "If we're lucky."

"Ezra, pull up at Willow Crick. They can get some exercise while we repack these wagons."

They pulled up under a large tree beside a flowing creek. Blake jumped down, then immediately flattened himself against the wagon wheel as a two-wheeled cart almost ran over him. It creaked to a stop, sending swirls of dust everywhere. He coughed and tried to fan the dust away with his hat. He saw a flurry of black fabric drop from the cart. "We made it," said a familiar voice.

He wiped the dust from his eyes and groaned. "I might have known."

Millie caught hold of the cart's wheel for balance, then shook her skirt a couple of times, sending puffs of dust floating upward. "See?" she stated proudly, "I told you I could do it."

"Do what?" he gasped between coughs.

"Keep up." She pointed to her horse. "Dumplin' is a lot like me. We might not look strong, but we are."

"Dumplin'?" He looked around, then wiped his eyes and stared in horror. Looking back at him from under a tattered straw hat was the poorest excuse for a horse he'd ever seen. He stepped closer and ran his hand over the beast's swayed back, then down its hollow chest. The animal's head drooped as if he'd taken the last five miles at a dead run. Blake lifted the horse's head and checked its teeth, then rolled his eyes heavenward. The horse had to be at least twenty years old. "This bag of bones is Dumplin'? It'd be a kindness to shoot the poor creature and put it out of its misery."

Millie shoved past him and threw her arms around the exhausted beast's neck. "Don't you dare. I've had Dumplin' nearly all my life. He's family and perfectly capable of making it to Montana."

Blake stared at her "wagon"—a dilapidated old wooden hay cart. The left wheel had a large crack halfway to the hub. He doubted it'd last until they reached Hogan's ranch, much less Montana. "Are you out of your mind, woman? That thing isn't going any farther than our next stop. Neither is Dumplin'! You won't get five miles with that outfit."

She looked from her pet to the cart. Mr. Harkins had wanted her to replace the cart, but the circular said *wagons furnished*, so she'd decided not to spend good money on a wagon she might have to abandon. However it never crossed her mind she might have to leave Dumplin' behind. "But…but you said we could go."

Blake was hot, tired, and out of patience. He shook his finger at her. "I said you could go, but not in this…" he swung his arm, indicating her cart.

Before he could say more, a loud honking rent the air and a sound like sheets snapping in the breeze came from the top of the cart.

"No!" Millie screamed.

Something hit Blake between the shoulder blades, knocking him to the ground. He quickly rolled over, but was just as quickly hit on the side of the head. Bright lights and dark spots flitted back and forth before his eyes. He threw his arms up to protect his face from heaven only knew what, then swore when a large clump of hair was snatched from his head.

Blake ignored the yells and screams of the women, but as soon as he slapped at the attacker, Millicent was in the fight.

She screamed and hit him every time he tried to defend himself. He shoved her out of the way, then caught a glimpse of something coming at him. He reached out to ward it off, catching the monster by the neck.

They stared at each other, eye to eye. "A duck?" The biggest damned duck he'd ever seen.

It hissed and snapped at his nose. He squeezed the neck, only to receive a sound thrashing with its wings. He slung it away, then scrambled to his feet. Ezra and the scout, John Eagle, yelled encouragement, though it wasn't clear who they were encouraging. Blake crouched and braced for another attack. A feather floated down, landed on his nose, and he blew at it, turning this way and that. Where was that crazy duck?

The bird had circled around to attack from the rear, biting Blake's backside at the hip pocket. He yelped and whirled, protecting himself as best he could while fumbling for his knife.

Millie grabbed his arm. "Don't you dare," she screamed.

Cursing, Blake pushed her hard enough to send her tumbling to the ground. "Damn it, woman, get out of the way."

He pulled his knife, but saw nothing except a press of people as the women circled around him. "Get back before that damn bird hurts someone." He'd never heard of a duck going crazy, but evidently this one had.

All he saw were faces, streaked with tears of *laughter*. Ezra tried to talk, but could barely breathe between guffaws.

Finally, the old cowboy stepped back and pointed.

Blake looked in the direction the old cowhand indicated and did a double-take. Millicent was huddled under a nearby oak tree, fighting to hold on to a huge brown speckled bird. Ezra's deep-throated laughter drew Blake's attention from the girl and fowl. He was surrounded by a dozen tittering females and a wornout old coot, all weak from laughter. Even John Eagle seemed to be having a hard time keeping a straight face.

Blake turned his back on them, sheathed his knife, and walked menacingly toward the culprits. The bird hissed threateningly.

He stopped a few feet from Millie, trying to decide whose neck to wring first. Finally, he pointed toward the bird. "What is that?" he demanded through clenched teeth.

"A…a goose. A watch goose," Millie stammered.

"Yours?"

She nodded.

"Why did he attack me?"

"She. Honey's a she. I'm… I'm sorry, Mr. Donovan. She was only protecting me."

"Honey?" Blake threw his arms in the air and let them fall, slapping his thighs with his hands. "*Dumplin'*, and now *Honey*. Lady, do you have any more pets that I should know about?"

She hugged the goose closer and shook her head.

"Well, thank God for small favors!" He glared at her. "If that bird ever attacks me again, we'll have an early Thanksgiving."

Ezra shoved past the brides, who'd gathered around Millie and her pet. "C'mon, Donovan, ya've been at the little lady since the minute ya laid eyes on her." He slapped Blake on the back.

"Where's ya sense of humor?"

Blake angrily shrugged Ezra's hand away. "Sense of humor?" He backed the old cowboy up by jabbing him in the chest with his finger. "I was publicly compromised at the train depot, nearly run over by a rickety hay cart, and attacked by an overgrown duck." He continued to jab Ezra's chest. "If there's one thing I'm all out of, it's humor."

Blake snatched up his hat, slapped it against his leg a couple of times to shake off the dust, then crammed it onto his head and stalked off toward the creek. *A jinx. That's what she is, a damned jinx.*

Chapter Three

Ezra rubbed his throbbing chest and chuckled. "That young feller's already ridin' with a short fuse and the trip ain't even started yet." He spit a stream of tobacco juice, barely missing the boots of the cowhand next to him. "That little gal shore sticks in his craw."

John Eagle jumped out of Ezra's line of fire, then shook his head and looked after the angry wagon master. "I've ridden with Blake since we were kids. Never knew any woman to make him so touchy." He watched Donovan stalk away, then turned to Ezra. "I'm John Eagle, scout for this outfit."

The old codger nodded, and they walked over to where Millie sat, squatted beside the girl, and reached out tentatively a couple of times before the goose allowed them to rub its neck.

Ezra ran a finger up and down the large bird's head. Honey didn't seem to mind the attention at all. "What'd ya mean, she's a watch goose, Missy? Never heerd of such."

Millie watched Blake disappear down the creek bank, then turned her attention to the cowhand. "That's what Aunt Lavinia called her. My aunt saved Honey from a chicken hawk when she was little more than a ball of fluff. Ever since then, Honey's protected us as if we were family."

She stroked her pet's long neck. "She's better than a

dog. Not only does she tell me when someone is near, she gives eggs."

John Eagle grinned and rubbed under the goose's bill. "That'll sure be welcome on the trail."

Ezra got slowly to his feet. "Well, ladies, if ye'll 'scuse us, Johnny an' me'll see about shiftin' that thar load so's ya got more settin' space. We still got 'bout two hours of travel left 'til we reach the ranch."

After the wagons were reloaded, Blake climbed up beside Ezra. The old cowboy whistled and slapped the reins against the horses' rumps. The wagon lurched forward. Blake winced as his sore backside jarred against the hard wagon seat. Thanks to that damned bird his butt felt like he'd been attacked by a dozen wildcats.

He looked back to see if everything was all right and that all the wagons were following. Millicent's cart brought up the rear. Honey sat in a nest between the rockers of an overturned chair. "That damn goose acts like she's sitting on a feather mattress." He turned around and resettled his hat to keep the sun from his eyes. "How long 'til Thanksgiving, Oats?"

****

At last, Blake thought. They'd been riding on Hogan's spread about three quarters of an hour when they topped a hill and rolled into a peaceful valley. The sunlight sparkled off a small lake on the far side of the basin. Horses and oxen grazed peacefully off to one side. Between the water and a copse of trees stood a dozen large covered wagons. Several wranglers, directed by several young women, were unloading three freight wagons.

Ezra and John Eagle pulled their wagons to a stop in the shade, then hurried to help the women down. Blake extended his hand to several of the women in his wagon. "We're here, ladies. You can get down and claim your things."

Emily Peterson shook the wrinkles from her skirt, then dabbed at her perspiring face with a lace handkerchief. "We're where?" She looked around in total bewilderment. "Where is the ranch house? We're tired and grimy, Mr. Donovan. We need a bath and a good night's sleep in a real bed." The other women murmured their agreement.

Blake shoved his hat back as Millicent pulled her cart to a stop beside the freight wagons. At least she didn't try to run over him this time. He glared at the bird perched regally on top of its nest. "Well, Miss Peterson, there's a whole lake, just perfect for bathing, and I know where you can find a goose with enough feathers to fill two beds."

Emily glared at him as if his pants were slipping, then, grumbling, jerked her carpetbag from the cart.

Blake turned as Jim Hogan hailed him. The men shook hands. "Hi, Jim. Did you get Miss Hannah settled in okay?"

"Don't I wish. My sister-in-law's impossible. She insists on staying out here with the rest of the women." Hogan glanced over his shoulder. "And I'll tell you something, Blake. Riding herd on all those women might sound like a dream come true to some, but it's been nothing but a nightmare to me." He lowered his voice to a deep growl. "Do you know, in the week my group of women have been here, there's one over there that I swear ain't stopped talking since we left Mississippi. I surely don't envy you the task of taking 'em on to Montana."

Blake shook his head and followed Hogan to the coffeepot. If he hadn't promised Ed… "Wait a minute, Jim. Ed's your brother. Seems only fitting that you take his wife to him."

Hogan handed Blake a steaming cup. "Forget it, son. I have a ranch, a wife, and two beautiful little girls to keep me busy right here. I only agreed to help you collect and work the rough edges off these fillies. Herding 'em to Montana territory is your problem."

Blake exhaled and squatted in the shade. "Well, it was worth a try." He sipped his coffee and watched the women climb all over the wagons and unload their gear. "How many did you get in Mississippi?"

Hogan blew into his steaming cup. "Twenty-two. How many did you get?"

"Twenty-four. That's forty-six of the fifty we need, and we lost one when her Pa caught up with her. Believe it or not, she was only fourteen. We'll probably lose a few during the pre-trip training. But we picked up Mrs. Watts, there. Maybe we can pick up a few more on the way."

Hogan shook his head. "I'm not sure I go along with your idea of only taking stout women. They'll each eat more than a wrangler at roundup."

"Yeah, but they'll have a better chance of making it than if they started out as skin and bones."

Jim Hogan froze as his cup reached his lips. He watched a slender blonde cross to the water barrel. "Is that what you meant by stout? Boy, I shore misunderstood ya."

Blake followed his gaze. "No, that's Millicent Watts. I got uh…bamboozled into taking her along. We figure a half dozen or so will give up before we even leave. Hopefully, she'll be one of them."

"You'd better do more than hope. If ever I saw a likely candidate for buzzard bait, she's it."

Blake and Hogan finished their coffee, then helped the men unload the rest of the wagons. When they got to Millicent's cart, Blake's hand hovered over his gun as he and Honey glared at each other. The goose suddenly turned her back on Blake, stretched to her full height, flapped her wings and honked loudly several times. Then, as if deciding Blake had been put in his place, she fluttered to the ground and waddled, honking, toward Millicent.

Ezra chuckled. "'Pears she don't think ye're worth another tussle. Ye gonna he'p me with this trunk or ain't ye, boy?"

As soon as he was sure the goose wasn't going to circle around behind him, Blake grabbed the other end of the trunk. While the men unloaded the wagons, the women headed for the lake. Honey, wings spread and neck stretched out, raced past the women, honking loudly until she rushed into the lake.

"She's got the right idea." Millie laughed as she dropped to the ground to strip off her shoes and stockings. Then, hitching up her skirts, she waded in after her pet. The cold water no sooner covered her foot than she was back on shore. She shivered. "Oooh, that's cold!"

The others joined her at the water's edge. They dipped their toes in a little at a time.

Blake groaned. "That's just great. Already *Mrs. Jinx* is assuming leadership of the flock." He dragged a large trunk off the cart and dropped one end onto his foot. Swearing, he hopped around for several seconds before sitting down to pull off his boot and rub his throbbing toes, rolling his eyes heavenward. "Why me?" he groaned. "Why me?"

****

Blake swallowed the last bite of apple cobbler and set his plate aside, leaned back, and rolled a smoke. The cook Hogan had furnished was one of the best. He certainly hoped the man was a good teacher, too. Unless he missed his guess, very few of these women had ever seen a bite of food before a slave or servant placed it on the table. He looked around camp as he lit his cigarette. The ladies had spent a lazy afternoon. He'd asked nothing of them except to organize their things so they'd be accessible.

John Eagle squatted beside Blake and accepted the makings for a smoke. "You know, Blake, some of these ladies are okay. They're not all as green as we feared."

Blake handed his cousin the matches. "Yeah, I was noticing some of them didn't seem as uncomfortable in camp as the others. What about that Peterson girl? The one who wanted a bath and a featherbed?"

John Eagle shook his head. "Near's I can figure, she's one of the green ones, but she was over trying to give Cookie a hand. I think she's willing to learn."

Blake nodded. He took a couple of puffs and let his gaze wander from group to group. He stopped at Millicent and her pet. "What about *Mrs. Jinx* over there? Does she know how to do anything but cause trouble?"

"Don't know. She seems friendly enough, but she doesn't volunteer any information. Guess we'll just have to wait and see."

"Yeah, that's what I'm afraid of." He took one last puff, then dropped his cigarette and stepped on it. "Well, as soon as I speak to Miss Hannah, we'll get started."

Across the camp, Emily Peterson nudged Millie. "Wonder what that's all about?"

Millie looked where Emily indicated. Mr. Donovan and Miss Hannah were deep in conversation. Miss Hannah was probably in her forties. She was almost as tall as Mr. Donovan's shoulder and, like the rest of the women, certainly hadn't missed many meals. Though every inch a lady, the woman had a very definite air of authority, but that probably came from teaching school for so long before she married Mr. Hogan.

Mr. Donovan, on the other hand, was a very rugged individual, tanned from hours in the sun. His eyes were a rich chocolate color. His hair was thick and dark brown, all but the white streak down the middle, slightly to the left side. He had broad shoulders, trim hips and his body—her cheeks burned when she remembered being trapped on top of him at the train depot—his body was fine.

Millie dragged her thoughts back to the present, "My goodness, Miss Hannah and Mr. Donovan, they're…blushing…both of them."

Finally, Blake nodded and went to the largest group of women. "Ladies, would all of you join us over here, please?"

The women moved up to sit in front of Blake, every eye turned in his direction. They all looked so sweet and trusting. Suddenly, before his eyes, they took on the appearance of a gaggle of geese, two dozen Honeys eyeing him with malice.

He shuddered, swallowed, and shifted from one foot to the other. "Ah, Miss Hannah has something to say." He hastily stepped back and stared toward the wagons as if they were in danger of some kind.

Miss Hannah looked uncomfortable, but took a deep breath and plunged in. "Ladies, this is going to be a long hot trip. Mr. Donovan feels…ah… She straightened her shoulders and started again. "We're going to need all our strength just to make it to Montana alive. My father always said nothing worthwhile ever came easy." She looked at each of the girls. "My Ed is worth anything I have to do to get to him. And if you'll take my word for it, the men you're going to are just as good. Well…" She shrugged and grinned. "Almost as good."

Everyone giggled, then became quiet as she continued. "The important thing is to get there, and we're going to have to change some of our ways to do it. One of those ways is doing work men usually do, and some things we use in polite society just aren't practical, such as our clothing. To make this short, we need to dress comfortably and as functionally as possible. That means leaving our petticoats and uh…other binding undergarments packed away until we get there."

Blake sneaked a glance at the women. The shocked expressions, deep blushes, and lowered eyes made him glad he'd insisted Miss Hannah make that last suggestion. They'd have lynched him for sure.

He hurriedly took Miss Hannah's place before the young women recovered. "Ladies, how many of you have camped out before?" He nodded as eight hands went up, then he frowned. One of them belonged to *Millicent the Jinx*. That meant she'd be that much harder to discourage.

He looked to the other side of the group. "Fine. From now on, ladies, we'll be living as if we're already on the trail. We'll sleep under the stars at night, cook our meals over the campfire, and during the day, you'll be taught to do all the things involved in getting this wagon train to Montana Territory."

Murmurs circulated around the group. The women glared in his direction. Again, they seemed to take on the image of a gaggle of angry geese. However, no one came forward with an objection.

Blake raised his hands for silence. "Ladies, I know this is hard on you, but we have to start sooner or later. The sooner you learn what we have to teach you, the sooner you'll be on your way to your new homes and husbands. Now, get your bedding ready. Those of you who know how, help the others, and we'll meet here at first light tomorrow."

****

"More coffee, Mr. Donovan?"

Blake smiled and extended his cup for a refill. "That was a very good breakfast, Miss Peterson. I guess you've done a lot of campfire cooking."

Emily Peterson blushed and reached over to refill John Eagle's cup as well. "No, sir. This is my first time, but I've always loved to cook. I just couldn't pass up a chance to try."

"Well, some lucky man in Montana's gonna eat good with you around, Missy," Ezra added as she refilled his cup.

Blake pitched the last sip of coffee on the ground and dropped his cup in the dishpan. He looked around the camp. It reminded him of one big outdoor bedroom. Those who'd brought beds had the mattresses made up as if they were still at home. Some even had lanterns sitting on small crates or trunks beside their beds. Still others had bedrolls spread on several quilts for comfort.

Women. They'd put ruffles on the trees if you'd let them.

He also noticed most of the ladies had put away their petticoats, and several seemed to be without their—uh—binding undergarments. Then Millicent came into view. Her, he wasn't sure about. She looked as thin as ever, but if he remembered correctly from their encounter at the train depot, she didn't wear a corset. Hell, why should she? She didn't have anything to cinch in.

He readjusted his hat and hitched up his gun belt. "Guess we'd better get going." Ezra and John Eagle nodded and dropped their cups into the washpan too.

"All right, ladies. If you'll join me over here, we'll get started," he called. When the women were gathered together and quiet, Blake continued. "First, I'd like to introduce the men who'll be helping us for the next three weeks. You've already met Cookie. He's the best cook in the territory. Mr. Hogan loaned him to us at great sacrifice." A grizzled old man of about fifty ducked his head and kicked at an imaginary stone. "Cookie will teach you the ins and outs of cooking over an open fire.

"Cooper here, is a blacksmith. He'll teach you how to make any repairs to your wagons, care for the animals, even fix holes in your pots and pans."

Cooper flexed his arms several times, making the muscles ripple beneath his chambray shirt. His red hair barely covered the top of his head as he leaned over and picked up a heavy anvil with no apparent strain. The ladies gasped as he carried it to the other side of the camp. The shirt's fabric stretched across his muscle-corded back like a second skin.

"You know Ezra, who'll be showing you everything about the wagons—how to hitch and unhitch them, how to load and unload them, how to repair the harness and fix anything else that might go wrong.

"John Eagle here," Blake continued, "besides being our scout, will teach you how to take care of yourselves both on the trail and in the wilds. Now, we don't plan on any trouble, but it's better to be prepared.

"Ben, over there, will teach you the care and use of firearms and later, with John Eagle's help, to hunt."

He looked around. "Let's see, seems like I've missed someone. Oh, yeah. That tall, lanky string bean in the chaps is Reb, one of Mr. Hogan's top wranglers. He'll do his best to teach you to use a lariat." Blake paused when Dumplin' wandered over and nudged Millie for a lump of sugar. "Not all the stock will come ambling up in their Sunday bonnets when you need them."

Millie laughed with everyone else. Blake didn't know which was more aggravating, *Millicent the Jinx*, or her damned pets. One way or the other, they were definitely not making this trip.

Blake cleared his throat. "Now, we'll divide into groups of six each and get started."

After they broke into their groups, John Eagle motioned to Blake. "Boss, I've only got five women. We need an even number to get this started."

Blake nodded. "Okay, I'll take care of it." He did a quick count of each group. Cookie had seven students. He strode over. "Ladies, I know Cookie, here, is one handsome fellow, but we really don't want to hurt poor old John Eagle's feelings." He spotted Millicent Watts in the cook's crowd. The last thing he wanted was to have *Mrs. Jinx* anywhere near anything he was going to eat. "Mrs. Watts, would you join John Eagle's fighting squad?"

Millie started to refuse, but the glare he gave her was enough to turn the strongest heart to mush. With a nod she went slowly toward the group he indicated. "This is just wonderful," she muttered. "I finally get a chance to show everyone I'm not such a clumsy ninny and what happens? I'm sent to the one activity I can't possibly live through." Each of the women was twice as big as she. They'd break her in half on the first try. That man intended to get rid of her, one way or the other.

When Millie's group went on to target practice, she remained behind at John Eagle's request. He said anyone could defend themselves, even a featherweight like her. She certainly hoped so. If she'd been able to defend herself, her life might have been so different. For one thing, she wouldn't have had to run and hide every time Pa staggered home.

After everyone left, she and John Eagle squared off. He lunged at her. She sidestepped, tripped him with her foot, clasped her hands together, and brought them down as hard as she could on the back of his neck. John Eagle fell in a heap at her feet. His head struck a root with a loud crack.

"Oh, no!" Millie dropped down beside the prone man. "Mr. Eagle, I'm so sorry! I didn't mean to hit you so hard." She quickly rolled him over, pulled his head onto her lap, then gently patted his cheek. "Wake up, please."

A shadow fell across Millie and her victim. She looked up and squinted against the glaring sun. However, she didn't have to see the face to know it belonged to Mr. Donovan. His legs were spread and his fists planted on his hips. She'd even seen that furious stance in her nightmares. The man had an annoying habit of being on hand whenever things went awry.

"Mrs. Watts, what do you think you're doing? Compromising me isn't enough for you? Now you have to kill my chief scout, too?"

Millie shook her head. "No," she protested. "I…it was an accident, Mr. Donovan. I didn't mean to hit him so hard, honestly."

John Eagle groaned. Blake stooped down to rub his friend's shoulders and neck until he came to, then pulled John Eagle to his feet. "You okay, cousin?"

John Eagle rubbed his neck, then gently touched the side of his head. "Sure, Boss. I guess so. Everything still works, as far as I can tell." He accepted a dipper of water that Millie had hurriedly fetched for him, took a sip, then leaned over and poured the rest over his head.

Millie offered him the dampened towel she'd intended to lay across his neck. "I'm so sorry, Mr. Eagle. I didn't mean to hurt you."

He wiped the water from his face and returned the dipper to her. "I'm not hurt, Miss Millie. And my name is just John Eagle. No 'Mister.'" He glanced speculatively at Blake, then back at Millie. "Do you think you could do that again, Miss Millie?"

"Why, I suppose so, but shouldn't you rest some first?"

"Yeah, but I was thinking of you doing it with another partner." He stared pointedly at Blake.

Millie looked from her teacher to the wagon master. She smiled sweetly. "Oh, and who did you have in mind? Mr. Donovan, perhaps?" She would certainly enjoy giving this arrogant cowboy a crack on the head.

Blake drew himself to his full height. "Teaching hand-to-hand combat is not my job, Mrs. Watts.

However, you're holding up the shooting class." He jammed his hat down firmly on his head. "Kindly come along and stop wrecking our schedule," he said as he started toward the waiting group.

Millie glared at his back. How dare he treat her as if she were an errant school girl! "Thank you, but I don't need shooting lessons. I can manage in that department quite adequately."

Blake turned on his heels and glared at her. "Mrs. Watts, I will decide who needs lessons and who doesn't. You wanted to join this group, so you will do everything the others do."

Millie's cheeks burned. She hadn't meant to be snippy, but he'd been so rude she just couldn't help it. She sighed, handed the empty dipper back to John Eagle, and followed the wagon master. As they passed her cart, she grabbed her gun and shot bag. Why were men always trying to push her around?

Blake walked over to the tall, thin man in faded gray army pants. "Reb, Mrs. Watts feels she doesn't need any further instruction in the art of firearms. I think we should allow her to demonstrate her skill."

Millie calmly loaded her gun. Oh, this man was asking for it. She was sick and tired of his belittling attitude.

Reb set up the targets and stepped out of the way. Blake Donovan bowed and smiled mockingly. "All right, Mrs. Watts, Whenever you're ready."

She aimed at the bottle several yards in front of her. From the corner of her eye, she saw a squirrel in the tree to her left. She didn't stop to wonder why the critter hadn't cleared out with all the firing they'd been doing, she just swung the barrel around and fired.

36

Blake ran his hand down his face and shook his head. "Mrs. Watts, the idea is to fire at the target. Waving the rifle around like that is likely to get someone hurt."

"Mister Donovan. It's been years since I've missed a shot that easy." Without turning her back to the wagon master she spoke to Reb. "Would you please look at the base of that tree over yonder?"

Millie smiled knowingly at Donovan while Reb limped over and shoved aside the bushes at the base of the large tree. "Well, I'll be da...darned." He reached down and lifted a squirrel by the tail. "She hit it, shore 'nough."

Chapter Four

Millie wiped her forehead on her sleeve. It was certainly warm for the end of March. She stretched her neck and rolled her shoulders back and forth to relieve the tension. As she finished wringing the rinse water from her blouse, tossed it toward the rest of her laundry, and missed, Blake Donovan rode by.

It'd been a week since the shooting lesson. He had scarcely said a word to her, but he never seemed to be far away…especially when something went wrong, like now. She'd tossed at least a dozen articles into that Arbuckle Coffee box and he had to be riding by the first time she missed. Drat the man. She snatched up the blouse and began rewashing it. What was he doing on this side of camp anyway?

Every time she did well at something, he seemed to become angrier. It was almost as if he were disappointed that she was keeping her end of the bargain. Of course, she'd been a little clumsy when they first met. She groaned. *A little clumsy.* The man made her so nervous she turned into a bumbling idiot at the very sight of him.

Millie tossed the garment into the box. *Well, all that stops right now.* She picked up the crate and headed for the clothesline. She was as good as any of these other women. She'd show Mr. Donovan she could do anything they could do.

Cooking over an open fire was no problem. Her

family had been too poor to own a stove, so until three years ago when she'd moved in with Aunt Lavinia, she'd always cooked over the fireplace or a campfire.

Hunting was second nature to her. For years before Ma died it was hunt or starve. Pa never lifted a finger. She glanced around the campsite. Mr. Donovan was helping Ezra untangle several sets of reins from rope someone had dumped into a box.

Although she'd never hitched six oxen to a wagon, she had hitched horses to Aunt Lavinia's buggy almost every day for the last two years. It didn't take much to learn to add several more animals, and she certainly knew better than to toss all the harnesses and ropes together in one box.

Millie took down Emily's dry laundry and began hanging up her own wet things. Over the top of a sheet, she watched Blake Donovan smile and nod to Esther Huggins. He never smiled at her like that. As far as she could tell, she was no worse than the other women at the tasks set for her, and better at some than most. She exhaled deeply. He just didn't want her along. She folded the end of a petticoat over the line and stabbed it with a clothespin. Whether Mr. Donovan liked it or not, she would not be driven away.

****

The stew was some of the best Blake had ever eaten. He watched *Millicent-the-Jinx* refill plates for several others. Not only was she one of the best shots on the wagon train, she could cook. He joined the line for seconds. Even so, he had to find a way to convince her to give up this trip. She'd been a burr under his saddle since day one, but he would not have her death on his conscience.

He stepped up to the stewpot. Millie ladled another helping onto his plate. "Thanks," he muttered as his gaze met hers. Her blonde hair hung across her shoulder in one long braid. The flush on her cheeks from the heat of the campfire was very becoming. Strange, he'd never noticed how pretty she was.

Millie nodded and quickly dropped her gaze. "There's apple cobbler when you're ready."

Blake returned to his seat beside John Eagle. What was it about that girl that irritated him so? Even the fact that she was a handsome woman aggravated him. He jabbed a piece of meat with his fork, then stopped inches from his mouth when he saw Honey sitting in the shadows nearby, eyeing him as if he were a big, juicy worm. *That damn bird.*

He shook his fork as if it were a finger. "See this, *Duck*? If you don't want to end up on this fork, stay out of my way."

John Eagle shook his head. "What's eating at you, cousin? I've never seen you so grouchy."

Blake shoved the forkful of meat into his mouth so he wouldn't have to reply. The mere sight of that girl and her pet goose made him want to…something. Damn, his insides seemed to be constantly tied in knots these days.

The scout followed his boss's gaze to Millie. "She's quite a woman. She'd make a damn good warrior. Any man would be lucky to have her cover his back."

Blake gulped down his bite whole, then choked as he glared at his cousin. "Are you out of your mind? She's a woman!"

John Eagle shrugged. "Some Apache tribes have women warriors."

Blake slammed down his fork. "Well, you're not

Apache. You're Kiowa. More or less," he mumbled.

John Eagle got up. "So? I sure as hell wouldn't want her fighting against me."

Blake watched John Eagle return for dessert. The scout didn't hand out compliments like that very often. He watched Millicent dish out helpings for several others. Warrior Woman? Naw. Witch Woman? Maybe.

He mulled it over for several minutes. Yeah, she was trouble, plain and simple. The sooner she went back to wherever she came from, the better. Eventually, someone else would have to carry her load. Deep in thought, when a large portion of apple cobbler was plopped onto his plate, he nearly dropped it. He grabbed the dish with both hands.

Millie smiled. "We had a little dessert left, and I thought you might have room for some." Without waiting for his comment, she returned the pan to the clean-up crew, then picked up her own plate and a cup of coffee before joining a group of women on the other side of the campfire. A southern girl was describing the last lavish ball she'd attended.

Millie listened for several minutes before her mind began to wander. The women, northern and southern, didn't seem to want to continue the war as so many of the men did. They took turns telling what their lives and homes were like before the war. One thing they all seemed to have in common was hardship. Whether from the North or South, life during and after the war had not been easy for any of them. They all seemed to want the same things—husband, home, family.

Millie sat quietly. With all their hardships, most of them had one thing she didn't. A loving family. Millie was able to share some amusing times with the other women, but was careful to keep it light. What would they think if they knew that, back home, her pa was called white trash? Would they feel the same about her? She'd worked her heart out trying to keep up with these women. She'd gone to bed every night aching all over rather than admit she couldn't keep up.

Her gaze wandered across the camp to Blake Donovan. She'd done everything she could think of to convince that man she wouldn't be a drag on this train, but he still wanted her out.

She didn't know what she would do if, at the last minute, Mr. Donovan did put her off the train. Now that she was away from Pa, she certainly wasn't going back.

****

Blake opened his eyes but didn't move. Something was wrong. His horse, Thunder, was better than a watchdog. He didn't nicker and stomp for no reason. Blake looked around as best he could from where he lay. Then, sliding his pistol from its holster, he eased from his blankets and into the trees. After several minutes he spotted a shadow moving toward the picket line. Whoever it was wanted the horses.

He crept silently from tree to tree in the same direction until he was close enough to jump the intruder. However, as a cloud rolled away from the moon, he recognized the slight shape of *Millicent the Jinx*. As soon as she passed his hiding place, he stepped out in plain view. "What are you doing up at this hour?" he demanded in a hoarse whisper.

She whirled, stumbling back against Dumplin'. Her hand flew to her mouth, stifling a yelp. She leaned against the horse, gasping for breath.

"Mr. Donovan! You nearly scared me to death."

"I nearly did more than that! I nearly shot you for a horse thief," he said, shaking his pistol at her.

"A horse thief!"

Slowly he shoved his gun under his belt. "But who in his—or her—right mind would want to steal that piece of crow bait?"

Dumplin' laid his chin on Millie's shoulder. "Dumplin' isn't crow bait. He's a sweet, loyal friend."

Blake shook his head. Millie's hair hung loose down her back. In the moonlight he could just make out the shadow of her long lacy lashes against her cheeks. She wasn't half bad-looking.

In spite of himself, he couldn't control a feeling of admiration for her. She'd done everything he'd sworn she couldn't, and without an air of "I told you so."

He scratched the old horse between the ears. *What's the use?* He grinned. It was hard to stay angry at a woman as cute as a day-old calf, or at a crazy, sway-backed nag with a silly straw hat perched between his ears. "Lady, you have the strangest friends. Don't you know any normal people, or animals?"

Millie rubbed Dumplin's neck. "That depends on what you call normal."

She glanced at Donovan from under her lashes. Why was he suddenly being so friendly? He hadn't said two civil words to her since they'd met, and he'd given her every dirty job he could possibly think of. Shooting her was probably exactly what he wanted to do. He'd tried about everything else.

She gave Dumplin' one last pat. "Good night, boy. See you in the morning." Millie nodded good night to Mr. Donovan, then backed away several steps. "I...I'd better get to bed. Morning comes early around here." She darted behind one of the wagons and hurried back to her own.

Blake watched her disappear into the darkness. *She never did say why she was out here at this hour.* He shook his head and returned to his own bedroll.

After breakfast, Blake called everyone together. "Ladies, according to Cookie's poor old bones, we're in for some rain. Now, as a rule, I don't pay much attention to such omens, but Hogan assures me those old bones are never wrong."

"Besides," he added, "it smells like rain. Anyway, we're going to push up our time schedule a bit. We've been together about three weeks. The time's come to decide once and for all who's going to Montana and who's not."

The women began whispering among themselves. Blake raised his hands and called for silence. "Ladies, ladies, please." When they became quiet again, he continued. "I know you signed a contract, but we realize you didn't really know what you were getting into. What you've been through these last few weeks is just a small sample of what lies ahead.

"The men in Montana territory want willing wives, not captive ones. Once we're under way, there will be no turning back. So if this isn't what you expected, now's the time to say so."

He paused, waiting for any who wanted out to come forward. Three hands slowly went up, but Millicent's wasn't one of them. He glared at her. *Come on, lady, give it up.*

"Ladies, it's no disgrace to change your mind. But if you're going to do it, please, do it now." Again, he looked in her direction, but she looked him in the eye and raised her chin stubbornly.

"Damn." He turned to Ezra and swore under his breath again. "Thought you said we could discourage her," he snarled through clenched teeth.

Ezra spit a stream of tobacco juice to one side. "Guess I jest ain't a good judge of she-male character. Ye'll jest have ta make do, Sonny."

Blake clutched the brim of his hat with both hands to keep from wrapping them around the old codger's neck. Make do? He rolled his eyes heavenward. He'd been making do for three weeks. She'd practically driven him to drink as it was. He'd be a babbling lunatic by the time they got to Montana. He had one more week to get rid of this jinx. He put his hat on and adjusted his gun belt. He could do it. *One skinny, frail little woman isn't going to defeat me. No siree. Not by a long shot.*

He took a deep breath and turned back to the ladies. He tried to smile. He could manage that, too, as long as he didn't look at her. "Fine. The rest of you ladies take a few minutes and choose a partner, someone you'll be sharing a wagon with for the trip. Then we'll load all your things before the storm hits. Oh, one more thing. These wagons will hold only so much, so those who have a lot of things, try to team up with someone who has less than you do. The oxen surely will appreciate it."

"Those who are going back, meet with Ezra and Ben over yonder. We'll try to get your things together and into town as soon as possible."

****

Millie and Emily managed to load the last trunk on their wagon just minutes before the storm broke. Since neither had a great many possessions, there was plenty of room. They spent the rest of the day arranging and rearranging, trying to make their wagon as homey as possible.

On the second rainy morning during a lull in the downpour, Millie took her turn at tending the animals. Honey and Dumplin' followed her as usual. She untied the lead rope from the picket line to move two of the oxen to better grazing. Suddenly, Honey's loud honking rent the air. The goose rushed at the feet of the nearest oxen. Dumplin' pawed the ground and neighed loudly. The oxen bolted, moving faster than Millie thought possible for such large, lumbering beasts.

She screamed as the lead rope jerked through her hands. Millie teetered for a brief moment, then Dumplin' charged past, knocking her backwards into a large mud puddle.

Blake rushed around Millie's wagon just as the oxen ran right toward him. He tried to jump back, but slipped on the slimy ground and fell before the charging beasts. He rolled under the wagon just seconds before he would have been trampled. Two wranglers ran out to corral the oxen.

Blake slid and crawled slowly from under the wagon. He looked down at his wet, muddy clothes, then retrieved his hat. He thrust his fist through a large hole in the crown. It couldn't have looked worse if a herd of buffalo had run over it. Blake glared from the hat to Millie. "I might have known." He opened his mouth to say more, then snapped it shut, jammed the muddy hat onto his equally muddy head, and stalked in her direction.

Millie pushed herself up. How could Dumplin' do this to her? When she tried to stand, her foot slipped and she sat down hard, again, in the puddle. The cold water quickly seeped farther through her clothing. Her hand stung from the rope burn. She reached out expecting Mr. Donovan's help, only to see him stalk right past her. "Ohhh." Blake Donovan was the rudest, most irritating man she'd ever met. He obviously blamed her for this, too. She'd seen the hole in his precious hat. *Too bad his head wasn't in the hat when the oxen stomped it.*

Ezra grabbed Dumplin's halter. "Whoa. Easy now, boy." As he fought to calm the old horse, he looked back at where the animal had been stomping. He emitted a string of cuss words that made Millie gasp, then ran his hand over the horse's chest and down first one foreleg, then the other.

Millie struggled out of the puddle with the help of one of the wranglers, then gingerly pulled her soggy skirt away from her body. She shivered but hurried toward Ezra and Dumplin'. "Is he all right?"

"Yes, ma'am. Near as I kin tell."

"I don't understand what made Honey and Dumplin' act that way."

"Thar's the reason, Missy." Ezra held up a dead rattlesnake—or what was left after Dumplin' had stomped it. "No wonder they's so 'cited. This here's the biggest varmint I seed this year. Ya shor' have loyal pets, Missy."

Tears filled her eyes as she sank to the ground beside her horse. Honey rushed into her lap and Dumplin' nuzzled her neck. She stroked the goose with one hand and the horse with the other. "You crazy beasts. That snake might have killed you! What would I ever do without you?"

After a cold bath in the lake and a change of clothes, Millie rinsed out her muddy dress and hurried to join the morning's work. The storm had left the day humid. She strained to help Allison Shiels move a crate from one side of the wagon to the other. "Allison, are you absolutely positive there's only material in this crate? It feels more like rocks, to me," Millie said as she stopped long enough to rest her tired back.

"'Tis not just material, Millie. There are perhaps a dozen bolts o' cloth in here. They were a gift from me parents, along with the new machine for sewing."

Millie looked at the blanket-draped cabinet that doubled as a headboard as well as a table. "My, that's a wonderful gift. They must love you very much."

The girl smiled and shoved a long, chestnut-colored ringlet off her shoulder. "They wanted me to have a way to support meself until I selected me future husband."

"Was it hard to learn to work it?"

"No. I was nervous at first, but now it's so much fun. Would you believe I can sew a dress in just a few days?"

Millie looked longingly at the machine. "Oh, that must be wonderful. I'm afraid it takes me forever by hand—well, weeks anyway. I just don't have the patience to sit and sew."

They each took an end and started moving the crate again. Allison backed up two steps, then tripped on the hem of her skirt. She screamed and fell off the end of the wagon, barely rolling out of the way as the large crate followed her to the ground.

Angie Pollard ran over to help Allison up. "My goodness, are you hurt, child? You're supposed to hitch up your skirts when you do this kind of work."

Allison clung to the older woman until she stopped shaking. "Aye, I'm all right, just a wee bit scared. I did hitch up me skirt, but it just won't stay. That's the second time I've tripped this week." She rubbed her hip and climbed back into the wagon. "There must be a better way."

After lunch, Miss Hannah filled her teacup, then sat beside Millie and Emily. She handed Millie a sheaf of papers. "I've been checking the supplies all morning. What does that look like to you?"

Millie, with Emily reading over her shoulder, studied the list. "Looks like the men did the shopping," Millie answered.

"Some very unimaginative men," Emily added. "If this is what we're to live on, starvation would be more exciting. Surely this isn't all they bought?"

"That's all," Miss Hannah assured them. "I think we should circulate this list and get some suggestions for a last-minute shopping trip."

"Will Mr. Donovan agree to that?" Emily asked.

"He'd better." Miss Hannah tapped the list. "I don't intend to cross this country for the next four or five months eating beans, hard tack and biscuits. And look at all the coffee. I don't know about you ladies, but I'm a tea drinker and what they've got isn't enough for me for a month, much less anyone else, too."

Millie made a quick mental calculation. "If none but the men drink coffee, that's over twenty pounds each. I agree. We need to make a few adjustments, but you're going to have to ask him. If Mr. Donovan thinks I had anything to do with this, he'll balk for sure."

They sat sipping tea and jotting down notes. "You know," Emily said thoughtfully, "we might make a list of what everyone else brought before we go shopping."

The older woman looked up. "What everyone else brought?"

"Yes. We have many fruit trees and a huge kitchen garden at home. I brought dried fruits and quite a bit of canned vegetables." Millie nodded, "I did, too. The neighbors who helped me pack also loaded all the canned goods from our root cellar."

"Hmm," Miss Hannah looked at each girl thoughtfully. "I hadn't thought of that. All right, would you two mind taking this list around? You can find out what each one brought as you get suggestions."

Millie gathered up the list and a lead pencil while Emily rinsed out the teacups. "We can discuss everything over supper tonight."

****

Millie shivered from the evening wind. Since the sun had gone down, the combination of cool wind and wet feet had chilled her to the bone. *Not even the warm campfire seems to help.* She reached for the coffeepot. Suddenly she was tackled from behind. The coffeepot flew through the air as she hit the ground. She screamed and clawed at the hands that roughly rolled her back and forth on the damp, muddy ground.

"Stop! Let me go. Help!" Why weren't the others helping her? When she finally stopped rolling, she was horrified to see Blake Donovan practically sitting on her. "Mr....Donovan. What...do you think...you're doing?" she demanded between gasps. "Kindly get off me! I was under the impression...you wanted...nothing to do with me."

Donovan's eyes narrowed as he hurriedly got up, pulling her with him. "You're so right, Mrs. Watts." He grabbed the back of her skirt and pulled it around so she could see it was smoking. "But the stench of burning flesh tends to spoil one's appetite." He turned on his heel and left as suddenly as he'd come.

Millie looked at her burned skirt, then stared after Blake Donovan. Why did he do that? He'd saved her, then acted as if she'd caught her skirts on fire intentionally. The man was impossible.

She was still dazed when several of the women hurried her back to her wagon for a change of clothing. She pulled on her last clean skirt, then held up the burned one and shuddered. That was too close. "I'm beginning to think these skirts are more dangerous than any road agents or wild Indians we'll meet on this trip. If we were smart, we'd wear britches like the men do. You don't see them catching fire or stepping on their hems," she muttered to no one in particular.

After supper, she lingered over a last cup of coffee with several of the women. "You know, I was just talking earlier, but now that I've had time to think it over, wearing britches on this trip might not be such a bad idea. I used to wear them on the farm and they're very practical."

Several of the women gasped. "Surely you jest! We couldn't wear britches. It's not decent," Angie Pollard protested.

"Why not?" Nancy Cleary demanded. Who'll see us but a few deer and some Indians? I, for one, think it's a very good idea. Look how hot these dresses and petticoats are here, and we haven't even gotten to the desert yet. Just think what a nuisance these long skirts will be going up hills or down ravines. Miss Hannah, you said we needed to adjust our thinking to what was practical for the trip."

****

The next morning Blake noticed a kind of nervous

51

excitement among the women all during breakfast. After the dishes were done, the men awaited their students, but none came. They watched in surprise as the women hitched up several of the freight wagons and saddled some of the horses. John Eagle caught the reins of the front wagon. "Good morning, Miss Emily. Where are you ladies going?"

"Into town. We have some business to attend to before we pull out for Montana."

He shook his head. "Sorry, but that's impossible. We still have a lot of work to do."

Blake held the reins of Millie's wagon. She met his gaze. "You can either come, or stay, but we *are* going, Mr. Donovan."

Blake looked from one woman to another. They were deadly serious, but he couldn't let them go. Shopping would take all day, and they had a lot to do before pulling out tomorrow. "Tell you what, ladies, make your lists. Ben will go into town for you."

"Thank you just the same, but there are some things a lady has to do for herself," Nancy Cleary assured him from her perch beside Millie. "Now, kindly step aside, sir."

Miss Hannah, perched beside Emily, tried to hide a smile. "I suggest you do so, Mr. Donovan. These ladies mean business."

The men finally released the reins, stepped aside, and watched the wagons and horses amble up the road. "She's behind all this," Blake insisted. "I knew she'd be trouble the minute I laid eyes on her. Her and that damned *duck*!"

He turned to John Eagle, but the scout was already at the corral. "What in hell are you doing?" Blake demanded.

John Eagle hoisted the saddle onto Patches and cinched it up. "Going to town. They don't know the way. They'll be lost inside of two hours. Besides, I want to see what's so important to so many sweet little ladies."

"Sweet little ladies," Blake muttered as he hurriedly saddled Thunder. Maybe, if he were lucky, a certain one of those sweet little ladies would decide not to come back, or would get thrown in jail for the next thirty-six hours. They could be long gone in thirty-six hours.

Chapter Five

Blake pulled up as the women stopped at the edge of town.

He'd worried over the problem like a dog over a bone. "Still can't figure why they insisted on coming to town," he muttered to John Eagle.

"Why don't we split up," Millie suggested. "Cookie says there are three mercantiles in town. If we hit each one together, this will take all day."

"Good idea," Miss Hannah said. "Why don't you take the first one we come to? My wagon will stop at the second, and you riders take the last one."

****

Blake stood aside as Miss Millie and the other ladies from the first wagon stepped inside Ferguson's Mercantile. She took a deep breath. "The smell of spices and freshly ground coffee brings back pleasant memories of shopping trips back home," she said to Emily. The women wandered from table to table looking at the bright array of ribbons, lace, and blankets. She noticed Mr. Donovan lurked in the men's hat corner.

"Good morning, ladies," the clerk said. "What can I do for you?"

"Good morning," Millie began, "we'd like to see some…" She glanced at Mr. Donovan, who seemed to be deeply engrossed in selecting a new hat. "That is… Just a minute." She moved hesitantly to the wagon master, "Uh, Mr. Donovan?"

Blake put aside the black hat he was inspecting. "Yes, Mrs. Watts?"

She cleared her throat, then smiled up at him. "We appreciate your bringing us into town. We wouldn't have made such good time without you. However, I'm sure there are things you'd like to do before we pull out tomorrow, so you go ahead, and we'll meet you back at the wagon in about an hour or so."

Blake stared at the woman, not sure he believed what he heard. He'd politely, but definitely, been told to leave. There was nothing else he could do but go. "Sure, I, uh, do have a few things to do. See you at the wagon."

He paid for the hat, then walked up the boardwalk toward the saloon. He didn't have anything to do. He might as well have a beer while he waited. After pushing through the batwing doors, he ordered a beer, then took a seat at an empty table by the front window. Just as the bartender brought his beer, he saw John Eagle and Cookie coming down the boardwalk. "Bring two more beers," he told the barkeep. He tapped on the window and motioned them inside.

By the time their drinks were served, the other four men who'd followed them into town had pulled up chairs, too. "What are you doing here, cousin?" asked John Eagle. Blake looked at his scout and shook his head. "I was politely told to get lost before I could find out anything."

John Eagle thumbed his hat back. "Yeah, me too."

"Well, not me." Ezra spit a stream of tobacco juice into a nearby spittoon. "They's nothing p'lite 'bout the way that Miz Pollard tol' me ta get lost. I swear, the way that woman looks at me gives me the willies."

Blake took a swallow of his beer. "Got any idea what those women are up to?"

John Eagle shook his head. "No. Can't remember ever running up against so many secretive women. Usually, they can't keep quiet for five minutes."

"We tried hangin' around Beauler's. Thought maybe we could see something through the window," Reb commented, "but that big farm woman, Elsa, I think, told us to git. And she was plum definite about it, too."

The men talked for the next hour, going over everything that could possibly be used on the trail, but couldn't think of a thing they'd forgotten to pack for the trip. "We even bought each of them wimens a bar of that perfumy soap Miz Fitzgerald said was so pop'lar back East," Ezra complained. "What more could they be a hankerin' fer?"

Reb looked out the window. "I don't know, but looks like they're coming back. Maybe we'll find out now."

They gulped down the last of their drinks and hurried to the wagons. The women were in deep conversation when the men approached. John Eagle sauntered up to the group. "Hello, ladies. Did you get everything you wanted?"

Millie tried to suppress a smile. *Ahhh. Men are just as curious as women.* "I'm not sure one ever gets everything she wants, but we did get what we came for, thank you. Ezra, maybe you could help us. It's late, and we're hungry. Is there someplace in town we could pick up something to eat along the way back to camp?"

Ezra scratched his bearded chin thoughtfully. "Yeah. I think I ken take care of it. C'mon, Reb, Ben. Gimmee a hand."

Blake and John Eagle eyed the bundles the ladies carried, but no one breathed a word about their contents.

"Could I help you with your packages, Miss Emily?"

"That's very kind of you, John Eagle, but I can manage nicely, thank you."

Millie and some of the ladies window-shopped for the next hour. When Ezra returned with four large boxes of food, they all mounted up and headed back to camp, stopping at the edge of town long enough to pass out fried chicken and jars of lemonade.

Blake chewed on a chicken leg as he and John Eagle rode ahead of the wagons. "Did you manage to get any hint as to what this trip was all about?"

The scout tossed his chicken bones away and licked his fingers. "Uh-uh. Never met such closed-mouthed women. Guess we'll just have to wait until they decide to tell us."

"Somehow, that's not too reassuring. I don't like surprises."

****

Millie stood beside Jim Hogan and Miss Hannah while Jim's two little daughters rubbed Dumplin's nose. "They certainly do love that horse of yours, Miss Millie. I'm glad you finally agreed to let them have Dumplin'."

She swallowed the lump rising in her throat. To part with Dumplin' was like giving up a part of herself. She would never have agreed if John Eagle hadn't convinced her it was best for the horse. Dumplin' was old. He'd need to stop and rest every hour or so, and the wagons wouldn't be able to do that. It would be kinder to leave him here than to abandon him on some lonesome plain where he'd be at the mercy of wolves.

She blinked back a tear. "You're sure Dumplin' will be happy? It's just that he's been with me since I was four years old. I can hardly bear to lose him."

"I can understand, Miss Millie. Believe me, we'll take real good care of your pet. He'll have a whole herd of mares to keep him company in his old age, and two little girls to dote on him. He'll be the best loved and most pampered horse this side of the Mississippi."

Blake walked up near the end of the conversation. "What about that overgrown *duck*? Wouldn't your little girls like to have her for a pet, too?"

Millie gasped. "No!" She couldn't hold back the tears. "Isn't the loss of one's home and loved ones enough? Do you have to take all that's dear to me? Honey is the last bit of family I have left, and I won't leave her. I wouldn't leave Dumplin' if there were any other way." She hurried to Dumplin's side. Hugging the old swayback, she put her head against his neck and gave way to the sorrow that filled her heart.

Miss Hannah shook her head. "Not long on tact, are you, Donovan."

Blake jammed his hands into his pockets. He'd seen Millicent Watts in a lot of different situations during the last three weeks, but never in tears. How was he to know she'd break down like that over some mangy old plug and a pile of hissing feathers? "Guess not," he admitted. "Say, you don't suppose she'll change her mind at the last minute and stay here, do you?"

****

Blake shook his head in dismay as he rode toward the lead wagon. Everyone was ready to go, but with the fancy seat cushions and sidesaddles, it looked more like they were heading for a picnic.

The wagons were about to pull out when two men raced across the floor of the valley. Millie saw them pull up in front of Mr. Donovan and exchange a few words. She stood up and readjusted the cushion she'd fashioned from the remnants of her burned skirt. That was one disadvantage to being thin, no extra padding between one's bones and these wooden seats.

She sat back down, then jumped up as she recognized one of the horsemen riding slowly toward her wagon. "Pa." She quickly climbed down and turned to face a very angry man.

Willard Tanncr dismounted with a thud and descended upon his daughter.

Millie took a fortifying breath. It was obvious he'd had just enough to drink to be mean, but she wouldn't back down. She had set her course, and no one, least of all her pa, was going to change it. "What are you doing here, Pa?"

"What am I doing here? Is that all you got to say to me, daughter?" Before she could answer, he grabbed her arms. "Jest where'd you think you was goin'?" He shook her like a rag doll. "How dare you sell *my* home an' then sneak off with the money!"

Millie jerked free of her father's grasp. She rubbed her arm. If she didn't stand up for herself now, she would be doomed to this kind of treatment, or worse, for the rest of her life. "It was never your home, and I didn't sell it, Aunt Lavinia did."

"That don't matter. The point is you stole the money and ran."

"I did not steal the money. Aunt Lavinia left it to me. Your name never entered into it."

Tanner stepped closer to Millie. She nearly gagged

at the smell of his whiskey breath.

"That's the thanks I get for spending the best years of my life taking care of you?" He grasped her arm again and dropped his voice so no one but Millie could hear. "As your pa, it's my duty to take care of you and your property. Now gimme that money, girl. You got mighty uppity living in that fine house with Lavinia. Now you're going to do your duty toward your pa and your new husband."

Millie's mouth dropped open. "Husband!" she managed to squeak. "What husband?" Dear God, surely he wasn't planning to go to Montana and live with her and the man she finally wed.

"Yeah, Rupert here's to be your new man. You're a headstrong girl, and you need the strong hand of a good man to show you the way."

Millie glanced up at the man who'd ridden in with her father. He was big and mean-looking. So mean, it seemed, that even soap and water were afraid to go near him. *Marry that piece of trash? Any man in Montana has to be better. I'll take my chances.*

"That's it." She whirled to face her father, then shoved at his chest several times. He stumbled backward several steps with each shove. "Now you listen to me, Willard Tanner! That money was left to me, not you. And you are *not* responsible for me. You haven't been *responsible* for anyone in years. I'm going to leave with this wagon train, and you can marry that dirty oaf yourself."

"You'll do as you're tol', girl." Willard raised his hand to strike Millie. She grabbed his arm, hooked her toe around his right foot and pushed with all her might. He staggered back until his horse broke his fall. He rushed forward, fist upraised. Millie ducked, turned sideways just as he swung, and rammed her elbow into his ribs. As he fell forward, she raised her knee to give him a swift jab in the stomach, but misjudged her distance and caught him, with all the force she could muster, in the groin. He doubled over and fell to the ground.

Rupert jumped down from his horse and started toward her. Millie grabbed the pistol from her father's holster and pointed it at the man. At the same time, the sound of guns being cocked filled the air. Rupert froze, then slowly looked around. Not only was he facing her gun but also the rifles of several other women.

Millie stooped beside her father. She raised his chin with the barrel of the pistol. "It hurts, doesn't it, Pa? That's only a small sample of how it hurt Ma every time you came home drunk and beat on her. It's not even a twinge compared to my pain the night you stood by and watched Otto kick me in the stomach. The night I lost my baby, thanks to you two."

She poked the barrel of her gun a little harder under his chin. "I've learned something these last few weeks, Pa. I've learned I can protect myself from the likes of you. From now on, I'm taking care of myself. From now on, I have no pa. I'm a widow and I don't have to answer to you." She grabbed his ear. "Look at me," she ordered.

When he opened his tear-filled eyes, she continued. "I don't care what you do, or where you go, but it'd better not be anywhere near me. If I ever see you again, I'll shoot you. And Willard, so help me, I won't miss."

"And neither will we," said several voices from the crowd.

Millie stood up looking squarely at the man standing

a few feet away. "You can consider yourself rejected. Now take this poor excuse for a man and get out of here." Rupert reached to help Tanner up. "I'd better not see either one of you again—ever."

As soon as her uninvited visitors were gone, Millie's legs began to tremble. She reached back to grab the wagon wheel but clutched a muscular arm instead. She turned in time to see Donovan holster his gun.

He gently took the pistol from her hand, dropped it on the wagon seat, then eased her to the ground. Millie leaned her head against the wheel. Her breakfast threatened to leave her stomach, and she closed her eyes to quell it. *Just one more hour. One more hour and I'd have gotten away. He wouldn't have followed me into the wilderness. He couldn't stay away from a saloon long enough.*

A sob escaped her as she covered her face. So close," she moaned. "I nearly killed him."

Blake put a reassuring hand on her shoulder. "But you didn't." She hoped he was beginning to understand why this trip was so important to her. "I know this is a bad time, but there's one thing I have to know. Is your husband really dead?"

She stiffened under his gaze. He cleared his throat. "Look, the whole purpose of this train is to take marriageable ladies to the Meandering Valley. If you're not free to marry, there's no reason for you to go."

Millie stood, straightened her shoulders, and looked him in the eye. "Oh, he's dead all right. I'll tell you something else. My next husband will be of my own choosing, and God help the man who ever raises a hand to me again."

Blake shivered, but he seemed to believe her. "It's

late. We'd better get going."

Millie's bottom lip trembled as she looked searchingly into his face. "You...you mean I can still go?"

Blake resettled his hat, looking embarrassed at her tears. "Not if you're going to make a habit of slowing us down," he growled as he headed for his horse. "We should have pulled out ten minutes ago."

She watched him ride toward the head of the train. Her hand shook as she wiped her cheeks. *I'm going... I'm really going...*

Emily Peterson tugged at Millie's arm. "Come on, Millie, or I'll have this big wagon all to myself."

Millie took the reins from Emily. They walked alongside the wagon as the train pulled out. Millie watched Dumplin' being hugged by Jim Hogan's two little girls. The big horse raised his head briefly, then followed after a carrot the oldest child carried. *Bye, Dumplin'*, she said silently as another tear slowly trickled down her cheek. *I certainly will miss you.*

After several minutes, Millie heard a loud hissing from inside the wagon. She handed Emily the reins and looked inside, but could see nothing. She checked on the ground on both sides of the wagon. "I haven't seen Honey since before Pa showed up. Have you?"

Emily threw her hands to her cheeks, nearly dropping the reins. "I almost forgot. She was ready to attack to protect you, so I threw a quilt over her and anchored it down with some crates. I was afraid she'd go for Mr. Donovan and he'd have her for supper."

Millie climbed inside the moving wagon and released Honey. The goose rushed out from under the quilt, hissing and honking and fluttering around inside the wagon in an angry snit for several minutes.

She laughed at the bird's antics. "Come here, you big bully," she said between peals of laughter. She held out her arms. After several more minutes of hissing, the goose finally settled into Millie's lap. She hugged and stroked the bird. Tears suddenly flowed down her cheeks. "Oh, Honey, I don't know what I'd do if I lost you, too."

****

Millie rolled out from under her wagon and, looking around, took a deep breath. They'd been on the move for about two weeks, and she still couldn't get over the thrill of being a part of this wagon train. The early morning was her favorite time of day. The dust-free breeze gently swayed the tall grass. Nature's creatures sang their songs. Everything seemed so…new. She built up the fire and filled the teapot.

Something barely audible, almost like a whisper of distress, floated by on the wind. Millie turned slowly until she heard it again. It seemed to come from outside the wagon circle.

"Oh, my, what have we done?"

Millie hurriedly stepped over the wagon tongue and outside the circle. Agnes Smythe stood several feet from the wagons. Her hands cupped her plump cheeks as she stared off into the distance. Millie had never seen such distress on anyone's face.

She quietly stopped beside the short, plump woman. "Agnes, what's wrong?"

Agnes continued staring into space and shook her head. "What have we done?" she whispered again.

Millie rested her hand on Agnes's arm. "I don't understand. What are you talking about?"

Agnes slowly moved her gaze along the horizon. Her face was drawn and pale. "Look," she whispered. The sun was beginning to rise. The tall grassy plains were gently bathed in golden sunlight. The birds twittered and the crickets sang in greeting of a new day.

"There's nothing around us. We're all alone…in the middle of nowhere," Agnes wailed. "It's like the rest of the world just dropped off, leaving us all alone. What will we do? What will become of us?"

Millie started to answer, then shut her mouth and looked around again. She'd spent most of her life out away from people. Even though there were no trees, to her it was still beautiful. It never occurred to her that others might not share her love of nature. She tried to see it as this poor frightened woman did.

"It's all right. We have each other. If we were in town, what would you have?"

Agnes swallowed. "People. Buildings and houses. Animals. Businesses operating as usual."

"Well…" Millie desperately tried to think of a way to calm her fears. "Look at it this way. If you were in that town, what would be outside it?"

Agnes wiped her tears and looked questioningly at Millie. "Country, I suppose."

"That's right. Now turn around and look behind you. What do you see?"

Both girls turned to look behind them. "Wagons?"

"Yes. Wagons. Our town, our homes for the time being, and people. Lots of us all living and working together to get some place, just like those in a town do. And all around us is country. So you see, we're not alone. We're a town on wheels. But unlike a town, we don't have to see the same scenery day after day."

Trying to smile, Agnes drew a ragged breath. "We don't?"

Millie laughed. "Well, I guess it has been the same for a long time. And will be for a while yet, but not forever. As long as we have each other, we'll be all right."

Agnes threw her arms around Millie. "Thank you, Millie. I'm sorry I was such a ninny. It's just that, well, for a minute everything seemed to close in on me."

"I know. Come on, help me get breakfast started. Everyone will be up soon."

****

They'd been traveling for three weeks. The day was hot and dusty. Millie wet her neckerchief before taking a sip from her canteen. *This won't last forever*, she kept telling herself. Sooner or later, they'd get out of these grassy plains and into mountains, with trees, she hoped.

Though she loved the country and this sea of grass, enough was enough. To her way of thinking, it was past time to move on to some different scenery.

Even though John Eagle had warned them what to expect, it became harder and harder every day to believe there was more out there than merely grass and sun.

Every evening, seeing Mr. Donovan point his wagon tongue north, using the North Star as a guide, wasn't very comforting. Lately, under cover of darkness, she'd heard crying coming from nearby wagons.

She watched John Eagle ride toward the lead wagon. He had a deer slung over his saddle. Now there was an interesting man, white, but raised by the Kiowa until he was in his early teens. According to Miss Hannah, Blake's and John Eagle's fathers were brothers, and when Blake went to school, John Eagle went with him, right on through college.

Millie snapped the reins against the oxen's rump. She really didn't blame them for wanting to slow down. It was a hot, dry trek. She'd almost sell her soul for a dip in a nice cool creek. A shadow fell across her, bringing her back from her reverie.

Blake Donovan tipped his hat. "Good afternoon, Mrs. Watts."

"Good afternoon, Mr. Donovan."

"John Eagle just rode in. Says there's a likely looking camping spot just ahead. Since he got us a deer, we've decided to camp early."

She smiled. "I think most of us can go along with that."

"Good."

He tipped his hat and rode on to the next wagon. Millie watched him until she stumbled over a stone. She quickly righted herself. "Watch where you're going, you ninny," she chided herself. "The last thing you need is for Mr. Blake Donovan to have to ride back and pick you up." She'd done very little, in his eyes, to please him. She certainly didn't need any more black marks against her as far as he was concerned. After all this time, he still didn't like her.

Chapter Six

Blake looked up from the map he and John Eagle were studying as Honey, honking loudly, rounded the back of the supply wagon. Emily Peterson chased the bird, swatting at the creature with a broom. Blake caught Emily's broom handle, hauling her up short. "Whoa, what is this all about, Miss Emily?"

Emily struggled for breath and scowled at the goose as it flapped its wings, raced into the campfire's light and headed straight for Millie. "Mr. Donovan, are you still interested in an early Thanksgiving dinner?"

Blake smiled as he released the broom. "You bet, but what did that overgrown *duck* do to you?"

She withdrew a large egg from each of her two apron pockets. "Do you see these? That *bird* had the nerve to lay them in my hatbox, right on top of my best hat!"

Blake's insides ached with suppressed mirth. "No!"

Honey rushed toward Millie, wings spread and honking piteously. Millie stooped down and pulled the goose into her lap. "Honey, what's the matter, girl? Who's after you?" She searched the dark beyond the campfire for the cause of Honey's distress.

The bird snuggled down in Millie's lap and hid its head under her mistress's chin as Blake and Emily stepped into the firelight. Millie hugged her pet closer. "Mr. Donovan, are you annoying Honey…again?"

Blake threw his hands up in surrender. "No, ma'am. That bird and I have an understanding. She leaves me alone, and I leave her alone."

Emily held out the two large eggs. "Well, I wish she had the same understanding with me. I just found these in my best hat."

"Wonderful. We can have flapjacks in the morning."

Emily huffed. "Millie, It's the only hat I brought, and it's ruined."

Millie set her pet aside, and got up to throw her arms around her friend. "Oh, Emily, I'm so sorry. Honey didn't know any better. I'll…I'll give you my hat. I really am sorry."

Emily sighed and gave the eggs to Millie. "Oh, Millie, I know it wasn't your fault. It's just that, well, I've never lived with a goose before and didn't realize that…well, she's not wagon trained. We've got to do something about her nesting anywhere she pleases."

"I know." Millie set the eggs on the work table. "I never gave it much thought when I brought her along."

"Maybe we could build her a…a coop, like the Blanton chickens have," Emily suggested.

"No. She's never been penned up in her life. I couldn't do that to Honey." Millie looked from Emily to Donovan, then back to Emily. "I just couldn't."

Blake looked thoughtfully at the goose. "Ladies, I think there may be a solution to this problem. Let Ezra, John Eagle and me discuss it over supper."

****

Millie looked back at her pet, which appeared to doze as everyone else worked. It had been nearly two weeks since Honey's run-in with Emily. The goose hadn't set one webbed foot inside the wagon since Blake

Donovan had mounted a nesting box on the outside of Millie's wagon beside the water barrel.

His sudden helpfulness was so out of character that, at first, Millie refused to allow him anywhere near her wagon. It took a lot of talking on Emily's part to change her mind. Millie still couldn't figure out why Blake Donovan was being so accommodating. He'd bear close watching until she could decide what he was up to.

She finished hitching the oxen to the wagon while Emily stowed their things in the back. Each day a different wagon led out. For today, at least, it was their turn to breathe something besides dust.

Blake Donovan rode up and tipped his hat. "Let's move out, Mrs. Watts."

Millie stood with her hands on her hips and glared at his back as he rode ahead. The man was impossible. He called everyone else by their Christian names, but not her. To him, she was *Mrs. Watts.* He was the most stiff-necked man she'd ever known.

Millie adjusted her bonnet as Emily joined her. "Are we ready?"

Emily tugged at her skirt, which was considerably looser nowadays. "Yeah. Let's go. I certainly hope we'll see something besides all this grass today. I'm beginning to think there's nothing else between us and the Pacific Ocean."

Millie snapped the whip above the oxen to start them on their way. "I know what you mean," she said as she walked beside the wagon. "I've been hearing a lot of grumbling."

Emily kicked a rock out of the way as she walked next to Millie. "Doesn't the monotony bother you?"

Millie shrugged. "I wouldn't mind seeing a tree or a

nice mountain, but this can't last forever. I just spend my time thinking about other things."

"Like what?"

She cracked the whip again. "Like how I'm going to fix up my home, and how I'm going to make a living when we get there."

"Make a living?" Emily swatted at a gnat. "Don't you think your new husband will be able to support you?"

"I'm not sure I'll take a husband."

"But you have to. You signed a contract."

Millie shook her head. "No, I didn't. I joined the group late. No one asked me to sign anything. I've been taking care of myself for years. I don't need a man to do that. Besides, from where I sit, men are grossly over-rated. They're lazy, mean and abusive."

"Oh, Millie, not all of them. You've just had bad luck with yours so far. Look at Mr. Donovan. He's just as nice as can be."

Millie made an unladylike snort. "Not that I've noticed."

They walked in silence for a spell. Emily plucked a blade of the waist-high grass. "Millie, I don't mean to pry, but...well...about your husband. I get the impression Mr. Donovan doesn't really believe he's dead."

Millie stared straight ahead. "Oh, he's dead, all right. I'm just sorry I wasn't the one who killed him."

"Millie. Surely you wouldn't have killed your own husband?"

Millie nipped at her bottom lip. She didn't like talking about her marriage. It was too humiliating. However, the dismay she saw on her friend's face changed her mind. Besides, she needed to talk to someone. Surely Emily would understand.

She cracked the whip above the oxen one more time. "Otto killed my baby." She didn't say *our baby*. It was hers. He'd never wanted it.

Emily gasped and stopped again. "Killed your baby? Oh, Millie, I'm so sorry, but surely he didn't mean to."

Millie shrugged. "No, I suppose he didn't. He just didn't care."

"That's horrible. How could you have married such a beast?"

Millie wiped away a tear. "Pa lost me to Otto in a poker game. It was either marry him or live in sin. At first it wasn't so bad. Pa gambled away our place, and we were living in a shack at the edge of town. Otto had a house and a couple of acres." She kicked at another rock.

"It was run down, but nothing that couldn't be fixed. And he had chickens. I repaired the coop and penned them in one place so I could gather the eggs. Then I planted a garden, and my aunt and uncle gave us a milk cow."

"Otto sold the cow the first month, and chickens disappeared from time to time, but I managed to save enough from the egg money to be ready to pay Doc when the baby came.

"One night Otto and Pa burst into the house demanding money. When I said there wasn't any, they both called me a liar. Otto slapped me around while Pa searched until he found my stash. Before they left, Otto gave me a kick in the stomach for causing him so much trouble."

Emily gasped.

"Aunt Lavinia hurried out to check on me after they raced past her house on their way back to the saloon. She saved my life, but not the baby's."

Millie wiped the tears and sniffled. "That same night someone bushwhacked Otto. It was more than a week before they told me. Then all I could do was cry because someone beat me to it. Six months later, Uncle James died. I lived with Aunt Lavinia for three years until she passed away, and then I joined this train."

Emily wiped tears from her own cheeks. "It's so hard to believe there are men in this world as cruel as that. Did they ever catch whoever shot your...Mr. Watts?"

Millie shook her head. "No, but from the snatches of conversation I heard between my aunt and uncle, I'm sure Uncle James did it. God help me, I often wished he'd taken care of Pa, too. "Uh, Emily, this isn't something I care to have repeated."

"Oh, I wouldn't, Millie. I don't blame you for feeling the way you do, but not all men are like that. Take my Gaylan. He was wonderfully gentle." She looked sad and dreamy-eyed. "He was an aide for General Lee," she explained in her soft southern drawl. "He came home three days before the end of the war. We had such dreams. We'd be married, then go out west. Gaylan was a teacher. He said a lot of people would be settling out west and he wanted to go too.

Millie glanced at Emily. He hadn't married her. Obviously, he wasn't any better than the men in her own life. "What happened? Did he decide it was too rough to take a wife along?"

Emily sighed. "No. He was killed an hour after leaving my home. In a way, this trip is rather like fulfilling our dream."

A shout from back down the line interrupted any further conversation. Millie halted her team, and she and Emily hurried back to see what had happened.

Donovan was inspecting a broken axle. He stood and glanced at the sun. "I guess this is as good a place as any to noon. You ladies tend to your stock, then rest while Ben and I fix this axle."

After watering their team, Millie gave Honey a drink while Emily prepared cold meat and biscuits for lunch. The sun was directly overhead, affording no shade.

Emily eyed the wagon for a minute. "You know, we could roll the canvas up for a cross breeze and sit inside the wagon."

"Good idea."

After lunch, they both stretched out on the bed for a short nap. Suddenly Emily yelped and quickly sat up, holding her nose.

What's wrong?" Millie asked anxiously.

"She bit me."

Millie looked where Emily pointed. Honey sat on her nest, her neck stretched over the wagon side. Her head rested on Emily's pillow. She gave Emily a soulful look and honked apologetically. Both girls burst out laughing.

Emily lay back down and rubbed the goose's neck. "If you really want to make amends, Honey, I need an egg. Cookies would be nice at our noonings, don't you think?"

"It's a little hard to make cookies without an oven."

"Not really. Cookie showed me how to. I can make them on the griddle."

Millie laughed. "Wonderful. I knew there was a

good reason for doubling up with you." She unhooked the waistband on her skirt. "Your cooking is putting pounds on me."

Emily tightened the rope around her own waist. "That's odd. I eat as much or more than you, and my clothes are getting looser. But," she hastened to add, "I'm not complaining."

Blake reined in Thunder beside the wagon. He looked down at Honey. "Hi, *Duck*." Then he tipped his hat. "Ladies, if you don't mind, let's move out. John Eagle says there's a creek about five miles ahead. It'll be a good place to make camp, providing we don't have any more breakdowns."

Honey honked her approval.

****

Emily was banking the fire when Blake walked by. "Good evening, Mr. Donovan. Have you eaten supper?"

"Evening, Miss Emily. Yes, thanks."

"Then please join us for peach cobbler and coffee."

"Peach cobbler. Where did you find peaches way out here?"

"Millie brought all kinds of canned and dried fruits. We're lightening our load as we go along."

Blake accepted a cup of coffee and a dish of cobbler. He took a good look at Emily when she returned the coffeepot to the fire. Her clothes seemed about two sizes too large. He smiled and watched several of the other ladies milling about camp. Yes, they certainly were "lightening the load."

His smile faded as *Millicent the Jinx* stepped into the fire's glow. Her clothes were bursting at the seams. Her rounded hips accented her tiny waist. Though modest, her blouse fit close enough to accent breasts he hadn't previously noticed.

Who'd have guessed anyone would pick up weight on a trip like this?

Millie filled her dessert plate and joined them. "Good evening, Mr. Donovan."

"Evening, Mrs. Watts. Got your stock all taken care of?"

Honey's happy honks drifted from the direction of the creek. "Yes, I think they're all very content, for now."

Emily poured coffee for several women who'd joined them, some bringing their own dessert. It had become a custom each evening for several ladies representing the members of the train to gather and discuss their problems of the day. To Blake's chagrin, Millie had been elected spokesman of the entire train. Whether he liked it or not, he had to deal with her every evening. It felt like he took his life in his hands every time he stopped at this wagon. The woman was a jinx, pure and simple.

He greeted each of the eight women and took note of their troubles. Tonight, the biggest concern seemed to be the oxen's sore feet. "John Eagle will show you how to wrap their hooves. After a couple of days, they'll be fine." He looked around. "Are there any more problems?"

Several of the women fidgeted and averted their gaze. Something was wrong, but for some reason, no one wanted to tell him. *Tell me what?* This wasn't like these women. None of them had been particularly shy in the past. "Well? Surely one of you can tell me what's wrong."

Millie sighed and stood up. "It's nothing that we

can't handle, Mr. Donovan, but there is something we'd like to know." She looked at the others, then continued. "These fields of tall grass we've been going through for weeks, is that how it's going to be all the way to Montana? Are there no trees, or mountains, or anything but tall grass between here and our destination? And what about when we get there?"

Blake leaned back and grimaced. So that was it. The great plains were finally getting to them. He'd wondered when it would happen. He'd seen women, and men, go mad traveling through these seemingly endless plains of grass. "No, ma'am, This isn't all you can expect in the way of scenery. The plains should end in a few days, a week at the most."

"That's a relief." Emily stood also. "Well, ladies, we have an early day tomorrow. We'd better turn in."

Blake drank his coffee. As soon as the other women left, he turned to Millicent. He wasn't fooled by the scenery question. There was something amiss and he'd bet his horse, *Mrs. Jinx* wouldn't hesitate to tell him.

"Mrs. Watts, I know there's another problem. If it's allowed to go unattended, it could affect the whole train. Since you're captain, it's your responsibility to tell me."

Millie carried the clean dessert dishes to the wagon. Blake followed her. She put them away, then turned back to the fire. He blocked her way. "I want to know, Mrs. Watts."

Millie bristled. "There is one thing, Mr. Donovan. I would appreciate it if you'd stop calling me *Mrs. Watts*. You're not that formal with anyone else. Why with me?"

Donovan lowered his gaze and toyed with the brim of his hat. "I'm sorry, ma'am. It just seemed…proper. What would you have me call you?"

Millie wanted to shake him. "You call everyone else by their Christian names."

He stepped aside, allowing her to pass. "Yes ma'am...Miss Millicent."

She glared at him, her fists braced against her hips. "For heaven's sakes, Mr. Donovan, Millicent was my mother. I'm Millie." She shoved past him, grabbed a bucket of water, and headed for her ox team.

He nodded and walked beside her. She washed the dust from her oxen's eyes and nostrils before feeding them.

"Miss...Millie, I know there's something else. Won't you please tell me what it is?"

She glanced at him, then returned her attention to her team. "It's really nothing to bother you with, Mr. Donovan."

"Anything troubling this train concerns me."

She sighed. "Well, I think it's more the terrain than anything. This endless grass wears on one's nerves. Everyone seems so...oh, I don't know, restless, I suppose you'd call it. They're beginning to squabble over trivial matters. Some of them want to change traveling partners, but the biggest problem is that others want to return home."

Blake grabbed Millie's arm and pulled her around to face him. "Return home?. They can't do that. They'd be lost in no time. And a wagon alone, or even in small numbers, would invite Indian attacks. No one is seriously thinking of turning *back* are they?"

A shiver raced through Millie at his touch. For a brief moment, all she could do was shake her head. "I...I don't think so. Maybe if they knew more about where they were going and what to expect, it would help. As it is, they're going blindly forward to who knows what."

The jolt from his grasp traveled from her arm throughout her whole body, turning her knees to butter. She swallowed and stared into his eyes as if mesmerized. When he finally released her, she felt lost. What was wrong with her? This man had been nothing but trouble since she'd met him. Why was she suddenly weak-kneed the moment he touched her?

Blake nodded. "That makes sense. I'll give it some thought." He tipped his hat and left. "Good night… Miss Millie."

****

Blake was trail-ready an hour before sun-up. Taking hold of Miss Millie's arm last night had been a mistake. All night he'd dreamed he'd pulled her into his arms. She'd rested her small hands on his chest, then smiled knowingly as he'd seen her do so often. Her eyes twinkled with devilment as he lowered his head to hers. Seconds before their lips met, a loud honking rent the air, and a ball of hissing feathers pounced on him.

Twice he'd awakened in a cold sweat, thanks to that dream. They'd been on the trail for two months. Why was he suddenly dreaming of *Mrs. Jinx*? Had she been working on him all this time? Why hadn't he noticed? Blake mounted Thunder. He'd do the scouting today. John Eagle could play nursemaid for a while.

****

Millie smiled and stretched. She didn't have to open her eyes to know this was going to be a glorious day. For the first time since the trip began, she'd slept all night. Not once did she dream of Blake Donovan putting her off the train at some rural outpost, or of Pa showing up with that trash he'd tried to force her to marry.

She peeked out under the side canvas. The first fingers of dawn were just crawling across the sky. Something hard nibbled at her fingertips. "Good morning, Honey. I'm surprised to see you here," she whispered. "What made you leave that wonderful creek?"

Emily raised up to pet the goose. "Good morning, you two. Is it time to get up already?"

"Just about." They both lay back for one more minute.

Emily stretched. "Is it my imagination or is there more room in this bed?"

"I was just wondering the same thing in reverse."

"I thought maybe I was imagining it, but my clothes seem so much looser, too. When we left Independence, I was such a butterball. Maybe I'll be a stick by the time we get to Montana."

Millie laughed. "Don't get too used to this extra room. You may become a stick, but the way I'm growing, I'll be the butterball." Millie grinned as they hurriedly dressed. "All my life I've wanted some kind of shape other than that of a broomstick. Now that I'm getting it, it brings a whole new set of problems."

"Such as?" Emily asked as she pulled the brush through her dark hair.

Millie sat on the tailgate of the wagon and pulled her long braid apart before brushing it out. "Such as what to wear. A few more pounds and I'll pop the seams of this skirt. Yet no one else is small enough to trade with me." She sighed. "I guess we've picked a good time to spring our surprise. Do you think the others will really do it?"

Emily shook the wrinkles from her pink blouse. "I think so. All except Miss Hannah and Mrs. Pollard, but they say they'll wear the split skirts Allison made for them."

Millie shoved the last hairpin in to secure her braid on top of her head. "If we don't fix breakfast and get ready to pull out, Mr. Donovan will leave us for slowing down his precious schedule."

****

The first flush of dawn was barely in the eastern sky when the camp slowly came alive. The tantalizing aroma of fresh brewed coffee wafted among the wagons. The men were dressed and drinking their first cup when the women began to emerge from their wagons.

John Eagle yelped when the coffee Ezra poured overflowed and burned the scout's hand. "Watch what you're doing!"

"I'm awatchin' somethin', but I shore don't believe it."

Blake glanced up and nearly choked on his coffee as several of the women descended from their wagons. Every man stared as the women went about their business as if nothing were amiss.

"Britches?" Most of the women wore britches! Blake's eyes couldn't help following Millie's backside across to the campfire. She might seem thin and frail in a dress, but in those trousers she looked like a—he choked—a woman. And her legs! She reminded him of a brand new foal. He'd never seen such long legs on a female. Not in pants!

This would never do. They couldn't travel across the country with women dressed in trousers. It was... indecent!

Blake tried twice before he managed to speak to the nearest woman. "Uh, ma'am, you don't plan to travel dressed like that, do you?"

"We certainly do," Allison declared in her soft Scottish burr. "I'm tired of nearly breaking me neck every time I trip on me own hem, or trying to cook while the wind whips me skirts into the flames."

"I understand that, but you can't travel dressed like that. It's just not done."

She filled her coffee cup, then smiled up at him. "Aye, and neither's leaving off our petticoats and other …personal items of clothing. But was it not you who said we'd have to change our way of dress if we wanted to make it safely to our new homes?"

"Yes, but…the men, you can't expect them to see you this way every day and… I mean…"

Allison tossed away her coffee, then faced him with her hands on her hips, coffee cup dangling from one finger. "Mr. Donovan, in polite society, gentlemen dinna appear before ladies in their shirtsleeves, much less totally shirtless, unshaved, or spittin' tobacco juice. Now if ye men want to return to propriety, of course we ladies will comply."

Blake started to protest, then slammed his empty coffee cup onto the Arbuckle box and stomped off. What's the use, they had him. In his anger, he barely missed plowing into Millie. He glowered at her, then hurried on. This was her doing. It had all the earmarks of a *Millicent the Jinx* scheme. Ohhh, that woman!

Millie rushed to the campfire just in time to catch hold of Allison's arm as the shaken girl's knees buckled. "Here, sit on this box. Are you all right?"

"Aye, at least I will be in a minute. I canna believe I talked to the man like that. It was like back-talking me da."

"Well, you did wonderfully. No one could've done better. How did you ever think of such a good argument?"

Allison accepted a fresh cup of coffee. "Me da always said I had a wicked tongue."

Millie studied all the women who'd gathered around them. "Okay, ladies, we've won the first round, more or less. We'd better be very sure we get this train moving on time. We have to justify our new outfits."

Murmuring their agreement, the women went about their assigned duties. Cindy Pollard eased up beside Millie. "Thank you for the britches, Miss Millie. I'll find some way to repay you."

Millie smiled at the sixteen-year-old girl. She and her mother, Angie, were traveling with little more than the clothes on their backs. "You're welcome, Cindy. And I know just how you can repay me."

"Really? How?"

"I purchased some yarn while we were in town. Do you think you could find time to make me a stole like your mother's? She said you knitted it for her last Christmas."

Cindy's face beamed. "Yes, ma'am. I'd be glad to."

****

Blake rested his boot on the tongue of the supply wagon. The other men gathered around. Now there'd be hell to pay. The women couldn't run around half dressed and expect the men to ignore them.

Reb shook his head, "Man, I never seed the like."

"Outside a cathouse, I never seen so much of a woman in my life," agreed Reb.

"As if this job isn't hellish enough," Blake muttered. "Regardless of how they dress, those women are still ladies. Ladies that we've taught to be damn fine marksmen, I might add."

Blake saw Reb's gaze follow Miss Millie's shapely figure as she walked across camp to pick up her rifle and head toward her own wagon.

"I see what you mean, Boss," Reb said.

After several minutes of uneasy silence, Blake pulled his hat down on his forehead. "Guess we'd better get going. I sure as hell don't want to have those females accusing us of delaying this train."

Blake saddled Thunder and began moving down the line, helping where he could. He pulled up near Emily's wagon. He tried not to ogle the woman, which wasn't easy. If she could see herself from his point of view, she'd get back into those skirts quick. Her legs, like all the others, resembled stuffed sausages, all but Miss Millie, that is.

"Good morning, Miss Emily. Is there anything I can do to help you?"

She finished watering the last ox, then wiped her hands on her apron. "Good morning, Mr. Donovan. We missed you at breakfast, but we put some biscuits aside for you. Millie? Will you please bring those biscuits we saved for Mr. Donovan?"

Blake stiffened as Millie came around the wagon with a plate of large flaky-looking biscuits. Good grief, had he become such a regular at her table that she held his meals for him? "No, thanks, ma'am, I'm not hungry." He put his heels to Thunder's sides and galloped toward the back of the last wagon. His stomach growled in protest. Even cold, Mrs. Wa-, er, Miss Millie's biscuits melted in your mouth. First pants, then food. Well, he dang sure wasn't going to get caught in her trap.

If he started putting his feet under Miss Millie's table regular-like, the next thing he knew, he'd be placing his boots beside her bed permanent-like. He shuddered. The thought of anything permanent with *Millicent the Jinx* was enough to turn a man gray...permanent-like.

"What do you suppose got into him?" Emily asked.

Millie tucked the napkin tightly around the plate and shrugged. "I don't know, but it's his loss. We'll eat these for lunch with some of that apricot preserve you brought."

****

Thunder rumbled as the dark clouds rolled in their direction. Millie tossed her slicker across the wagon seat. The rain had been expected all day. According to Mr. Donovan, when it hit, it'd probably last for several days. This next meal might be the last hot one they'd have for a while. They made camp early and began preparations for the rainy siege.

During the day, the men had shot and butchered several antelope. Each wagon was dealt a share. Millie sliced and broiled theirs while Emily made cornbread and biscuits. Miss Hannah, who shared their fire, rolled out several pie crusts and began cutting them into saucer-sized pieces.

Emily peered over the older woman's shoulder. "Are you making dessert, Miss Hannah?"

"No, I'm making pasties." She removed the stew pot from the fire and began ladling meat, carrots, potatoes, and gravy onto the crusts. Then she folded the dough over and crimped the edges. She handed the perfect little half-moon pastries to Emily. "Now fry these, girl, and tomorrow we'll have a meal fit for a queen."

Millie grinned. "Miss Hannah, if you'll roll out more of those crusts, I've got some dried apples…"

"Say no more. I'll be ready when you are."

Emily put away the last clean pan and dropped down beside Millie and Miss Hannah. She tightened her stole closer as a cool wind whipped about her. The fire crackled and swirled with each gust. "I don't think I've ever been so tired," Emily said with a sigh.

"Me neither," Millie agreed. She looked up at the moonless, starless sky. "But rain or no rain, we won't have to cook again for days."

The usual group of ladies arrived, each with her own cup and either a pot of tea or a dessert. Blake, John Eagle and Ezra joined them, each carrying his own cup and plate, but Millie noticed none of them saw fit to bring anything else but their appetites.

As they ate dessert, the women took turns stating the various concerns of the wagons they represented. The Jenkins' wagon had run out of axle grease. The doubletree on the Harvey wagon had rubbed a sore on the lead ox, and so on for the next hour. When all the problems were addressed, Blake got to his feet.

"Thank you, ladies. We'll see to all these problems first thing in the morning."

"Mr. Donovan."

"Yes, Miss Winifred?" The woman, though thinning down, still resembled and acted like the typical old maid. He couldn't imagine anyone wanting a woman who always found fault with everything. As far as he could remember, a smirk was the closest thing to a smile he'd ever seen from her.

"Do you think we should pull out in the morning if it's raining? Seems we'd be putting our animals to a great deal of work, what with the mud and all."

"That depends on how hard it rains and the condition of the ground. We can't afford to tarry. We have a ways to go to get to Montana before the winter sets in." He tipped his hat and hurried off.

He clamped his jaws shut. That woman was a constant complainer. She wanted to dally at the slightest provocation. If only she'd shown up at one of his meetings, he never would have allowed her to come along.

****

Blake opened one eye as the cock crowed, but that wasn't what woke him. He listened to a stream of swear words permeating the air, then groaned. He stuck his head outside his tent. "Damn it, Oats, watch your mouth. You'll have every lady in camp swooning. What's your problem?"

The sound of spitting and a mumbled "nothing" was all the answer Blake got. Just as he drew back inside and reached for a towel, a slicker-draped arm holding a steaming cup of coffee reached in. A flash of lightning illuminated John Eagle stooping outside the tent flap. Blake grabbed the tin coffee cup.

"Thanks. What's eating at Oats?"

The scout struck his most serious Indian pose. "Him heap crazy white man. Put wigwam in middle of natural runoff, then swear like crazy man when him get wet."

Blake grinned. "You're joshing." John Eagle chuckled and shook his head. Blake sipped his coffee. "I haven't made that mistake since I was fourteen. And Oats swore he'd been trail driving over twenty year."

Blake finished his cold breakfast, then mounted Thunder. He checked each wagon and told the ladies they wouldn't be pulling out for a day or two. Most of the women had presumed as much. Some were taking the opportunity to sleep a little longer.

Shortly after noon, he made the rounds again. The first two wagons were empty. He became concerned when the third was also unoccupied. Had someone snuck in and carried off six of his women without anyone knowing? He'd already checked the picket line, and the cattle. None of the missing women were there.

He pulled up at the fourth wagon and was relieved to hear voices. He frowned at hearing Mrs. Watts' voice. He couldn't be so fortunate as to have some foolish Indian haul her off. He knocked on the tailgate.

Miss Emily peeked from behind the flap. "Mr. Donovan. Won't you come in out of the weather?"

He tipped his hat. "No, thank you, Miss Emily. I just wondered if you'd seen the ladies from the first three wagons. They've disappeared."

Her face dimpled sweetly as she stepped back to pull the flap open. "Certainly, they're here."

Blake nearly fell from his horse. The ladies were gathered together as if having a Sunday social in their parlor at home. Some were brushing their hair, others doing needlework, while Miss Hannah read to them. His gaze stopped at Millie. Her blonde hair hung loose about her shoulders, short wisps curling about her face. Her work shirt had been exchanged for a frilly white blouse. He'd never seen such a lovely sight in his life. And instead of cleaning her rifle, she sewed on needlework.

"Mr. Donovan?"

Blake cleared his throat, then dragged his attention back to Miss Emily. "Yes, ma'am? Oh, I was just concerned when I found them missing. Everything's just fine." He glanced back at Millie. "Just fine," he muttered as he tipped his hat and rode on.

Emily dropped the flap. "Well, he stared at us as if we were in our wrappers." The ladies giggled, but Miss Hannah grinned at Millie as if she were hiding a secret.

Millie shifted uncomfortably, returning to the quilt top she embroidered. "Did you notice Mr. Donovan is still wearing that same battered hat the oxen trampled? Guess he's not taking any chances with his new one. I've never met such an accident-prone man. Whoever takes him for a husband will certainly have her work cut out for her."

As Miss Hannah resumed her reading, Millie sighed. Never had she felt such contentment. These women accepted her for herself, not for who her family had been.

Aunt Lavinia had been right—about so many things. She'd always said Millie would fill out if she could get away from the worry of a no-good pa and nursing a sick old lady. Millie certainly did miss that sick old lady, but not her pa. And she truly had begun to fill out.

She sighed again as Miss Hannah finished reading the book of Ruth from the Bible. What a touching story. But life wasn't like that nowadays. Men were brutes. She'd have to depend on herself. A small part of her yearned for a home and children. If only it didn't include a husband.

Chapter Seven

Millie squeezed what water she could from her hair, then sat down with Emily and Miss Hannah to let the sun finish drying it. With the wagon master's decision to noon late in order to reach this stream, Miss Hannah had convinced Mr. Donovan to lay over until the morrow.

The stream resembled one big bubble bath, with the women washing themselves, their hair, and their clothes. She doubted any of them would actually get clean, but no one seemed to care. The last stream they'd crossed had been muddied by a wagon train just ahead of them. Mr. Donovan altered their course so there would be plenty of fresh water for them, and grass for their animals.

Now they were trying to get everything done at once. As soon as they finished, the men would wash, and then the animals would be allowed to soak.

Honey honked and swam among the women, ducking under as she was splashed. "Guess Honey thinks she's people," Emily said with a giggle. She wiggled her bare toes in the warm sunshine. "I heard someone crying again last night."

Millie nodded. "I've heard it several times, but lately it's gotten so much worse. Who do you suppose it is?"

Miss Hannah drew a comb through her nearly dry hair. The gray strands gleamed in the sunlight like a rich vein of silver through dark brown clay. "I don't know, but we should find out."

Millie nodded. "If it happens again tonight, I'll go."

Miss Hannah dropped her brush into her lap and eyed Millie and Emily. "Everyone seems depressed and out of sorts, except you two. I haven't noticed you snapping at each other. What's your secret?"

Emily shoved her hair back, "I don't know if we have a secret exactly. My father had every scrap of information available on this trip—the route, the geography, everything. I more or less knew what to expect before we left."

Millie glanced at Emily, then back to the pond. "Me, too. My aunt's lawyer did all that for us. Before I agreed to come out west, he showed me everything he'd gathered for my aunt. Besides, we keep busy thinking about other things."

"Such as?" Miss Hannah prompted.

Emily grinned self-consciously, "It's silly, really."

"It can't be too silly if it works," Miss Hannah insisted.

"Well, I've been mentally decorating and re-decorating my cafe. And planning menus."

"Your cafe? Do you think your husband will allow you to start your own business?"

Emily ran her fingers through her hair and looked at Miss Hannah. "I'm not married yet, ma'am. I have no interest in marrying a stranger. Until I get to know the man I want to marry, I need to earn a living. Millie and I have talked about being partners. She's very good at plain cooking. And my French Grandma on my mamma's side taught me to do wonderful things with spices and sauces. We should make a good team."

A shadow fell across Millie. She looked up. "Hi, Cindy. Come join us."

Cindy nodded a greeting to Miss Hannah and Emily, then sat beside Millie. "I just wanted you to see what I've knitted on your shawl so far. If the pattern isn't to your liking I can change it."

The kelly-green yarn Millie had purchased in the last town they'd passed through was working up beautifully. However, this definitely wasn't going to be a triangular shawl. It started out rounded at the neckline and got larger with each row. "What is this, Cindy? It's not the same as your ma's."

"No, ma'am, it's going to be more of a cape. That way your hands would be free for carrying. But if it's not what you want, it's no trouble to make it the other way."

"No. I love the idea!"

Miss Hannah ran her finger over the pattern. After several stitches the yarn puffed up about the size of a thumbnail, in a ball. "What do you call this stitch, Cindy? I've never seen anything like it."

"I don't know, ma'am. It's just something I made up."

"I'd love to learn to knit," Emily said, wishfully.

Cindy's face lit up. "Really? I could teach you."

"All right, and I'll teach you to make those griddle cookies you like so much."

Cindy's smile broadened. "That's a deal. Then I could trade Miss Allison some cookies for altering my britches on her sewing machine."

"That's it!" Miss Hannah jumped up. "Child, you're a genius!"

All three girls stared at Miss Hannah. "I'm a what, ma'am?" asked Cindy.

Miss Hannah laughed. "Never mind. I'll tell you after supper. By then I should have most of the details worked out."

They watched Miss Hannah hurry toward the wagons. Finally, they scooted closer together while Cindy tried to teach them a simple knitting stitch.

****

After supper, Miss Hannah called a general meeting. Millie refilled all the coffee cups, and Emily passed out the cookies Miss Hannah had asked her to make earlier that afternoon.

"Ladies, my husband always said a woman just isn't happy unless she's nesting. Well, we've all been bickering as if we were a bunch of nestless hens. At this rate, we'll be cutting each other's throats before we reach Fort Laramie."

"As I see it, we have too much time to think and nothing to think about. Men talk about their prized cutting horses, or their cattle, or crops, but women talk about home and hearth, of which, at the moment, we have none. So I propose we turn this wagon train into a moving city. "First, we should decide what kind of town we want, then set about helping each other become the kind of neighbors we'd like to have."

She watched the dubious reactions of her traveling companions. "What I mean is, we all come from different areas of the country and from different backgrounds. Some of us are farm raised, some city bred. Some can cook all manner of fancy dishes and some of you never even had to get your own glass of water. Some of you are educated and some can't read a lick. So I'm proposing we teach one another. Then by the time we reach the valley, we'll already be a real community."

Emily grinned. "You mean like Cindy's teaching me to knit in exchange for my teaching her to make griddle cookies?"

"Exactly. If we pool our talents, by the time we get to the valley, we'll have a community to be proud of."

Winifred Fugit, amply endowed, pushed her way from the back of the group. She squinted her close-set eyes, her little nose pointed upward, as she asked, "This fine community you're talking about, how many saloons does it have?"

"Saloons?" Miss Hannah looked questioningly at Blake Donovan.

Blake shrugged. "As far as I know, none."

She drew herself up to her full five feet four inches.. "Then why are we taking a saloon girl with us? That's just asking for trouble."

Everyone began talking at once.

"What?"

"No!"

"You're daft!"

She pointed to Cora Kerns, a stockily built brunette Millie had thought painfully shy. "She worked in a Saloon in St. Louis. My brother saw her there."

The crowd parted, leaving Cora standing alone, looking from one woman to the next, humiliation and horror on her face as she licked her lips, took several steps back, and turned to flee.

Reb stepped from the shadows to intercept her. He held her securely by the shoulders. "Ain't no place to run, gal. Either make your stand now or work in saloons the rest of your life."

She raised her tear-stained face to his. "You knew?" she gasped.

"Yes, ma'am. But it don't make no difference." He handed her his handkerchief, then turned her back toward the women. "Now, stand and fight for what ya want," he told her softly.

Cora twisted the kerchief nervously. The women were staring at her like a lynch mob. Finally, she dried her eyes, raised her chin, and looked straight at Winifred Fugit. "Your brother's right, I worked in that saloon, and several others before that. But no more."

"Don't you believe it," Winifred stated righteously. "Once a…a loose woman, always a loose woman. They can't be satisfied with one man. It's in their blood!"

Cora clenched her hands as she glared at the sanctimonious woman. "And just how do you know? Have you had several men?" Cora pressed her advantage. "Have you ever had even one man?"

Winifred's mouth gaped as her eyes widened. "Certainly not! I'm a decent, God-fearing woman."

"Are you saying that any woman who's had a man ain't? Miss Hannah or Millie, they've had a man. Does that mean they can't be trusted around other men?"

"Well, of course not!"

"Then how can you stand there and say something so dumb? No one's born a whore. I want to live like everyone else. I want a husband, one for me, that I don't have to share. A house, not a dingy room over a smelly saloon, and…" She stifled a sob as she added softly, "maybe a couple of kids."

Millie's heart went out to the girl. She knew what it meant to be trapped by circumstances, to desperately want another chance for a family.

"I don't believe her. I demand she be put off at the very next settlement," Winifred insisted.

Cora's hands were nearly colorless from being tangled so tightly in Reb's hankie. She seemed frightened as she shook her head. "No, please," she whimpered.

Millie stepped to the front of the group. "Wait. You can't do that. She signed a contract just like the rest of you did. You can't just put her off somewhere. Besides…" She looked at several faces in the crowd, stopping at Winifred's. "There's not a one of us who hasn't done something she's ashamed of. Aren't we all going to the Montana territory for the same thing, to start a new life? We should all leave the past behind us, and work together for a new future."

Everything was deadly quiet. Even the night creatures seemed to be pondering Millie's words. Finally Emily stepped forward. "I agree with Millie. All our lives have changed because of the war, very few for the better. We should start now to make our future husbands and children proud of us. And tomorrow after we make camp, I'll be happy to hold a cooking class for anyone who wants to learn."

"We'll push me sewing machine out," Allison McLeod offered, "and I'll help alter some of your loose clothes. With all this exercise, I've almost walked out of me own britches several times."

Everyone snickered as Blake breathed a sigh of relief. Then the ladies broke into small groups to make plans to share their skills.

"But, but, but what about…?" Winifred sputtered. She was left standing alone.

Blake straightened and tipped his hat as Miss Hannah stopped beside him. She dabbed her brow with a white lace hankie. "Goodness. For a minute, I thought we were about to have a civil war of our own. Thank the Lord for Millie Watts. I don't know what we would have done without her."

Blake clamped his mouth shut and stared at Miss Hannah. Thank the Lord for Millie? Not by a long shot. Granted, she helped avert a bad situation this time, but that didn't offset all the disasters she had caused, or the ones she most assuredly would cause in the future.

Miss Hannah squeezed his arm playfully. "Come on, Donovan, join Millie and me at our wagon. We're starting anew, remember?

Blake snorted. "I'm staying as far away from that jinx and her ornery pet as I can get. Besides, Miss Winifred isn't going to forgive and forget, especially where Miss Cora's concerned." He tipped his hat and walked away.

Hannah smiled. "We'll see, Mr. Donovan. You can bet we'll see."

****

Blake couldn't believe what he witnessed. For days now, the ladies who weren't driving walked in groups. Some had yarn coming from their apron pockets as they knitted with Cindy Pollard.

Many had slates from Miss Hannah's school supplies. They were learning their numbers and letters. Even in the evenings, after supper, the lessons continued. Many were learning to read from the Bible.

There were even classes on manners, grammar, and needlepoint. But what really bothered him was that there hadn't been any bickering since all this began. The atmosphere felt eerie and unnatural.

Blake nudged Thunder up beside John Eagle's horse. "It's just not right. All these women and not one argument in a week. And when it comes to a head, it'll be worse than a raging prairie fire."

The scout glanced over his shoulder. "I hope you're wrong, but in case you're not, I won't be here to see it. We're only a couple of days from the Platte. I think I'd better locate the best fording, then make arrangements to camp near Fort Kearny."

"Good idea. I'm sure the ladies need a few things from the post store. And it wouldn't hurt to go over these wagons. We've had only a few breakdowns. And to tell the truth, that makes me a little nervous, too."

John Eagle grinned and shook his head. "When did you get to be such a nervous ninny?"

Blake resettled his hat and surveyed the distance. "Since I started herding women instead of cattle."

"Yeah, well, see ya soon."

Blake watched as John Eagle rode off. "Coward," he mumbled. He looked back at the wagons, then at the extra horses and cattle bringing up the rear. Everything seemed to be doing fine. So why did he feel so uneasy? His gaze moved back up the line, stopping at Millicent Watts' wagon. *Why, indeed!*

****

Millie stretched, then rubbed her lower back. She'd been baking cookies all morning. In the past two days, while they'd been camped outside Fort Kearny, they'd all made enough money to last a year at home. The men here seemed starved for creature comforts, and many of the women were mending the men's clothes. She and Emily sold cookies and cakes as fast as they could make them. And by the time Mr. Donovan finished with all the wagon repairs, the women should have enough money to buy a year's worth of supplies and still have money left over.

Emily spooned batter onto the griddle. "This is better than a gold mine. If this is any indication, our cafe will do very well."

Millie groaned. If digging gold was as hard on the back as this, why wasn't the precious metal more scarce?

Emily looked critically at Millie's britches. "You should think about getting another pair of britches before we leave. I don't understand how you can keep gaining weight while the rest of us are losing."

Thank goodness. As much as Millie hated to admit it, Mr. Donovan had been right. She hadn't had an ounce to spare. "You're right. Everyone's been trading britches, but I'm still so much smaller than the others. Guess I'll make a trip to the post store before we leave."

She took her cup of tea and sat down. At least she didn't have to cook supper, too. They must have mixed over twenty batches of cookies today. Actually, she'd lost count, but it had certainly been a lot. She didn't want to see another cookie as long as she lived.

She peered over Elsa Hern's shoulder as the German woman thumbed through her picture album. "Who's this?" Millie asked.

"Das ist *mein* da. My father."

The picture was of a man standing beside a brightly painted wagon with a rounded wooden top. Flowers were tied in the horse's mane, and curtains hung from the small window cut in the side of the wagon. It seemed more like a house on wheels than a wagon. "What kind of wagon is that?"

"Oh, dis vas taken in the old country. Dat is a gypsy vagon. I think it vas taken at a fair. Gypsies live in dese kinds of vagons."

"Are you a gypsy?" Emily asked as she took a seat on the other side of Elsa.

"*Nein.* By the time ve get settled in dis country, Mamma say she feel like one."

"Hmmm, looks real homey," Millie said between sips of hot tea. "Guess if you move around a lot, you might as well make yourself comfortable. Come to think of it, we'll be in our wagons for months yet. Maybe we should add some personal touches, make them more homey." Everyone laughed. "I can just see a whole train of decorated wagons traveling across the country," Miss Hannah said as she wiped the tears from her cheeks. "If Mr. Donovan made a fuss over our britches and sidesaddles, think what he'd say about wagons like that."

Emily studied the picture for a long minute. "You know, it's not such a bad idea. Why not make our wagons homelike? We could probably get paint at the post store with the money we made selling all the baked goods this morning."

Miss Hannah struggled to her feet. "Somehow, I doubt Mr. Donovan will allow it, but we can discuss it later. Right now, we'd better get busy. The Army is hosting a dance in our honor in just two days. I don't know about you girls, but it's been years since I attended a dance, and I don't have a thing to wear."

Everyone giggled, then sobered. "You know, she's right," Cindy said. "I've lost so much weight, I'm not sure I could keep my best skirt on unless I tied it with a rope."

"That wouldn't look very nice," Miss Hannah said. "Let's go try on our finery and see what we can alter in the next two days."

A short time later, Millie pulled her green dress over

her head, then tugged at the front of it. "Oh no! I've been saving this dress for a special occasion, and now I've gotten so fat I can't even gather it together, much less hook it. Guess I'll just have to stay here."

Emily dug through her trunk. "That's a good one. No one will ever be able to call you fat! You're going to that dance if I have to sic Honey on you."

"Well, I don't think they'd like my coming in britches."

Emily giggled. "No, I don't imagine they would." She handed Millie a dark rose-colored skirt. "Here, try this on."

Millie pulled it over her head and down around her waist. The skirt wrapped around her one and a half times. She looked up at Emily and shrugged. "Thanks anyway, but I don't think this will do."

"Of course it will. We'll just take it in a little."

"A little! Emily, you'd have to cut away a third of it. You'd never be able to wear it again."

Emily examined the skirt thoughtfully for a minute, then snapped her fingers. "Of course, we need a seamstress. I'll get Allison." She hurried from the wagon, but returned almost immediately.

Allison repinned the skirt several times before she was satisfied. "Aye, me thinks we can gather it all to the back like a bustle, so we can take it out later."

Chapter Eight

Blake tied his string tie, then unpacked his new hat. He'd been wearing the one the ox trampled. Under no circumstances was he going to give *Mrs. Jinx* a chance at this new one. He turned as the other men stopped by the supply wagon. "Are we all ready?"

Reb nodded. "The women are meeting us at Miss Hannah's wagon. They surely are somethin' to behold."

As soon as he saw them, Blake whistled under his breath. They weren't the fat sheep he'd signed on back in Independence. These were capable women. Though still hefty, they weren't the giggling, blushing, creampuffs he'd started out with. They held themselves with pride and confidence, and they were darned good-looking to boot. He tipped his hat. "Ladies. You all look beautiful tonight. It will be our pleasure to escort you to the dance."

With a lot of laughing and talking, they hurried through the main gates and to the fort's mess hall where the dance was to take place. He glanced at Millie several times, but with her all bundled up in her long cloak and hood it was impossible to see what she looked like, not that it mattered. He'd seen enough of *Mrs. Jinx* to know he still wasn't interested.

Major Kirkland, a jovial man with a wide girth and graying hair, met them at the mess hall door. He stepped back to admit them all, nodding to the ladies and shaking hands with the men. "Welcome. We're honored you could join us." He turned to the band. "Let her rip, boys!" Strains of "Blue Tailed Fly" set the beat for a lively evening.

The ladies had barely removed their wraps when the soldiers rushed toward them. Blake glanced at Millie as she removed her hood and cloak, then stared. Her hair gleamed in the lantern light like spun sunlight. It was pulled back loosely and secured in some kind of knot with three curls hanging down on the left shoulder. When she turned, her cheeks were rosier than the pink blouse she wore. How did she get so pretty without him noticing?

Blake watched as she whirled past in the arms of a tall red-haired lieutenant. He couldn't take his eyes off her. During the past weeks, she'd gained weight, and in all the right places. Her green eyes twinkled like dew on new pine needles.

The major nudged Blake's arm before shoving a cup of punch into his hand. "Here, boy, this'll put hair on your chest." He winked, then lowered his voice. "It's been doctored. Sip it slowly," the major warned, handing one to John Eagle.

The scout took a swallow. His eyes opened as wide as quarters. Tears rolled down his face and his mouth gaped open as if he were gasping for breath. Blake slapped him on the back. "Hey, you okay, partner?"

After several long seconds, John Eagle nodded and gulped in several deep breaths. "Man, when you said doctored, you meant *doctored*." He wiped his face. "I think I'll stick to the stuff in the regular punch bowl."

"I think I will, too," said Blake with a chuckle. "Thanks anyway, Major, but I guess we've been on water too long." He turned toward the dance floor as Millie waltzed by in the arms of another soldier. Her whole face glowed as she smiled. Lord, she's a looker, he thought as she disappeared in the crowd.

John Eagle followed the direction of his cousin's gaze. "She heap pretty woman."

Blake glanced over his shoulder at the scout. "She heap big trouble, too, Chief. Any man would look, but only a fool would touch. And believe me, that big a fool I'm not."

John Eagle slapped his cousin on the back. "Of course you're not, Boss. Of course you're not."

Blake glared at his scout's receding back. Now, what did he mean by that? Never mind. Blake knew exactly what he meant. It had taken him several weeks, but he was pretty sure Miss Emily and John Eagle were doing their damnedest to push him and Miss Millie together. He turned back to watch the dancers. Well, they could just forget it. There wasn't a more mismatched pair in the world than he and *Mrs. Jinx*.

Millie glimpsed Blake several times during the evening. He'd danced with nearly every woman in the room. Everyone but her. She sighed. Why couldn't they become friends? On the other hand, the last thing she wanted was to have her life complicated by another man. Pa and Otto were enough men to last her a lifetime. From now on, she'd look after herself. She didn't need anyone else. Especially not a man.

"Miss Millie?"

Millie looked back at her partner. They were standing in the middle of the dance floor. She hadn't even noticed when the music stopped. "What? Oh, I'm sorry. I...I guess I got caught up in the lovely music.

What did you say?"

He grinned down at her. "I said thank you for the dance. I hope you'll save me another before the evening is over."

She smiled at him. "Thank you, I'll do my best."

John Eagle suddenly appeared at her elbow. "If you'll allow me, Miss Millie?"

Millie smiled and placed her hand on his arm. He led her onto the dance floor. They whirled around the floor several times. "Where did you learn to dance, John Eagle? Surely not while living with the Indians."

"No, ma'am. But I've lived with Blake since I was fifteen."

"You have? How did that happen, If I'm not being too inquisitive?"

John Eagle whirled her around the floor as if he'd been doing it all his life. Finally he shrugged. "When my mother died of a fever, Dad brought me to the home of his brother, Blake's father. A couple of years later, when Dad was killed in a hunting accident, Uncle Warren more or less became my father. He educated me, even sent me to college with Blake."

"College? Then what's all that dumb Indian talk you've been handing us?"

He grinned, then leaned closer. "It goes with the image," he whispered.

"Oh, you!" Millie laughed, then sobered. "I'm sorry about your family. So it was your mother who was Indian. What tribe did she belong to?"

He twirled her, then brought her back into his arms. "No. My mother was white. She'd been captured as a baby and didn't know any other life but Kiowa, so Dad chose to live with her people until her death."

"Do you ever go back to visit?"

"Sure," he answered as the music stopped. "Thank you for the dance, Miss Millie." He bowed over her hand as her next partner stepped forward.

Two dances later, Millie breathed a sigh of relief when it was announced that the band would take a breather. She made her way to Emily, who was talking with Mr. Donovan and John Eagle.

"Oh, Millie, isn't this wonderful? It's been such a long time since we've had this much fun! Do you suppose it'll be this way at each fort we come to?"

Millie smiled. "It would be nice, but I wouldn't pin all my hopes on it if I were you."

Emily sighed deeply. "You're probably right." Then she grinned. "But one can dream."

Millie laughed with them, then followed as John Eagle and Blake led them to the punch bowl There was a plate of cookies at each end of the table. "Uh-oh," said John Eagle. "Miss Emily, don't look now, but someone has been sneaking around our camp."

She looked at him in surprise. "What? How do you know?"

He pointed to the sweets. "Those look and…" he stopped long enough to take a bite of one, "taste an awful lot like your cookies."

She blushed and swatted at him playfully. "Of course they're mine. Did you really think we could come to a gathering this large without bringing something?"

The band tuned up, indicating the start of another set. Before Millie could put down her cup, two soldiers were vying for her next dance. Blake watched as she waltzed off with a redheaded sergeant. "How could she enjoy dancing with a man old enough to be her father?"

he muttered. "He's one big freckle with ears."

John Eagle winked at Emily. "Sure makes a man wonder, doesn't it, cousin?"

Blake gave his scout a glare that would wilt well-established cornstalks. "Not really. I'm just glad it's him and not me. That soldier doesn't know what kind of danger he's flirting with."

Emily set her cup down, then gave the scout a conspiratorial smile before turning to Blake. "Well, I for one love to dance, and dancing with a handsome man makes it even more enjoyable."

John Eagle quickly set his cup beside her. "Well, that lets me out, Boss. Guess I'll go mope in a corner while you and Miss Emily take a turn around the floor."

Blake's mouth dropped open as John Eagle suddenly disappeared among the dancers without a backward glance. He turned back to the lady at his elbow. She watched the dancers as if she hadn't heard a thing. Something wasn't right here, but he'd be hanged if he could figure it out. He cleared his throat. "Uh, would you care to dance, Miss Emily?"

She looked at him from under her long dark lashes. "Why, thank you, Mr. Donovan. I'd love to."

Blake looked at her suspiciously as he whirled her onto the floor. The hairs on the back of his neck were beginning to prickle. Whenever Miss Emily took on those innocent southern airs, there was mischief afoot. They hadn't danced halfway around the floor when someone bumped into him. He turned around, preparing to apologize for his carelessness.

"Why, Boss," said John Eagle with an air of total innocence. "Fancy meeting you here. Sorry I was so clumsy." He turned and danced away.

"Hey," Blake found himself protesting to a crowded dance floor. He turned to Emily, but faced Millie instead. "Sorry, Miss Millie. John Eagle seems to have grabbed the wrong partner. Would you care to finish this dance with me?"

Millie swallowed. She tried to smile as she nodded and stepped into his arms. What were Emily and John Eagle thinking? They knew how much this man disliked her. How could they leave her in this predicament? If Mr. Donovan decided to leave her standing alone in the middle of the dance floor, she'd die—right after she murdered him.

She glanced up. His frown immediately turned into a smile, but not quickly enough for her not to know he was thinking along the same lines as she. His smile would warm the coldest of hearts. She discovered it was easy to smile back.

He whirled her away. He was as good as Uncle James on the dance floor. Where had a backwoodsman learned all the newest steps?

"You must have done a lot of dancing in the past, Mrs. Watts."

She smiled. At least he didn't say something like how light she was on her feet. "No, there wasn't any place for women to go to dance except the local saloon. Uncle James and Aunt Lavinia loved music and dancing, though, and we spent winter evenings singing and dancing in the parlor. Do you dance a lot in Montana?"

He shook his head and whirled her past several other couples. "No, there aren't any women in the valley. I learned at finishing school."

Millie cocked a brow. "I thought only women went to finishing schools."

"Yeah, that's true, but Dad used to tease us about going off to college as rough cowhands and coming home as plantation gentlemen, although sometimes he grumbled that I didn't learn the gentleman part very well."

Millie grinned. There were times she agreed with his father, most of the time, in fact. But now wasn't one of them. He'd been a wonderful partner, and they'd not had a single argument or mishap since they'd traded partners with Emily and John Eagle. If only it could stay this way.

"What's the town like?"

"Town?"

"Yes, the town you're taking us to. Are there already buildings, or will they be built as needed?"

"Well, when I left, they were busy building. They hoped to have the town ready by the time we got there."

"How wonderful. What kind of buildings were they erecting?"

Blake bumped into another couple, mumbled excuse me and whirled around the floor several times. "Let's see. The church was the first one built, followed by the school. When I left they were finishing the hotel and the jail. Then they planned to start on a strip of stores. They should have everything pretty well finished by the time we get there."

"I think that's lovely. It's very exciting being in on the beginning of a town. Do you think there'll be any shops to rent?"

"Rent? For what?"

"Well…" She wasn't sure she was ready to tell her own plans yet. "Let's see, Allyson wants to open a dressmaker's shop. We were wondering just the other day if there'd be a place for her to rent or at least a house she could work out of."

Blake nodded. "I'm sure we could find something. It would be up to her husband, of course."

Millie bit back a strong retort. No man would tell her what she could or could not do, and she'd bet Allyson felt the same way. However, she wasn't going to ruin the first pleasant time she'd had with Mr. Donovan since bumping into him in Independence. "I'll tell her that," she said primly.

The music stopped. Immediately a master sergeant stepped up, switched his wad of tobacco from one cheek to the other, and bowed to Millie. "May I have this here dance, ma'am?"

"It would be my pleasure," she said, flashing an *I'm sorry* smile in Blake's direction. Oddly, she meant it. She hadn't enjoyed anything in a long time as she'd enjoyed dancing in Blake Donovan's arms.

Blake watched as Millie hopped away, trying to keep up with her new partner's uneven gait, then winced as the man stomped her foot. Lord, that clod would cripple her for life if he kept that up.

Before Blake had taken two steps forward to rescue her, John Eagle was tapping the sergeant on the shoulder. Good.

Blake turned to retrace his steps, but bumped into a tall, stocky lieutenant. Before he could apologize, Miss Emily stepped into his view. "Thank you for the dance, Lieutenant." Then she turned toward Blake. "Why, Mr. Donovan, how nice to see you again." She stepped forward, and before he knew what had happened, he was back on the dance floor.

"Are you having a good time, Miss Emily?"

Her eyes twinkled. "Oh, my, yes. This party is a

girl's dream come true. I don't think I've missed a single dance. I honestly can't remember when I've had such a lovely time."

He grinned at her enthusiasm. She was such a warm, bubbling person. The man who married her would never suffer from the lack of joy in his home. He noticed Millie at the far end of the room. She was laughing, but it was a dignified, reserved sort of laughter. Why wasn't he drawn to Miss Emily instead of *Mrs. Jinx*? And as much as he hated to admit it, he *was* drawn to the woman.

After a few more turns, he was bumped from behind. He didn't have to turn to know he'd end up with Miss Millie. He had caught on to the pattern. John Eagle and Miss Emily were still trying to play cupid.

"This is beginning to be embarrassing," Millie admitted as she stepped into his arms.

"I know what you mean. I think those two are plotting against us."

Millie was astounded at how easy it was to talk to this man. Suddenly, the prospect of living in Montana was much more than just a means to get away from her father. It was the beginning of a new life. And all the men in the valley became more interesting.

"What do you do in the valley, Mr. Donovan? Are you a rancher too?"

"No, ma'am…well, yes, in a way."

"No? In a way? I don't see how it can be both," she teased.

His smile was enough to make her legs turn to jelly. She hardly noticed anyone else in the room as he whirled her around the dance floor.

"John Eagle and I are partners in a horse ranch. Town living doesn't suit him, so we put the house on his half. I'm going to live in town, at least for a while."

"Really? What will you do there?"

"I'm the town's sheriff."

"You are? I think that's exciting."

"You do? Most women shy away from lawmen."

"I don't know why. Without lawmen, our society would be in a pretty pickle."

Blake began to relax. Maybe his notion of an enforced solitary life wasn't his only option after all. More and more, he began to realize what an extraordinary woman Miss Millie was.

The last strains of "Oh! Susanna" faded out. Breathing hard, Millie fanned herself vigorously while Blake swiped at his brow with his shirtsleeve. "Would you care for some punch, Miss Millie?"

Millie's heart skipped a beat. He'd finally used her Christian name. "I'd be most grateful, Mr. Donovan."

They joined a group near the refreshment table, and Blake excused himself to fulfill his offer.

"Oh, Millie. I couldn't believe it when I saw you dancing with Mr. Donovan," Cindy exclaimed. "Isn't he wonderful?" She looked in his direction, dreamy eyed.

The ladies laughed.

Cindy's mother tweaked the Cindy's nose. "He's entirely too old for you, young lady."

"Oh, Ma."

Blake picked up two cups of punch, then looked at the plate of cookies. What he needed was a third hand. He looked up at John Eagle. "Hey, how about taking that plate to Miss Millie?"

"To Miss Millie? You mean *Mrs. Jinx*? The woman no smart man would get involved with?"

"All right, you overeducated redskin. Keep that up

and I just may stake you out over an ant hill."

Chuckling, John Eagle picked up the cookie plate and walked beside Blake toward the ladies. "Come on, Blake, you've got to admit she's not a bad dancer."

"No," Blake conceded, "she's not, but her dancing has never been the problem."

"No, but you've been dancing with her all evening, and nothing has happened so far."

Blake shook his head, "Well, cousin, the night is still young. And don't think for one minute that a few dances are going to make any difference. I'm just trying to make this a pleasant evening."

John Eagle stopped beside Millie and Emily. "Miss Millie?"

Blake stepped up to Millie from the other side. As she turned to acknowledge John Eagle, she bumped Blake's arm. Red fruit punch flew from the cup to the front of his light blue shirt.

"Oh, no!" Millie looked on in horror as the red liquid trickled down his shirt. "I'm so sorry!"

Miss Hannah grabbed some napkins from the table. "Here." She shoved them into Millie's hand.

Millie quickly began to dab at the front of his shirt. "I'm terribly sorry, Mr. Donovan."

"That's quite all right, Mrs. Watts." He took the napkins from her. "Thank you, but I'll do it." After several more dabs, Blake set the napkins aside. He plucked at the wet fabric sticking to his chest. "If you'll excuse me, I'll go change my clothes."

He stopped only long enough to retrieve his hat, coat and gun. "I knew it was too good to last," he muttered as he slammed the door behind himself. "She's a jinx, pure and simple."

Chapter Nine

Millie tied down the wagon cover. "There. That should do it. No one will see the paint until we're ready to use it. Now all we have to do is wait until John Eagle and Mr. Donovan go off for a while."

Emily pulled the top taut over the wagon hoops and tied it off on her side. "I can't wait. You know, every time I want to visit with someone, I have to count the wagons so I can find my way home. It'll be so nice to have them all different."

Millie nodded. Yes, it certainly would—but would Mr. Donovan understand? Somehow she didn't think so. Men were so…unimaginative.

John Eagle stopped his horse beside their wagon. "Good morning, Miss Millie, Miss Emily."

They both looked up with a start. Millie's heart did a half flip. What an odd time for him to ride up. "Good morning, John Eagle. We expected you were out scouting by now. We're almost ready to pull out."

"Fine, Miss Millie. I'm leading you today. Blake decided he needed some exercise. He's out there in my place. Are there any last-minute problems I can help you with?"

"No, we just have a few more things to put away and we'll be ready to go."

"We'll pull out as soon as I check the horse herd." He tipped his hat and touched Patches with his heels.

"Well," Emily exclaimed. "You'd think in the three days since the dance Mr. Donovan would have spoken to us at least once. Do you suppose he's still peeved over the accident with the punch?"

Millie shook her head as she pulled the chair Emily handed her into the wagon. "Emily, you certainly have a way of understating a situation. I really don't think peeved is exactly how Mr. Donovan felt about getting punch spilled all over his new shirt."

Emily dusted her hands together. "Well, I'm making an apple cobbler for supper tonight. If he wants to be a sourpuss, he can just do without."

John Eagle galloped by. "Let's go, ladies."

They traveled all day, seeing no one other than an occasional glimpse of Mr. Donovan on the horizon. Emily shaded her eyes and watched him ride along the ridge some distance ahead. "How long can one man hold a grudge? He acts as if he's the only man in the world who's ever gotten punch spilt on him."

Millie shook her head. "That man is accident prone. It's almost as if accidents hang around waiting for him to step in their way. He'll certainly be a trial to the poor woman who takes him to wed."

****

John Eagle tightened the cinch on Patches' saddle. "You sure missed a good supper last night, Blake. That cobbler was the best they've made so far."

"Don't worry about it. I had a nice peaceful evening."

The scout looked across his animal's back at his cousin. "Speaking of which, peace isn't what I feel in the air around here these days. What do you suppose those women are up to this time?"

Blake shook his head as he tied a bedroll behind his saddle. "I don't know, but I'm glad you noticed it, too. I was beginning to think I was paranoid."

"Naw, I've given it some thought. Can't put my finger on exactly why, but I know they're up to something."

Blake stepped into the stirrup and hoisted himself onto the saddle. "Me too, but I'll tell you right now, it'll be Oats' problem. I figure it'll take at least a couple of days to get enough meat to last for a while. And I intend to stay away every minute of it." If anyone got caught in one of *Mrs. Jinx*'s disasters, it wouldn't be him this time.

John Eagle swung up onto Patches and followed Blake out of camp. As soon as they passed, Cindy stepped from behind a boulder. She watched them disappear into the distance, then ran to find Millie.

"Millie? Millie!"

"Whoa!" Millie caught Cindy's arm. "Slow down and catch your breath. What's the matter?"

Cindy leaned over, struggling to breathe. Finally she straightened. "Mr. Donovan," she gasped, "and John Eagle just left. I heard them say they'd be gone for at least two days."

"That's wonderful!" Millie turned to the several women who'd hurried up to see what the matter was. "Now's the time. Pass the word. We have a lot to do in the next two days. Let's get started." Instead of loading up to pull out, the ladies began unloading their wagons.

Ezra galloped into camp. "Whoa, what's goin' on here? Why ain't you ladies loaded and ready to go? We have a fer piece to travel before sundown."

Miss Hannah set down her end of the table she was helping Emily move. "We've decided to stay here and take advantage of the good weather and the creek for some much needed repairs and cleaning."

He shook his head vigorously. "No, ma'am. Donovan said we was to meet him at the next crossin', and that's about two hard days' travel from here."

"Well, Mr. Donovan will just have to wait for us, or come back here."

"But ma'am, we jest spent a week at the fort. We shouldn't need no repairs or cleanin'."

Hannah cringed at his neglect of proper grammar. "Nonetheless, we do. There's water for washing, plenty of sun to dry our things."

Elsa stepped from the crowd. She looked up shyly at Ezra. "Ya, ve have things to do that ve did not feel right doing in front of all those soldiers."

Several other women murmured their agreement. Ezra scratched at his beard and looked around the cluttered camp.

"We're not moving, Mr. Oats," Miss Hannah assured him. "A couple of days more aren't going to hurt. However, if you think you can catch enough fish, we could manage a big fish fry tomorrow night. We ladies might even have enough time to make a pie or two."

Ezra's face lit up, before he squinted his eyes and glared. "'Course I can ketch 'nough fish. What kind of a question is that? C'mon, Ben. Let's get outta here 'fore they put us to work fetchin' water or some such."

As soon as the men were out of sight, the women, giddy with excitement, quickly finished unloading and began scrubbing down their wagons.

After two hours, Miss Hannah straightened up, rubbing her back. "I could use a cup of tea."

Millie dried her hands on her apron. "That's a good

idea, and while the sun dries our wagons, we can decide how we want them decorated."

By late afternoon, the wagons were painted and nearly dry. Millie and Miss Hannah surveyed the vehicles. No two were the same color. "This is lovely," Miss Hannah said. "Now all we have to do is remember who lives in which color."

"*Nein*, that no problem. I paint names on each one," Elsa offered. "Come, I show you."

They followed her to a dark green wagon. On the side, just above the front wheel, she'd painted her name and that of her wagon mate, then surrounded them with birds and flowers, giving it a cameo effect.

"Elsa, that's beautiful. I didn't know you were so talented. Could you do that to our wagon as well?" Millie asked.

"Ya."

"Mine too," Miss Hannah added. All of the women examined her work and enthusiastically agreed.

Elsa blushed. "Ya, I do all."

As they walked past Cindy's wagon toward their own, Millie noticed three unpainted wagons sitting to one side. She sighed. "Every town has its slums, but it's a shame our wagon master has to live in one."

"Hmmm." Miss Hannah thoughtfully stared at them for a long moment. "Why don't we see if we have enough paint to do those, too?"

Millie flatly refused. "Not me. No matter what color we use or how nice it turns out, if I have anything to do with it, Mr. Donovan will hate it."

"I'll do it," Cindy offered.

"Fine, child," Miss Hannah agreed. "See if you can find enough paint to do the job."

Several minutes later Cindy stopped by Millie. "Millie, there might be enough white to do all three, but it'll be close."

"White?" No, that'll look dirty right away. Maybe you can find a little color to mix with it."

"All right, I'll ask around."

Miss Hannah watched the girl hurry off, stopping at each of the other wagons. "I don't know where that child gets all her energy."

Millie shook her head. "Me neither, but right now I could certainly use some of it."

They all laughed as they began washing and hanging out their personal clothing. As the day moved on into evening, the women lit the fires and started a late supper.

Emily peered into the gathering dusk. "I wonder where the men are? I halfway expected them to show up for supper."

It was well after dark when Ben and Ezra stumbled into camp. "Boy, it sure do get dark out here. Plum forgot there weren't no moon tonight."

"My goodness," Emily said. "We thought ya'll were spending the night out."

"No, ma'am, we got to fishin' and talkin' and jest lost track of time. Shor' hope you still got somethin' in that there pot. I got a powerful hunger right about now."

Emily hooked her arm through Ezra's. "Well, of course I do. Ya'll don't think I'd forget about you now, do you?"

Ben pulled off his hat and sat down beside Ezra. "No, ma'am. You never have before." He looked around. "It's awful dark out there, but as near as I can tell, you ladies have everything back in the wagons. You should have waited for us to come back to help with the heavy stuff."

Emily set plates of vegetables and leftover roast before each man. "Thank you, Ben, but you men were busy providing meat for our table. We didn't want to bother you with woman's work. Did you get enough fish for supper tomorrow?"

"No, Missy, we'll go back first thing in the morning. But don't you fret none, we'll have enough by tomorrow night," Ezra managed to say between bites.

Morning was at its darkest when Millie heard Ben and Ezra leaving camp. "Why'd you want to get up before dawn?" Ben demanded in a hoarse whisper. "Now we don't get breakfast."

"I kept thinkin' what if some varmint gets that string of fish we left in the water? We'd have to ketch 'em all over again."

Millie made a mental note to take breakfast to them so they wouldn't return to camp early. She lay there for a while, mentally rearranging the wagon and trying to decide what decoration would look best on the side of their wagon. It was a pretty color. She and Emily had wanted a light honey color but had accidentally mixed too much brown in with the yellow. However, it didn't look too bad, as near as they could tell in the waning light. As soon as the sun came up, she'd get a good look at it now that it was dry.

Emily had slipped out just before dawn. Millie could hear her moving toward the tent they'd erected to offer a measure of privacy while taking care of their personal needs. She'd just drifted off when Emily shrieked, "Oh, no!"

Millie's eyes flew open and her feet hit the floor at the same time. She scrambled from the wagon. "What's the matter?"

Emily's face was pale as she pointed toward the three wagons Cindy had painted. Millie gasped. One was beige, one light pink, and one pale lavender.

The other women, in various forms of undress, scrambled from their wagons. "Saints preserve us," several mumbled.

Cindy shoved her way to the front and stood between Emily and Millie. "Oh, no," she gasped. She looked at the stricken faces around her. Finally, she cleared her throat nervously. "Those didn't turn out half bad. It was so dark by the time I finished, I wasn't sure what they'd look like."

"Half bad!" Miss Hannah cried. "Are you crazy? Child, those men are going to sell us all to the first band of Indians we come upon."

Millie swallowed, trying to control the war that was suddenly waging in the pit of her stomach. "Cindy, please tell me the beige wagon is Mr. Donovan's."

"No, that's Ben's wagon. I tried to make the second wagon a little darker, but it was almost dark and I guess I added the red instead of the brown paint."

"Well that explains the pink," said Miss Hannah, "but what about the lavender?"

Cindy shrugged. Obviously beginning to feel the unrest in the crowd. "Uh, I was running out of paint so I tried to add the rest of the brown. Guess I got the blue instead."

Millie grasped the girl's arm. "Cindy, please tell me the pink one isn't Mr. Donovan's." Not that he'd like the lavender one any better.

"I can't. Unless someone moved the wagons during the night, that pink one's where I left his."

"Maybe we can mix the rest of the paint and redo them," suggested Cora.

Cindy shook her head. "I…used…every bit…of it."

Groaning, Millie walked slowly toward the back of her own wagon. "He's going to kill me. Doesn't matter that I didn't do it, he's going to kill me."

****

Blake lifted his hat and wiped his forehead on his sleeve. "I think this is about all we can haul. Guess we'd better head back. Can't say I won't be happy to eat someone else's cooking. You never were the best in the kitchen."

John Eagle cleaned his skinning knife on a tuft of grass. "You're not so good yourself. Sure hope Miss Millie saved us some of her biscuits."

"Humph," Blake said as he emptied the coffeepot. He was starving for some female cooking, but not necessarily hers.

"Since we're a day early, maybe the wagons aren't too far ahead. If we push it, maybe we'll be in time for breakfast."

As they topped a hill, both men drew up and stared. "What in hell…?"

"I've never seen anything like that in my life," John Eagle declared.

Wagons were circled in the valley below. Colored wagons—every color in the rainbow and then some. "Those are our wagons, aren't they?" Blake asked as they rode down the hill, then slowly around the circle, looking at each wagon as if it were something from another planet.

Miss Hannah nodded from her red wagon. Miss Millie and Emily proudly stood beside their dark honey-colored one. Yellow-and-brown calico curtains hung from the front and back of the wagon. The seat had been removed and two chairs with matching cushions sat in its place.

Every wagon, including the supply wagon, was a lively color. There were even flowers and birds drawn on some of them along with the occupants' names. When he got to his own wagon, he let loose a string of swear words that made Miss Hannah gasp.

Pink! His wagon was pink, with red flowers and birds. And his name on each side by the front wheels. How could they? "Who did this!" he demanded. Then turned and glared at the honey-and-brown wagon. Who else? "Mrs. Watts!" he bellowed.

Millie cringed. She'd been afraid he'd react that way. She stepped from the crowd that had gathered. "Yes, Mr. Donovan?"

Her soft gentle answer didn't fool him for one second. "Don't '*Yes, Mr. Donovan*' me! This is your doing! How could you?"

She didn't bother to deny any part in it. If he believed her, which he most certainly wouldn't, his wrath would be turned on Cindy. Maybe she could bluff her way through. "You don't like it?"

"Like it?" Blake waved his arms. "This whole train looks like a gypsy caravan. We'll be laughed off the face of the earth, the butt of all the jokes clear across the country."

When he stopped for a breath, Millie tried to reason with him. "Oh, really, Mr. Donovan? That's what you said about our wearing britches, but who's to see us, way out here?"

"Who? Who?" For several minutes he seemed to be

at a loss for words. Then he grabbed her arm and jerked her around to face his wagon. "Painting your wagons was one thing, but how dare you do it to mine!"

She jerked her arm from his grasp. How dare she? How dare he lay hands on her? She took a deep breath, trying to hold onto her temper. "We didn't intend to, but it looked so bad after ours were painted, we decided to finish the job."

"But pink? Why didn't you paint it black, or brown, or at least blue?"

She shrugged. "We didn't have enough of any one color. We mixed the two largest amounts we had left, red and white, to make enough. I'm sorry if you don't like it."

"Don't *like* it! You're damned right I don't like it. And what's more, You're going to fix it."

Millie glared at him. He was the most ungrateful wretch she'd ever met. The wagons had been ugly, now they were homey. Everyone's spirits were up. This gave each one of them a certain amount of pride. "Mr. Donovan, these are our homes. No one wants her home to look like her neighbors'. It's not as if we can plant flowers and trees around them. This way each of us has her own unique place."

He seemed ready to explode. Millie swallowed, then smiled as best she could. "Don't worry, Mr. Donovan. We'll re-do your wagon just as soon as we pass a town and can buy some more paint." She turned to make a hasty retreat, but he caught her arm.

"Oh, that won't be necessary. We'll just unload and trade wagons. I'll take yours."

"Mine! Now, wait a minute. If you don't care for the pink wagon, you could…move into the supply wagon."

"The supply wagon? No, I can't. It's specially built to keep things dry and varmint-free. And it's..." He looked around. "It's purple!"

Emily laid a comforting hand on his arm. "No, It's lavender. Isn't it a lovely shade?"

Blake flung his arms up, then dropped them against his sides. "Oh, yes. Just lovely." Then he leaned down until he was almost nose to nose with her. "But I don't intend to live in it, either, so get busy!"

"You can't just..." Millie began.

"Oh, yes, I can." Glaring, he took a step toward her. She swallowed and backed up each time he moved forward. "Now get started," he said in low even tones.

Emily caught Millie's arm and pulled her into the crowd of women. "We'll do that, Mr. Donovan. It won't take long. C'mon, Millie. We'll all help."

Blake stomped toward the horse herd. He'd known she was up to something, but never in his wildest dreams would he have thought of painting the whole damn wagon train. He could have taken the blue wagon, or the green one, but it was only right that he take hers, since this was most certainly all her doing.

He spotted Ezra and Ben climbing the hill from the creek. Each carried a fishing pole in one hand and a mess of fish in the other. "Oats," he yelled. "I wanna talk to you."

Ezra and Ben exchanged looks, then changed direction and walked toward the wagon master. "Hey, Donovan, glad to see you're back. How was the huntin'?" Ezra asked.

"Never mind the hunting, Oats. Suppose you tell me why you allowed those women to paint my wagon pink."

Ezra looked as confused as Blake felt. "Paint? Pink?

What're you talkin' about, boy?"

Blake pointed toward the wagons. "That."

Oats followed Blake's gaze. His mouth dropped open. His pole and fish fell to the ground as he hurried toward his own brightly colored lavender wagon. "What the...? That's my wagon? Who done that?"

Blake stopped slightly behind Ezra. "The women, that's who. You were supposed to be watching them. Whatever possessed you to go fishing?"

The old cowboy grasped the sides of the wagon as if to look inside, then jerked his hands back like they'd been burned. He wiped them on his shirt, then carefully peered inside without touching anything. "Galdarnit!" They's even painted the insides."

He dropped down onto the ground, rested his elbows on his crossed legs and held his head in his shaking hands. "How could they do that to me?"

"To *you*? Look what they did to me! My wagon's pink!"

Ezra glanced up, then shook his head. "That's understandable. They don't like you. You're always after eatin' that there goose, but me! I ain't never done nothing to them little ladies. And Miss Elsa!" His eyes widened as the full impact dawned on him. "Why, she lied to me. Made me believe they was goin' to wash them fancy she-male doo-dads. Sent me off fishing so we could have a big fish fry t'night!"

Blake dropped down beside the old cowboy and watched the women who hustled to unload his wagon. Could they really have done this...maliciously? Just because he teased about an early Thanksgiving? Nay, he decided. It was all that man-hating jinx's fault. She just plain didn't like him.

John Eagle squatted beside them. "Good thing I was riding Patches—they might have painted him to match one of those wagons."

"Very funny, cousin."

Ben stooped beside Ezra. "I guess I got lucky. My wagon's kind of a whitey- brown with light flowers and birds painted on the tailgate. I can probably hang something over the end to hide those."

Finally Ezra got up and, shaking his head, walked slowly to his wagon. "I won't do it," he muttered over and over. Stopping several feet from the offending vehicle, he snatched off his hat and threw it on the ground. "No, sir! I won't do it. Galdarnit, I won't drive no lie-lack wagon."

Blake waved at his new wagon. "Then do what I did. Pick a color that suits your fancy and the ladies will reload for you."

Ezra shook his head."Cain't do that, boy. You know this here wagon's special made and sealed special to hold our extry supplies. Cain't none of these other sissy wagons keep our grain and meal dry." He turned and glared at the women who were nervously pretending to be busy elsewhere. His gaze finally settled on Elsa, the one he felt had betrayed him the most. "Them womens painted it, they's gonna drive it."

Chapter Ten

Millie sat on the tailgate scraping the mud from her boots. Seemed like that was all she'd done for days. That and wringing the water from her clothes every hour or so. It had rained constantly for the last week. The only one on the whole train not squawking like a soaked hen was Honey. She was in goose heaven.

Millie looked up as Honey waddled around the end of the wagon, honking at the top of her voice. The goose seemed to be doing a little dance, flapping her wings and shaking one webbed foot, then taking a couple of steps before shaking the other. Finally Millie realized her pet was trying to shake the mud from her feet, too.

"Well, ol' girl, looks like you've finally had too much of a good thing. There's a lot to be said for sunshine and a little dust, isn't there?"

The goose eyed her mistress, then spread her wings and honked. "No!" Millie screamed. Honey flew into Millie's lap, muddy feet and all, knocking her mistress backwards into the wagon bed. Millie struggled to gather the large bird into her arms and sit back up. A masculine chuckle made her skin prickle. She peeked from under a large speckled wing.

Blake Donovan, hat thumbed back and hands on his hips, stood not three feet away, an amused smirk on his face. "Ain't pets wonderful," he said between chuckles, then pivoted around and left.

Millie fell back, burying her face in Honey's breast feathers. "Ohhh, that man…"

As he walked away, Blake shook his head. The woman was a menace even to herself. How she'd lived this long without a keeper, he'd never understand.

He walked down the line of wagons until he met John Eagle coming from the other end. "How are things back there?"

"Not bad." The scout thumped the water from the feather sticking out of his hatband. "There are three sewing groups and two reading sessions in progress. These women are certainly determined. By the time we reach the valley, they'll be a well-educated bunch. Heaven help their husbands."

They turned back toward the head of the train. "Then there's Miss Winifred."

Blake looked up, then cursed as his foot sank to the boot top in a mud puddle. He pulled his booted foot out of the puddle and shook the excess muddy water from it. "What's she up to now?"

"Nothing much, just wants to know if this delay might keep us from making it through the mountains before snowfall. She feels maybe we should turn back and try again next spring."

Blake snorted just as they passed Millie's wagon. She was washing the mud from Honey's feet. "Between Miss Winifred and *Mrs. Jinx*, I wouldn't do this again next year if my life depended on it."

Blake cringed as he stopped beside the lead wagon. That lavender color still made his innards shiver. "By the way, Reb rode in a while ago. Looks like the storm's over. He says it hasn't rained to the northwest in the last couple of days. If the sun comes out this afternoon, maybe we can push on in the morning."

John Eagle pulled his jacket from the back of the supply wagon. "Think I'll saddle Patches and check out the fordin' at the Platte. With all this rain, we might have to use the ferry."

****

Blake flexed his tired shoulders, then rubbed the back of his neck while awaiting the next wagon. The river was so high grown men would have had a hard time fording it. It was another half day farther to the ferry, but they decided it was safer for the women. He'd haggled all yesterday afternoon over the price and gotten nowhere until Miss Hannah stepped in. She talked the ferryman down to half what he was demanding and threw in domestic services for the rest.

The women invaded the ferryman's cabin shortly after breakfast. He'd looked in after lunch and couldn't believe his eyes. The place was spotless. Everything was washed, swept, and put away. They'd taken the flour sacks used to cover the windows and transformed them into attractive curtains. There was even a stew cooking in the fireplace.

Donovan watched as each wagon was rolled onto the barge, the toll was paid, both in coin and canned or baked goods. The ferryman obviously hadn't done a thing about his personal hygiene all winter, yet as her turn came, each woman paid her toll, then smiled and curtsied to him as if he were a Greek god.

The women drove the herd of horses toward the water while Ezra tightened the cinch on his saddle. "You know, Oats," said Blake, "the only thing stranger than seeing a woman in pants, riding sidesaddle, is seeing one in pants doing a cowpuncher's job from a sidesaddle. I just don't see how they stay balanced on one of those things."

Ezra spit, then climbed onto his own saddle. "Me neither." He got comfortable, petting his horse's neck. "Makes me gladder ever' day I ain't no she-male."

The horses, urged forward by Miss Millie and Miss Elsa, plunged into the rushing waters. Blake turned his attention back to the last three wagons. "Bring that wagon up, Miss Winifred."

Winifred slapped the reins against the oxen's rumps, and the wagon bumped down the slope toward the river. She stopped at the bank and stared in horror at the rushing water. All her life she'd been terrified of the water. Even crossing a bridge left her feeling faint. She couldn't get on that barge. What if something happened? What if it sank in the middle of the rushing water? The livestock would run her down.

Cora stepped up on the wagon rung and reached for the reins. "Here, I'll do it. Water don't scare me none."

Winifred came out of her stupor. "What? What do you think you're doing? I can drive my own wagon, thank you." She yanked the lines aside and slapped them smartly against the oxen. Cora barely had time to jump out of the way. "The idea!" Winifred groused. "There's nothing in the world that trollop can do that I can't do just as well if not better."

At the edge of the barge, the oxen were unhitched and the wagon rolled forward until it was at the far edge of the vessel. The brake was set and blocks wedged against the wheels. As the other women had done, Winifred and her wagon mate, Olive, paid their toll, then got on the barge with the wagon.

The water slapped at the barge. Winifred clutched

the side of the wagon as the barge bounced and bucked across the angry water. Suddenly the barge jerked to one side. The wagon bounced forward, sending both women flying into the air.

Winifred screamed as she hit the water. The current sucked her under. She bobbed up, gasping for breath and grabbing for anything to keep her afloat. All she grasped was air. Over and over the waves covered her head.

Millie looked up just in time to see Winifred, Olive, and their wagon plunge into the swollen river. The gray wagon floating between the two women kept Millie from seeing Olive, but Winifred bobbed up and down like a log.

"Oh, dear Lord," Millie gasped as the wagon, carried by the swift current, swept within inches of Winifred.

Millie dug her heel into her horse, urging him along the bank at top speed. As soon as she was several yards ahead of the bobbing woman, she dismounted almost before her mount stopped. After yanking off her boots and hat, she dove into the rushing water, coming up just a few strokes from Winifred. She half swam, half floated with the current until she could grab the drowning woman's blouse.

She looked up just in time to see a large log bearing down on them. Millie yanked the woman below the water just as the log whizzed overhead. They both bobbed up, gasping for breath.

"Easy, Winifred. I've got you. Just relax, and we'll be on shore in no…time—" Suddenly, Winifred had managed to turn and throw her arms around Millie, taking them both down again. Millie broke the hold and was almost up to the surface when a hand grasped her collar and propelled her upward. A strong arm grasped her across the chest.

As the current picked up, Blake was thrown against some rocks, losing his hold on Millie. He fought to stay afloat while frantically searching for her. He spotted her several yards ahead, floating face down in a current of water that slammed her repeatedly into more rocks. "Damn," he muttered. With strong steady strokes he cut through the stream toward her.

He managed to grab her belt and pull her back into the center of the river. A shrill whistle pierced the water's loud roar. Blake looked up to scc Ben whirl a rope in the air and let it fly in their direction. It landed close enough for Blake to grab. He pulled the loop over Millie's head and down under her arms, then grabbed hold and gave the signal to pull.

As he reached shallow water, Blake dragged Millie onto shore, then flopped her face down on the muddy bank. He pressed on her back. "Breathe," he muttered, "breathe, damn it."

Finally, Millie coughed several times, water gushed from her mouth, and she began to struggle.

Miss Hannah pushed her way through the crowd to kneel beside them. "Move, Donovan. I'll take her from here."

As soon as the women took Millie away, Blake dried his face on the end of a blanket someone had put around his shoulders. He looked around to see if John Eagle, who'd jumped in almost the same instant he did, had made it out okay. Finally, he spotted the scout on the other side of the river. Using Indian sign, Blake asked after Miss Winifred. He was relieved to learn she was alive. However, from the way everyone was hustling around, he wondered if she were hurt. Then he asked after Miss Olive. John Eagle shook his head and gave the thumbs-down sign.

Dead. He dropped onto the rock beside him. Dead. He swallowed the sick feeling rising from his gut. He'd known they weren't likely to get everyone there, but he'd hoped…prayed.

****

Millie stood with bowed head as the last spade of dirt was spread over Olive's final resting place. How tragic that someone as quiet and sweet as Olive should come to such a senseless end.

Miss Hannah finished the prayer, then led everyone in singing "Rock of Ages." After less than half the first verse, only sobs could be heard.

Slowly, Millie became aware of soft notes riding the gentle breeze from the far left. She'd never heard "Rock of Ages" sung with such deep feeling, such sincere sorrow. Soon all the sobbing ceased. The exquisite vocal ability expressed everyone's sorrow, yet instilled in them a joyful hope for the future. She slowly turned her head to see who had so perfectly expressed all their feelings. She gasped. "Cora?" The ex-saloon girl who seemed to have nothing to offer the community but trouble? Not only had this fallen woman, as Winifred insisted on calling her, brought peace and tranquility to Olive's passing, but she sang every word and every note perfectly.

After the song ended, there was a long moment of silence. Miss Hannah cleared her throat. "Come on, ladies. We have to get going. There's a lot of time to make up if we're to reach the valley before the first snowfall."

Millie fell into step beside Miss Hannah. "How is Winifred this morning?"

"All right, I suppose. She was asleep when I left the wagon this morning. As near as we can figure, she has several cracked ribs and a badly wrenched knee. It'll be a while before she's up and around."

Heaven help us all. "How long will she be staying in your wagon?"

"Until hers dries out, I guess. Thank goodness they were able to save the wagon and most of her things."

Millie rolled her eyes heavenward. And thank goodness Winifred wasn't staying with Emily and herself. She stumbled on the uneven ground and immediately asked forgiveness for her unchristian attitude. But honestly, she thought, Winifred was the most negative person she'd ever known. The woman saw the dark side of everything.

****

By the middle of May, the days had grown longer and warmer. Millie made her bed under the wagon with Emily's. They slept head to head so they could talk while taking advantage of the cooling breeze. Millie heard the sound of crying and running feet. She scooted clear of the wagon, but before she could get up, someone tripped over her. Millie grunted, but scrambled to her feet. She recognized Cindy's flyaway red hair and reached toward the crying girl.

"Cindy?" When the sobbing girl lay there, making no effort to rise, Millie stooped down beside her. "Cindy, where are you hurt? Shall I send for your ma?"

Cindy shook her head as she sat up. "No. I'm…I'm not hurt. It's…" She pointed toward Winifred's wagon, which had been moved in between Millie's and Miss

Hannah's.

"It's that woman! I...I can't stay with her anymore. She's horrible!"

Millie grinned as she slid her arm around the girl. "I know what you mean," she whispered. "You say there's a cooling breeze, she'll say it'll muss her hair. Mention it's warm and sunny out, and she'll insist it's just nature's way of making her sweaty and freckled."

Cindy smiled as she wiped her face on her sleeve. "You must think I'm an awful crybaby, but I just can't stand it any longer."

"Any longer? Girl, you've lasted three days. That's two and a half days longer than most. Look, you go on back to your own wagon and leave her to me. It'll do her good to spend one night alone. Tomorrow we'll pin her ears back."

Millie watched as Cindy hurried off, then turned to glare at Winifred's wagon. How dare that foul-tempered old biddy browbeat a sweet kid like Cindy!

Millie met Miss Hannah when she stepped down from her wagon. "I need to talk to you." She took the older woman's arm and quickly hurried her away from Winifred's wagon.

"What in the world...? "Miss Hannah dug her heels in and pulled Millie to a halt. "My dear girl, I'm not exactly dressed for an evening stroll."

Millie's cheeks burned. She'd been so angry, she'd failed to notice Miss Hannah was dressed only in her night clothes. She wasn't even wearing a wrapper. "I'm sorry. It's just that I'm so angry I could wring that woman's neck."

Miss Hannah looked in the direction Millie glared. "My gosh, you too? Is there anyone she hasn't offended?"

"I don't know about the others, but poor Cindy Pollard just raced by me in tears. Because Winifred's hurt, we've all tried to overlook her rudeness, but in truth, she's always rude, even on her good days."

"I know. I'd hoped Cindy was faring better than the others, since she's lasted so long."

"Well, she didn't. Now, who in her right mind would even consider staying with Winifred?"

"I would."

Millie and Miss Hannah jumped and whirled to see Cora standing several feet away.

"I'm sorry. I was listening and heard what happened to Cindy. Miss Winifred's accident was my fault, so I'll take care of her."

"What do you mean, 'your fault'?" Miss Hannah asked.

Cora plucked nervously at her shirtsleeve. "Well, I knowed she was skeert of the water, so I tol' her I'd take the wagon acrosst. But I guess she thought I was a-poking fun at her, 'cause she wouldn't let me. Now she's hurt and Miss Olive's dead, and it's my fault."

Cora looked so miserable Millie's heart went out to her. "Oh, Cora, it wasn't your fault, unless you cut the ferry's cable."

"No, ma'am. I'd never do such a thing—not even to someone as deserving as Miss Winifred."

Miss Hannah took each girl by an arm and urged them several steps farther from the wagons. Even in the pale moonlight, Millie could see a devilish gleam in the older woman's eye. "How tough are you, Cora?"

"If you'd seed some of the places I've worked, you wouldn't ask that."

The older woman dropped her voice to a whisper. "How would you like to help that woman *and* teach her a lesson at the same time?"

"Well, I might. What did you have in mind?"

****

Millie scrambled one of Honey's eggs, then put a portion, along with two biscuits dripping in butter and jam, on the plate Cora held. "As soon as you give this to her highness, come get yours."

Cora nodded, picked up a cup of tea, and walked slowly toward Winifred's wagon. She stopped, glanced back at Millie, then took a deep breath. "Well, here goes," she muttered and climbed into the wagon.

"It's about time, girl. Where have you been? I'm starving." When Cora looked up, Winifred gasped. "You. What are you doing in my wagon?"

"Bringing you breakfast. I'll be seeing after you from now on."

"You'll do no such thing," Winifred said in a voice loud enough to be heard all over camp. "I'll not have a whore anywhere near me."

Cora ignored the insult and pulled the covers down to the foot of the bed. For someone in such pain, the woman moved with surprising swiftness to pull them back up. "Stop that!"

"You've been in that same nightie for the last two weeks. Even whores have ta change at least once a week." ·

"I didn't know whores used nighties."

Cora yanked the covers back down. "For a God-fearin' woman, ya sure know a lot 'bout a whore's ways." Winifred sputtered, but Cora interrupted. "While you eat, I'll bring you some hot water. Then you get out of that bed, wash, and put on some clean clothes. Or everone'll see ya in yer dirty nightie."

"What do you mean?"

Cora glared at her. "I mean, I'm a-rollin' up them wagon aides an' airin' it out as we go. It stinks in here."

"What!"

Cora left the woman sputtering and joined the others for breakfast. "This is really good, Miss Millie. Do ya have eggs ever' mornin'?"

Millie looked at Honey. "No, the stingy bird only gives us one egg a day, so we save them up and have a treat every once in a while."

Emily took her plate and sat down beside Cora. "What are you going to do about Winifred? Do you think you can stand caring for her?"

Cora shot Millie a conspiratorial glance and grinned. "Oh, I ain't gonna take care of her. She's made ever'one who tried miserable. From now on, I'll be there to do the heavy work, but she's gonna take care of herself. We git to that valley, she or me's gonna be a different person."

Millie smiled to herself. This was too good to miss. Those two would mix like water and hot grease. She collected the dishes, then began packing up their gear while Emily washed, dried and put away the dishes.

Cora shoved two buckets of warm water inside Winifred's wagon, then climbed in. "Well, are you done with breakfast?"

Winifred tugged at the corner of one of her pillows. "Yes. It was surprisingly good. With all your other— duties—when did you have time to learn to cook?"

Cora poured the water into the hipbath Ben had brought earlier. "Oh, you'd be surprised what us whores learn, day and night. Come on, we'll be pulling out in about an hour."

"Don't be ridiculous. I'm not able to bathe. I'm hurt, remember?"

Cora set down the bucket, then stood with fists on her hips, glaring at the woman. "You better hurry, woman, or I'll strip you, and with this top rolled back, your bare bosoms'll be kissed by the sun and nuzzled by the wind."

Winifred clutched the covers to her chest. "You wouldn't dare!"

Cora snatched the bedding, pulling it down to the woman's waist. In the process, she ripped the gown down the front as well.

"Nooo!" Winifred grabbed the pieces of her gown together.

"You'd better get cracking. We ain't got much time." Cora turned and, with all the dignity she could muster, left the wagon. As soon as her feet hit the ground, her legs seemed to turn to string. She grabbed the wagon wheel for support. How could she have done such a thing, even to that woman?

Winifred was so stern, so judgmental. Like an avenging angel hovering, always ready to strike. From the beginning, Cora had stayed as far away from Winifred as possible, trying hard not to draw the woman's attention. Look at her now! Not only was she Miss Winifred's main focal point, but without any conscious effort, her own unruly tongue seemed to work overtime to antagonize the woman. *Lord, deliver me from my own foolishness.*

Millie, followed by Emily, dropped what she was doing and hurried to Cora's side as the girl stepped away from the wagon. She took Cora's arm. "What happened to make Winifred scream like that?"

Cora took several deep breaths, then straightened her shoulders and shook her head. "Nothing's wrong. Would you please help me roll back this canvas? It's very stuffy in there."

"No! Wait," came the cry from inside the wagon. "I'm…I'm taking a bath." Movements from inside shook the wagon. "You have to give me more time."

Emily smiled and winked at her companions. "Well, well." She hooked her arm through Cora's and led her farther away. "How in the world did you manage that? None of the others could get her to so much as sit up by herself."

"Oh, it's jest a matter of understandin'. Is there anything I can do to he'p ya while we wait for her highness ta finish her bath?"

"No," Millie answered, "but I'll help you hitch up her team."

When everything was done, Cora climbed into the wagon. Winifred sat on the side of her bed, in a clean nightgown, brushing her freshly washed hair. Without a word, Cora dumped the water out the wagon's back end. She'd just dried out the hip bath when Ben knocked.

"Are ya ready for me to take the bathtub back to the supply wagon?" he asked.

"Yes, thank you." She watched his muscles bulge as he picked up the tub and swung it from the wagon as if it were made of paper. "Oh, Ben, when you're through, would you help me roll this wagon covering back?"

"Yes, ma'am. Be right back."

As soon as he'd left, Winifred turned an indignant glare at Cora. "You cannot expose me to the elements this way. It's not good for my condition."

"I'll tell you what's not good for your condition—sitting here day after day. Your knee needs exercise and so does your middle. You've grown some heavier in the last two weeks."

Winifred gaped at the saloon girl. "Well, I never! Just who do you think you are?"

"Nobody. Jest the only person on this train who ain't afraid of your sharp tongue." Cora reached over to untie the wagon top.

"It's 'isn't.' "

"What ain't?"

"The word is 'isn't.' Honestly, you sound like you've never had any schooling."

Cora stopped on the tailgate and looked at Winifred for several minutes. "It's a deal."

Winifred stared, open-mouthed. "What's a deal?"

"You learn me to talk right, and I'll learn you manners." Cora jumped down from the wagon.

"Of all the nerve! I don't need lessons in manners, and it's 'teach,' not 'learn,' " Winifred shouted from within the wagon.

Just before they pulled out, Ben and Reb rolled back the canvas, completely ignoring Winifred's protests. She pulled the covers up to her neck. "This is an outrage. You can't do this. I'm hurt."

Blake rode up, tipped his hat and smiled at the disgruntled woman. "Good morning, Miss Winifred. You're looking a good deal better this morning. Hope to see you up and around soon."

"Thank...thank you, Mr. Donovan. I am feeling a mite better."

Blake winked at Cora, then turned his attention to Millie and Emily. "Ladies, it's about time to pull out. Is everything ready here?"

Emily picked up the reins. "Good morning, Mr. Donovan. We're ready when you are."

Chapter Eleven

Millie dabbed at her forehead, then shoved her hankie into her back pocket. The last several days had been one blur into another. Nothing happened to break the routine, or the heat. Thank goodness they weren't fighting those long skirts and petticoats. But what she wouldn't give to shed these hot britches and sink into a nice cool stream.

She slapped the reins against the oxen's rumps. They still had several hours before dark. *Oh, how I hope there's a stream where we camp tonight.* Millie looked off into the distance. There were those two Indians again. Whether the same two or two different ones, they'd been appearing on the horizon every couple of hours for the last several days. They never came any nearer, just followed and watched. Though there hadn't been any trouble, Mr. Donovan had doubled the guards at night.

Cindy walked up beside Millie and looked in the Indians' direction, too. "They make my skin crawl. Just watching and waiting. What do you suppose they want?"

"I don't know. Mr. Donovan says they're probably fascinated by our gypsy caravan. I think maybe they're just curious about us, like we'd be about them if they were passing through our town."

Cindy shaded her eyes and watched as the Indians disappeared over the horizon. "Maybe, but they still scare me."

"Me, too," Millie admitted. "They're gone now. That scares me even more. I guess we'll have to trust Mr. Donovan and John Eagle to take care of them. The extra guards they've posted make me feel better."

When they finally camped, it was beside a gurgling stream. After the women finished their swim, they started supper while the men and then the animals took their turn in the water.

Millie hung the stew pot over the flames. Female chatter and laughter sounded all over camp. The boisterous sounds of men horsing around drifted up from the stream. She stopped to listen to Honey's happy honking as she swam with them. Evidently, Mr. Donovan wasn't interested in an early Thanksgiving dinner at the moment.

The extra couple of hours' layover had lifted everyone's spirits. All but Winifred. She was her usual grumpy self. She'd complained until they dropped the sides of the wagon cover, then insisted they raise the side by her bed so she could see what everyone was doing.

Millie shook her head. She wouldn't be surprised to wake up tomorrow to learn Cora had cut out Winifred's tongue.

****

Millie replaced the coffeepot over the hot coals. It was a beautiful morning, but of course, Winifred only noted that it'd be another scorching day. Obviously, Cora hadn't gotten around to Winifred's tongue. She would soon, surely.

"Mr. Donovan! Mr. Donovan!"

Millie whirled from the cookfire as Cindy ran screaming from the creek. Two Indians rode their horses at a slow walk behind her, while Honey ran toward the girl, hissing and honking.

Millie grabbed her long gun and raced toward the terrified girl. She helped Cindy into the wagon's circle, pointing her rifle at the Indians as she did so. They stopped several yards away.

Blake hurried to the group of women. "Excuse me, ladies." He squeezed past them and stopped just inside the wagon circle. Ezra joined him. "Where's John Eagle?" Blake whispered to the old cowboy.

Ezra shoved his hat back and scratched his chin whiskers. "Don't reckon he's back yet. What kind of injuns ye reckon they is?"

Blake untied the leather thong around his leg, then unbuckled his gun belt and let his weapon drop to the ground. "Kiowa, I hope. At least we're in their territory." He stepped over the wagon tongue, giving the peace sign and moved forward. After several minutes' discussion, he turned and called for Cindy to join him. She swallowed nervously but slowly did as he bade.

Blake took her arm and pulled her to his side. "Say nothing," he whispered. "Just let me do the talking, and I'll do my best to get us out of this without any trouble."

"Wha-What do they want?" she asked nervously.

"You. Seems the young one there thinks your red hair is good medicine. He wants to trade for you." Cindy's eyes widened, and she began to tremble.

He squeezed her arm reassuringly. "Now, hold on. Don't panic. He's a reasonable man. I'm sure something can be worked out."

Elsa Herns hurried up to Millie. She was a large, serious-looking woman who also carried a long gun to this meeting. "Ve shoot, if'n them redskins tries to took Cindy."

"Good idea," Millie agreed. "You pick a spot over there, and I'll do the same here. That way we'll have them in a crossfire, more or less."

"Ya. Dat's goot."

Millie moved behind the wagon to her right. She rested the gun barrel between the wagon wheel and tailgate, then lined a straight bead on her target. *If he sells her,* she thought, *it'll be the last thing he ever does.* She watched as the Indians talked to Mr. Donovan, though she couldn't understand what they were saying.

Both Indians slid off their horses. The younger one walked slowly around Cindy. He squeezed her cheeks, forcing her mouth open to check her teeth. He felt her arms, fingered her bright red hair, and then Cindy gasped as he ran his hand over her backside.

"She strong. Make fine woman. Give Black Hawk many sons." He signaled his friend, who came forward leading three horses.

Blake walked over and took his time inspecting the horses, then he returned to stand beside Cindy. He looked at her thoughtfully. "Three horses for a woman is a damned impressive offer. He must really have taken a fancy to you," he muttered.

Cindy could hardly breathe. "Please, Mr. Donovan, don't sell me. Please!"

"Take it easy. I won't, but I have to make him think I'm taking his offer as seriously as he means it."

Angie Pollard pushed her way to the front of the group of women. "Oh, my Lord! Winifred said some Indians were trying to buy my baby, but I didn't believe her. I'll put a stop to that right now!"

Miss Hannah caught Angie by the arm. "Don't interfere. Mr. Donovan knows what he's doing. If we offend these Indians, we may have real trouble. Let him handle this. It's what he's paid for."

As the haggling continued, it became clear the Indian was not going to take no for an answer. Angie Pollard slipped back among the wagons. She caught Cora's arm, saying, "Come with me, quick."

Blake shook his head. "I'm sorry, Black Hawk, but she's not mine to sell. She belongs to my chief, and he'd skin me alive if I returned without her. She's his favorite. What would your chief do to you if he left his women in your care and you sold one?"

Before the brave could answer, a loud cackling came from behind the wagons. Angie Pollard hurried toward them with an uneven gait. Her usually well groomed, graying hair hung loose around her head like a wild mustang's mane. Her regal posture was hunched over, and her black dress, now several sizes too large, hung on her like a shroud. Her long graceful fingers were extended like talons. She rushed forward. "Take me, too! Take me, too!" she insisted in a high, squeaky voice. Then she leaned toward the Indians and shrieked like a mad woman.

Black Hawk and his companion jumped to their feet, shook their heads and backed up several steps.

Blake also jumped to his feet. *Damn the woman. What did she think she was doing?* However, noting the Indians' reaction, he almost felt sorry for them. He knew the woman, and his scalp still prickled. He grabbed Angie's arm and pulled her away from the braves. "This is the girl's ma. Take one, you have to take the other."

The braves looked at each other, then back at Angie. With a final shake of their heads, they leaped on their mounts and, with the three extra horses, rode away as if

Satan himself were after them.

Blake turned his attention to Angie Pollard. "Dammit, woman, are you trying to get us all killed?" Before she could answer, Cindy burst into hysterical sobs. He turned around in time to wrap his arms around the sobbing girl before she fell to the ground. "You did fine, girl. They're gone now. Take it easy." Angie took her daughter and half carried her into the safety of the wagon circle.

A stream of tobacco juice brought Blake's attention to Ezra. "That shore was a clost call. Wonder if'n that buck would've left without the gal if'n her ma hada stayed outta sight?"

"I don't know, but we were damned lucky. Those two could have done a lot of damage. From now on, we'd better make arrangements for someone to cover us if we're ever approached like this again."

"Oh, you was covered. That Miss Elsa was coverin' them bucks from over yonder. And Miss Millie had her long gun over t'uther side." He spit another tobacco stream and shoved his hat forward. "Only she weren't pointin' at no injun," he said as he ambled off.

Blake stared at the old codger's back for several seconds, then slowly turned to look where Millie was said to have been standing. In his mind's eye, he traced a line from that spot to where the Indians had been. He grabbed the wagon wheel for support as his legs buckled. He'd been directly in her line of fire. If anything had gone wrong, *Millicent the Jinx* would have drilled him right between the shoulder blades. She wouldn't even have given him a chance to explain.

Blake slowly slid to the ground. He shivered from a cold that no one else felt, while perspiration beaded on his forehead. After several minutes, he shakily pulled himself to his feet, wondering if Reb still had any of that whiskey left.

Emily fell in step beside Millie as they followed Miss Hannah toward the Pollards' wagon. "Millie, from where I was standing behind you, it looked like you'd have hit Mr. Donovan if you'd fired."

"As sure as I'm breathing."

Emily gasped. "You really intended to shoot him?"

"Only if he sold Cindy." She certainly hoped Emily didn't hear the uncertainty in her voice. Or notice how her hands were shaking.

"He wouldn't have done that. You know he wouldn't."

"Do I?" A month ago she wouldn't have had any doubts, but now, when it got right down to it, she wasn't at all sure what Mr. Donovan would or wouldn't have done. Donovan hadn't given her any reason to suspect he'd sell or mistreat anyone, except maybe herself. Nor was she sure she could have pulled the trigger. Thank goodness she hadn't had to make that decision.

They stopped at the edge of the group of women crowded around the Pollard wagon. "How is she?" Emily asked.

"She'll be all right. She's jest scairt," Cora assured them. "Wasn't that a grand idea Miz Pollard had? When she tol' me to help her get messed up that-a-way, I thought she'd taken leave of her senses, but she shore knowed what she was about."

Millie pushed her way through the crowd to Miss Hannah. "Ma'am, we're all glad Cindy's safe, but maybe we should move on. We still have a lot of daylight left. And those Indians could decide to come back and bring their friends."

Everyone agreed and rushed toward their wagons. Miss Hannah hurried up to Blake just as he took a large swig of Reb's whiskey. "Mr. Donovan! Are you drinking at a time like this?"

Blake choked on his swallow. He coughed several more times, then removed his hat and turned toward the woman. "Yes, ma'am, under the circumstances, I felt I needed it. What's all the commotion?"

"We thought maybe we should push on. It's still early, and we were concerned that the Indians might return with reinforcements."

Blake recorked the bottle and returned it to Reb. "That's exactly what I was thinking, and the sooner, the better."

She nodded. "Fine, we're ready when you are."

Blake mounted Thunder, rode to the head of the column, and gave the signal. The wagons pulled out. After several minutes, he rode back down the line until he reached Miss Hannah's wagon. He turned Thunder and rode beside the wagon.

"Did you need anything, Mr. Donovan?"

"Yes, ma'am. I was wondering whose idea it was to pull out."

Miss Hannah looked at him for a long minute, then urged her oxen on. Blake could almost swear he saw a shadow of a grin on her face before she turned away saying, "Why, I believe it was Millie's."

Blake readjusted his hat. Of course, who else? Not only was the woman planning to do away with him, she was now taking over his job. He'd have to do something about her, but what? Everyone was blinded to her threat. And to be honest, she didn't seem to be a danger to anyone…but him.

It was late when Blake called a halt to the day's traveling. They'd made extremely good time, traveling nearly eighteen miles. The landscape was changing, the terrain wasn't so flat, and the tall grass was thinning out. Fort Casper shouldn't be but about another week or two ahead.

So far they'd been lucky, only one injury and one death. He just hoped the next death on the wagon train wasn't his own, aided by *Millicent the Jinx*. Probably the only way to be sure of that was to change jobs with John Eagle.

****

Blake crawled from his tent and stretched. It was about an hour before dawn. The sky was clear, but it still smelled like rain. He'd hope for the best, but expect the worse. That way he'd avoid any unpleasant surprises. Blake picked up a bucket and headed toward the creek.

He looked toward the northwest as he returned to camp. John Eagle should be back sometime this morning. He'd been gone two days. Blake splashed a little water on his face before stoking the banked fire. He filled the coffeepot, then hung it over the coals.

As soon as the coffee began to boil, the aroma brought the other men stumbling out of their tents to join him. The women would be getting up soon, but right now was the men's time, the only peace they'd have all day. He poured himself a cup of coffee, then ambled over to the picket line to check on Thunder.

He stopped suddenly. Patches, John Eagle's paint, stood beside Thunder. A small noise made Blake whip around, dropping his coffee cup and reaching for the gun he'd forgotten to put on.

John Eagle stepped out from behind a tree and into the pale morning light. "Morning, cousin. It's about time you got up."

"Galdarnit, Johnny, one of these days you're going to get yourself shot, sneaking around like a pesky Indian."

John Eagle smiled and swatted Blake on his gunless hip. "Not by you, hot shot. Besides, I am a pesky Indian. How about a cup of that coffee?"

Grumbling, Blake snatched up his cup and led the way to the coffeepot. He filled two cups, then handed one to the scout.

"What'd ya see out there?" Blake asked as they squatted by the fire.

"Everything's just the way we like it. No wagon trains this way so far. There's plenty of grass for the stock, and the hunting is excellent. Near's I can figure, we're about ten or twelve days out of Fort Casper.

The slender fingers of dawn crept across the sky as the women began moving about the camp. "Good morning."

The men looked up and nodded. "Morning, Miss Millie."

Millie poured herself a cup of coffee. "Nice to have you back, John Eagle. Is everything all right up ahead?"

"Yes, ma'am. Sure looks like it."

"That's wonderful…"

"Ah, mein Gott!" Elsa Hern whispered. She began beating on the bottom of a pan with her spoon. "Kommen Sie! Come, everybody. Look!" She pointed toward the west.

The women rushed to her side. "What's the matter?" They looked where she pointed. Gradually, the sky lightened and several of the women gasped. "What is that?"

Millie stared for several long seconds, then her heart beat faster. "Why, it...it looks like mountains!" She turned to John Eagle and Blake. "Are those mountains? How far away are they? Why didn't we see them when we camped last evening?"

Blake looked off into the distance. "Yeah, those are mountains. It was too foggy to see them yesterday. They're still a good many days off, but the scenery is about to change, ladies."

The camp buzzed with excitement as breakfast was finished and the wagons were made ready to roll. The day flew by. Each of the women kept an eye on the horizon, trying to judge the distance they traveled by how much closer the mountains looked. By the end of the day, the women fell into a depressed silence. They didn't seem any closer to the mountains than they had been that morning.

Chapter Twelve

After supper, Millie wandered along the creek bank
with Honey honking at her heels and a full moon lit her
pathway. She stopped in a small clearing. It was almost
like stepping from a hallway into a sitting room. There
were boulders here and there like chairs. The bushes
along the creek bank split in the middle, making a
window, and the moonlight sparkling off the water
offered a breathtaking mural.

She stood still, absorbing the peace. Even Honey
seemed to hold the place in reverence. Millie had spotted
this place while swimming earlier in the day. If she
remembered correctly, behind the bushes immediately to
her right, there should be... She squeezed between two
large bushes. Yes, there it was. A boulder shaped like a
chair, surrounded on three sides by shrubs. She sat down
and drew her feet up. Wrapping her arms around her legs
and resting her chin on her knees, she gazed out across
the water.

Honey stretched her long neck toward her mistress.
After several minutes of being stroked, she tentatively
placed a webbed foot in the water, then glided away,
honking with pleasure.

Millie smiled. *Enjoy yourself, Honey.* This might be
the last creek for some time. She leaned her head back
against the rock and stared across the water. It was such
a beautiful, romantic place. It was almost a sin to sit here

without a sweetheart. *My gosh. Where in the world did that thought come from?*

She hadn't dreamed of having a man in her life since she was fourteen. Men were nothing but trouble. First her father, then Otto Watts, the husband her father had forced on her. How could two different men be so alike? So cruel?

Unbidden, Blake Donovan's image popped into her head. Now there was a confusing man who didn't seem to fit into any niche. He'd disliked her from the minute he laid eyes on her. He rarely had a civil word for her. Yet he was such a gentleman with all the others. He was even patient with Winifred, though Millie could tell it was an effort.

She sighed and closed her eyes. It was certainly a good thing she didn't need a man to make it in this world. Pa's neglect had taught her self-reliance. His brutality toward her mother had strengthened her own backbone. Ma, sweet gentle Ma, taught her to dream. Aunt Lavinia, Ma's sister, had taken in a wild hellion and taught her to be a lady and a homemaker. Finally, there had been good-natured Uncle James. He'd taught her to laugh, and that all men weren't brutes.

Where were the Uncle Jameses in this world? And why didn't any of them come into her life she wondered as she dozed off.

Millie shifted slightly. Her bed was awfully hard. Voices? *Was someone in her room? What were they saying?* Little by little, the dream receded and reality intruded upon her time with Aunt Lavinia and Uncle James. She slowly opened her eyes. Water? There wasn't any water outside her window. Then she remembered where she was. She looked around. The voices were louder now.

"My pa was a preacher."

"I've heard some men of God were as mean as Satan when they felt called to save the world. It must have been pretty bad at home for you to turn to…to salooning."

"Not my pa. He was a very gentle man. It was hunger what turned me to salooning. Until the war, life with Ma and Pa was wonderful. In fact, I dreamed of being a preacher's wife."

Millie started. *That's Cora.* She turned and peeked through the branches. Cora and Ben were sitting on the rocks just behind her. What should she do? They were deep in conversation. If they saw her, they'd think she'd deliberately been eavesdropping, but there was no way Millie could slip out of her hiding place unnoticed. Maybe they'd walk on in a minute and never know she'd overheard anything.

"Pa went to war with the militia from our county," Cora continued. "He thought them boys would need his counseling, but he got kilt right off. Ma and me were doin' pretty good until the fightin' moved closer to our place. One side or the other was always raiding our storehouse. And then they come…" She sighed and looked down at her feet.

Ben reached over and took one of her hands. "You don't have to tell this. It's none of my business."

She gave him a half smile. "It's all right. I want you to understand." She stared out across the calm water. "Ma and me tried to put in a crop. The last raiders took the only thing we had left, our old mule. So we took turns pulling the plow, but we weren't strong enough. Then one night while we was saying our prayers, they come."

"They?" Ben prompted gently.

Cora nodded. She squeezed his hand tighter. "Two of 'em. One a Yankee and one a Reb. It seemed strange at first, them two bein' together, but Ma said they was probably family and just couldn't fight each other no more. She stepped out on the porch to offer 'em the use of the shed for the night. But that weren't enough. They demanded food, then money. When we said we didn't have neither one, they slapped us around and…and…" She dropped her voice so low Millie could barely hear. "And took their comfort from Ma, then me."

Millie could hear the tears in the girl's voice. How awful. Millie was grateful for what little protection she'd had back then.

"When Ma tried to protect me, they kilt her. They stayed all night, usin' me, over and over and…" Her voice cracked.

Ben put his arm around her shoulders. "It's okay. You don't have to say any more."

Cora sobbed against his chest for some time. Finally, she wiped her eyes and continued her story. "When they left the next mornin', they shot me, too, though I was already more dead than alive. Someone, I don't know who, found us. They buried Ma and took me into town. Not one of them good ladies would admit me into their prim and proper homes. I was soiled goods. The only ones who'd tend me was the whores in the saloon.

"For a long time I just didn't care. Zeke, the piano player, and me became friends. Over the next couple of years, he taught me to sing and play the piano. And little by little he brought God back into my life through the music. In his own way, he was as good as my pa."

Ben pulled out his bandanna and wiped her face.

"Where's this Zeke now? Why didn't he come with you?"

"He liked to play poker ever' now and then. One night he got into a game with some cowboys that were terrible players and even worse losers. He won all their money, but when he tried to quit the table, they accused him of cheatin' and shot him. Ed, the bartender, shot the killer, but that didn't help Zeke none.

"Before he died, he give me his money poke and told me to get away as far as I could. He had one of Mr. Donovan's ad papers. I decided that must be what Zeke wanted me to do, so here I am."

Cora sniffed again. "I miss Zeke, but that cowboy done him a favor. Zeke had the lung sickness. It was bad. He was dyin' by inches. We'd talked about leavin' together, but he kept puttin' it off. I guess he just didn't have the strength to travel."

"Gal, this here Zeke gave ya another chance. You take it. In fact, we have a preacher in our valley, and I think you and him might hit it off real well. I'll introduce you to him when we get there."

Cora gave his hand one last squeeze before getting to her feet and shaking her head. "Thank you, Ben, but no man of God will ever want me now. A whore ain't got no place in the church, exceptin' maybe on the sinner's bench."

Ben put his arm around her shoulders again and they slowly walked on along the creek. "Don't be silly. Seems I remember something about Jesus and a whore at a well. Besides, this here preacher weren't no pillar of society himself, before he got the call."

As soon as they moved on, Millie got slowly to her feet. Her left leg refused to hold her and tiny little pinpricks shot up and down it. She rubbed the leg for a few minutes, then peeked from her hiding place, before limping back to camp.

How awful. Cora's past made her own seem like a party. If Cora wanted to be a minister's wife, she'd need a little more polish and education. Millie could help her get that.

****

Millie handed Cora a plate of warmed-over fish stew from last evening's supper. Aunt Lavinia would have been horrified at the thought of eating this for breakfast. As soon as Cora left, Millie wrinkled up her nose. Fish stew was barely tolerable at the best of times, and breakfast certainly wasn't one of those times. They needed some real meat, badly.

Cora climbed into Winifred's wagon. "Lean back against them pillers. I brung breakfast."

"*Those* pillows, and it's 'I *brought*.' Honestly, one would think you'd never had any education at all," Winifred grumbled.

Millie grinned and turned back to the cook fire. Well, well. Wouldn't it ruffle ol' Winnie's feathers if she knew how she was helping with Cora. Millie took a bite of fish stew and gagged. She scraped the food onto the ground and dumped the plate into the washpan, then grabbed a couple of biscuits and smeared them with some of Emily's apricot jam. This would have to do until lunch.

****

Blake rode in at midafternoon and slowed beside her as Emily walked at the back of her wagon. He tipped his hat. "Afternoon, Miss Emily."

"Good afternoon, Mr. Donovan." She looked at the

bundle draped across his saddle. "What's that wrapped in your slicker?"

Blake grinned. "Well, ma'am, this antelope just jumped into my line of fire while I was practicing, earlier. It didn't seem right to let its sacrifice go to waste, so I thought maybe you could suggest someone who'd appreciate a little fresh meat."

"Oh, I think I can help you put that dear, sweet creature's sacrifice to good use. In fact, I know a little ol' southern gal, well maybe not so little or old, but anyway, I've been told she cooks a mouth-watering roast. Would you like a dinner invitation for this evening?"

Blake slid the animal onto the tailgate of her wagon. "I'd be much obliged, ma'am." He smiled and tipped his hat. "See you tonight."

Millie watched Donovan ride off, then turned back to her driving when Emily joined her. "Mr. Donovan certainly is friendly when he's around you. What was that he put in the wagon?"

"Would you believe that sweet ol' thing brought us an antelope for supper? And I do believe I could eat the whole thing by myself."

Sweet ol' thing, indeed. The man was just doing his job. Each man was supposed to keep four wagons in meat. Millie had to admit Blake Donovan had never allowed them to go too long without fresh meat, but he was anything but gracious about it, at least when he had to deliver it to her. However, he was all peaches and cream with any of the other women.

Millie snapped the reins against the far oxen's rumps as she walked beside the wagon. "Guess you'd better start gathering buffalo chips if you expect to have enough heat to do that roast justice."

Emily grimaced. "Now, that's the part of this trip that I dislike the most. If there were any alternative other than eating it raw, I'd never touch those nasty ol' things."

Millie nodded. Driving these animals was slow, boring work, but there were times when the job had its advantage.

Cindy walked up beside Millie. "I see you got some meat, too. John Eagle wanted me to tell you he'd like the skin if you don't mind."

"He's been collecting a lot of skins lately. What in the world is he doing with them?"

"He says he needs new winter clothes. A woman in his tribe will sew them for him if he has extra to pay her with."

Millie looked disbelievingly at the girl. "You're kidding, aren't you? He really does wear animal hides for clothes?" She'd seen several mountain men in such clothing, but John Eagle was civilized. He'd been wearing regular clothes on this whole trip. An alarming thought came to her. "Cindy, you don't suppose all the men in the valley dress like that, do you?" Cindy stared at Millie in horror. "No, surely not. Miss Hannah wouldn't wear that kind of thing, and I can't see her going where she might be expected to, do you?"

"No, of course not. I wasn't thinking, I guess." Millie looked at the shawl Cindy was knitting. The girl was never without the bag hanging from her left side and the knitting needles clicking furiously in her hands. Millie didn't see how the girl could knit, walk, and talk all at the same time. "How's your knitting coming along?"

Cindy held it up. "Fine. It's almost finished."

"Who's this one for?"

She lowered her voice. "I'm not supposed to say, but I guess it won't hurt to tell you. Ben asked me to do it. Would you believe he even bought the yarn himself at the last town we passed through?"

Millie was touched. The yarn was a rich shade of burnt orange. She had no doubt it was for Cora. The color was perfect. She wondered if Ben cared more for Cora than he let on. Did he still plan to introduce her to the preacher?

****

The Wagon School, as it had been named, was doing very well. Those who couldn't read or write were learning rapidly. The sewing classes and quilting bees were almost a nightly activity. By the time they arrived in the valley, everyone who wanted one would have a quilt top and a new stole.

Millie even enjoyed sewing since Allison had taught her to use the sewing machine. When they got to the next town of any size, she intended to order one for herself. Maybe it would arrive in the valley by next spring. After all, it was her money. She could spend it any way she wanted. At least it was a useful purchase, not like throwing it away on drink or losing it in poker games.

Millie sighed. Would she ever be able to spend a penny without thinking of Pa? Hundreds of miles between them, and he still intruded on her life.

Cindy looked at Winifred's wagon. It seemed to be driving itself. "How did you train those dumb oxen up there to stay in line all by themselves?"

Millie laughed and snapped her lines. "We didn't. Cora told Winifred her days of lying around being waited on were over."

"You mean she's driving her own wagon? How did

Miss Cora get her to agree to that?"

"Cora hitched up and drove the wagon out of the line. Then she told ol' Winnie to get up on that seat and drive—or be left behind." Millie couldn't suppress a giggle any more now than she had earlier. Winifred had argued, cried, pleaded and finally resorted to a few unladylike words, but in the end, she struggled onto the wagon seat and took up the reins. "Cora has school this morning. She said Winifred would just have to manage until after lunch."

Cindy shook her head in admiration. "If I'd tried that, Miss Winifred would have pinched my head off."

"Well, somehow, I don't think she dares try that with Cora." The woman still snapped at Cora every chance she got, but in truth, Millie thought Winnie might be as intimidated by Cora as Cora was by Winifred.

****

Blake Donovan and Ben sat astride their mounts, their heads together. Millie certainly wished she could have the same kind of rapport and be able to carry on a friendly conversation with Mr. Donovan. It was quite uncomfortable to have to deal with him every evening knowing he didn't like a thing about her. She sighed. More and more, she wondered what kind of life she could look forward to in Montana. Everyone else speculated on what their husbands would be like… What kind of home they'd have… Would it be in town or on a ranch…

Would any man want her? Not that she necessarily wanted or needed a man, but after all, there was nothing wrong with her. She knew the social graces, was a good cook, and would make a passable homemaker. Even if she chose not to accept, every girl needed to be wanted.

Blake Donovan rode by her without a word. He'd stopped to speak briefly to everyone else, but he merely tipped his hat to her and kept going. On the other hand, she thought, if all the men were like Mr. Donovan, she'd count herself lucky indeed if no one even looked her way.

Passing Millie and hurrying toward the back of the train, Blake hoped it didn't appear he was snubbing her, but he'd spent too much time talking this morning. Besides, he still hadn't gotten over how close he'd come to being shot in the back by that woman. The best thing for him to do was stay as far away from her as possible.

Anyway, he'd be putting his boots under her table at supper tonight. He'd hear her problems then. Right now, he needed to hear from the others about any problems with the wagons or teams before that new storm broke.

He just hoped the rain held off until after supper. That pot roast Miss Emily had spoken of made his mouth water. And all things considered, Miss Millie made the best pies he'd ever laid a lip on. If he wasn't mistaken, he'd seen her put the finishing touches on one this morning. He hoped it was peach, but he wouldn't turn it down whatever it was.

He tipped his hat to the lady in the last wagon and headed toward the horse herd. The ladies certainly had come a long way since they'd left Hogan's ranch. They no longer wasted his time with complaints about lack of baths, privacy, or sand in their food or beds. Now he was asking them whether any of the animals had sores on their bodies or hooves, were there any problems with the wagons or did the harness need mending, and so on. And most of those things the ladies had learned to take care of themselves.

Yes, sir, these were women to contend with. Every one of them would do their husbands proud… Well, nearly all of them. Heaven help the man who chose *Miss Jinx*. Although she could cook and was one of the most self-reliant women he'd ever met, there were more important things than getting a woman who could make a good meal. The one thing she was best at was getting into trouble. Thank goodness he wouldn't have to worry about that. A lawman had no business being married, and that's what he planned to be—the sheriff. Even a self-reliant woman like Millicent Watts wouldn't want a man who'd always be in danger… *Would she*?

Chapter Thirteen

"So we'll be hunting tomorrow. We have to get our meat when we can. Besides, it will take a couple of days to smoke all the meat. I propose we split up into groups and do as much as we can here today, then tomorrow will be used for hunting and the next day to finish up and be ready to roll again." Blake finished laying out his plan and left with the other men.

The meeting was over almost before it'd begun. Millie picked up her load of laundry. "It's easy for him to say. He doesn't have two weeks of clothes and all this bedding to wash. What do you suppose he does about his laundry?"

Emily shrugged and picked up the other clothes basket. "I can almost taste that fresh meat. I can think of about ten different ways to cook it."

"Does that mean you intend to join the hunting party?"

"Oh, Millie, you know I'm not worth a fig with a gun." She looked sideways at her friend. "But you are. I'll make a deal with you. I'll do the laundry if you'll go get us one of those little ol' antelopes."

Millie laughed. "Emily, one of those *little ol' antelopes* weighs a couple of hundred pounds, at least. Besides, to me hunting is fun. I'd feel kinda guilty leaving you with all this work."

"Don't be silly. You know, I've been so hungry for

fresh meat that I actually looked longingly at Honey yesterday."

Millie stopped dead in her tracks. "At Honey? To eat?"

"Oh, I know what you're thinking, and I'm rightly ashamed of myself. But I promise, no matter how hungry I get, I'd never eat Honey. Honestly."

"I sincerely hope not." Millie looked at her friend and then at the creek. Though she knew Emily would never eat Honey, Mr. Donovan was another matter entirely.

"Well, all right, for Honey's sake, and if you're sure you won't think I'm trying to push all the hard stuff off on you, I'll go."

"Hard? Sugar, hard is lying in those bug-infested bushes waitin' to kill some cute little animal, then skinnin' it out and packin' it back." Emily made a face and shuddered. "Compared to all that, washin' is a breeze. Please, I'd almost promise my soul for a pot roast."

Millie laughed at the longing on her friend's face. "All right, you convinced me. I'll get you a pot roast, but only for Honey's sake. After all, one person looking for an early Thanksgiving is enough."

****

Blake shook his head in resignation when he found himself paired with Millie for the hunt. The fates certainly seemed to be against him. Surely, as long as he stayed just behind her, she couldn't shoot him.

They dismounted and worked their way as close to the antelope herd as possible before stretching out on their stomachs behind some brush at the edge of the clearing to wait. As several of the herd grazed toward them, Millie and Blake took aim.

He shot two to her one. For some reason known only to her, she stubbornly resisted giving up her single shot Hawken. He levered another shell into the chamber, then took aim at another antelope. Before he could pull the trigger, Millie's scream was almost drowned out by a roar that sent chills up his spine. He whirled in time to see a large brown bear on two legs looming over Millie.

Blake fired, putting a bullet in the bear's heart. The animal roared and staggered backward. He fired twice more. The beast toppled forward. Millie screamed again as the mountain of fur landed with a thud between them, falling so close to Millie that Blake couldn't see her.

He felt weak all over as he exhaled deeply. That was close. Too close. *That woman's even bad luck for the animals.* "You can get up now, Mrs. Watts."

When she didn't respond, he snorted in disgust. "Just like a woman. Have a little excitement to break the monotony and she faints." Blake reloaded his rifle. Should he bring her to, or enjoy the peace? He glanced up to see the vultures circling over the freshly killed animals. "Hey." He fired several times, killing two of the huge birds and chasing the others off. That wouldn't last long. He'd better wake up the *Jinx* or they'd be eating jerky again tonight.

Blake hurried around the bear. The woman was nowhere in sight. "Where the hell…?" He looked around, then saw the toe of a boot showing from under the animal's thigh. He stared. "Naw, that wouldn't happen in a million years."

He grabbed hold of the bear's front paw and raised it enough to confirm the unbelievable. She *was* under there. Blake dropped the leg and pushed at the front end.

The bear wouldn't budge. He had to get her out before she suffocated, if she hadn't already.

Blake jerked off his right glove, put two fingers to the corners of his mouth and let out a long, shrill whistle. Then he returned to pulling and shoving at the dead animal. Within minutes Thunder galloped up to his master. Blake snatched his lariat from the saddle, slipped the loop over the bear's head and legs, and quickly tied the other end to the saddle horn, then pushed against Thunder's chest. "Back up, Thunder! Back. Back." When the bear was moved enough, Blake pulled Millie free. "Okay, boy, whoa." The horse stopped pulling, letting the bear plop back with a dusty thud. Thunder walked forward several feet until he could nudge the unconscious girl.

Blake shoved the animal's muzzle away. "Get back, Thunder." *Might have known.* He sat on the ground beside her. *She's even bewitched my horse.* He tapped her cheeks. She was still breathing. *Must have knocked the wind out of her.*

She lay on the ground beside the dead beast. She seemed so small, yet so hardy. Strange he'd never noticed how long and dark her lashes were. The lengthy wheat-colored braid she usually kept wrapped around her head had come down and draped across her shoulder. Without thinking, he caught hold of it. *Soft, but thick.* The braid was as big around as the neck of his saddle horn.

John Eagle rode up and leaned forward on his horse. "Hey, Boss. Don't you think you could save your sparking until after we get this meat back to camp? Those vultures aren't going to leave us much if we don't hurry."

Blake looked over his shoulder and glared at the

scout. "Sparking? With *Millicent the Jinx*? Are you *loco?*" He looked down at the unconscious woman. But he'd certainly been thinking along those lines. Thank goodness he was saved from that mistake. "Gimme your canteen."

The scout tossed it over. "What happened?"

"Bear got her."

John Eagle dismounted, rushed over and squatted down beside them. "How bad's she hurt?" The whole front of her shirt was covered in blood. "Lord, I never saw so much blood. We'd better stop that bleeding and get her back to camp."

Blake poured a little water in his hand and bathed her face and neck as much as was proper. "It's not her blood. It's the bear's. As tempting as it is, I wouldn't let the animals get her." *I think too much of the wildlife for that.* "I shot it, but she just sat there and let the damn bear fall on her."

John Eagle looked from the bear to the girl. He shook his head. "That's one of the largest bears I've seen in a long time. It's a wonder every bone in her body isn't broken."

Blake swore. "I hadn't even thought of that. Better go bring that wagon up. We may need it."

*****

Millie took several shallow breaths. She stretched, then groaned. Every spot on her body hurt. *Hot, it's so hot.* She tried to open her eyes, but they were so heavy. Then moisture began to sprinkle her face. *Rain. So cool.* Drops fell on her face, her neck, trickled between her breasts.

Slowly she became aware of someone touching her body. Hands. Hands on her neck, on her shoulders, down her arms, down each of her legs, then slowly up the sides of her stomach and up her ribs. When they reached high under her breasts, her eyes popped open.

Millie glared into the face of Blake Donovan. She pushed away from him, then groaned. The sudden movement sent new pains through her entire being. She did her best to ignore them. "Just what do you think you're doing?" She slapped his face smartly. "How dare you make free with my body! I may be a lot of things, but a strumpet certainly isn't one of them."

Blake grasped her shoulders and got to his feet, pulling her up with him. "That's ridiculous. The bear fell on you. I was only trying to be sure nothing was broken. Believe me, making free with your body never entered my mind."

She shoved his hands away and shakily stepped back out of his reach. "Of course not. You were too busy trying to kill me. I knew you were planning something the minute you so kindly brought me a horse for this hunt."

Blake raked his fingers through his hair. "That's not true. I shot the bear before it could get you, didn't I?"

Millie stepped farther from his reach. "You most certainly did. Letting it crush me to death was much cleaner. When that didn't work, you let your baser instincts take over."

"Baser instincts?" Blake slammed his fists onto his hips. "Woman, where you're concerned, I don't have any baser instincts."

"Fine! In the future, we'll both remember that." She turned on her heel and limped toward the downed antelope.

Blake stared after the retreating woman. "Well, if

that don't beat all! Try to help a woman and that's what you get."

"The wagon's on its…way." John Eagle struggled to retain his balance as Blake shoved past him.

"The next time you need meat, count me out if you count her in. She's crazy! Plumb crazy!"

Blake pulled his skinning knife from his boot scabbard and began working on the bear. "Well, no one will go hungry for a long time now. That is, if we can get all this meat back."

He looked up at the staring, open-mouthed scout. "Well, don't just stand there. Get busy. By the way, how did you and your partner do with the antelope?"

"Fine. I got two, she got none," he answered as he pulled his own knife and stooped to help with the bear. "But it looks like we'll have enough for a while. The hunting should be a lot better now that we're getting into the mountains."

Millie had just finished gutting her kill when Elsa pulled up with the wagon. "Yoo vant I help yoo wi'd put animal in de vagon?"

"Yes, thank you. I'm not sure I can lift it by myself."

When Millie stood and turned around, Elsa's eyes got bigger. She gasped and scrambled from the wagon. "Vat happen to yoo? All dat blood! Vhere yoo are hurt?"

For the first time Millie noticed how bloody the front of her blouse was. "Oh, dear." She looked up at Elsa and smiled. "I'm all right. Mr. Donovan shot a bear, and it fell on me. I'm not hurt, at least not seriously. But I can't say the same for this blouse." Honestly, every time she got near Blake Donovan, something happened. The man was nothing but trouble.

It was late in the day by the time they returned to

camp. Millie grinned. Camp? It looked more like a fort, with walls of ladies' unmentionables. The women had stretched ropes from one wagon to another and filled in the spaces with wet laundry hung to dry. Now if it just didn't rain for a couple of days, they'd have enough clean laundry to last a week or so.

Emily was beside Millie before the wagons stopped. "My goodness, Millie! Are you all right? I've never seen so much blood." Before she could answer, several others echoed Emily's concerns. Millie sighed. Blake Donovan did this to her on purpose. "I'm just fine, really. It's only animal blood. It'll wash out." *I hope.* "We got six antelope and a bear. That should hold us for a while. How did the fishermen do?"

"Oh, they caught some big ones," Emily answered. "I saved you some. Wash up and you can eat while we divide the meat."

"That sounds great. I've never been so hungry."

Millie cleaned up as best she could. As soon as she'd eaten, she picked up her skinning knife and went back to the wagon full of meat, but there was nothing for her to do. Already a man and a woman worked on each carcass, so she decided to take advantage of their preoccupation and take a much-needed bath.

She stopped by her wagon to get a clean wrapper, soap, and a towel. "Come on, Honey. Let's go try out that water."

Millie laughed as her pet waddled, honking loudly, wings outstretched, as fast as it could toward the water. She stopped behind some bushes and stripped off her bloodstained clothes, then looked around to be sure she was alone before wading into the cold water.

The initial shock was weakening, but she was soon

used to it. Honey glided across the water at Millie's side. They'd been swimming together for years. It was almost like old times.

As she glided across the water, a deep inner peace settled upon her. Being out in the wilderness always made her feel like this. The sun had disappeared behind the mountains, but it wasn't quite dark. The birds had long since settled down for the night except for an occasional good-night twitter here and there. The crickets and water insects were in fine voice. At times like this it wasn't hard to believe in God. Who but a supreme being could have created such a blissful scene?

****

Blake stooped at the water's edge to wash his hands. Except for Honey's contented honking from somewhere on the other side of the reeds, the night was quiet and peaceful. He sat back on the bank, closed his eyes, and listened to the noise of the night creatures.

After several minutes, his eyes flew open. Suddenly everything was deadly quiet. Not a sound could be heard. Without moving, he looked around and waited. He was in the shadow of a large tree and couldn't be seen easily. After several seconds, Honey appeared in the middle of the lake. Something seemed to be keeping pace with her, but he couldn't make out what it was. The goose waded up on shore, and just then a cloud moved from over the moon.

Blake gasped as the moonlight fell on Millicent Watts…all of her. He swallowed as she rose from the water and stepped on shore. He'd been with his share of whores, but this was no whore. While not flaunting her nakedness, she was more intent on picking her way barefooted to the bushes than hiding her lack of clothing.

He should leave, or at least make his presence known, but he couldn't so much as blink—he didn't dare. She'd swear he was spying on her. He blinked his eyes and she was gone. The bushes rustled.

He'd caught little more than a glimpse of her, but that was enough. She was evidently getting dressed behind those bushes. He quietly took his leave. The last thing he needed was for her to catch him gaping like a schoolboy. How could a woman have so many different appearances? In a dress, she looked like a broomstick. In pants she suddenly took on some very feminine curves, but just now, naked, she was all woman.

Chapter Fourteen

Blake glanced around from behind the wagon. Seeing no one looking his way, he casually stepped over the wagon tongue into the circle, then strolled toward the supply wagon. His pulse raced as he nodded to several of the women. Just as he reached the lead wagon, John Eagle climbed from the back end.

"Hey, Boss, I thought you went to the river to take a bath. You can't be done already."

Blake's heart almost stopped beating. "No, I, uh, I lost my soap. Had to come back for another bar." *Goldurnit, why am I acting like a naughty schoolboy? It isn't as if I deliberately set out to spy on the woman.*

The scout grinned. "Isn't that it in your shirt pocket?"

Blake looked down at the end of the bar sticking from his shirt. "Well, I'll be… Guess that bear thing rattled me more than I thought." He shrugged. "Let's get a cup of coffee, and then I'll head that way again."

****

Millie followed her honking pet into the firelight and sat on an empty coffee box beside the warm blaze. As she began rubbing the towel over her wet hair, she glanced toward the campfire near the supply wagon. Blake Donovan set his cup down and walked toward the river. She shook her head. "You know, Honey, that's the strangest man I ever met."

She was mending her torn blouse when Blake returned. His damp hair glistened in the firelight, all but the light streak. How could a man get gray in only one spot like that? As far as she could tell, there wasn't a single strand of gray anywhere else on his head.

Emily handed Millie a plate of antelope roast and potatoes, then dropped down beside her. They ate in silence for several minutes. "This is wonderful," Millie said as soon as she finished the last bite. "Are there any seconds?"

"Sure are. I just can't thank you enough for getting us that little ol' antelope. We should have enough meat for a while. In fact, I'd say this day has been a big success for all of us."

"Oh? How?"

"Well," Emily said as she refilled Millie's plate, "y'all brought back enough meat for everyone, plus all that bear. John Eagle got all the hides for his lady friend, and I washed and dried all our laundry."

Millie rolled her eyes upward. "Well, I guess it was worth nearly getting crushed by a bear. My, what does that leave for us to do tomorrow?"

Emily grinned. "Oh, I don't think that'll be a problem. We still have to wash out the wagon and grease the wheels, mend the harness, and—"

Millie made a face. "Stop. That's an awful ending to an equally awful day." But the day hadn't been all that awful. She could still feel Blake Donovan's arms around her, his hands moving slowly over her body. Until now, a man's touch had never meant anything but pain. Would Blake Donovan really be that gentle…all the time? Or would he revert to the violence she suspected he was barely keeping in check?

She sighed. "I'm going to bed. I can't remember ever being this tired. Good night, Emily." She groaned as she got to her feet. She was sore all over. Tomorrow, she'd probably feel like Ma must have felt after one of Pa's beatings. As God was her witness, no man would ever lay a hand on her like that…at least not more than once, she vowed as she climbed into the wagon.

****

Millie took a deep breath of rain-fresh air. There was nothing like a good slow rain to give everything a new lease on life. The close call with that bear last week had taught her something. She would be buying a new rifle at their next stop at a fort with a general store.

Back home, her single-shot Hawken was fine. And it was special since Uncle James had given it to her for her eleventh birthday. But out here, where life was a struggle, at best, an empty gun could cost one her life. She would have been killed if it hadn't been for Blake Donovan. She shuddered. Being beholden to that man was almost as bad as being attacked by the bear.

The wagon shook as Emily climbed inside. She was covered with mud from head to foot. "What in the world happened to you?" Millie exclaimed as her friend climbed in and let the curtain drop over the opening.

Emily shoved a wet strand of hair from her face, then plucked at her muddy clothes with two equally muddy fingers. "Well," she said, exasperation dripping from her voice as she began unbuttoning her blouse, "I was on guard duty and heard a noise in the bushes near the horses. When I went to investigate, a certain web-footed bird flew at me."

"What?" Millie couldn't help giggling. "And I suppose she had a bucket of mud under each wing?"

179

Emily pulled her arms from the blouse and threw the muddy garment at her wagon mate's feet. "She might as well have. I was so startled, I whirled around, tripped over a wagon tongue, and fell practically face first in a mud puddle."

Millie swallowed hard to keep the laughter under control. "If you fell face first, how come the back of you is as muddy as the front?" She grabbed the soiled britches from her friend's hand before those were sent flying at her, too.

Emily glared at Millie. "Just as I managed to get to my feet, that pet of yours ran at me—whether to harass or apologize I really couldn't tell. Anyway, I slipped and fell backwards in the same puddle."

Millie struggled to keep a straight face but lost the battle. Peals of laughter burst from her. She lay back, helplessly laughing until tears filled her eyes.

Emily harrumphed, but the laughter was infectious. She finally collapsed onto the end of her bunk, tears making trails down her muddy cheeks. After several minutes, the girls were able to pull themselves together.

A gust of wind blew in from under the back wagon flap. Emily rubbed her hands up and down her bare arms. "I declare, it gets so cold in these parts at night." She began scrubbing at the drying mud, then gathered her long hair over the wash basin, before feeling around for the water pitcher.

Millie choked back her mirth and quickly got up. "Here, let me help you." She began slowly pouring water over the muddy hair.

"Ohhh, that's cold!"

"I'm sorry, but this place is just too wet to get a fire started. You'll have to make do with a quick, cold rinse until we reach a drier area."

Emily began squeezing the water from her long tresses. "When we do, I reserve the first use of that bathtub." She took the towel Millie dropped over her head and began rubbing vigorously.

"You know, more and more, I'm tempted to join Mr. Donovan at his early Thanksgiving," she said from under the towel.

"Emily. I can't believe you'd even joke about that."

Emily straightened up and peeked out at her friend. "Well, you have to admit, that bird has been a trial…most of the time."

Millie knew her friend was teasing, but there also was a certain amount of truth in what she was saying. Honey had done her share of mischief on this trip. "Well, I will admit that where Honey is concerned, things haven't been dull."

"Oh, my, no. Things on this trip have rarely been dull."

****

John Eagle finished saddling his horse, then tied his bedroll behind the cantle. "I should meet up with you in a couple of weeks or so. That is, if everything goes as planned."

Blake, on the other side of Patches, leaned against the horse. "That sounds good. We'll keep heading northwest, and you be careful."

John Eagle mounted, barely missing Blake's hat, then leaned down, rested his arm on the saddle horn, and grinned. "Be careful? I'm only riding through hostile Indian country. You're the one staying behind with *Mrs. Jinx*."

Blake whacked his hat against Patches' rump. "Get

outta here." He watched the scout ride out of sight, but John Eagle's laughter hung from the low rolling clouds. Finally, Blake put his hat back on and turned toward the wagons. Unfortunately, the parting taunt wasn't so wrong. He still had Millicent to deal with. *God help me.*

Chapter Fifteen

John Eagle dismounted beside a running brook. He'd spent the last hour scouting this wooded area before deciding it was safe for the night. He unsaddled Patches and staked him and the pack horse where grass and water were plentiful. It was still about two hours until dark. He set up camp a bit back from the stream, then roasted the rabbit he'd shot earlier. After eating his fill, he stripped and waded into the cold creek. He'd left the wagon train almost a week ago, but if the wind shifted, they'd probably still be able to smell him wherever they were.

Finally, he waded out and dried off with his only blanket. He pulled on fresh buckskin britches and a faded blue shirt, then rolled up his soiled clothes and stuffed them into his saddlebag. Starting now, he would dress like the Indians.

The wind wasn't cold, but it wasn't exactly warm, either. He put his gun and holster under the blanket within easy reach, then stretched out and looked at the sky. The night was clear and the stars bright. He guessed the cool weather was due to his getting closer to the mountains.

Before first light, John Eagle finished his second cup of coffee, then put away his supplies and broke camp. He buckled on his gun and knife, hung his hat on the saddle horn, then opened his shirt down to his breastbone, exposing an amulet given him by Chief Red Cloud.

He'd no sooner swung up on his horse than he dove off the opposite side. Everything had suddenly become still, too still. The birds had stopped singing, the insects stopped buzzing. Even the wind seemed to hold its breath. Patches looked toward the west, his ears perked forward, and John Eagle gripped his knife tighter as he crouched behind a deadfall.

He waited for more than five minutes until nature began to move again. When Patches and the pack horse resumed their grazing, John Eagle slowly got to his feet. Whatever it was seemed to have passed, though it was still too dark to see much. He took the reins and walked slowly to the edge of the woods. Everything still seemed to be progressing naturally, so he remounted and, after looking around once again, rode on.

He rode due north toward the Sioux reservation. Though he was white, he'd been raised with the Kiowa since infancy. Sometimes it was hard to know where his loyalties should lie, but not now. This time he was doing something for both sides. By taking Chief Red Cloud's nephew to him, John Eagle would be helping to get a child off a starving reservation and reuniting him with his family. At the same time, he was ensuring the safety of these white women who had to travel over the Bozeman Trail to start new lives in Montana Territory.

The biggest problem would be keeping the boy out of the hands of the soldiers. Red Cloud and his tribe more or less had a death hold on the Bozeman Trail. The soldiers wouldn't hesitate to use the boy as a pawn to gain control of that war zone. To his way of thinking, children shouldn't be used like that.

Patches' ears suddenly perked up. John Eagle quickly scanned the horizon. He looked to the west just as two mounted Indians raced over a small rise toward him. All he had time to notice was the war paint on the braves' faces.

John Eagle touched his heels to Patches and the horse raced forward, his pack horse in tow. He fired a couple of pistol shots over his shoulder at his screaming pursuers but didn't expect to hit anything. After several minutes, he raced the horses behind a group of boulders, leapt down almost before they were stopped, and ground-reined both animals. Then he climbed into the rocks—close enough to keep an eye on them but far enough away to be sure no stray bullets hit his mount.

The Indians dismounted and ducked below the base of the clustered boulders. He fired at them several times, but only one returned his fire. Where was the other? Did he get lucky with one of his first shots?

After he'd traded shots with the one attacker for several minutes, Patches began to snort and stomp. John Eagle raised up to see what his problem was only to feel the wind of a bullet near his ear. He quickly ducked down.

While the first Indian kept him pinned down, the second was trying to slip around and steal his mounts. John Eagle grinned maliciously. That sorry son-of-a-gun was in for a big surprise.

He returned his attention to the first attacker, who was beginning to move toward his friend. Though still pinned down, John Eagle heard an aggravated whinny and knew the Indian had mounted Patches. *Big mistake.* John Eagle put his fingers to his mouth and let out two short, shrill whistles.

Patches suddenly threw his back feet in the air. The surprised Indian flew over the horse's head, landing with a loud thud. He nimbly rolled to his feet, shook his head, then rushed forward to grab the reins again.

Patches had evidently had enough. He reared, striking the would-be horse thief in the head with his hoof. As the first Indian whirled and pointed his rifle at the horse, John Eagle stood, aimed, and fired in one swift motion.

By the time he climbed out of the rocks, both Indians lay dead within a few feet of each other. He rolled his kill over with the toe of his moccasin. A *Crow* warrior. He did the same to Patches' victim. A *Navajo*? John Eagle turned to rub his horse's nose and gave him a cube of sugar. "Well, boy, there's only one reason for a Crow and a Navajo to be together. They're renegades."

He gathered their weapons, ammunition, and knives, stowed them on his pack horse, then mounted up. He rode off a few steps before turning to look behind him. There was no reason to let perfectly good horses revert to the wild. He rode slowly back toward the two riderless mounts.

****

About dusk on the third day after the incident, John Eagle neared a stand of scrub oaks. A lone Indian emerged and stopped his mount almost nose to nose with Patches. His hair was generously peppered with gray, his face aged by years in the weather, and his body, though straight and proud, was very thin. He eyed John Eagle's amulet a minute before raising his hand in the sign of peace.

John Eagle returned the greeting, then sat with his hands carefully folded over the saddle horn. The old man's eyes were alert. The markings on his clothes identified him as Sioux. John Eagle's gaze moved to the horse. As old as the warrior was, that horse looked at least ten years older. If this were a sample of the mounts the army allowed the reservation Indians to keep, no wonder they couldn't hunt for themselves.

Finally, he nodded and motioned for John Eagle to follow him. Though it wasn't quite nightfall, the deeper woods held little light, and by the time they reached the Sioux camp, they were riding in pitch black darkness. They picketed their mounts beside two more of the poorest excuses for horseflesh John Eagle had seen since leaving Miss Millie's sway-backed pet Dumplin' back East. Two braves and a young boy sat near a small fire.

The older of the two men looked about fifty, with more gray than black in his hair. He motioned for John Eagle to join them beside the fire. "I Charlie Bear," he said, then introduced the others in his party.

John Eagle introduced himself and sat, cross-legged, across from the old man. The boy handed a piece of rabbit on a leaf to John Eagle. He hated to take what little food they had. All three Indians looked like they hadn't had a good meal between them in some time, but to refuse would be an insult. When he'd finished his second helping and waved away the offer of a third, he pulled a pouch of tobacco from his shirt pocket. The old chief accepted the offer and filled his pipe, then passed the pouch to the two braves. After several minutes of contented smoking, John Eagle broke the silence.

"I didn't expect to meet with you for several days yet. Did you have any trouble leaving the reservation?"

Charlie Bear shook his head. "We leave in night. Think soldier learn who is uncle to Little Feather. They not know boy come."

John Eagle looked at Little Feather. He was small

for his twelve years, a testimonial to the shortage of food on the reservation. "How will you explain your disappearance?"

"We go hunting many time."

"How is the hunting around the reservation?"

Charlie Bear took a long drag from his pipe. "Not good. Soldiers take good horses, weapons. Must go far for game. Can not carry much back."

John Eagle shook his head, then excused himself and retrieved the captured weapons from his pack horse.

He returned and set the rifles and ammunition belts before Charlie Bear. "I took these guns off two renegades who made the mistake of trying to relieve me of my horses. I would like to make a gift of them to you and ask if you'd do me the honor of allowing me to join your hunt. The game seems to be plentiful in this area, and it's been a long time since I've hunted with anyone but women."

"Women?"

John Eagle explained that he scouted for a wagon train of women. The Indians asked many questions. The only white women they'd seen were the army wives who stayed behind the stockade wall, or those who drew their skirts aside in distaste whenever an Indian passed.

At the end of three days, the small party had killed, skinned, and smoked five antelope. Little Feather proved to be a good provider and managed to keep squirrel or rabbit roasting at all times.

By the time they were ready to break camp, it took John Eagle's pack horse plus the two he had collected from his attackers to carry all the meat and skins. They traveled together to within two days' journey of the reservation. "This far enough, John Eagle. Must not allow soldiers to see Little Feather."

John Eagle nodded. "If you and your men would like to come with us, I'm sure we can make room for you on the wagon train."

Charlie Bear shook his head. "Is good thought, but no. Our women still on reservation. Time of war is much past for us. We stay, help our people as we can."

John Eagle nodded. These were wise men. The children on the reservation would also need someone to teach them of their heritage.

He handed the lead ropes to all three packhorses to Charlie Bear. At the old Indian's protests, John Eagle grinned and pointed out the Crow and Navajo markings on two of the horses. "I liberated those at the same time I got the rifles. When the soldiers notice the strange animals, they'll think maybe you're not as weak and defeated as they thought. It will do them good to worry some."

This left John Eagle with only Patches, but most of his supplies were gone, and the boy was so light, he didn't think Patches would have any trouble carrying them both. He also felt certain they could live off the land until they reached the wagons.

Charlie Bear nodded and grasped John Eagle's arm. "May Great Spirit watch over you and Little Feather, John Eagle."

"Thank you, Charlie Bear. I wish the same for you."

After saying their goodbyes, the Sioux braves slowly headed back to the reservation. John Eagle glanced at the boy they left behind. He was such a small thing to be such an important pawn.

"Well, come on, Little Feather, mount up and let's put some miles behind us before nightfall." The words were no sooner out of his mouth than the boy turned and fled into the woods where their noon camp had been. Little Feather was probably scared to death and didn't want to be seen crying. He'd lost his parents, been restricted to a reservation, and now he was being handed over to a stranger to be sent to an uncle he hardly knew. His whole way of life was being shattered—enough to terrify the bravest of warriors. He'd give the boy time to pull himself together.

John Eagle busied himself adjusting Patches' trappings. The boy was back in almost no time. Instead of tears, he grinned proudly and held up two rabbits.

"Din-ner."

****

Dark clouds rolled overhead like steam from a kettle. Neither moonlight nor twinkling stars showed through. Millie stopped in the shelter of the trees. Shivering, she pulled her coat closer against the cold wind. Thank goodness it was almost time for the watch to change. She suddenly stilled to listen. Were those hoofbeats? She waited, straining to hear even the smallest noise. Yes, there it was again. There was definitely someone out there. She eased deeper into the shadows in case the cloud decided to drift away from the moon. She could barely make out a horse and rider heading her way. As soon as they were slightly past her, she cocked her rifle.

"That's far enough."

The rider pulled up. He raised his hands and waited.

"What do you want here?" she demanded. "Why are you sneaking around in the dark?"

"I'm not sneaking. It's not my fault if it got dark before I could get here. I work for Donovan."

Millie could barely hear him over the wind, but finally the cloud drifted away from the moon and she recognized John Eagle, or thought she did. He looked more Indian than white, dressed in buckskin pants and moccasins. His coat was wrapped around a young child hunched against his back.

So he'd been out visiting his relatives and having a good time while they'd been worried sick that something had happened to him. She smiled to herself. Well, she'd just give him a taste of his own medicine. She drew her coat collar over her mouth and dropped her voice an octave. "Sure you do. Get down, slowly."

"Now wait a minute…"

"I said get down, *Indian.*"

John Eagle tensed. The way she spat out *Indian* made him mad. He couldn't quite place her voice. He was almost sure it was a woman, but none of the ladies in this group would use that tone with him. Why did she stay in the shadows? "Easy. Just don't get nervous with that gun." He swung Little Feather down, then slid to the ground.

"Now, leave the horse and head toward camp, both of you. I'll be right behind you."

John Eagle looked down at the scared child. "It's all right, just head toward the campfire."

Blake jumped to his feet as they stepped into the firelight. "Good grief, Johnny, it's about time you got back." When the scout didn't respond, Blake looked past him into the dark woods. "Why are you standing there with your hands in the air?"

John Eagle nodded to Ezra and Ben, then turned his attention to his cousin. "Hi, Blake. I'd appreciate it if you'd tell Miss Sharpshooter back there to put that gun away. It makes me damn nervous to have an armed woman behind me."

"Woman? What woman? There's no one behind you."

John Eagle looked over his shoulder, then dropped his arms as he whirled around. "Well, she was there." He'd taken just one step toward the woods when Little Feather tugged at his belt. John Eagle looked down and the boy pointed back toward the campfire.

Millie strode into the firelight from the opposite side. "Hello, John Eagle. We wondered if you'd deserted us or just got captured by some jealous husband." She poured a cup of hot coffee and handed it to him. "Elsa unsaddled Patches and gave him some grain. Who's your friend?" She smiled at the boy and offered him a bowl of stew from a big kettle.

At John Eagle's nod, Little Feather accepted the bowl and, in one fluid motion, sat cross-legged beside the fire and began eating as if he hadn't had a bite in weeks.

"Was that you back there?" John Eagle asked. "How did you get to the other side of camp so fast?"

Ignoring his questions, she replaced the cover on the stew pot, then stretched. "Help yourselves to the stew, gentlemen. I'm going to bed." Millie passed close to the scout as she left the group. "The next time you worry us like that, you surely will have reason to fear an armed woman at your back."

He watched her leave. *The cheek of the woman.*

Ezra slapped his knee and laughed as soon as she was out of sight. "She out-injuned ya, that's what she done. Guess ye're out o' practice, boy."

John Eagle turned and glared at the old man, then

squatted beside the fire and calmly sipped his coffee. "I prefer to think of it as being a credit to her teacher. She learned well. I told you she'd make a good warrior woman."

"Warrior Woman," Little Feather repeated under his breath.

Chapter Sixteen

Millie watched John Eagle and Little Feather ride away from camp. John Eagle had volunteered to get the meat for the evening's festivities and to keep the boy busy while the ladies bathed.

With a sigh of relief, Millie and Emily picked up their soap and towels and headed for the river. The sun sparkling off the water against a backdrop of mountains and trees gave one the feeling that all was right with the world. "This would be a perfect day, if the wind would just go away," Emily commented. "But I suppose that sounds greedy."

Millie laughed. "Greedy or not, after almost a solid week of wind and rain, a little still sunlight really doesn't seem like too much to ask. What does your soap smell like?"

"Lilacs, how about yours?"

"Roses. It certainly was thoughtful of the men in the valley to get this fancy soap for us. I plan to make sure there's some left for when we pull into the valley. I don't want to smell like the back end of an ox the first time we arrive at our new homes."

"I declare, Millie, you are a caution. I thought you didn't care about getting a husband."

Millie sat down and began pulling off her boots. "I don't, but there's no use slamming the barn door before you see what's inside."

"Slamming what barn door?" Miss Hannah asked as she dropped her things beside Emily's.

"Oh, we were just talking about this sweet-smelling soap the men in the valley sent us. Come to think of it," Emily added thoughtfully, "I know it's not improper for a lady to accept perfume from a gentleman, but what about perfumed soap? Isn't that rather personal?"

Miss Hannah stopped and looked thoughtfully at the girl for a moment. "Now, that's a good question, Emily. I'll have to think about that for a while, but I don't think so, in this case. These men were trying to give us what little comfort they could on our long trip. I'm sure there were no lecherous motives involved."

"Lecherous? Who's lecherous?" Cindy asked as she joined them at the water's edge.

"Oh, you. You're entirely too young to know what lecherous is," Millie teased as she pushed the girl toward the river. "Get in there and cool off."

Cindy screamed playfully when she hit the water. She bobbed up, spitting and sputtering. "Hey, that wasn't nice. I thought you old ladies were supposed to set a good example for us younger ones."

Millie and Emily looked at each other. "Old?" they repeated together.

"We'll show you *old*," Millie threatened. "Get her!" She and Emily dove in together and swam after the fleeing girl.

They played in the water, accompanied by Honey's antics, for almost two hours. After a leisurely picnic lunch, they spent some time napping, resting, and being at one with nature as it surrounded them. With a glance at the descending sun, Millie sighed. "I certainly hate to see this pleasant afternoon end, but we have a lot to do to get ready for tonight."

Reluctantly, they pulled on their shoes and stockings. As they walked, the girls listed the things they needed to do. "I certainly hope John Eagle has returned with the meat," Millie said. "We need to put it on right away if it's to be ready by evening."

"I have to get my cookies started," Emily added.

Millie stopped long enough to retrieve the soap she'd dropped. "Miss Hannah and I plan to put apples and peaches on to cook for the pies. I think Allison is bringing some kind of Scottish dish. And, heaven help us, Winnie is bringing a family favorite of hers."

Emily groaned. "With her sour disposition, it'll probably be made from prunes."

They both laughed. As they neared the camp, Miss Hannah, who was walking a little ahead of them, stopped so suddenly Emily bumped into her back. "What's that I smell?"

Emily rubbed her nose, then sniffed. "I declare, it smells like roasting meat."

Emily looked at Millie with apprehension. "If it is, that means John Eagle had good luck this morning." Then her expression changed to one of alarm and she began looking around. "If that's the case, where is Little Feather?"

"Don't worry, child," Miss Hannah said soothingly. "John Eagle will keep the boy out of mischief. I'm sure he's much too busy to fall back into his old habits."

As they approached camp, they were happy to see the meat already on a spit, being turned slowly by none other than the little offender himself. "Would you look at that," Millie said. "The meat is almost done. John Eagle must have gotten lucky early this morning."

"I wonder what it is?" Cindy muttered.

Millie hung her towel over the tailgate of their wagon. "I really don't care, as long as it's not bear."

****

Blake removed his hat and wiped his forehead while Thunder drank from a small brook. He'd spent the morning scouting the trail for tomorrow's move toward Fort Casper. They'd been camped for almost four days. Their schedule was already cut pretty close by the detour to pick up Little Feather, and now this rainstorm. *Heaven help us if there's an early snowfall in the Rockies.*

He picked up the reins and swung up onto Thunder's back. "Come on, boy. We still have ground to cover before turning back." He'd never be forgiven if he missed the supper and dance tonight. Those things meant a great deal to the ladies. Unless he wanted to eat Ezra's cooking the rest of the way to Montana, he couldn't afford to be late.

Blake was about ready to turn back when he spotted an Indian pony grazing just below the rise Thunder stood on. He looked around carefully but could find no sign of the rider. It could be a trap, though he didn't feel threatened. He rode slowly toward the pony.

Every time he reached for the stray, it shied away several feet. Finally, he shook out his riata, twirled it over his head twice, and dropped it over the animal's neck. After several minutes of protest, the horse settled down.

Blake looked around once more, then pulled his rifle from the saddle boot and dismounted to check the quivering animal. "Where's your rider, boy?"

There was no fresh blood on the horse. Blake studied the pony's tracks. Finally, convinced it wasn't a trap, he swung onto the saddle and began backtracking. He saw where the horse had come out of a ravine, but the sides were high, and with all the rain they'd had—and what was still falling in the hills, he wasn't about to ride down there. The wilderness was dangerous enough without getting caught in a flash flood due to stupidity.

He dismounted and studied the ravine and the surrounding terrain. Blake secured the Indian pony's lead rope to his saddle horn, then looped Thunder's reins around his pistol handle. Still carrying his rifle, he began walking along the upper rim of the ravine. "Come on, boy, let's go for a stroll."

Every once in a while, he stopped and studied the area, then moved on. Finally, he dropped to his belly and crawled to the rim of the ravine. On the far side lay an Indian boy. He was young, in his middle to late teens, Blake figured. He wasn't dead, but he lay as still as a rock. A large rattlesnake sat coiled near the boy's face.

How had he gotten himself in a situation like that? Blake quickly shifted positions so the angle of a bullet would travel past the boy's head rather than toward it. If he missed, chances were good that the serpent would strike, killing the boy anyway.

He took a deep breath and gently squeezed the trigger. The snake's head and the bullet both slammed into the side of the ravine.

The boy was on his feet before the snake's head hit the ground. He threw himself against the side of the ravine and frantically looked for the source of the shot.

Blake exhaled slowly, then quickly got to his feet. He pulled the pony to the rim and stood with his rifle resting on his hip until the boy spotted him. Their gazes locked for several long seconds, then Blake touched his fingers to his hat, mounted Thunder and rode off, leaving the pony grazing on the ridge.

The trip back to the wagons was uneventful. It was late by the time Blake returned. He just had time for a quick dip in the river. John Eagle and Little Feather were already in the water with none other than Honey. Blake dropped his towel, stripped off his clothes, and waded in. After bathing, he and John Eagle dressed and sat on the bank, talking, while Little Feather swam with the goose.

"He certainly didn't have any trouble making friends with that overgrown duck," Blake complained. "I must be the only person in the world that critter wants to do away with."

John Eagle laughed and shook Blake's shoulder. "Keep trying, cuz. You'll make it." He tried to dodge as Blake tossed his towel over the scout's head.

They sat in comfortable silence for several minutes. "We should be able to leave in the morning," Blake commented. "It's pretty dry up ahead. Saw plenty of game, but I was too far out to bring any back. Did shoot a rattler, but I left it for the Indian boy's lunch."

John Eagle's head snapped around in Blake's direction. "Snake? Indian boy? What are you talking about?"

Blake stood up. "Come on, I'll tell you about it on the way back to camp." He put two fingers to his mouth and gave a sharp whistle. "Come on, Little Feather, or those hungry females will have everything eaten before we get there." The boy scrambled out of the water, quickly dressed and, with Honey hot on his heels, raced past the men toward camp.

Someone began beating on a pan, indicating supper was ready. Blake tucked in his shirt and hooked up his britches, then grabbed his hat and followed John Eagle to the supper fire.

Ezra was just ahead of them. "Boss, can't you think of something that will keep Ezra busy until after everyone else is served?" asked John Eagle. "If he gets there first, the rest of us will go hungry."

Blake laughed. "The way that man's moving, he'll already be half loaded before I could get to him. We'd just better hurry."

Several of the wagons had been turned tailgate-in and the food was set out so everyone could help themselves and then sit down at the tables. The ladies wore their best dresses. Some of them hung loosely, others had obviously been altered. Blake turned to mention how nice they looked, but John Eagle was intently whispering in Little Feather's ear. The boy's face was serious for several minutes, then it lit up like a firefly's tail. He nodded and darted past the nearest wagon.

"What's that all about?" he asked the scout.

"Oh, nothing," John Eagle answered. "He'll be back in a few minutes."

Blake and John Eagle were putting their full plates on the table where Miss Hannah, Millie, and Emily sat, when Little Feather ran up. The boy stopped several feet away, then walked slowly to Miss Millie. Shyly he held out a fistful of wildflowers. "Flowers give much pleasure on table?"

Millie's face turned a pleasing shade of pink as she took the gift. "Why, yes, Little Feather, they certainly will. Thank you very much."

The boy held himself ramrod straight and took a step or two backward. "Warrior not pick flowers for woman!"

He glared in Blake's direction, then hurried off to fill his plate.

Millie looked from the disappearing boy to Blake then back to the flowers. Blake glared at the retreating child, then to John Eagle, finally looking uncomfortably at Miss Millie. He had the distinct feeling he'd been set up.

Emily quickly tossed out last night's wilted flowers and shoved the empty vase into Millie's hands. "I declare, those are even prettier than last night's." She nudged Millie with her elbow.

"Uh, yes. Yes, they certainly are. I can't think of anything nicer." She hurried to the water bucket to fill the vase. What in the world was happening? Why was Mr. Donovan suddenly giving her flowers? Even though Little Feather handed them to her, it was obvious who they were really from. The man had been acting strangely for some time…ever since the hunting incident with the bear. She put the flowers in the water, then returned to place them in the middle of the table.

For the first several minutes of the meal, conversation was rather strained. Without looking up, Millie could feel everyone's gaze moving from her to Blake and back. However, Emily and Miss Hannah began chatting, and before long everyone was talking as if nothing had happened.

After supper, the women did the dishes while Blake and John Eagle put the tables away and moved the chairs to accommodate an audience for the dancing and Ben and Ezra laid boards as the dance floor and the musicians tuned up. Miss Hannah frowned as Winifred took her place as self-appointed committee of one to mind the dessert table. "It'll be interesting to see how many people brave her sharp tongue for a sweet."

Millie laughed. "I suppose that's one way to keep the fat off our hips."

After about two hours of dancing with several different women each dance, Blake dropped to the ground near the dessert table. Millie filled several cups with punch and took one to him. "Thank you, ma'am." He took a quick sip. "You ladies certainly amaze me. Where did you get the makings for this, way out here?"

Millie smiled. "You'd be surprised at the amount of canned foods and juices we still have from what we brought on this trip. Some of the women lost everything they had during the war. The only things some had to bring to a new home were their canned goods, remember."

"Did you lose everything, too?"

Millie shook her head. "No, we were lucky in Pineville. The war didn't touch us in that way. However, before her death, my aunt sold everything she owned. She left me a little money and a whole cellarful of canned and dried fruits and vegetables. I think she felt it'd be easier to carry money across country than heavy furniture."

Blake nodded. "She was right about that. But are you carrying a lot of money with you now?"

"No, our lawyer sent it ahead to a bank near the valley. He said he didn't want word to leak out and encourage road agents."

Blake took another sip. "This lawyer, is he a tall, distinguished gentleman with dark graying hair? Wears a black suit with a string tie?"

Millie nodded. "Why, yes. Have you met him?"

"No, but we saw such a gent at the meeting in Cairo,

Illinois. We were wondering who he was." If he'd known what trouble the old guy represented, he might have shot the lawyer on sight.

Blake set his cup on the table. The idea didn't really appeal to him, but since there were only five men on the whole wagon train, he felt he ought to dance with as many women as possible. "Would you care to dance, Miss Millie?"

Millie looked up in surprise. "Oh. Yes, I'd like that."

Blake circled the dance floor with her. She was surprisingly light on her feet. It wasn't due to her size. It was more like a natural grace. She seemed to follow him as if... Well, she fit well in his arms. It was scary. After all these weeks when the most casual passing turned into a major disaster, here he was having a very pleasant evening with her in his arms.

He looked down at her. Her eyes were beautiful. They usually flashed daggers in his direction, but tonight they sparkled like a dew-covered field at sunrise. Her soft-spoken voice was pleasant. Unlike some women he'd met, she wasn't a featherbrain, chattering constantly and saying nothing. He liked that. And most importantly, she didn't make him feel like he had to be there to protect her all the time. She was the most competent woman he'd met in a long time, when she wasn't involved in some disaster or other.

Meanwhile, John Eagle whirled Miss Emily around the dance floor several times. "My goodness, would you look at that," she said as he completed the last round.

"What?" He turned to follow her gaze.

"Millie and Mr. Donovan are actually dancing together."

"Yeah," he said in astonishment, "but we didn't

arrange it this time, and I don't see any trouble brewing anywhere."

"Maybe this is just what they need. If they'd only get to know one another, they might find they have a lot in common. Oh, fudge, someone just cut in. That's too bad."

John Eagle cocked a brow and lowered his voice to a conspiratorial tone. "Well, maybe we could 'help' them again and have some fun in the bargain. Are you willing?"

"Why, Mr. Eagle, you have that cat-that-stole-the-cream look on your face." She giggled and lowered her voice to match his. "The same as we did before?"

Millie felt a tap on her shoulder. She stepped out of Blake Donovan's arms to allow someone else a turn with him. No sooner had she turned to leave the floor than John Eagle stepped in front of her. "May I have this dance, Miss Millie?"

Millie smiled. "Certainly, I'd be honored." She'd lost count how many times he'd done this during the course of the evening. She no longer had to look to know Emily was dancing with Mr. Donovan. After less than half a turn around the floor, Millie found herself back in Blake Donovan's arms, watching John Eagle whirl away with Emily.

"You know, those two have been together a great deal this evening. Do you suppose there's something brewing between them?"

Blake nodded absently. "I was just thinking the same thing." But he suspected rather than a romance brewing between John Eagle and Miss Emily those two were once again trying to promote one between himself and Millie. John Eagle could be damned sneaky when he wanted to be.

Blake turned his attention back to Millie. Odd how relaxed he'd become with her. When she wasn't threatening him with a gun, she was surprisingly fun to be with. Could be John Eagle and Miss Emily were just tired of him and Miss Millie always scrapping. Maybe this was their way of establishing peace on the train.

Not a bad idea, at that. Blake had come at her like an angry bull the first time they'd met. Why, he'd probably scared her half to death. That could explain all the accidents every time he came near her. He probably made her as jumpy as a frog in a hot skillet.

"You're certainly a good dancer, Miss Millie. You must have been the belle of many a ball back home."

She blushed. "Thank you, Mr. Donovan. Actually, I went to very few dances. However, some of my fondest memories are of the evenings in the parlor with Uncle James and Aunt Lavinia. They did love to dance." Her eyes became so misty he thought she might cry. Could she be homesick? Just as quickly, her mood changed to happy again.

She smiled up at him. "You're not such a bad dancer yourself. Did you attend a lot of barn dances?"

He grinned back. "No, ma'am, my memories aren't as fond as yours. As John Eagle would say, I come from a large tribe that included ten girls."

"My!" she gasped. "You have ten sisters?"

"No, thank heaven. I was an only child, but my father had two brothers and a sister, and between them they had ten girls and three boys. Seems there was always a girl or two who needed an escort to some kind of gathering. I got plenty of practice on the dance floor."

"Do any of them live in Montana?"

Blake shook his head and lowered his voice to a whisper. "No, I'm hiding out."

Millie looked at him in surprise. "Why? I think it would be wonderful to have cousins to do things with."

"Well, so did I, at first. Then they all started getting married and having babies. When they started wanting Uncle Blake to come over and babysit, Uncle Blake headed for the mountains."

"Oh? Don't you like children?"

"I don't know. I didn't stay around long enough to find out."

Finally, Blake and Millie staggered to the refreshment table and dropped into two vacant chairs. "I may never stand again," she complained with a laugh.

"Me neither. Would you like something to drink?"

Millie fanned herself with her hand. "Yes, please."

He knew it was too good to last. He'd asked out of politeness, but if she were considerate, she'd have refused the drink. He looked around. Of course, there wasn't anyone in sight to act as waitress. With a sigh, he struggled to his feet and headed toward the punch bowl.

Just as Blake returned with two cups of punch, Emily plopped into his chair beside Millie. John Eagle dropped to the ground in front of them.

"Are you two quitting already?" Millie asked.

"Are you kidding? I don't know about Miss Emily, but I couldn't dance another step."

Blake handed one cup of punch to Millie, then offered the other to Emily before going back for two more. Upon his return, he handed a cup to John Eagle. Seated beside his cousin on the ground, and leaning back, he rested his shoulders against a wagon wheel and sighed. "Ahhh, I may never get up again."

"My goodness, Mr. Donovan, surely you're not tired already?"

Blake peered up at her through one half-opened eye. "Miss Emily, would you care to dance?"

"My, how gallant of you, kind sir. I would be most pleased." When he started to get up, she laughed and placed a restraining hand on his shoulder. "After you've rested, that is. I don't think I have the energy right now, either."

He scooted to a more upright sitting position. "Thank you most kindly, ma'am. I really don't think I'd have been able to get up. Five men to fifty women really puts a strain on a man's endurance. Remind me to hire more men the next time."

Millie reached over and snagged the cookie platter. "Do you plan to go back East for another group of women?"

Blake's hand hovered over the plate briefly before taking a sweet. He looked up at her. "No, ma'am! Not if I live to be a hundred!"

John Eagle nudged Blake in the ribs. "Look over there. For an old man, Oats seems to be having an awfully good time."

Blake looked over at the dance floor. "Yeah, he certainly does. Thought Miss Elsa scared him."

"Maybe that's why he's danced the last four dances with her. He's too scared to turn her down."

Blake watched them for several minutes. "He certainly doesn't look scared. In fact, that pleased look on his face is almost indecent. We may have to have a shotgun wedding before we ever get to the valley."

Millie laughed with the others, but wondered if they weren't close to the truth. For weeks now, Ezra had been spending a lot of time near Elsa's wagon. She'd seen him heading that direction several mornings with strings of fresh fish, or in the afternoons with a small animal for supper.

"Wouldn't that be exciting," Emily said.

"Sure would, but maybe we should wait a little longer. Maybe we'll make it a double wedding," the scout added, looking pointedly at Blake.

Blake jabbed John Eagle in the ribs, then hurriedly got to his feet. "Not in a hundred years," he mumbled through clenched teeth before hurrying back to the dance with Miss Emily in tow.

Chapter Seventeen

Blake's evening had been going great until John Eagle made that remark about marriage. Some friend. John Eagle knew good and well that no matter what a woman said, she was always interested in marriage.

Marriage to *the Jinx*? Blake shuddered. All he needed was for her to start looking at him with that on her mind.

Blake stepped aside while John Eagle put the tailgate up. "Let's check the horses." They walked toward the picket line. As soon as they were out of hearing range of the closest wagon, Blake turned and dropped John Eagle with a well-placed blow to the jaw.

The scout fell flat on his back. "Hey, why'd you do that?" he demanded as he rose up on one elbow and rubbed his jaw.

Blake stood over John Eagle. "Why? After the way you stabbed me in the back, you ask why? You've played some pretty rank jokes on me over the years, cousin, but this is the worst. We're family, damn it!"

"Now you remember." John Eagle sat up and wiggled his jaw back and forth.

Blake paced up and down. "Of all the women to push at me, *Millicent the Jinx*? How could you do that to me? How could you do that to her? I thought you liked her."

John Eagle just sat there. As soon as Blake came

close enough, John Eagle's feet suddenly shot forward, kicking Blake's legs out from under him and knocking him on his butt. "There, that's better. I was getting a crick in my neck," John Eagle said. "Now, you listen to me. She's exactly right for you."

Blake scrambled to his knees, rubbing his hip. "You're crazy!"

"No, I'm making perfect sense. You don't like clinging women, right? And you don't think a lawman is a good risk for a woman out here, right?"

"Right on both counts," Blake said before John Eagle could take a breath. "I still intend to be the sheriff in the valley, so nothing's changed."

"Yes, it has. You don't want to be alone all your life. Miss Millie's your best choice. She can take care of herself and you too, if need be."

Blake's mouth dropped open, and then he sprang to his feet. "You're daft, you know that, Johnny? Absolutely daft."

Blake turned on his heel and marched toward a rise several yards from the circle of wagons. Johnny had finally lost his mind. Of all the crazy ideas! To even consider having a close relationship with that jinx was crazy enough, but to suggest he *marry* her? That was the most ridiculous thing he'd ever heard.

He dropped down and crawled to the top of the rise. Lying flat, he scanned the distant horizon for a campfire or anything out of the ordinary. It wouldn't do any good to be interested in Miss Millie, even if he were so inclined. Which he wasn't. Her *watch goose* wouldn't let him anywhere near the woman. The whole idea was insane.

Blake turned his attention to the landscape. He

raised the binoculars and slowly surveyed the surrounding area. If anyone was out there, they were running a cold camp. The only flickering lights were a few stars in the sky. He looked from left to right, but he couldn't keep his mind off that blonde-haired *Jinx.*

She was right capable when the chips were down. She was a crack shot and good hunter. He didn't know anyone, except maybe John Eagle, that he'd rather have back him when there was trouble, as long as he was sure she was on his side. Though he'd accused her several times of needing a keeper, when trouble came, he'd never once thought she couldn't take care of her share.

And her looks weren't hard to take, either. She'd gained weight on this trip, in all the right places, as Ezra had pointed out several times. Her long blonde hair looked like it had been kissed by the morning sun. Her green eyes, framed with those thick dark lashes, haunted his dreams, day and night.

He put the field glasses down and rested his head on his arms for a moment. Damn the woman. She was driving him crazy. Maybe if he spent some time with her, they could get all this craziness between them settled and be able to go about their business.

He raised his head and took one more look around. It was all useless speculation anyway. That overgrown *duck* practically attacked him every time he went near Millie. Finally, he scooted back until he could stand up without being outlined on the horizon and headed back toward the wagons. He checked the picket line, then all the night guards. Assured that all was organized and going as expected, he pulled his bedroll from the supply wagon and spread it on the ground across the fire from Ezra. Blake probably wouldn't get any sleep with the old coot snoring that way, but he adjusted the saddle, then stretched out with a sigh. *How does one make friends with a duck?*

****

Blake handed his empty cup and breakfast plate to Miss Hannah. "Thank you, ma'am. That was a real treat."

"You're quite welcome, Mr. Donovan. And thank you for hitching my team this morning."

"My pleasure." As he tipped his hat and turned to leave, his gaze fell on the remaining three biscuits. "By the way, could you, uh, spare one of those for the road?"

"Certainly. Help yourself."

Blake took a biscuit and hurried toward Thunder. He mounted and headed down the line. When he reached the Watts wagon, he slowed Thunder's pace. He took a bite of the biscuit, then tipped his hat to Miss Emily. "Good morning. You ready to pull out?"

Emily smiled. "Just about. Millie is helping Cora hitch up. As far as I can tell, everything's just peachy."

Blake grinned as he nudged his horse. *Just peachy.* Now that's a phrase he hadn't heard in a long time. He stopped beside the nesting box hooked to the side of the wagon. The goose immediately stood up and honked threateningly.

"Well, here goes nothing," he muttered. "Hi, *Duck*. I've been thinking it's time you and me stopped feuding." He broke off a piece of the biscuit and started to hand it to the goose. When she hissed, he thought better of his plan and tossed the bite into the nest. "Call that a peace offering."

Honey looked at the bread, then back at Blake suspiciously.

"Come on, *Duck*, surely you aren't going to hold a grudge indefinitely."

****

Millie looked up from mending the harness in time to see Blake Donovan toss something to Honey, which the greedy goose gobbled right down. She'd seen him do that several times in as many days. What in the world was the man up to? He obviously wasn't trying to poison her or she'd already be dead. As soon as he left, she looked over to find Emily looking askance at her. "What do you suppose he's up to?"

Emily shook her head. "I don't rightly know, but he's been doing that several times a day for the last two weeks that I know of."

"Do you suppose he's trying to fatten her up for his early Thanksgiving?"

"I don't know, but if she gets much fatter, she'll be popping her feathers."

Both girls laughed, but Millie still worried. "You don't suppose he's trying to make friends with her, do you?"

"I hadn't thought of that, but why would he?"

Millie put down the finished harness, then followed to help Emily make supper. "I don't know, but I don't like it. He's up to something. I haven't figured out what, but I will."

John Eagle pulled his horse to a sliding halt, sending dust and dirt flying in all directions. Emily slammed the cover down on the stew pot. Millie, coughing and sputtering, tried to fan the dust away with her hand. "John Eagle," she cried, "there's enough dirt in our food without your adding to it."

The scout tipped his hat and looked contrite. "Sorry,

Miss Millie. I didn't want to be late for one of your good meals. Hope I didn't ruin anything."

"No, you didn't ruin it, but the pie might be a little crunchier than I'd planned."

"Good. I mean, I'm glad I didn't ruin it. I'll take care of Patches and get cleaned up." He beckoned to Blake as he passed.

Blake fell into step beside the scout. "Man, you like to live on the edge, don't you? If I'd raised a dust like that, Miss Millie would have skinned me alive." He helped John Eagle strip the saddle off his horse and rub him down. "What's up?"

John Eagle looked around to be sure they couldn't be overheard. "Fort Sedgwick is about two days west."

"Good. I'm sure the ladies would enjoy a little rest."

"Not this time. I'd suggest we swing north and bypass it completely."

"Why? And what happened to you? Your face and hands are bruised and your shirt's torn."

John Eagle looked down at his torn shirt. "Yeah, guess I do look pretty bad. I should have cleaned up before coming into camp." He looked around again. "I wanted to get to you before you told the ladies about the fort. You haven't told them, have you?"

Blake stopped rubbing and looked over the back of the horse at the scout. "No, but why not?"

"There are some hard cases there calling themselves mountain men, but I'd guess they're more like fugitives hiding out in the mountains. I doubt they've been near a woman in months. In fact, they've been such strangers to soap and water, I had to get outside just to breathe. Someone must have overheard me talking to the clerk in the store. One of them followed me outside and started asking questions about the wagon train, like how big it was, how many men we had, where we were coming from, where we're going. Things like that. I finally told him it wasn't any of his business. That made him fightin' mad." He touched his bruised cheek gingerly. "And I *do* mean fightin'. I got in a lucky punch and lit out of there. Rode northeast for a day and a half before coming here. They're bad news, Blake. The ladies are right handy at taking care of themselves, but this kind of trouble we don't need."

Blake stared off in the distance thoughtfully. The South Platte Trail was a little longer, but he'd decided to take it because it was easier traveling for the ladies. They were running a little low on supplies, but the hunting was pretty good. They could manage until they reached Fort Laramie. He turned back to the scout. "Maybe you're right. This trip has been surprisingly trouble free, and I'd like to keep it that way. I was counting on using Latham's Ferry, but I guess we'll have to do it ourselves. You'll have to go out again in the morning and find us a crossing place."

John Eagle nodded as he finished graining his horse. "Just let me get a good meal under my belt and one full night's sleep first."

"I think we can manage that. I noticed Miss Millie working on a pie when you rode in. Don't know what kind it is, but I've never known one of hers to be bad."

John Eagle brushed the dirt from his hands. "Me neither. Let's hurry. I'd like to get there ahead of Oats."

Blake laughed and caught his cousin's arm. "Whoa! Miss Millie isn't about to let anyone put his feet under her table who hasn't had a bath"—he sniffed, then wrinkled his nose—"in a long time."

The scout looked down at his clothes. His pants and boots were splattered with mud. His shirt was dirty, torn, and had a few bloody spots on the sleeve. "I guess you're right. I didn't realize those so-called mountain men had messed me up so badly."

He snatched up his saddlebags. "All right, I'll take a quick dip in the river, but you find something to keep Oats busy. That man can inhale food faster than anyone I've ever seen."

Blake laughed as John Eagle raced toward the water, only slowing down long enough to grab a towel from the supply wagon.

"You weren't planning to keep that information to yourself were you, Mr. Donovan?"

Blake whirled around just as Miss Hannah stepped from the bushes. "What? Miss Hannah, how long have you been standing there? I'm surprised at you, ma'am. How many times have I heard you tell Miss Cindy that a proper lady doesn't eavesdrop?"

"I was here first, and there are times when a proper lady doesn't call attention to herself. Besides, Blake Donovan, my actions aren't being questioned here. Yours are. I insist the ladies be warned of the possible danger."

"Now, wait a minute. We're not sure there is any. We don't know that they've followed John Eagle. Let's not start a panic for no reason."

Hannah allowed Blake to escort her back toward the campfire. "Well, you may be right, but I think we should alert the night watch. If they *are* following John Eagle, they'll show up sometime between now and tomorrow, right?"

Blake thought a minute then nodded. "Could be.

And you're probably right about alerting the night watch, too. Okay, we'll do that, but there's no need to get everyone stirred up until we know there's a need."

She patted his hand before taking her leave. "Fine, I'll leave it to you, then."

Blake watched her until she'd joined the others, then turned to intercept one of the men. "Ben, pass the word for all the men to join me for coffee at Miss Hannah's fire right after supper. John Eagle's back, and we need to talk."

"Sure, Boss. I'll tell Ezra to put on an extra coffeepot."

After supper, Millie helped Emily clear the table, placed a dish of cobbler before John Eagle and Mr. Donovan, then took her seat. John Eagle took a big bite. As soon as he swallowed, he grinned from ear to ear. "Miss Millie, this is your best yet. Where did you get the blackberries? And the sugar. I thought we were nearly out."

"We are, but my aunt and I canned a great many jars of pie fillings."

John Eagle washed down his bite of cobbler with a large swallow of coffee. "Pie filling? You mean fruit to be made into pies, don't you?"

"No, well, we did put up fruit, but we canned fruits with all the sugar and spices for pies, too."

"All blackberry?"

Millie laughed. "No, we have peach, apple, cherry, strawberry, apricot, and I don't know what all else. I didn't realize the cowboys who helped me pack cleaned out the root cellar and put it all in the wagon. By the time we get to Montana, I'll have a very light load, but we'll certainly eat well in the meantime."

Everyone laughed. Millie turned her attention to Blake. "Mr. Donovan, I've noticed you feeding Honey for the last several days. May I ask why?"

Blake nearly choked on his coffee. He set the cup down and looked at all the interested faces now turned toward him. "Well, I...uh, every time I ride past, that *duck* hisses at me. It makes Thunder nervous. So I decided if we were friends, she might not do it anymore."

Millie nodded, not at all convinced. "Seems to me, if she makes your horse nervous, Thunder's the one to make friends with her."

Her face was deadly serious. Blake didn't know how to answer, until finally, her eyes began to twinkle. His mouth twitched as he nodded. "Yes, ma'am, I'll tell him that. Maybe he should be sharing his oats instead of me saving biscuits."

Everyone around the table broke into peals of laughter. Emily got up and removed the plate from in front of him. "Mr. Donovan, remember that old saying, *'Be careful what you ask for, you might get it.'* Being friends with Honey is no bed of roses, believe me."

While the women cleaned up the dishes, Blake and Ezra unloaded the sewing machine and the small pump organ. As soon as the supper things were cleaned and put away, the women sat in groups, mending, altering clothes, trying out new hair styles, and singing.

Blake and the men gathered around the coffeepot at a fire some distance from the women. John Eagle drew a small map in the dirt by the fire. "We're here, and we need to bypass the fort. That means we have to find a place to ford the Platte again, someplace that's not so close to the fort but where the ladies won't have too hard a time. If anyone has any suggestions, I'd sure be obliged to hear them."

As Blake listened, the night creatures chirped in chorus with the organ and the ladies' singing. It still amazed him how well all these women got on together. If the men in the valley got along with the women as well as the women got along with each other, this community shouldn't have any trouble at all.

Finally, the last of the coffee was gone. Ezra banked the fire. Reb headed back to check on the stock and Little Feather. Ben and Reb went to help the ladies put away the organ and sewing machine while Blake and John Eagle got the night watch set up. All was quiet when Blake finally crawled into his tent.

****

Morning came too early to suit Millie, but she struggled into her clothes and splashed a little cold water onto her face. "Brrr! It's enough to make a person give up washing altogether," she mumbled. She put the coffeepot on and had the biscuits baking by the time Emily joined her.

Millie had finished hitching the last ox to her wagon when Blake stopped Thunder a few feet away. She looked at him over the rumps of the lead oxen. "Good morning, Mr. Donovan. Did you stop to see me or Honey?"

He grinned good-naturedly and tipped his hat. "'Morning. I stopped to see you this time."

"Well, I'm flattered." She smiled. "Did you bring me a biscuit, too?"

Blake snapped his fingers. "Shucks, I knew I forgot something. Maybe next time."

Millie laughed and moved to his side of the wagon, checking the lines and yoke as she went. "What can I do for you this morning?"

The smile faded from Blake's face as he dismounted. "You might like to wear your pistol for the next several days. And keep a sharp eye out. There probably won't be any trouble, but it never hurts to be prepared."

Millie nodded. "I heard you telling the night watch about those men, last night. Do you really think they'll come?"

"I don't know, but white women are rare out here, and unattached ones are almost nonexistent. I've been surprised we haven't had unwanted visitors before now."

Millie pulled her pistol from under the wagon seat and strapped it on. "How far do we have to go before we no longer need to fear these men?"

"I'm not sure. Even if they don't show up, we're getting into hostile country. From now on, we'd better all be on our toes. Guess we'd better pass the word along the line."

Millie nodded. "What's up ahead?"

"The North Platte River is two or three days away. John Eagle and I have been this way a few times and have a pretty good idea where to cross. He's gone on ahead to be sure it's as we remember it." Blake mounted Thunder and tipped his hat. "As soon as we get underway, I'll warn the others to be watchful."

He put his fingers to his mouth and let out two short and one long, shrill whistle, then waved his hat over his head several times and gave the signal to pull out.

****

Just before noon on the second day, John Eagle rode up beside Blake. He raised his hat and sleeved the perspiration from his head. "Hi, Boss. Any trouble?"

220

Blake shook his head. "None. How about you?"

"Same here. We should reach the crossing in about an hour. Must have been a lot of rain upriver somewhere. Water's higher than I expected, but we've no choice. It's here or at the fort."

Blake nodded and turned almost due west. "The ladies can probably manage all right. They're pretty seasoned."

At the river, the men stretched two ropes across, anchored by a horse at each end. The cattle and extra horses were taken across first. Then the wagons were floated across the river between the ropes.

Finally, Ezra and the supply wagon brought up the rear. As he reached the middle of the river, a snake swam by. The lead mules bucked and brayed. The wagon jerked from side to side, almost tipping over before Ezra could get the animals under control.

As soon as they were dragged ashore, Blake groaned. Water poured out of the wagon bed. Millie, with Miss Hannah a few steps behind, hurried up to the tailgate as Blake climbed inside. "How much damage is done to the supplies, Mr. Donovan?"

Blake shook his head. "Looks like we lost more than half of it."

Millie groaned. Things had been going so well, too.

"Will we have enough to make it to the next supply stop?" Miss Hannah asked.

Blake climbed back out. "I don't know. It depends on how much you ladies have in your wagons. We'll have to check when we get to the new camp."

Millie wiped her forehead. "If we don't have enough, what will we do?"

"Eat a lot of meat," he said with a smile. "The game

around here is plentiful, if not varied. We won't starve. And there are settlements here and there. We might have to stop at several to get enough, but we'll do all right."

Miss Hannah leaned over to wring the water from the hem of her split skirt. "I'm not at all certain how only meat for every meal will set with everyone. Certainly hope he was right about those settlements here and there. Besides, I'd like to have a nice meal that didn't have sand in it."

A gust of wind blew across Millie's damp clothes, and she shivered. "Yes, and maybe a hot bath that someone else heats and pours for me." They both laughed. "I suppose it doesn't hurt to dream, but a hot bath really does sound heavenly," Miss Hannah agreed. "Speaking of hot, Emily went ahead to set up camp. If we hurry, she might have supper ready by the time everyone gets there. I could certainly use a cup of tea."

"That does sound good," Millie agreed as she allowed Mr. Donovan to help her mount. She followed the dripping supply wagon the last three miles to the new camp.

Emily already had supper cooking and the table set, complete with yellow clover flowers. Millie unsaddled and rubbed down her horse, then staked it out to graze for the night. She could hear Emily and Miss Hannah talking as she poured water into the basin.

"It seems we're either tromping through dusty plains or swimming. It brightens up the day to see flowers and trees again, Emily. I'll pick the flowers for tomorrow's table."

"That'll be nice. I should have thought to pick some for tonight."

Miss Hannah finished putting flowers in a can of

water. "You didn't pick these?"

Emily shook her head. "Maybe Little Feather left them."

Millie looked at the flowers over the towel as she dried her face. Who were the flowers for? If Little Feather left them, was it on his own, or had someone put him up to it? He'd said picking flowers was not warrior's work. No, of course not. He was only being helpful before.

If they were from Mr. Donovan, he would have handed them to Emily, not just dropped them and run. But under no circumstances would Mr. Donovan leave her flowers. Although they'd been getting along well lately, she had no illusions about their relationship.

****

Blake wiped his forehead, then replaced his hat. He sat in the shadows, watching the camp activity. His thoughts kept returning to John Eagle's preposterous suggestion. And it was preposterous. How could anyone think he and *Millicent the Jinx* could have more than a working relationship…an uneasy one, at that? Even if he were willing, which he certainly was not, she couldn't stand him and neither could her *pet*. Though, now that he thought about it, things didn't seem as bad as they'd started out to be. She didn't seem to draw him into as much trouble as she did at first.

He rubbed his thumb across his unshaved chin as he watched her rub down her horse. She rubbed the mare between the eyes and gave her a hug before leading her off to graze. Her way with animals was amazing. She wasn't a bad cook, either. She wasn't too swift of foot where bears were concerned, but that situation wouldn't arise again in a lifetime.

His thoughts wandered back to the dance a while back. Even now, he could almost feel her in his arms…almost as if she belonged there.

Thunder snorted and stomped his hoof impatiently and Blake snapped his attention back to the present. What was he thinking? The whole idea of him and Miss Millie was out of the question. He reined the horse around toward the end of the train. "Come on, Thunder, before my mind and John Eagle get me in more trouble than I can handle."

Chapter Eighteen

John Eagle scratched a crude map in the dirt. Putting an X at the bottom of a line, he said, "We're here. If what I heard at Fort Sedgwick is true, there's a small settlement about here." He pointed with the stick in his hand. "We should reach it in about three days or so."

Blake nodded. "All right, we can send most of the wagons on, with you in charge, while Oats and I can take two supply wagons into town for whatever they can spare."

****

Millie strapped on her gun and holster. It looked a little odd with her blue skirt, but she'd traveled armed for so long she felt undressed without it. Besides, it was difficult to shop with a rifle in her hand. With trouble always lurking in the background, none of them were going unarmed. She shrugged into her coat and glanced at the sky. There was a chill in the air and heavy dark clouds to the north. *If the weather will just hold until we get the supplies and rejoin the train...*

While the wagon train hurried to get as far as possible before the bad weather set in, she, Emily, and Miss Hannah were going into town for supplies with Ezra and Mr. Donovan. After a general meeting, it was decided those mountain men would probably spend time in the nearest saloon licking their wounds. However, the women thought it might be prudent to put as much distance as possible between them.

Ben helped Millie onto her horse. She arranged her skirts over her ankles and sighed. It seemed so strange to be back in a skirt again. In a way, it felt nice, too. Going to town was exciting. *And Mr. Donovan is such a handsome escort.* She gasped. Why in the world would she think something like that? The man was pig-headed and bossy!

Emily climbed onto the seat of the lilac-colored wagon, followed by Ezra. Miss Hannah drove the pink supply wagon. Blake tipped his hat to them. "If you're ready, ladies, we'd better get going."

With Mr. Donovan in the lead, Millie was free to ride along or disappear into the trees, which she did often. If anyone was following them, they wanted to know about it. It was almost noon by the time they stopped outside the little settlement. Ezra insisted on riding Millie's horse into town.

The few people on the street stared in open surprise at the gaily colored wagons. Millie grinned when she noticed Ezra had dropped back almost two wagon lengths from the group. The town's business district wasn't much, just one short street. Two saloons and a livery stable stood at one end, and a feed store, an emporium, and a cafe at the other.

Millie sat beside Emily. "Look, a doctor's office. I'm surprised this town is large enough to support a doctor." There were several side streets boasting three or four crude homes each. A half-built church sat at the west end of one street and a newly started jail occupied the east end.

"What do you suppose ever possessed these people to settle way out here?" Emily asked.

Miss Hannah shook her head. "I don't know, but it's not too difficult to understand why one would fall in love with this valley. Look at those mountains."

"This really is a beautiful place," Emily said. "But I'm not certain I'd want to live out here in the middle of nowhere."

Millie looked around. "Well, isn't that what we're planning to do in Montana Territory? Start a town in the middle of nowhere?"

Miss Hannah nodded. "Yes, I guess it is. Somehow, the magnitude of it didn't strike me until now."

"Me neither," Emily said. Then her stomach growled loudly. She giggled. "Oh, dear, I'm afraid my stomach isn't impressed with all this beauty. I'm starving."

Miss Hannah nodded toward a building up the street. "There's a cafe right next to the emporium. Suppose we eat before we start our shopping."

"That's a wonderful idea." Emily pulled up to the hitching rack in front of the emporium.

Blake and Ezra dismounted and helped the three ladies down. "I could eat a mite myself," Ezra said as he hitched up his britches and led the way into the cafe.

They took a table by the window. Millie looked around the room. The blue calico tablecloths and matching curtains gave the room warmth, something that had been lacking in her life during the last few months. She was surprised how much she'd missed civilization.

The waitress smiled at them. "Good afternoon. Welcome to Peaceful Valley. I'm Sharon. What can I get you?"

"We'd like vittles without dirt in it that someone else 'sides me cooked," Ezra answered.

The girl raised one brow in his direction, then grinned. "I think we can manage that. What would you like to have?"

Ezra scratched his chin. "Whatcha got?"

"Our venison stew is very popular."

Ezra and Blake both shook their heads. "We get plenty of deer and mostly stew."

"Well, we have beef steak, or fried chicken complete with mashed potatoes, gravy and green peas."

"How about a large steak," Blake suggested. Ezra nodded.

"For all of you?" The men looked askance at the ladies, who were shaking their heads. Emily grinned. "I don't know about y'all, but I surely do have a longing for some of that fried chicken and all the trimmin's."

Both Millie and Hannah agreed.

"Thank you. I'll bring it in just a few minutes." Then she smiled at Ezra. "And I'll be sure to tell the cook to leave out the dirt."

Ezra grinned. "Thank ye, Missy."

While they waited, they watched the town's people hurrying about their business. "Shore is busy round here fer a place so far out into nowheres," Ezra commented. "'Pears maybe it was a good place fer a town after all."

Blake leaned across Ezra and looked out the window. "There's a feed store and a blacksmith. Do you see a hardware store anyplace?"

Miss Hannah looked up the street from her place across the table. "Not that I can see. Let's ask the waitress when she comes back." She pulled a list from her handbag. "Maybe we can split the chores and be able to catch up to the wagons before dark."

"No, ma'am, we won't be able to do ever'thing afore

dark," Ezra said. "We'll have to spend the night here. That is, iffin we can find a hotel. Do you 'member seeing one when we come into town?"

Blake shook his head. "That's another thing we'll have to ask about." He thought a minute. "Let's see. We need to take the wagons in for repairs, need some feed for the stock. They can't be expected to go indefinitely on only grass, which may only get sparser from now on. We need to get more parts for wagon repairs along the way, too, so that means a hardware store."

Miss Hannah checked her notes, then looked at Millie and Emily. "We need to go to the emporium next door for supplies. Can you think of anything else that's not on this list?" They passed the list around the table, each perusing it.

"I'd like to replenish our medical supplies, if I can," Emily answered.

"And we could use more ammunition, if that's possible," Millie added.

Hannah looked around the table. "Anything else?"

They shook their heads.

Blake nodded. "Fine. Oats and I will take the wagons to be repaired, get the ammunition, and find a hardware store. You ladies can see to the supplies and medicine."

Their waitress, Sharon, arrived with their lunch. "Medicine? Is someone hurt?"

"No, we're just restocking some of the supplies we lost on our last river crossing."

The girl placed the heaping plates on the table, boardinghouse style, then gave Miss Hannah a quizzical look. "Last crossing?"

"Yes, we're from a wagon train not far from here.

Our supply wagon sprang a leak and we lost most of our extra provisions during a river crossing several days ago. Maybe you can give us directions for the things we need."

"I'll try."

"Hey, girl, you gonna serve us, or do we have to get up and do it ourselves?" a gruff voice demanded from the other side of the room. Two men looking more like barflies than ranch hands glared at the table of newcomers.

"I'll be right there." She turned back to Miss Hannah. "Let me take care of the other customers, and I'll be back before you're ready to leave."

When the last bite of cake and the last drop of coffee were gone, Ezra leaned back and sighed. "That shore hit the spot. Now we need to find a shady spot to take a little snooze."

Millie laughed with the others. "Somehow, I don't see that happening anytime soon, Ezra."

He grinned. "Me neither, Missy, but it's still a nice thought."

Sharon returned with the coffeepot. "How was everything?"

Ezra looked at her seriously. "Everything was fine, Missy. And you can tell the cook I said the lack of dirt didn't hurt his cooking one little bit."

They all laughed.

"I'm sure he'll be pleased to hear it," she said. "More coffee, anyone?"

The men declined and, after asking directions, excused themselves. Millie and the other two ladies accepted a final refill. The other customers had left the cafe. "Could you get a cup and join us for a bit?" Miss

Hannah asked. "It's been a long time since we've talked to anyone other than those on the wagon train. I'm afraid we're a little behind on the news."

Sharon looked around. Seeing nothing pressing to take care of, she reached behind the counter and returned with an extra cup and a plate of cookies. She took Ezra's empty seat. "Traveling across the country must be exciting. I'd love to hear about it."

Millie stirred a little sugar into her coffee. "All right, and we'd like to hear about living way out here in the middle of nowhere. That's what we'll be doing, and we'd like to know what to expect."

They spent the next hour exchanging news and experiences. Finally, Sharon got up. "I've really enjoyed this, but it's time I got ready for the supper rush. Would you come back tonight? We're having a roast that I promise will melt in your mouths. And absolutely no dirt."

"I don't see why not," Miss Hannah said. "Ezra said we'd probably have to spend the night."

They walked next door to the emporium, and Millie pushed open the etched glass door. The smell of spices and fresh ground coffee greeted them as they stepped inside. Emily took a deep breath. "My, that does make me a bit homesick."

Millie nodded. "Aunt Lavinia and I used to go to town every Saturday for lunch and a bit of shopping, as she referred to it. She always said a lady needed to get out and socialize. Men had the saloons, but women had the stores."

Miss Hannah nodded. "My Ed always threatened to cut off my credit, but he never did."

Millie wandered down the clothing aisles, finally

stopping at the boy's britches. She really needed a new pair. Even with all the weight she'd gained, she still wasn't large enough to swap with any of the other ladies. Besides, none of them had lost enough to fit into hers either.

She glanced around the room. Miss Hannah and Emily were keeping the clerk busy, and no one else was in the place. She quickly shook out a pair of britches and held them up to herself. They were way too large. After several tries, she found a pair that looked just right. With a satisfied nod, she folded the ones she didn't want and replaced them on the shelf, then took a black pair of the right size, and a brown pair a size larger. Surely, she wouldn't gain any more than that.

On her way back to the front counter, she noticed a sale on children's shirts. She was staring thoughtfully at them when Miss Hannah stopped beside her. "What's wrong, Millie?"

Millie shook her head. "Nothing's wrong. I was just thinking. It would probably be safer for Little Feather if he got out of those reservation clothes."

Miss Hannah nodded. "I think you're right." She selected a bright yellow shirt. "This will go well with his coloring."

"Yes, ma'am," Millie said thoughtfully, "but it'll certainly show the dirt. And will be too easily seen if he has to hide out along the way. Maybe the dark blue or black would be more practical."

"You're right again. Why don't we get one of each color?"

"Sounds good, and maybe an extra pair of britches, too."

After gathering their purchases, Millie and Miss

Hannah joined Emily at the counter. "What's all this?" Millie asked, pointing to several skeins of yarn.

"Oh, I found a wonderful bargain. Ten skeins for fifty cents!" Emily whispered. Then she giggled. "As slow as I knit, I'll be lucky to have the afghan finished by the time I've been married for five years."

Millie looked at the shades of brown, yellow, and orange. Aunt Lavinia always said things made by hand, with love, made a house a home. Millie had always been too busy just keeping body and soul together to indulge in such nonsense, but since she'd been traveling with all the other ladies, she took pride and pleasure in handwork. It might be nice to carry on Aunt Lavinia's traditions. "Will that be all, ladies?" the clerk asked.

"Let's see." Emily began reading off the list as Miss Hannah and Millie accounted for the items. Finally, Emily looked up. "Well, there are a few medical items still missing."

The clerk shook her head. "We don't carry such things. You'll have to check with Dr. Aims. His office is just above the cafe. The stairs are on the other side of the building."

"Thank you," Miss Hannah said. "Could we leave these things here until in the morning?"

"Surely. We open at seven."

Millie stopped in front of the cafe. "Miss Hannah, you and Emily go ahead and get the medicine. I'll wait for you inside, with a pot of tea."

Chapter Nineteen

Ezra pushed his supper plate aside and, leaning his chair on its two back legs, patted his stomach. "That little gal shore was right. That roast jest melted in my mouth."

Blake shook his head. "How would you know? The way you shoveled it in, it went from lips to gullet, never resting long enough in between to melt or anything else."

The older man dropped his chair down on all fours and harrumphed. "It ain't often I gits to eat someone else's vittles. I don't in-sult 'em by bein' picky, young feller."

They all laughed. Millie suspected Ezra wasn't as old as he made out to be. She was about to ask him his age when Emily stifled a yawn. "Oh, my, I didn't realize how tired I was. I can't wait to stretch out in a real bed."

Ezra winked at Blake. "Ye need some company, Missy?"

Though she had seen the wink, Emily couldn't stop the blush that burned her cheeks. However, she leaned forward and tugged gently on his beard. "Why, Mr. Oats, are you volunteering to fluff my pillows?"

Ezra's eyes widened, whether from surprise or swallowing his tobacco wasn't clear, but everyone laughed.

Ezra coughed several times, then glared at the girl. "'Course not, Missy. I jest thought if all you she-males wanted to turn in, us men might stop off at the saloon for a bit."

"That sounds like a good idea," Miss Hannah said as she picked up her purse and shoved back her chair. "I plan to soak in a hot tub for at least an hour while Millie reads to me from the new book she got this afternoon."

Emily sighed. "After a short rest, I'm going to prop myself up in that bed and start on the new afghan I bought the yarn for today. If I start now, it might be finished by my fifth wedding anniversary."

Blake paid their bill, and then he and Ezra escorted the ladies to the hotel. When they stopped at the desk for their keys, Blake ordered hot water and a tub sent to the ladies' room. He stopped just inside their doorway after ushering them that far. "Will you ladies be all right for the evening?"

Millie removed the gun and holster from under her coat and put it beside the bed she and Emily were to share. "I don't see why not. You go ahead and have a good time. Just remember, we're leaving early in the morning, hangover or not."

Blake bit back a sharp reply, jerked his hat on his head and, with a nod to the other two ladies, stomped down the stairs with Ezra right on his heels. She had no right talking to him that way. A man could darn well have a drink or two without having a hangover the next day.

He yanked open the hotel door and rushed out onto the boardwalk. The cool evening breeze hit him as he crossed the street and walked toward the end of town. By the time he reached the saloon, he'd cooled off a bit. Remembering her pa, he figured Miss Millie came by her feelings about drinking honestly.

****

The hotel clerk glared at Hannah Hogan. "Now, look, lady. I done hauled two loads of water up here already. I ain't gonna bring another. There's nothing wrong with that there tubful."

Miss Hannah stood with her hand on her hips. "It's been used."

"Well, it ain't like you ladies've been wallowing in a mud hole. You can take two to a bath."

"Mister, you charged Mr. Donovan twenty-five cents *each* for us to have a bath. Not twenty-five cents for us to *share* a bath. We paid for three baths and we're going to *have* three baths."

The balding, portly little man shoved his chest out and glared back at Miss Hannah. "Not here, you ain't."

Millie slowly pulled her pistol from the holster and thumbed back the hammer. "I hear there's going to be a beautiful sunrise tomorrow. I'm sure you'd want to see it, wouldn't you?"

Running his finger around his collar, he swallowed and held out his other hand in a placating gesture. "Now, don't do nothing we'll all be sorry for. I'll…I'll see what I can do. But my help has already gone for the night."

"That's fine. You see what you can do," Millie said as she uncocked the pistol. She stepped to the door and called after the man about to descend the stairs. "But that's my bath and you've got five minutes before I come looking for you."

"Yes, ma'am," he said as he hurried down the steps, mumbling to himself.

As soon as Millie shut the door they fell into a fit of giggling.

"I thought he was going to bust a gut when you demanded another tub of water," Millie said between giggles.

"There was a good possibility I might've busted him *in* the gut, if you hadn't cocked that gun when you did. Imagine, twenty-five cents for a bath? That's outrageous! He's lucky we didn't string him up," Miss Hannah said.

****

In the morning, Millie groaned at the persistent knock on her door. She staggered to the door. "Yes? Who is it?" she mumbled without even opening her eyes.

"It's me, Donovan. We'll meet you ladies downstairs in about thirty minutes. Will that be long enough?"

"Yes, we'll be there." She yawned and leaned against the door, feeling that if she let go she'd dissolve into complete nothingness. Finally, she pushed away from the door and went to the washstand. She'd take care of her needs, then wake the others. No sense in everyone getting up until absolutely necessary.

Half an hour later, Mr. Donovan and Ezra stood as Millie and her companions descended the stairs to the lobby, each carrying a small bag.

The men took the bags and Donovan stepped up to the desk. "How much do we owe you?"

The portly clerk slapped a piece of paper down before the wagon master. "Mister, you owe for three rooms and two extra baths."

Miss Hannah stopped what she was saying in mid-sentence and shoved past Millie to Donovan's side. "Blake Donovan, don't you pay another cent for those baths." Then she turned on the desk clerk. "Yesterday, standing right here, Mr. Donovan asked you how much for a bath, and you said twenty-five cents, in advance.

Isn't that right, Mr. Donovan?"

Blake winced and rubbed his temple. "Yes, ma'am," he whispered.

"And you paid him seventy-five cents. I saw you. That's for three baths. Last night Millie almost had to shoot this little weasel to get hers." She reached over and poked the clerk's chest. "With all the stomping in and out and men coming in at all hours, singing at the top of their voices, you're lucky we don't charge *you* for the inconvenience of staying here."

The man backed up a step and rubbed the tender spot on his chest. "I beg your pardon, madam. The only people stomping through here, singing at the top of their voices, were…"

"Never mind," Blake said threateningly. "The lady's right. I paid for three baths. If I'd known you'd given them a hard time about it, I'd have shot you myself." He looked at the bill, then dropped the payment, minus the extra bath money, on the desk. "Come on, ladies, let's get out of here."

Without a backward glance, they turned as one and, with heads held high, walked out of the hotel and down the boardwalk to the cafe.

They took the same table they'd used the day before. Emily couldn't contain her giggles any longer. They all burst out laughing, while Blake and Ezra grabbed their heads.

"Please, Missy, could ya laugh a little quieter?"

"A lot quieter," Blake added.

Millie looked at him with mock concern. "What's the matter, Mr. Donovan? Do you have a headache?" she asked in a louder than necessary voice.

He glared at her briefly. "No. We just don't need the

whole town thinking we've lost our minds. Now, what do you want for breakfast?"

The cafe was surprisingly full for such an early hour. Sharon placed cups of coffee in front of each of them. "What can I get you?"

Millie grinned. "We'd better all eat hearty. No telling how long we'll have to travel to catch up with the others."

"Oh, I agree," said Sharon.

****

Ezra pushed his empty plate aside and drank the last of his coffee. "Well, ladies, the boss and me'll go get the animals and wagons, and we can load up and leave. If we hurry with the loading, we should be on the road before noon."

Ezra escorted the women to the emporium just as the proprietress opened up for the day, leaving them there while he and Mr. Donovan went for the supply wagon.

****

Blake clamped his mouth shut. He didn't want to push her too far. He wiped his forehead, then replaced his hat. "Miss Millie, we're ready to pull out," he called from the doorway.

They all said their goodbyes. Miss Hannah and Emily climbed on the wagon, Blake boosted Millie onto her saddle, and they pulled out.

Dark clouds rolled, far back in the mountains. Occasional flashes of lightning streaked the sky. When they finally topped the ridge of Peaceful Valley, the air was fresh, and so moist Millie could almost feel it. She looked back at the town. It would rain there soon. The sky on the other side of the mountain seemed clearer. Finally, as they rode along flatter land, the sky became lighter. The clouds were white and fluffy. They'd managed to move out of the path of the storm, but now they'd have some heat to contend with.

****

They'd been traveling three days at an easy gait when Blake galloped up from a scouting trip. He reined up beside the pink grain wagon, now dark blue, which was in the lead, and touched the brim of his hat. "Ladies, looks like we're slightly north of the wagon train. Find a shady spot at the edge of those mountains, and we'll wait for them."

Emily looked ahead. "My, can we make it that far before dark?"

"Yes, ma'am, they're only about a mile or two off. We shouldn't have much trouble."

Before she could say anything else, Blake touched Thunder's flanks and rode ahead. They had made very good time. They'd angled northwest to intercept the wagons and still managed to be ahead of them. He supposed two wagons traveled faster than twenty-odd ones.

Chapter Twenty

Cassandra tightened the cinch on the horse she was saddling.

Since she'd ridden, half dead, into their camp several weeks ago, these women had nursed her back to health.

As the days stretched into weeks, she'd regained her health. Hunting and working with the horse herd had helped build back her strength. For the first time in her life, she had lady friends. It was a good feeling. Maybe by the time this wagon train got where it was going, the ladies would let her stay in their town.

Cassie, as they called her, led a saddled horse to a group of ladies at the head of the train. "You know, I ain't never seen anything like you ladies. You dress in britches, but wear those frilly shirts. You shoot and hunt and do most of the chores that men usually do, yet you ride sidesaddle. Do you know how silly it looks to see all them ladies in britches sitting sidesaddle? First time I seen all of you on horseback, I nearly split a gut laughing."

Miss Hannah took the reins, stepped on a boulder, climbed onto the saddle, then leaned down, raising a brow at the girl. "First of all, Cassie, a lady doesn't *split a gut*. She may die laughing, but she never *splits a gut*. Second, if you thought it was funny, any bad element might think so too, and then before he could stop laughing one of us *ladies* would've shot him between the eyes."

Cassie lowered her head in embarrassment. "Sorry, ma'am. Guess I have lots of talents, but none of 'em is very ladylike."

"Don't worry about it," Miss Hannah assured her. "We'll teach you what you don't know. As I'm sure you've noticed, this wagon train is a school on wheels. You'd be surprised what we learn from each other."

Millie cracked the whip over her oxen as Miss Hannah rode past the lead wagon. They were finally out of the tall grass. The terrain was a lot more than rolling as they moved deeper into the mountains. The sun was bright, but the breeze was downright nippy in the shade. Millie adjusted her newly knitted cape. Cindy had done a nice job. It fit around her shoulders like a short cape and tied neatly at the throat. They'd had no more trouble since Cassie had joined them, but still she felt uneasy. It was almost as if someone were watching them, but they'd seen no one. Maybe she should speak to John Eagle about it when he returned from his scouting trip.

She smiled as Little Feather galloped toward the end of the train. Today he had hunted on behalf of the last four wagons. Looked like they were having rabbit tonight. Between helping with the horses and hunting for the various groups, he seemed happy as a lark, and much too busy to spy.

****

When the supper dishes were washed and put away, the women formed small groups according to their interests. Emily draped her apron over the tailgate of her wagon, then stopped beside Cassie. "Come on, it's time you learned to do something besides curry horses and clean guns."

"No, I don't think so. I never took to needlework."

"Oh? You've been watching us knit for over a week now. If you weren't interested, you wouldn't be over here. Now, come on. I'm a beginner myself. Besides, it's very satisfying to take a string and make something useful out of it."

After three hours, Cassie held up a slightly lopsided square. She looked at it critically. "Not bad. What's it good for?"

Cindy looked up and smiled. "Well, you can make about nineteen more and have a nice cover for the winter."

Cassie's mouth dropped open in surprise. "Are you crazy?"

Several of the ladies laughed. Cindy tried to stifle her snickers at her pupil's reply.

"At three hours each, I'll be old and gray before it's done."

"You get faster with practice," 'Cindy assured her. "I'm sure you didn't learn to shoot those guns right off."

Cassie looked at her dubiously but picked up her ball of yarn, found the end, and began casting on.

"If it'll make you feel better, you can make a couple of pillows. It only takes two squares for each pillow."

Cassie smiled. "Now that's more like it."

Blake rubbed his hands together over the fire. While the ladies enjoyed their sewing groups, the men sipped coffee around one of the campfires and talked about the day's events and problems. He accepted a cup of hot coffee from Ezra, then wrapped both hands around the warm cup. "The days are cooler and the nights are getting downright cold. You can sure tell we're out of the lowlands. It's like coming home."

Ezra nodded as he poured himself a cup. "Yep, looks like the ladies 're gonna git some use out of them fancy wraps they's been knittin' up."

John Eagle eased up, reached over Ezra, and took the cup of coffee from his hand.

Ezra whirled around. "Hey!"

The scout grinned and took a sip. "Hmmm, this hits the spot, Ezra. Thanks."

Ezra snatched the hat off his own head and threw it on the ground. "Goldarnit, ye damn injun! Why do ya always have ta sneak up on a feller like that?"

John Eagle laughed and hung his arm around the older man's neck. "Glad to see you, too, old man."

John Eagle sat down beside Blake. "Should be smooth traveling up ahead. The ladies will be pleased to know they won't have to collect buffalo chips for a while. There's plenty of wood along the way."

Little Feather moved over beside John Eagle. "What you do about men who follow?"

John Eagle looked up sharply. "What men? Are you sure?

"The boy nodded. "Me sure."

Blake glared past John Eagle to Little Feather. "How long have they been following us?" he demanded. "Why didn't you tell me?" Did this boy even know what he was talking about? How old was he, eleven? Twelve? He seemed awfully young to be reading signs.

Little Feather shrugged. "See tracks last two mornings. John Eagle not come back yet."

"Damn it, boy…" Blake began.

"Are you certain, Little Feather?" John Eagle asked. At the boy's nod, he thought a minute. "How many?

What can you tell me about them?"

Little Feather held up three fingers, then brought down two of them. "One much big. Leave big tracks—deep." He raised another finger. "One high like willow."

Blake frowned. "High like willow? What does that mean?"

Little Feather thought a minute, then reverted to the Sioux sign language to explain. John Eagle translated. "The second man has long, narrow feet and his stride is long, so Little Feather thinks he's tall and thin."

John Eagle smiled at the boy. "That's very good, Little Feather. You're a credit to your fathers. What about the third one?"

"He not like other mans. Has small, wide feet. Short steps. Much nervous. Stop, make circles, look behind much times maybe."

John Eagle smiled, squeezed the boy's shoulder reassuringly, then turned to Blake. "That's a pretty fair description of the three from the fort. Guess they did follow me, after all. From the questions they asked, I couldn't tell if they were interested in the women or just anything they could get their hands on. Must have taken the big one longer to heal from our fight than I expected."

Blake looked back at the wagons and swore under his breath. The camp had been haphazardly set up with no thought given to safety. "Let's get some order to this camp and be ready for them. If we're lucky, they'll try coming in peacefully at first."

John Eagle got to his feet. "Come on, Little Feather, show me those tracks. We'll tell the women to keep their guns handy, too."

****

Ezra had just poured himself a fresh cup of coffee

and given a stir to the stew he'd hung over the fire when a call came from the shadows.

"Hello the camp. We's peaceful. Can we come in and set a spell?"

Blake glanced around to be sure everyone was ready, then put down his coffee cup and faced the direction the voice came from. "Sure, come on in, neighbor." Three men stepped into the firelight. He'd never seen such scruffy specimens in his life. The leader was as tall and big as he was dirty. His clothes, like the others, were a mix of storebought and hides. Each visitor stood with a rifle cradled across his chest, finger on the trigger.

"I'm Blake Donovan. That's Ben, and the guy at the fire is Oats." He waited a moment. When the men didn't offer their names, Blake prompted them. "And you are?"

The biggest man, whose gaze had darted about the camp, focused back on Blake. "Oh, guess I plum near forgot my manners. Jest never seen so many colored wagons. They call me Moose." He chuckled, but the mirth didn't reach his eyes. "Guess you can see why. He's Scar, and the othern's Hairy."

Blake nodded to each man. Scar was tall and thin. He'd probably gotten his name due to the long, jagged scar on the left side of his face from the edge of his nose to below his chin. The name "Hairy" was evidently a joke. The third man was short, pudgy, and bald as a newly hatched bird. True to Little Feather's surmise, the man jumped at everything that moved.

"Sit down," Blake invited. "How about some coffee and stew?"

"Say, that's right neighborly of ya. It's been a coon's age since we et anything but ol' Hairy's cookin'." The three visitors each pulled a cup from his possibles bag. Moose took a noisy slurp of the coffee Ezra handed him, then set it aside in favor of the plate of stew. Holding his spoon overhand, he began shoveling the food into his mouth as fast as he could. Suddenly, he stopped in mid-bite. The other men did the same. Blake turned to follow his line of vision. The men were leering at Emily and Cindy.

"Hot damn, I never seed wimmins in britches afore. That ain't hardly decent."

Blake stiffened, then slowly stood. "Neither is the way you're leering at them. Now that you've finished your stew, I think it's time you move on."

Moose narrowed his eyes, glaring at Blake. "And that ain't hardly friendly. We was hoping to stay by yer far tonight."

"Sorry. There's no room. If you hurry, you can travel some distance while the moon's up."

Hairy and Scar shifted their gaze between the women and Blake. Scar scratched his crotch, practically drooling. It was all Blake could do to keep his hands from around the man's neck.

"Seems ya got some wimmins to spare, Donovan. Why be so stingy? The code of the mountains is ta share with yo' feller mans."

Ezra stepped forward. "These here are *our* wimmins. We ain't got none to share with the likes of you."

Blake looked around. John Eagle stepped out of the shadows. "You didn't get enough back at the fort?"

Moose whirled around. "What're you doin' 'ere?"

"I work for these people. Surely you remember. You asked enough questions the last time we met."

Moose suddenly reached for his gun. A shot bit into the dirt at the edge of his foot. He jumped back, looking wildly around.

Millie stood at the edge of the firelight, the rifle in her hand still smoking. "Understand one thing, mister. We choose who we're with. You are not to our liking. Come near any of us, and you'll never be any use to a woman again. Is that clear?"

Moose glared at her, seemingly forgetting about the men. "No one threatens me. 'Specially not no woman." He started to take a step forward, but Hairy caught his arm.

"Moose, look."

Moose cast a quick glace in the direction Hairy indicated. The wagon master and his men were standing back, arms crossed in a casual stance with amused grins on their faces. Moose slowly turned around in a circle. He and his men were encircled by gun-totin' women. Their guns were primed and pointing directly at him.

Moose swallowed and then, with a sickly grin, turned back to Millie. "Shucks, ma'am, we didn't mean no harm. All we wants is ta set by the far, enjoyin' yer company. It's been a long time since we seen such purty wimmins."

Miss Hannah stepped forward. "Well, gentlemen, that's kind of you, but we've had a very hard day. We really don't feel like entertaining this evening."

Moose looked her up and down in a most insolent manner. She calmly raised the pistol she had hidden in the folds of her split skirt. "Goodbye, gentlemen."

The men looked around, then turned on their heels. "Thanks fer the grub," Moose muttered as he and his companions disappeared into the darkness.

When Millie looked around, John Eagle and Little Feather were nowhere to be seen. She turned back to Blake. "Should John Eagle take Little Feather with him to follow those men?"

Blake nodded. "The boy's earned the right."

Millie turned to the women. "Hitch up, ladies."

Blake caught her arm. "What do you mean, hitch up? We're not going anywhere."

She shook her head. "No, but we're not leaving these wagons in this undefendable position, either. From now on, we'll always be on guard."

Blake released her arm. "Good idea. We'll help you."

****

Millie snapped the lines against her team's rumps as she walked beside the wagon, shivering. These cool mountain mornings would take some getting used to, although the change was more than welcome. The scenery was pretty, too. In fact, this whole adventure had been wonderful, for the most part. Never in her wildest dreams had she imagined such beauty existed out here. She felt a twinge of sadness. Aunt Lavinia and Uncle James would have loved this.

John Eagle and Little Feather had spent the night making sure the three unwelcome men kept traveling. Now they slept in the supply wagon. Hopefully, they'd not cross paths with those men again.

As the day wore on, Millie tossed her wrap onto the wagon seat. She wiped the perspiration from her face, then dropped back to get a dipper from the water barrel. She took a moment to stroke her pet's head. "Hi, Honey. Getting kinda lazy, aren't you, sitting on this nest in the middle of the day? Why aren't you walking like the rest of us?"

Millie took a drink, then offered the dipper to Honey. The goose drank her fill, then nestled down and closed her eyes. Millie stroked her again. This wasn't like Honey. That goose had spent the whole trip harassing first one and then another on the wagon train. Millie shook her head, replaced the dipper, and returned to driving the oxen. *I hope Honey isn't sick.*

As Blake rode past, he noticed the worried look on Millie's face, and turned back. Dismounting, he walked beside her. "Something wrong, Miss Millie?"

"I'm not sure. It isn't like Honey to ride in her nest all day. She's usually such a…well, a pest."

Blake looked back at the snoozing bird. He walked back to look at the goose. "Say, *Duck*, what's eating you? I wouldn't take kindly to you dying and cheatin' me out of my nice Thanksgiving meal." He reached out to stroke the bird, then jerked his hand back when she hissed and snapped.

He walked back to Millie's side, counting his fingers. "Can't see there's much change in her temperament. Same ornery ol' *Duck*, as far as I can see. Maybe she's just tired, or lonely."

Millie glanced at him before cracking her whip over the far ox's rump. "Lonely?"

"Sure," he answered. "We all have each other to talk to. Maybe she'd like another goose for company."

"That's crazy, but even if it were true, where would I get another goose way out here?"

"Good question." Blake swung back onto Thunder. "I'll give it some thought." He tipped his hat and rode down the line.

Emily walked up to spell Millie with the driving.

"What's the matter with Mr. Donovan? He just rode by so deep in thought he didn't even return my greeting."

Millie handed the whip to Emily. "Oh, among other things, he's afraid Honey is going to, as he put it, die and cheat him out of his Thanksgiving supper."

"Honey? Why would he think that?"

"She just sits on that nest without moving. That's really not like her."

"Mr. Donovan also suggested she might be lonely for another goose."

"My, do geese get that way, too?"

"I hope not. If she's lonely, I don't know what we could do about it out here. I'm going to those boulders for a few minutes of privacy."

****

Millie finally stood and blinked several times in confusion. Good grief. How long had she been wool-gathering? The last wagon had passed her by. She hurried toward the horse herd, which was coming abreast.

Reb rode up beside her, tipping his hat. "Afternoon, Miss Millie. What are you doing way back here, and on foot?"

"Hello, Reb. I was exploring and time got away from me. Could you give me a ride up to my wagon?"

"Sure thing." He reached down and, wrapping his arm around her waist, hoisted her onto the saddle in front of him. "Little Feather just rode in, said something about a herd of antelope to the northeast of here. If I didn't have to wrangle these jugheads," he said indicating the horses, "I'd go get us a couple. Sure would taste good this evening."

Millie smiled. "Well, *if* I had a horse, I might be

persuaded to ride over there. It's been a while since we've had something besides hoppin' chicken.' "

Reb pulled up beside a middle wagon and set her down. "I'll be right back." He wheeled his mount and galloped back to the horses.

Millie looked up to see whose wagon she was beside. Cassie stopped and waited for Millie to catch up to her. "Hi, come visitin'?"

"Looks like it. Reb was giving me a ride back up front, but abandoned me in favor of an antelope."

"What?"

Millie laughed. "He went back to get me a horse. Seems there's a herd of antelope near here, and I'm elected to go get one."

"Want company?"

"Sure, but what will you do for a horse?"

Cassie stepped away from the wagon, turned toward Reb's back and let out a shrill whistle. Reb looked over his shoulder, and at her wave, pulled up and turned her way. She pointed back and forth from Millie to herself, then held up two fingers. He nodded and continued back to the horses.

Millie shook her head and grinned. "Now that's something I'd like to learn to do."

"What? Whistle?" Cassie shook her head. "Nothing to it, but don't let Miss Hannah hear you. She'd have boxed my ears if she'd heard that. That woman is determined to make a lady of me."

Millie giggled. "Well, being a lady does have its advantages. It certainly can confuse the enemy when a sweet little lady turns into a raging gunslinger."

Cass shook her head as Reb came up leading two mounts and two pack horses. "Well, I've certainly got the gunslinger part down pat," she whispered.

"Here you are, ladies. I'll send Little Feather out to lead you in as soon as we make camp."

****

About an hour before sundown, Little Feather showed up to help the women load the three antelope they'd shot. "Much good feast tonight," he said between grunts. "What you do with skins?"

Millie exchanged glances with Cassie. "Hadn't given it much thought," Millie answered. "Why?"

"Cold come early in mountains. Little Feather need coat and new moccasins."

"Help us skin these animals," Cass said, "and the hides are yours."

"Deal," he said with a grin.

****

Ezra leaned back and rubbed his full belly. "That was some feed, ladies. Don't know when I et better."

Millie picked up the empty plate. "I'm glad you liked it, Mr. Oats. Are you sure you can't eat any more?" she asked, trying hard to keep a straight face. "You've only had four helpings."

He got to his feet and stretched. "No, ma'am. I think that'll hold me 'til breakfast. Could use another cup of that there coffee, how-some-ever."

Emily brought the steaming coffeepot over and refilled his cup. "How about another piece of pie?"

"No, ma'am. I don't have room for nary another bite. Thank ye, though."

They watched him disappear around the supply wagon, then doubled over in laughter. "Four servings! How could you have said that with such a straight face?"

Millie shook her head and gasped for breath. "I

don't know. Where do you suppose that man puts all that food?"

"I have no idea, but what do you bet he goes down to Elsa's wagon and eats some more?"

Millie untied her apron. "Come on. Let's follow him and see." With Emily in her wake, Millie stepped over the wagon tongue and hurried along the outside of the wagons toward Elsa's. They stopped in the shadows and watched. In a very few minutes Ezra showed up, with hat in hand. "Howdy, Miss Elsa. You're looking mighty purty tonight."

Elsa blushed. "Yah, thank ye, Mr. Oats. Vould you care to sit for some strudel?"

Ezra took a seat at her table. "Thank ye. I'm jest starving for a piece of your strudel. Is it apple?"

Millie stifled a giggle. Emily glared at the back of the man's head. "Why that old fibber," she whispered. "That's the last time he puts his big feet under my table, at least this week."

They hurried back to their wagon and sat down in time for the regular evening meeting with Mr. Donovan and John Eagle. The men tipped their hats. "Ladies. We thought maybe you'd forgotten about the meeting."

"Oh, no," Emily said breathlessly, "we just had an errand to run. We're sorry if we kept you waiting."

Blake shoved back his hat. "Ladies, are there any problems that can't wait until tomorrow evening to take care of?"

Millie thought a minute. "No…yes, one. The single-tree on Amy's wagon probably won't last much longer. I'm surprised it's lasted this long."

Blake nodded. "We'll take care of it first thing in the morning. We should reach Fort Phil Kearny by sundown tomorrow. We can take care of any other repairs there."

Emily looked up excitedly. "My, that's wonderful, Mr. Donovan. I had no idea we were so close to civilization. What's it like?"

John Eagle shook his head. "Not a place you'd want to spend any time in, Miss Emily. It's been under almost constant siege by Red Cloud and his Sioux since opening up last year."

"Then maybe we should go around it," Emily suggested.

Blake shook his head. "Would if we could, but we can't. However, we shouldn't have any problems with the Indians. We have something they want."

"We do? What?" Millie asked.

"Little Feather."

Both girls gasped. "How dare you!"

"Absolutely not. We're not trading that sweet boy's life for ours," Millie said indignantly.

John Eagle shook his head. "You don't understand, ma'am. We won't be trading his life. Little Feather is an orphan. Singing Dove, Red Cloud's niece, is the boy's only living relative. That's where we're taking him."

"Oh." Suddenly Millie sat up, alarmed. "Oh, but what if the army finds out who he is and decides to use him to bargain with?"

Blake rubbed his finger along his jaw. "We thought of that. That's why no one, until now, has known who Little Feather is. As far as anyone knows, he's Johnny's ward."

Millie looked John Eagle in the eye. "He's not full Indian, is he?"

John Eagle cocked an eyebrow in obvious surprise, then shook his head. "I don't know, ma'am. His mother was Indian. He grew up with the tribe. Because he looks more white than Indian, when they moved the tribe to the reservation, the army planned to find his white family. But he ran away."

John Eagle sipped his coffee, then grinned and continued. "The little bugger hid out, finally rejoining the tribe after about a week away from the fort. No one ever suspected. He just faded back into the mist of his people. His uncle, Red Cloud, is my blood brother. I couldn't very well refuse his request to bring the boy to him, especially since it is on our way."

Blake got up and poured everyone another cup of coffee. "We'll keep the boy with the horse herd as much as possible. If the army spots him, Johnny may have to leave suddenly. That's why we're telling you this now. If that happens, we'll have to start out without him. He'll meet us a ways past the fort."

Millie nodded. "We'll worry about that if it happens. We're certainly going to miss that boy."

"Me, too," John Eagle said.

Chapter Twenty-One

At their noon break, the women had changed into their skirts so as to be presentable when they arrived at the fort. Emily laughed as she commented, "I've lost so much weight, I'll probably walk right out of it."

Millie's problem, on the other hand, was just the opposite. She'd gained so much, she couldn't get the top two buttons hooked. "Mine will probably fall off 'cause I can't hook it," she replied, giving a laugh also.

The ladies circled the wagons outside the fort, and Millie looked around as she unhitched the oxen. Everything was peaceful and beautiful, no sign of Indians anywhere. Fluffy white clouds floated lazily over the green, rolling hills.

The fort was the only blight on the landscape. It stood, tall and forbidding, on the top of the rise. Its high log walls were like a prison. The enemy couldn't get in, but neither could the inhabitants go out. How sad to have to live that way, Millie thought as she put the gear away.

After helping Emily unload the wagon and set up camp, she leaned over to set a box of supplies down, and in doing so she stepped on her skirt hem. "Darn," she mumbled under her breath. It had been so long since she'd worn skirts, she'd almost forgotten how cumbersome they could be.

The wind had become rather nippy in the last half hour. Emily started water boiling for tea and also some for coffee. She drew her shawl closer, then took a deep breath. "My, the smell of snow is so strong you can almost reach out and touch it. Seems like we didn't have much summer, despite all those hot days not so long ago."

Millie shivered as she also drew her wrap closer. "From what I'm learning, the summers in these mountains are a lot shorter than those back home. However, the thought of being stuck in a wagon during a snowstorm isn't exactly the dream of my life." She gazed around her again. "Can't you just picture cattle peacefully grazing all over those hills?"

"Red Cloud would rather see buffalo grazing there," said a familiar voice from behind her.

Millie whirled to face John Eagle and a very handsome lieutenant. "Oh! You startled me."

"I'm sorry, Miss Millie. May I introduce Lieutenant Collins?"

"Lieutenant, this is Mrs. Watts, and yonder is Miss Emily Peterson."

The lieutenant touched the brim of his hat. "Ladies."

"Do you know Red Cloud, Lieutenant?" asked Emily.

"No, ma'am. That's one gent I avoid at all costs."

"Gentlemen, may we interest you in a cup of hot coffee?"

"Yes, thank you, Mrs. Watts."

"Sounds good to me, too," said John Eagle.

"What did you mean about the buffalo, John Eagle?" Millie asked as she handed them each a steaming cup.

John Eagle took the cup and sampled it. "This really hits the spot, thanks." Then he indicated the surrounding area. "The Indians claim this is their hunting grounds.

They say that when the white man built this fort and opened the Bozeman Trail, the buffalo stopped coming. The Indians believe the buffalo will return if we leave."

"Will they?"

He shook his head. "I don't know, but I doubt it."

Emily shook her head. "How sad."

The lieutenant handed his empty cup back to Emily. Their fingers touched briefly as she took it. "Thank you, ma'am."

Emily blushed and quickly withdrew her hand.

The lieutenant cleared his throat, then plunged on as if nothing had happened. "Colonel Carrington isn't in the fort at present, but the ladies would like to invite all of you for luncheon tomorrow."

"Why, that's very nice," Emily said in her best southern drawl. "Please tell them we'd be honored. May we bring something?"

"No, ma'am. Just yourselves."

Millie struggled to hide a grin as Emily blushed and became all smiles and dimples. "Thank you, sir. We'll be there about noon?"

"That'll be fine." He tipped his hat and followed John Eagle.

Dreamy eyed, Emily sighed as she watched the lieutenant and John Eagle cross the camp. "My, isn't he the most handsome man you've ever seen?" she asked in a near whisper.

Millie grinned and nudged the girl in the ribs. "Emily, you say that about every new man we meet."

"I do not! I never said that about those awful mountain men."

Millie sobered slightly. "I apologize, Emily. You certainly did not." Then she burst out laughing. "But you

259

are right about this one. Lieutenant Collins certainly is handsome."

****

Miss Hannah called a meeting the morning of the luncheon.

"John Eagle tells us the Indians have prevented supply trains from getting through, so the fort's supplies are very low. Under those conditions, fifty extra mouths to feed would be a terrible strain," she said. "I'm thinking maybe we should each take something."

"Wouldn't that insult them?" asked Winnie.

"During the war, the things to go first were the extras. You know, like jelly, sugar to make pies, things like that," said Cora.

Miss Hannah grinned. "That's a very good idea."

The camp was bustling from breakfast until time to leave for the fort. The ladies went armed with jellies, canned fruits, and dried fruit pies from their dwindling supplies. There was even an elk stew.

The offerings were accepted with deep gratitude, but more than the delicacies, the women of the fort were starved for news from the outside world. It was nearly suppertime before Millie and her friends returned to the wagons. "For a place short of food, I've never seen so much of it, or eaten so well," Emily said as she pulled on her britches. "I don't think I'll have room for supper. Sure hope the men don't mind fixing their own this evening."

Millie wiggled into her britches. "Same here. I think I'd better spend this evening altering my skirt."

Before retiring for the night, Millie and Miss Hannah went to every wagon, making a list of needed repairs. Several animals needed re-shoeing. It would take

Ben a week to get to all of them. Even the little pump organ needed attention.

****

As soon as the breakfast dishes were done, Millie emptied the dirty dish water. The breeze smelled of rain. She looked up into the overcast sky. *Lord, don't let the weather change.* They'd been working on the repairs for five days. If nothing changed, they'd be ready to leave in the next day or two. They were too close to their destination for delays now.

"Hey, he's got Little Feather," someone yelled.

Millie whirled around. Little Feather was on the end of a rope, running to keep up with a soldier cantering in front of him. The boy fell, but the soldier never slackened his speed. "That no good..." Millie grabbed her rifle, jacked a shell into the chamber, then rested her arm against the nearest wagon, took aim, and fired. The rope snapped in two. Little Feather lay still.

She had no time to wonder whether the boy was all right or not. Blake Donovan, appearing at her side, snatched the gun from her hands. "Are you crazy? You can't fire at the U.S. Army."

"If I'd fired at him, he'd be dead. I'd never miss a target that big."

The soldier, a corporal, galloped up, yanked his horse to a stop, leaned down and snatched Millie by the hair. She screamed. She tried to grab the hands pulling her hair.

Blake grabbed the man's wrist and yanked him out of the saddle, knocking Millie down in the process. "Army or no army, you touch her again and I'll slit your throat."

Millie struggled to her feet, gasping for breath as the

261

corporal grappled with Blake, yelling, "She can't fire on the United States Army!"

Blake yanked the man to his feet by the front of his blouse. "Mister, if she'd shot at you, you'd be hit. She could make that shot all day long and never miss."

The corporal jerked from Blake's grasp.

Millie shoved Blake aside. "Corporal, you're the poorest excuse for a man I've ever seen," she said as she doubled up her fist and socked the soldier in the eye.

Grunting, he stumbled back. She advanced for another shot, but Blake caught her around the waist and hauled her back several steps. "Woman, you are a caution. Save some of him for the rest of us," he said as he set her aside, whirled around and drove his fist into the man's middle.

The corporal had no sooner gasped and doubled over than Ben grabbed him by the shoulder, whirled him around, and gave him an uppercut to the jaw. The soldier staggered from Ben's blow to Ezra's before Miss Elsa clubbed him on the head with her rolling pin.

"How dare you do little boy dat vay!" she demanded.

Several soldiers rushed in to rescue their battered comrade. "Lady, that ain't no boy, he's a damned *injun*," one of them said through clenched teeth.

"He's probably been killing since he was six," another of them insisted.

Blake looked up as John Eagle rode in holding Little Feather before him in the saddle. He slid off Patches, leaving the boy slumped in the saddle, grabbed the corporal's shoulder, spun him around, and planted his fist in the man's face, as hard as he could. Before he could hit the soldier again, two army privates grabbed

John Eagle's arms and pulled him back.

The corporal pulled away from his friend's grasp and rushed toward John Eagle, his fist pulled back. However, the clicks of several guns being cocked brought him up short.

Miss Hannah stood with her pistol pointed at the corporal. Five other ladies backed her up with their rifles. "Now, *gentlemen,* you will stop acting like savages and discuss this in a civilized manner or we'll shoot the legs out from under each of you."

When John Eagle was released and she had all their attention, she lowered her pistol, though the other ladies didn't lower their rifles. "Fine. Now, will someone please tell me what's going on here?"

Gasping, the corporal glared at her. "Ma'am, we caught this here little savage skulking around your herd at the back of the wagons. He mighta run off ever' last one of them horses and cows if we hadn't-a caught him."

John Eagle glared at the man. "He wasn't skulking. He was doing exactly what he was told to do, minding the stock."

The corporal shook his head and glared back at the scout. "Man, that's like putting…" He paused to gasp for air. "…a chicken hawk in charge of the henhouse." Still doubled over and rubbing his middle with one hand and his jaw with the other, while trying to look intimidating through two already swelling eyes, he demanded, "How come you're having truck with a damn injun kid anyway?"

"He's my ward…"

"Ward?" The corporal glared at him. "You injun?"

"Indian enough to skin you alive if you lay a hand on him again."

"Yeah? Well, we thought he was one of Red Cloud's spies."

"He most certainly is not," Miss Hannah assured him. "Now, you get on your horses and get out of this camp before I shoot you myself."

Millie held her breath as the corporal looked from Little Feather to John Eagle and back to Miss Hannah's gun. He snatched his hat from a private, glared at the boy still slumped in the saddle on Patches, and then, with his men's help, mounted his own horse and galloped toward the fort.

Blake whistled. "That was close." He looked up in time to see Millie shaking her hand and disappearing around her wagon. He followed in time to see her bend over, clutching her hand to her stomach. "Miss Millie, you're hurt."

She whirled, then turned quickly away. But not fast enough to hide the tears running down her face. "I…I'm fine."

He turned her around and reached for her hand. "Let me see."

She gasped as he touched her thumb. "I…I think it's broken. But it was worth it," she said defiantly.

He tried not to grin as he gently felt each bone in her hand. "How did you hit him? I mean, how did you close your hand?"

"I don't know, I just did it."

He nodded toward her left hand. "Make like you're going to hit me." Suddenly realizing what he'd said, he caught her upraised fist. "I said make like, not really do it, woman!" Her fingers were curled around her thumb. "That how you clobbered the corporal?"

"I guess so."

264

He ran his fingers up and down her right thumb, then suddenly jerked it.

She screamed. Her whole body was alive with pain, and then her legs seemed to give way.

Blake caught her before she sank to the ground. He held her tightly against his chest. "Sorry. I know that hurt. You were lucky. It just dislocated your thumb. A little harder and you probably *would* have broken it." He held her for several minutes, rubbing his hand up and down her back. The top of her head fit nicely under his chin.

Millie rested against his chest. Her whole body felt as light as air. All but her right hand, which throbbed like blue blazes. After a few minutes, her legs began to regain their strength. But his arms felt so…safe. Almost like Uncle James's, but different. She began to tremble, and it had nothing to do with the pain in her hand.

What? Suddenly she stiffened. These weren't Uncle James's arms. They belonged to Blake Donovan. Blake Donovan held her. Her head rested on *his* chest.

She swallowed and stepped back. "I…I think I'd better check on Little Feather. Thank you for fixing my hand…and for coming to my defense against that bully."

Blake grinned. "Believe me, Miss Millie, it was my pleasure." They walked together to the other side of the wagon. "By the way, the next time you attack a man, double your fist like this…" he held out his hand and made a fist, "with your thumb on the outside."

She looked at it, then at her throbbing hand. "I'll remember that."

Millie hurried over to Little Feather. He was covered with scrapes and scratches, but it would have been much worse had he not been dressed in long pants and a jacket.

"I can't believe anyone would treat a child like that—or anyone else, for that matter," Emily exclaimed. "That corporal had better not ever find his feet under my table at mealtime."

Several snickers broke the tension. Blake laid a hand on Millie's shoulder. When she looked up, he nodded. "Nice shot." He squeezed gently, then walked off.

Millie watched him mount Thunder and ride toward the fort. He'd complimented her. He'd actually complimented her.

After letting Miss Hannah wrap her hand, Millie led Patches to the picket line. She watered and grained him, then turned to find Little Feather standing close by. She smiled. "Are you feeling better?"

He nodded. "Little Feather owe life to Warrior Woman."

Millie smiled and shook her head. "I was glad to do it." Then she thought a minute. "There is a way you can repay me."

Little Feather's face seemed to light up. "How?"

"There is a lot of cruelty and misunderstanding between your people and mine, Little Feather. I'm asking you to remember how scared and hurt you were today, and how grateful you were to be saved. Then the next time you come in contact with an enemy, remember that each person has a right to live as painlessly as possible. Respect gained through pain is really fear, and not worth having."

The boy looked questioningly at her for a moment, then nodded. "I remember."

"Good." Millie put her arm around the boy. "Come on. It's hard work being dragged up hill. I think this calls for milk and cookies."

****

It was late afternoon before Millie had her chores done. She stepped into her newly altered skirt and hooked it without effort. Then she put a freshly baked apple pie in a basket along with enough dried apples to make at least two more pies, and covered them with a napkin. Mrs. Winslow, a lieutenant's wife, was in the family way and craving apple pie. Millie had promised to see that she got some before they pulled out.

She buckled on her pistol, then buttoned her coat over it. Mr. Donovan had complained to the post commander about the corporal and insisted he be punished. The man was just the type to hold a grudge. If she were unlucky enough to run into him again, she'd be prepared.

After sharing a cup of tea and a piece of apple pie, Millie and Mrs. Winslow walked around the parade grounds. They climbed to the palisade for a good look around the countryside. The view nearly took Millie's breath away. She'd grown up in the Ozark Mountains where the trees were so thick one had to hack her way through them. The Rocky Mountains were intimidating and exactly as their name suggested, rocky. Good for nothing but mountain goats, Elsa had claimed.

However, *these* mountains, the Bighorn Mountains of the Wyoming Territory, were breathtaking. The surrounding landscape was a little more hilly than rolling. The grass was thick and lush, with trees scattered in clusters for several miles in all directions. Everything was green and peaceful, with a back drop of purple and deep blue mountains dotted with snow. If their valley was even half this beautiful, she'd be happy for the rest of her life.

Finally, she took her leave and headed back toward the wagons, mentally making a list of the things she needed to do. They'd be leaving in the morning. She looked around as she neared the wagons and sighed. This gypsy life was nice, but she wanted a home, a garden, and…a husband? No, she wasn't ready to go that far.

****

Shortly after sun-up, Blake gave the order to pull out. Lieutenant Collins and five of his men pulled up in front of him. "Good morning, Mr. Donovan. May we ask where you're going?"

Blake readjusted his hat. "On to our destination, Lieutenant. Our plans haven't changed."

"Well, I'm afraid they have, at least, been slowed down some. Colonel Carrington isn't allowing any wagon train of less than one hundred wagons to travel beyond this point."

Blake pulled his hat lower on his forehead. "Lieutenant, we're not in the army and we're not subject to Colonel Carrington's orders. We will go or come whenever we please."

"No, sir, you won't."

"You mean you'd shoot at defenseless women?"

The lieutenant looked at the women, shook his head, then looked back at Blake. "From what I hear, sir, they're not exactly defenseless. But to answer your question, no, we wouldn't shoot the women, only the oxen."

"Now, wait a minute…"

"No, sir, you wait. This is for your own good." He dropped his voice and leaned forward. "Dammit, man, surely you know what Indians do to white women."

"Certainly, I do, but we don't anticipate any problems with the local Indians."

The lieutenant shook his head. "I can't believe you said that. Nonetheless, you'll have to wait until another wagon train comes in."

Blake inwardly chafed at the delay. "When do you suppose that will be?"

"I don't know, but you'll have to remain here until one does come."

Blake started to protest further, but realized it would do no good. The soldier was merely following orders. He nodded and turned Thunder around and gave the order to wait.

"Thank you, Mr. Donovan." Lieutenant Collins looked around briefly. "I'll just leave my men here to...protect you."

Blake looked over his shoulder at the officer, then past him to his men. "Fine, but you'd better have them stay well away from these wagons...for their protection. The ladies are going to be madder than blazes at this delay."

Emily, Millie, and Miss Hannah met Blake at the head of the first wagon. John Eagle, with Little Feather beside him, dismounted immediately. "What's the problem?" he asked.

As soon as Blake finished his explanation, Miss Emily shot murderous looks at the soldiers sitting just out of hearing distance. "Did you tell them about Little Feather?" She quickly clamped her hand over her mouth. "Of course, you didn't. What a silly question."

"Maybe we could outrun them," Millie suggested.

Blake shook his head. "No. If these soldiers fired just one shot, killed one ox, the whole post would be on us before we got a new animal hitched up. We'll have to sneak off."

"Oh, certainly," Miss Hannah said with a snort. "These wagons are so quiet."

Blake nodded. "I'm not saying it'll be easy, but I think it can be done. Let's make a token show of setting up camp, and then we can make our plans. We won't be able to do anything until after nightfall."

****

It was the blackest part of the night when Millie, along with Blake, John Eagle, and Cassie, moved silently through the dark toward the soldier's camp.

A cold wind nipped at Millie as she huddled behind the brush at the back of the belligerent corporal. As soon as Mr. Donovan and the others were in place, they'd take care of these curs.

The five soldiers sat around a large campfire. "Hell, I don't see why we have to sit out here freezing," said one of the soldiers.

"If them people are crazy enough to go out there, I say let the Indians have 'em. It'd serve that gun-toting bitch right if every buck in the tribe rode her," the corporal grumbled.

Silently Blake stepped into the clearing. A fraction of a second later Millie shoved her gun in the corporal's ribs just as each of her companions did to the other soldiers. "You won't live to hear about it if you make one sound," she whispered in his ear.

The man froze, his coffee cup half way to his mouth. "And don't get any ideas about that coffee." She shoved the gun barrel firmly against the back of his head. "At this range, nothing would save you. Now, put the cup down, slowly."

When he'd complied, they motioned for the men to move back from the firelight. "On the ground," Blake ordered. Then each man was gagged and tied hand and foot. Finally, they tossed a blanket over each man. Millie tucked hers under the corporal's chin and tightly around him. "We wouldn't want you to catch cold."

He glared at her and mumbled something from behind the gag.

Millie shrugged. "Sorry, you're not speaking clearly enough. Maybe you should practice, so you can tell me the next time we meet."

When all the soldiers were taken care of, Blake led the way back to the wagons. Miss Hannah had everyone ready to pull out. Millie and Cassie mounted their horses, and they all moved, very slowly and quietly.

By first light, they were completely out of sight of the fort. "Do you think they'll come after us?" Millie asked.

"I don't know," Blake answered, "but from the sound of that gunfire, I'd bet Red Cloud and his band are covering our backs. I just hope he doesn't go scalp-hunting. I'd hate to be responsible for the deaths of those soldiers we left tied up."

Millie hadn't thought of that. She prayed for the men's safe release. Also, that she'd never see any of them again.

The wagons traveled for three days before two Indians appeared on the horizon behind them. By late afternoon Millie, like everyone else on the wagons, could stand it no longer. She rode up beside Blake Donovan. "Mr. Donovan, those Indians have kept pace with us for the last three days. Why don't they come talk to us?"

Blake shook his head. "I don't know." He looked into the distance toward the two mounted figures on the rise. "They're so far away, I can't tell what tribe they belong to. It could be they're just curious about us. They don't see wagons like these every day."

Her hand rested on the saddle horn as her gaze followed his. "I hope you're right."

He reached over and patted her hand briefly. "Don't worry. If they meant us harm, they'd already have started something."

Suddenly, as if realizing what he'd done, Blake jerked his hand back, cleared his throat, and tipped his hat. "Uh, I'd better ride back and make sure no one gets trigger-happy."

Millie pulled her horse to a stop as she turned to watch him ride off. Then she looked down at her hand. Did that really happen? Had he really touched her like that?

"Millie? Millie!"

Finally, she looked around at Emily walking beside their wagon. Millie rode over and dismounted. Leading the horse, she walked beside Emily.

"Is something wrong?" Emily asked.

Millie shook her head. "I don't know. I mean, I don't think so. Mr. Donovan just…well, he…"

"He what?" Emily prompted.

Millie took a deep breath, then told Emily what he had done. "I don't know what to think. Lately it seems he's gone out of his way to be nice to me. What do you suppose he's up to?"

"My goodness, Millie, why does he have to be up to anything? Maybe he's finally realized you're not so bad. Maybe he wants to get to know you better. After all, you *are* a nice person. In fact, I've often wondered what was wrong with him that he didn't see it from the beginning."

Millie smiled and hugged her friend around the

shoulders as they walked. In her own flighty way, Emily had very good insight where people were concerned…usually.

Mr. Donovan rode by for the third time in as many hours. Millie couldn't help wondering if he really did want to know her better? Until now, she had suspected he was waiting for her to make a mistake. She watched him out of the corner of her eye. Did she want to know *him* better?

Cindy Pollard hurried up beside Emily. "What do you suppose those Indians up there want?" she asked in a shaky voice.

"Mr. Donovan thinks they may just be curious about us," Millie answered as she looked at the girl. "What have you done to yourself? There's something different, but I just can't decide what."

Emily snapped the reins at the nearest ox, then scrutinized the girl. "It's your hair. You didn't cut it, did you?"

Cindy pulled a pair of scissors from her pocket and snapped them a couple of times. "No, not yet. It's just tucked up in my bonnet, but if any more Indians take a fancy to my hair, they can have it, but not me."

They all laughed. "I certainly hope that's not necessary," Millie said between giggles. Then she sobered. "You know, I can't help wondering why the soldiers didn't come after us. I was under the impression people didn't get away with crossing the U.S. Army."

"I heard John Eagle tell Ben he'd backtracked and heard a lot of shooting. He supposed they were busy with the Indians," Cindy said.

Millie glanced at Emily. Were the Indians really covering their back trail? *Please God, don't let this be a mistake,* she prayed silently.

Blake pulled up beside the women and tipped his hat. "Ladies. When you reach that stand of trees a ways up, we'll stop for a nooning. The hills are getting pretty steep. John Eagle is hunting an easier way over. Otherwise, we'll have to haul the wagons up one at a time."

"I certainly wish him good luck."

Donovan rode on down the line. Cindy returned to her own wagon to pass the news to her ma. "I'll go on ahead to see if there's any water," Millie said. "If those Indians weren't spying, a swim would be wonderful."

"It surely would," Emily agreed.

Millie rode with one eye on the rise where the Indians sat. Even knowing they had safe passage because of Little Feather didn't make her any less nervous. What were they waiting for? Why didn't they merely ride down, collect the boy, and be on their way?

When she reached the stand of trees, she drew her rifle from the saddle holster. She didn't know what she'd find in there, wild animals or unfriendly humans, but she'd be ready.

Millie rode slowly through the woods. It wasn't a very large stand of trees. She followed a trail, of sorts, but doubted their wagons could get through without widening it considerably. She decided to ride around the wooded area.

She turned back the way she'd come, thinking to check the distance from the train before wandering around. Two Indians sat on their ponies, blocking her way. She pulled up short. Where had they come from? She hadn't heard so much as a sigh.

Chapter Twenty-Two

She tightened her hold on the rifle. They made no move to attack her, so she sat still. After several minutes of staring at each other, she nodded a greeting. One of them nodded back, but still they made no move toward her nor did they move to allow her to pass. Finally, they turned their mounts and one after the other left the trail.

Millie sat for a long time, trembling, listening. Not even a twig snapped. Their moving through the woods like that without making a sound was extremely unnerving. Little by little, the birds began to chirp. The insects started their chorus. Until now, she'd not been aware they'd stopped. She was so relieved that things seemed to be back to normal, she nearly fell from the saddle. Millie grabbed her mount's mane, almost sobbing from the fear and tension.

Maybe exploring alone wasn't such a good idea after all. She headed back the way she'd come. She'd never been called a coward, but neither was she foolhardy. This wasn't her country. There was much to learn before she was capable of taking on the wilds by herself.

Millie pulled up on top of a rise. The wagons were several miles to the south of her. "Goodness, I hadn't realized I'd come so far," she said as she petted her mount. "Well, come on, we'd better get back before those Indians decide they've made a mistake in letting us go." She nudged the horse's flank and they started across country.

What had looked like flat ground, from the top of the rise, turned out to be rolling countryside. As she neared a swell, her horse raised its ears and nickered. Millie pulled to a stop. "What is it, Lady? What do you hear?" she asked, petting the animal's neck. She looked and listened, but could detect nothing. Finally drawing her rifle and loading a round in the chamber, she turned the horse slightly upwind and walked her slowly around the swell. Whoever was over there would have a fight on his hands if he thought to get her.

Millie went around the swell with her gun pointed in the direction of the horse's ears. There, peacefully grazing on the downward slope stood two antelopes. Without thinking, she took aim and fired. The buck dropped. She fired again, but missed the other animal. Well, they could divide this and all have plenty of fresh meat. She touched her mare's flanks and rode forward.

Millie started to dismount just as a shadow fell across her kill. She looked up and into the face of one of the Indians she'd seen earlier. She tightened her hold on the rifle as her body began to tremble. Where had he been hiding? What did he want?

He said something. She shook her head indicating, she hoped, that she didn't understand his language. After a few minutes, he pointed to the buck, then placed his hand on his own chest.

Millie took that to mean he was trying to claim her kill. Her first instinct was to let him have it, but that would show weakness, just what John Eagle said she shouldn't do. She shook her head and slowly lifted her rifle, being careful to keep it pointed upward. She pointed to her kill, then back to her gun. Anyone could see it was *her* kill, since he only carried a bow. They sat there looking at each other for a long time.

Her pulse raced through her trembling body. This was getting them nowhere fast. Finally, Millie indicated the animal, then took both hands and pretended to break something in half, offering half to him and keeping half for herself.

After a long moment, he nodded. In one fluid motion, he slid from his horse, drew his knife, and quickly began skinning the dead animal. Millie didn't know what to do. Should she get down and help? Would it be safe to do so? Her dilemma was short lived. The brave stopped and looked at her. He said something, then motioned for her to get down and do her part. She stared at him for a minute, then slid the rifle back into the saddle boot and dismounted. She supposed if he'd meant her harm, he'd have already made his move.

They worked together for over an hour, skinning and dressing the dead beast. Finally, he sat back on his haunches, as if waiting for her to indicate how they should divide up the spoils. Millie took her rain slicker from the back of her saddle and laid it on the ground. She divided the meat nearly in half. One pile had a little more than the other.

Millie indicated that he should take his pick. *Just like a man, to claim the largest half.* Then he looked at the skin. Millie had been giving all her skins to Little Feather. He had a nice pile of hides, from rabbit to antelope. He wouldn't go to his new family empty-handed. But he was home now. One skin, more or less, wouldn't make a difference. She nodded, indicating the brave should take the skin. She also gave him the stomach and any other body parts he wanted.

She wrapped her share in her slicker and dragged it to her horse. Try as she might, Millie couldn't lift it onto the mare. Much to her astonishment, a dark hand reached around her and hoisted the bundle onto the back of her saddle.

She watched as he secured his share in the skin, then mounted his own horse. They sat there looking at each other for a moment, then Millie smiled and tentatively waved goodbye. He smiled fleetingly and nodded. Then they each rode away, in opposite directions.

Millie held her breath. Would he shoot her in the back? He could have killed her anytime in the last hour. Had he just been waiting until she helped him with the work?

She rode back to the wagons without seeing anyone else—or getting an arrow in the back. She was never so happy to see anyone in her life as when she saw Blake Donovan. For some reason, he represented safety. As ornery as he was, she felt safe with him, most of the time.

"Where have you been?" he demanded. "Miss Hannah's been worried sick."

Safe? Well, from everyone but himself. "I ran onto an antelope, and invited him to supper, half of him, that is."

"Invited him…Half of him? What are you talking about?"

She grinned. It was good to see him confused for a change. But maybe this wasn't the time to exact her pound of flesh. She indicated the bundle of meat tied onto the back of her saddle. "I shot an antelope, but an Indian wanted half of it, so I shared. I think there's still enough for everyone."

"An Indian?" He began looking in all directions as fast as his head would turn. "Where?"

"On the other side of that hill, behind the trees. He went his way, and I went mine. I don't think he means us any harm."

"Oh, you don't? Just what makes you an authority on Indians all of a sudden?"

Millie drew herself up in the saddle. Now he was back to his old insulting self. "He had plenty of chances to kill me, if that's what he wanted. But all he was interested in was sharing my kill. I think he was very hungry." She started her horse toward the circled wagons. *Come to think of it, so am I. He can sit here and argue if he wants to, but I have meat to distribute.*

After another hour's travel, Blake Donovan called a halt. "Unless John Eagle shows up within the next hour or so, we'll camp here for the night." The wagons were circled and fire pits dug. The women went about their chores quickly and quietly, one eye on their tasks and one eye on the surrounding hills.

As the stew bubbled over the fire, Millie and the representatives from the other wagons held a brief meeting with Mr. Donovan to discuss any problems with the stock and wagons. So far, everything was in fine shape, thanks to the repairs they'd made at the fort.

When supper was over and the ladies were doing their handwork, Millie found herself the center of attention. What was the Indian like? Where did she meet him? Wasn't she scared?

She answered all their questions, but was relieved when the topic of conversation finally shifted elsewhere. When John Eagle rode in, she put down her knitting and went to dish him up a bowl of stew.

"Thanks, Miss Millie. I was hoping there'd be something besides Oats' coffee." He took a deep breath over the bowl, then smiled. "Doesn't smell like Oats' stew, either." He took a bite, then his brows raised in surprise. "That's not rabbit. What is it?"

"Antelope."

"You're kidding! Where'd you get it?"

Millie handed him a steaming cup of coffee. "I shot it this afternoon, but only brought half of it back."

He took a sip of coffee then set the cup aside. "Why's that?"

"That's what I want to talk to you about." She sat down beside him and told of meeting the two Indians in the woods and later sharing the meat with one of them. "Did I do the right thing? I don't know if I showed a weakness by giving him half or what. But I couldn't see him going hungry."

John Eagle finished his stew in thoughtful silence. Finally, he set his bowl aside and picked up his coffee cup. "Miss Millie, Indians are people, just like anyone else. I think, as much as anything, he was testing you. You showed strength by not allowing him to bully you. And you showed compassion by sharing with him. He'll remember it."

Millie heaved a sigh of relief. "Good. I didn't want to offend him, but neither did I want to lose the only fresh meat we've had since leaving the fort. Would you like some more stew?"

"No, ma'am. I've had plenty. It's time Blake and I put our heads together and worked up a plan for tomorrow. We've a lot of work ahead of us."

Before first light, the camp bustled with activity. All but the four women assigned to do the cooking were busy preparing to pull out. It would take all day to haul all the wagons over the hill. The incline was so steep they would need to hitch several teams to each wagon.

By noon, they had half the wagons on the other side of the hill and an evening camp set up. Millie wiped her forehead, then reached for the lines. This wasn't as hard as hoisting the wagons over a cliff as they'd done at Ash Hollow and several other places. They could move more than one wagon at a time. However, the mountain was so steep it took several teams to get each wagon up, and then they had to be anchored so they wouldn't roll down the other side at breakneck speed. And the teams had to rest before they could take another wagon over.

It was just past dark when the last wagon rolled down the hill and took its place in the circle. "I never be so tired," Elsa said as they finished tending the last team.

Millie splashed a little cool water on her face. "Me neither. All I want to do now is sleep."

****

It wasn't quite daylight when Millie finished hitching the oxen. As soon as the last ox took his muzzle out of the water bucket, she turned to toss out the remaining liquid. "Oh!" She all but screamed as she dropped the bucket.

The same brave who'd shared her kill the day before stood behind her. He'd almost gotten a cold shower. She swallowed and smiled tentatively. He nodded back. Though no smile touched his lips, his black eyes twinkled. He's as bad as John Eagle, she thought. Evidently all Indians enjoyed sneaking up on people. He stood with his arms crossed over his chest, his hands far away from his weapons.

"Goo-Good morning," Millie stammered. "I'm

sorry, I didn't hear you come up." He said nothing, merely stood there watching her. "Is there something I can do for you?" she asked.

Mr. Donovan had warned them to expect members of Red Cloud's tribe, but she hadn't expected them to suddenly turn up at her elbow. From the corner of her eye, she saw Emily heading toward the back of the wagon, loaded down with pots and pans. A yelp and the loud clatter of pans hitting the ground told Millie that Emily had seen their visitor.

Within seconds Emily backed into Millie, then moved to the side and stood at Millie's shoulder, still facing the opposite direction. "M...Millie, there's an Indian right behind you," she whispered without turning around.

"Really? There's one behind you, too."

Emily chanced a quick glance over her shoulder. "Oh, my! What should we do? My gun is in the wagon."

Millie tried to swallow the lump lodged in her throat. "I don't think they mean us any harm. Maybe you should excuse yourself and go find Bla-...Mr. Donovan or John Eagle."

Emily nodded, never taking her eyes off the brave behind Millie. "Ex...Excuse me, sir," she said as she eased away from the group. "I...I'll be right back." Then she turned and, completely forgetting her dignity, fled toward the lead wagon. "Mr. Donovan!"

Not knowing what else to do, Millie went to the water keg, filled a dipper full, and offered it to the Indians. The one she'd shared her meat with accepted first. He drank, never taking his eyes off her. When he returned the dipper, she refilled it and offered it to his friend, who reluctantly accepted. When he returned it a sip later, Millie was still alone with the braves.

She looked around for something else to do. Her gaze fell upon the cookie tin that Emily had filled last night. She retrieved it, lifted the lid, and offered each man a cookie. They didn't seem to know what they were being offered, so Millie took one and bit into it, then offered it again. Each brave took one, looked at it and smelled it before taking a bite. This time both braves smiled and nodded.

Blake rushed up beside her. "I see you're making our guests feel right at home."

Millie heaved a sigh of relief. "I wasn't sure what to do."

"You did right."

He turned toward the braves and began talking in sign language. Millie stared at his back. *That's twice. He's complimented me twice in the last few days. Is he sick?*

After several minutes, Mr. Donovan turned to Millie. "Pass the word to pack up, and we'll move out as soon as possible." She nodded. Her pulse raced as she hurried to do his bidding. This meant they were on the last leg of their journey. She was, however, sad that Little Feather would be leaving them. They'd all become very attached to the boy.

****

Millie snapped the reins against her lead ox's rump. They'd been traveling for the last two hours. The two braves sent by Red Cloud rode up front with John Eagle. All the women were frightened, and justly so after the horrid stories they'd heard about how Indians treated white women. However, John Eagle assured them they'd be safe. "At least you and Emily will be," he added in lower tones. "Seems they're impressed with your marksmanship, generous nature, and Miss Emily's cookies."

They certainly must have liked the cookies. The tin was almost empty. They'd each taken three extra cookies before following Blake to the head of the train.

She blushed at her slip of thought. *Blake*. When did she began thinking of him by his Christian name? Earlier she'd almost slipped in front of Emily. That would never do. Just about everyone seemed to be pushing Mr. Donovan and her together. She certainly didn't want to encourage that. She neither needed nor wanted a man in her life right now, and maybe never.

They'd been traveling lengthwise through a long, narrow valley. Now they were turning west around the edge of a large forest. *I certainly hope John Eagle is paying attention so we can get out of here*. She snapped the reins again. *This is beautiful country, but...* Her thoughts were interrupted when Emily hurried up and reached for the lines.

"I'm to drive. Cassie is bringing you a horse. John Eagle says there is game up ahead, and it would be polite if we arrived with some as gifts."

Millie nodded. She hurried to get her rifle and ammunition. She'd heard that the Indians were starving, but to hear the soldiers tell it back at the fort, they were the ones going hungry. She shrugged. It didn't matter. They took goodies to the fort, and she supposed it was only polite to do the same here.

Cassie rode up, astride, leading Millie's horse and two pack animals. Millie climbed onto her sidesaddle and took one of the lead lines. "We'd better get out of here before Miss Hannah sees you riding astride. She'll skin you alive."

Cassie grinned and nodded. "I've been in dozens of gunfighting situations and never raised a hair, but that woman terrifies me."

They galloped across country, then pulled up to a slow walk as soon as they could see the elk herd. Millie moistened her finger and held it up to check the wind's direction. "Good. They're upwind of us."

Before they could dismount, Little Feather, also leading a pack animal, rode up beside them. He dismounted, then held out his hand, indicating that he would hold the horses.

"How many do you think we should get?" Cassie asked as they crept nearer the herd.

"Well, I figure each pack horse can carry two, no farther then we have to go. We have three pack horses, and if need be, we can use Little Feather's horse, and he can ride behind you."

"Me? Why behind me?"

Millie grinned. "Have you ever tried riding double with a sidesaddle?"

"I see what you mean. Okay, eight. That's four apiece. Do you think we can get that many?"

Millie grinned as she checked her rifle. "We'd better come close if we don't want the men to make our lives miserable."

The herd grazed almost directly in front of them. Millie took the front of the herd, and Cassie took the back. They carefully selected the animals they wanted, then at a muttered, "Go!" from Cassie, they began firing rapidly. When the smoke cleared, the herd was gone, leaving six dead.

"A tie," Cassie said as she reloaded.

Little Feather hurried up with all the horses in tow. "That good shooting. Who win?" he asked breathlessly.

Millie reached for her horses. "No one. We each got three. Guess we'll have to settle who's better another time."

****

As soon as they rounded the far side of the woods, the Indian camp came into view. It was a large village of maybe one hundred tepees or more. They circled the wagons just outside the tepees, made camp, and set about making preparations for supper.

The Indian men stood at a distance and watched. The women, though bashful at first, eased forward until they were at the white women's elbows.

John Eagle introduced Spotted Elk, the young brave with whom Millie had shared her kill. He stepped from in front of a young woman plump with child. She wasn't quite as tall as Millie and had a ready smile. "This is Morning Dove, Spotted Elk's wife," John Eagle said.

The girl shyly acknowledged the introduction, then whispered something to her husband. He turned to Millie. All she could understand was the word "coo-kee."

John Eagle chuckled and translated, "Seems Spotted Elk saved one of your cookies for Morning Dove. She wants to know if you'll teach her to make them."

Millie grinned. "Of course. Let's go talk to Emily. It's her recipe." She stepped forward, then turned and motioned for Morning Dove to follow. The Indian girl hesitated only a second before falling in step behind Millie.

"How in the world are we going to do this?" Emily asked after Millie explained what Morning Dove wanted.

"I don't know. We'll have to think about this for a bit."

Blake and Little Feather joined Millie and Emily at the fire. "The women already have the elk you shot skinned and on the fire. There will be a big celebration tonight, so you don't have to worry about cooking. We've all been invited."

"That's very nice, but John Eagle said these people were starving. They can't feed us all. How about if we each bring something…make a big picnic out of it."

Blake nodded. Millie never ceased to amaze him. "That sounds good. Go ahead. I'll square it with the chief." He left Little Feather to translate for the women while he looked for Chief Red Cloud.

Blake's thoughts drifted back to Millie. He shook his head. As much as he hadn't wanted her along, he couldn't imagine what this trip would have been like without her. All the women on this trip had turned out to be extraordinary people, but Miss Millie seemed to be wherever a helping hand was needed. True, she was the cause of a lot of problems, but that only served to make the trip interesting.

He stopped dead in his tracks. *Interesting!* Had he gone loco? She'd damn near cost him his life, one way or the other. Until recently, she was a jinx, plain and simple…well maybe not so plain, and definitely not simple.

He jerked his hat low on his forehead. Brother, he was in trouble now. When he stopped thinking of her in any way but as a jinx, he'd had it. He might as well shoot himself in the foot.

Chapter Twenty-Three

The festivities started early. The Indian women added their feast foods to that which the white women put out, and everyone had a good time. The men, white and Indian, competed against one another in various games while the women conversed as best they could using signs and Little Feather's translating.

Morning Dove had helped Emily make several batches of cookies. Though Emily said each ingredient several times and had Morning Dove repeat it each time, she knew the Indian girl wouldn't remember. She even wrote down the recipe. Morning Dove wouldn't know how to read it, but might be able to show it to someone who could. With Ben's help, Millie found and traded Morning Dove a heavy griddle for a pair of soft moccasins.

The celebrating lasted well into the night. Millie could hardly drag herself out of bed at daylight.

Emily stifled a yawn. "It's entirely too early for morning," she grumbled.

"I know what you mean," Millie agreed as she felt around with one foot for her boots. "This may well prove to be the longest day of the trip."

As soon as they'd eaten and packed up, Millie mounted her horse. Mr. Donovan had invited her to ride point with him for a while. She couldn't imagine what had gotten into the man, but she intended to take advantage of it.

As fascinated as the Indian women were with the white women's long skirts and strange tepees on wheels, they let out whoops of laughter as Millie rode up beside Blake wearing her britches and riding sidesaddle.

Millie looked around, bewildered at the merriment. "What are they laughing at?" she asked.

Blake was evidently having trouble keeping a straight face himself. "At your sidesaddle." They think it's silly and that you'll break your neck the first time your horse takes a jump."

Millie stiffened her back. "Oh, really!" She could understand their attitude. They'd never seen saddles like this, but his grin was a totally different matter. She touched her heels to the mare's side and the animal raced forward.

The mare leaped over a dry creek bed, then turned and leaped back. Millie pulled up beside Mr. Donovan, smiled, and shrugged. "See, I'm still in one piece."

Shaking his head, Blake waved his hat in the air and gave the order to move out. Spotted Elk and Morning Dove rode up beside them.

"Where are they going?" Millie asked.

"They're giving us safe conduct out of here," Blake explained.

****

Millie snapped the reins absentmindedly as she walked beside her wagon. She had never seen such beautiful country. She and Emily had often wondered what made the men they were going to marry settle way out here in nowhere. Now she thought she understood. The land was hilly but green and lush. At the moment, there were yellow flowers everywhere.

Elsa, walking beside Millie, stopped and poked the toe of her boot into the ground, then stooped and scooped up some earth. She looked at it, let it filter through her fingers, then hurried to catch up with Millie. "Iss very goot earth. I hope de men have goot earth like dis."

"I was just noticing that. Look at those flowers. The hills are covered with them." It had been almost a week since they'd parted company with Spotted Elk and Morning Dove. The land was easy traveling and beautiful. There were no trees to shade them from the sun. However, they didn't miss the shade. In fact, the few times the clouds shaded them, it was almost cold.

Millie couldn't help wondering if it was this way all the time. It certainly was different from Missouri. Missouri. Home. She hadn't thought of Pineville since she'd left some months ago. Truthfully, she hadn't missed it and still didn't.

Her best friend had moved away when she was fifteen. Then Pa had forced her to marry Otto Watts, and she'd never gotten around to cultivating friendships with the other people her age. Not that any of them wanted to associate with Otto Watts, or her pa.

She watched the birds soar through the air. Of course, without Pa and her late husband, she hadn't had any trouble making friends. Aunt Lavinia had been right. She'd just needed to get away from the problems that plagued her.

Elsa had wandered off to visit other wagons. Millie reached into the wagon for a drink of water. As she replaced the dipper, Blake Donovan rode by and tipped his hat. He dismounted and, leading Thunder, walked beside her.

"Good afternoon, Miss Millie."

"Good afternoon, Mr. Donovan. Isn't this beautiful country?"

"Yes, ma'am. Is it to your liking?"

"Oh, yes. How could anyone not like this? Is the valley we're going to as pretty as this?"

He shoved his hat back and looked around. "Well, in a way it is, but at the same time different. I like the valley better because it has trees. My pa used to say I was a tree person. Seems I used to set up quite a ruckus when anyone cut down a living tree." He grinned. "Guess to me, they were meant to be climbed, not burned."

She smiled, glancing at him from under her lashes. This was the first time he'd stopped to pass the time of day with her. Well, he'd stopped a couple of times several weeks ago, but didn't say much or stay long. This was the first time he'd shared anything personal without her prodding him.

"I know what you mean. I've spent many a night in a tree, myself."

He looked at her in surprise. "You're kidding. Why would you do that?"

Millie shrugged and fidgeted with the reins. "When Pa was on one of his toots, he'd come looking for me. Up was the only place he never seemed to think of."

"Guess I was lucky. My pa was always there like a best friend."

"What about your ma?"

He reached down and pulled a flower as they walked, then casually handed it to her. "She died of a fever when I was three. I don't really remember her very well."

"Oh, I'm sorry."

"What about your ma? Is she still back in Missouri?"

Millie was surprised that he remembered where she was from. "No, she died when I was about thirteen. I lived most of the time from then on with Aunt Lavinia and Uncle James."

They walked in silence for a while. Millie was amazed they were sharing such intimate details of their lives. She chanced another quick glance his way. She wasn't nervous nor had she stumbled once in his presence.

Just as she was thinking things were changing for the better between them, Honey waddled up behind them. Suddenly, Blake yelped, with a sidestep, and Honey walked between them.

"What happened?" Millie demanded.

"She bit me. I don't think she likes me walking with you. Hey, *Duck*, I thought we were friends."

"Honey, shame on you," Millie scolded her pet. "Mr. Donovan is just being neighborly. Now you tell him you're sorry."

Blake moved a bit farther from the overgrown bird. He wanted to rub his thigh where she'd bitten him, but modesty forbade it. "She's looking at me as if I were a big fat worm," Blake said. "I think something needs my attention up ahead." Without another word, he tipped his hat, then swung up on Thunder and galloped away.

Millie sighed. "Oh, Honey, how could you? That was the first time since we've been with this train that he's been the least bit friendly. Why couldn't you behave?"

Blake rode up beside John Eagle. After several minutes, the scout glanced his way. "Well?"

"Well, what?"

John Eagle shook his head. "How's the courtship

coming along?"

"Courtship? What are you talking about?"

"Come on, Blake, don't play dumb. How's it coming between you and Miss Millie? I saw you talking to her."

When Blake opened his mouth to protest, John Eagle stopped him. "We've had this discussion before, so stop acting like a horse's ass. She's perfect for you, and you know it. Besides, if you don't start mending fences, some other lucky fellow in the valley will spot her, and you'll lose out."

Blake exhaled. "Well, it was going pretty well until that overgrown *duck* horned in. Guess she thought I was walking too close. She bit me and then shoved between us. Maybe I'd better spend a little more time winning her over before I start on her mistress." He shifted in the saddle to ease his sore behind.

John Eagle watched several pairs of birds soar through the sky. "You know, if Honey had a friend, she wouldn't have time to bother you."

"Yeah, I've thought about introducing her to a hungry fox, but she's my Thanksgiving supper, and I don't intend to share."

"I was thinking more in the line of a gentlemen friend, if you know what I mean."

Blake looked up at the birds, fluttering around each other, diving in, then sailing off. "Yeah, I know what you mean, but where do we find a gander brave enough to take her on?"

"I'll put the word out. Maybe we'll get lucky."

"Yeah, maybe. In the meantime, we'd better start thinking about camping. Is there water up ahead?"

Millie was thankful for the early stop. Actually, it

wasn't so early, it just stayed light longer out here. As soon as camp was made and the animals taken care of, the women started supper.

As was their usual custom, Blake and John Eagle joined the representatives from each group of four wagons for dessert at Millie's wagon. Millie could hardly keep her mind on the discussion. A breeze blew across Mr. Donovan into Millie's face. He smelled as if he'd just had a bath. Goodness, the very nearness of him gave her goose bumps. She got up to refill his coffee cup. He smiled up at her as if they'd been friends forever.

She caught her breath. His eyes had never twinkled at her before. Come to think of it, he'd smiled at her a lot lately. That smile, coupled with his dimples, made her heart soar. She returned the coffeepot to the fire, then looked across the distance, struggling to calm herself before rejoining the group.

The last thing she wanted was a man…this man, at any rate, she reminded herself. He was arrogant and bossy. She'd best remember that if she didn't want to end up with a man as bad as Pa, or worse.

The strum of a guitar floated on the breeze. It was quickly joined by the organ and then by a fiddle. The camp erupted in merriment. As soon as the supper things were washed and put away, the camp became a beehive of activity. Some gathered around the musicians, some brought out the quilting frame, and still others gathered around Allison's sewing machine. They'd have new clothes in which to meet their future husbands.

The camp meeting broke up. Millie and the women hurried to join their respective groups. The men sat around the fire too, doing men's work. Millie stitched on her new blue skirt. She had also bought a length of emerald green material. Like most of the women, she intended to start her new life without patches on her clothing.

She couldn't, however, keep her eyes from straying toward the men, Mr. Donovan in particular. He seemed totally engrossed in his harness mending. The task had his full attention, all but for his right foot. It seemed more interested in keeping time with the music. She couldn't hide the grin that kept trying to burst forth. Like Mr. Donovan, Millie couldn't keep her foot still either.

A shadow fell across her work as she whipped in the last few stitches on the hem of her new skirt. She glanced up, then started. The pair of legs standing before her were definitely male. Her gaze traveled up past the ornate gun belt, the blue shirt, over a broad chest, and stopped on Blake Donovan's face.

He held out his hand. "May I have the pleasure of this dance?"

Millie's mouth gaped open. She looked around, then back up at him. "Me?" she asked in a squeaky voice, then quickly cleared her throat and asked again. "Me?

"Yes, ma'am, you." He picked up her sewing and laid it aside, then took her hand and pulled her to her feet.

She felt every eye in camp looking at her. *What is this man up to now? You simply don't ask someone you don't like to dance. Why can't he stay in character?* But the thoughts fled as he gently pulled her into his arms and whirled her around the dancing area.

Millie had been on guard duty during the last two dances. She'd almost forgotten how it felt to be in Blake Donovan's arms. How could you dislike and distrust a man so intently and still feel so right in his arms? It must be the mountainous setting. Everything out here was so…romantic.

As the evening passed, Millie danced with all the men, and several times with Blake. Finally, she began to see a pattern. No sooner had someone cut in on the two of them than John Eagle would become her partner. They'd whirl around the dance floor only to, more often than not, literally bump into Blake, who would be dancing with Emily. They'd laugh and change partners. This was almost déjà vu. Now that she thought about it, this seemed to happen every time she attended a dance. These two were playing cupid. Was Mr. Donovan in on it too?

Blake whirled Millie around the dance area for the dozenth time. He'd thought to dance with her first and get it over with, so then he could dance with the other women, but he was beginning to suspect that the fates— by the names of John Eagle and Miss Emily—were against him.

Blake looked down at the small woman in his arms. He couldn't say he was sorry, though. She was pretty and good natured…well, maybe he wouldn't go that far, but she was self-reliant, and always there to do her part and more when needed. She felt good in his arms, too, almost like she belonged there. He couldn't help chuckling.

Millie looked up sharply. "What's so funny? Did I miss something?"

"No, ma'am. I was just thinking. It's certainly taken a long time for us to become friends. For months we've been circling around each other like a pair of fighting cocks. Now here we've spent a whole evening dancing and talking like two old buddies."

She grinned and nodded. "I was thinking the same thing. Do you think we'd have ever become friends if we'd stayed in Independence?"

He shook his head. "I seriously doubt it. I think fate just wore us down out here."

"Yes," Millie agreed. "Fate, in the form of John Eagle and Emily Peterson."

He turned her around in small circles. "So you noticed too?"

"Oh, I noticed. And you know, I don't think we should let them get away with this. I mean, they shouldn't be allowed to dictate one's life, no matter how good their intentions."

"I agree. It's just a matter of principle."

Blake saw timid fingers tap Millie's shoulder and turned to change partners. He didn't do so as reluctantly now, knowing Cupid's helpers would see to it that the sweet little jinx would be back soon.

Somewhere along the line, he'd get a chance to repay his cousin and Millie's wagon mate for their concern. In the meantime, he was beginning to enjoy Miss Millie's company.

Millie and Blake were among the last to retire for the night. As soon as the last of the chores were done, Blake walked Millie back to her wagon. The tailgate was down, though the wagon cover was drawn and tied against the chilly night air.

Blake removed his hat. His hands worried with the brim for a few seconds before he raised his eyes to her face. It was a sweet face, bathed in moonlight.

The silence between them grew by the second. Millie felt like she should say something, but what? Finally, she smiled and laid her hand on his arm. "Thank you for a pleasant evening, Mr. Donovan. I enjoyed it very much."

"You're welcome, Miss Millie. I've enjoyed it, too."
He set his hat back on his head, then placed his hands
around her waist. "Here, let me help you."

Before she knew what he was about, he kissed her
on the cheek, then set her up on the tailgate and tipped
his hat. "Good night, Miss Millie."

With her fingers gently touching the spot he'd
kissed, Millie peeked around the side of the wagon and
stared after the retreating wagon master until he was out
of sight.

"Millie, come to bed. We've got to start early
tomorrow," Emily whispered from inside.

Millie blinked, then shivered. She got to her feet and
climbed slowly inside, pulling the tailgate closed and
tying the covering behind her. She sat on the edge of the
bed for several minutes staring at nothing.

Emily reached over and shook Millie's shoulder
gently. "Millie? Are you all right?"

"Huh? Oh, yes," she answered with a deep sigh.

"Millie, what is wrong with you? Are you ill?"

Millie sighed again, then shivered, though not from
the cold. She slid off the bed onto the floor before folding
her arms on the mattress and resting her chin on the back
of her hands. "Oh, Emily, he—he kissed me," she
whispered.

"He what?"

"He really did. Right here," she said, tapping her
cheek. "I can still feel it."

Emily sat up suddenly, "That's wonderful! We'll
have to have a big party!"

Alarm bells went off in Millie's head as she sat up
suddenly. "A party? Whatever for?"

"To celebrate your engagement, of course. Just

think, you're the first one of us to become engaged."

"Engaged? What are you talking about? I'm not engaged!"

"But—but you must be. A lady doesn't kiss a man unless they're engaged."

"Well, I'm not! And I didn't kiss him. He kissed me. Emily Peterson, don't you dare tell a living soul about this. It—it was just a brotherly peck on the cheek." *Yes, that was it, just a brotherly peck. Surely, he hadn't meant any more than that.* "You know how I feel about getting married again."

Emily stared openmouthed at Millie.

"Oh, for heaven's sake, Emily. The way you're carrying on, you'd think the man just dragged me into the woods and had his way with me."

"Millie!"

"Well…"

Chapter Twenty-Four

Blake took the bucket of water from Millie. "Here, let me help you with that, Miss Millie."

Millie struggled to hold her temper. He'd been doing this for over a week. Ever since they left the Indians, Blake Donovan had been constantly under foot. She could hear snickers from the others every time he came near. He was making a spectacle of her, and it had to stop.

She followed him toward the creek. As soon as they were out of sight of the wagons, she snatched the bucket before he could refill it. "Mr. Donovan, this is very thoughtful. I know you began being helpful because I hurt my hand by socking that odious soldier for mistreating Little Feather, but," she wiggled her thumb, "it's well now. It's time we both started taking care of our own chores."

She stopped him as he started to say something, "Besides," she continued, lowering her voice, "it's giving the ladies the wrong impression. They're saying you're courting me."

He thumbed his hat back and grinned—the grin that Emily said would melt any lady's bones...the grin Millie vowed wouldn't affect her one whit. "Well, what's wrong with that?"

Millie gasped. "You mean you are? Courting me?" When he nodded, she dropped the bucket and stumbled back against a scrub tree growing beside the water. "You can't...I mean...I never agreed to this."

"You let me kiss you. What did you expect me to do?"

"I did no such thing. Kissing me was all your idea. I had nothing to do with it."

"Well, you didn't stop me."

"You never asked my permission. How did I know what you were planning?"

He glared at her, his hands now resting on his hips. "Mrs. Watts, the whole purpose of this trip to the valley is to take husbands."

Millie swallowed several times. She'd been afraid this would happen. Contract or not, they were going to insist she marry at the end of the trip. She'd have to be very careful how she responded to this. He still had the power to put her off the train. "Well, I'm...I'm not ready. And we're not in the valley yet. It's...it's not fair to the others. They don't have anyone to court them. You...you can't play favorites."

He snatched his hat off, slammed it against his leg a couple of times, then jammed it back onto his head. "What's the use?" He glared at her. "We leave in ten minutes, lady. You'd better be ready." He turned on his heel and purposefully strode back to the wagons.

Millie watched him go, then slid to sit on the ground. Her heart beat against her chest like a wild bird trying to escape a cage. She couldn't believe it. He actually thought she'd welcome his advances. The last thing she wanted was a husband. And never again would she place her life in the hands of someone with as volatile a temper as Blake Donovan's. She could take care of herself. She didn't want a man, especially not that one.

"Millie…Millie! Come on. We're leaving."

Millie looked up at Emily, who waved frantically from the edge of the trees. Millie sighed and reached for the water bucket. It wasn't there. She looked all around, then stamped her foot. *He* must have taken it. Blake Donovan was incorrigible. Millie hurried up the creek bank toward the wagon. Maybe she could sell him to some lonely Indian woman.

Millie walked alongside her wagon. As the day progressed, different groups of women joined her, chattering about nothing in particular, then left giggling. Drat Blake Donovan. He had every woman on the wagon train speculating about his intentions, or hers. Well, Aunt Lavinia used to say, "The more fuss you raise about something, the more people will harp on it." Fine. She wouldn't make any fuss where Blake Donovan was concerned. She'd merely pretend he didn't exist. Eventually, they'd all get tired and move on to some other subject. She hoped.

****

Emily finished smoothing the wrinkles from her bed in the wagon. Millie had been acting so withdrawn since she and Mr. Donovan had gone to the creek last week. "Millie, is something wrong?"

Millie pulled on her other boot. So far, she'd managed to avoid Emily's questions where Mr. Donovan was concerned. But it was getting harder. She jumped to her feet and grabbed her jacket. "Wrong? No, nothing except it's getting colder. I certainly hope it doesn't start snowing before we get to the valley. Let's hurry and get breakfast so we can get going."

Emily picked up her coat and followed Millie outside. "That's not what I meant, and you know it.

What's happened between you and Mr. Donovan? You haven't said two words to him in a week."

As soon as the coffeepot was filled and put on to boil, Millie looked at Emily. "That's silly. I've talked to him as much as anyone else has." At her friend's unladylike snort, Millie sighed. "Emily, I keep telling you, there's nothing between Mr. Donovan and myself. We are just friends, like you and he are."

Emily shook her head and stirred the vegetable soup left over from last evening. Millie heard her friend mumbling to herself as she worked on breakfast. Well, she couldn't help it if Emily was disappointed. As much as she and John Eagle had tried, there was nothing between Mr. Donovan and herself, and there never would be. The women on this wagon train would just have to pick someone else to match him up with.

Honey, loudly announcing her arrival, shoved her big orange bill into her owner's pocket. Millie laughed and shoved the big bird's head out of the way. "Hey, you big clown, where have you been?"

She stooped down and hugged her pet. "I certainly could use an egg right now. Do you think you could help me out? I want to make a cake tonight for supper."

The bird looked up and honked at Millie. "Well, I'd appreciate anything you can do between now and the time we stop tonight."

"Miss Millie?"

Millie turned in time to see Ezra hurrying in her direction with an armload of protesting bird. She got up and hurried toward him.

"Mr. Oats, where in the world did you get that wild goose?" she demanded. It was a beautiful beast, but not a bit happy at being toted around like a sack of meal.

He dodged a snapping beak, while fighting to hold on to the struggling goose. "I seen this here bird tangle with a hawk. That hawk musta been mighty hungry to attack something this size, but when they come down, I chased the other guy away. This here bird's got a broken wing. Probably won't never be able to fly very far again."

Millie tried to stroke the bird's neck and back. "Poor thing. What are you going to do with it?"

"I figgered maybe yer goose there might like a gentlemen friend."

Millie stared at Ezra in surprise. "Why, that's very thoughtful of you, Mr. Oats. Let's see if we can do something about its broken wing."

"Yes, ma'am. Then I'll rig another nestin' box on the side of your wagon. Who knows, maybe before long Donovan'll have a whole passel of little Honeys a-chasin' him."

Millie laughed at the thought. "Wouldn't that be something!" But surely they'd reach their destination before then.

She and Ezra watched as Honey got acquainted with her new roommate. It wasn't long before Honey was waddling throughout the camp, the wounded gander in her wake.

Blake strode to the fire, cup in hand. He stopped short as Honey stretched her wings and hissed at him. Then, mouth open, watched as the goose, followed by a bandaged gander, waddled off.

"What was that?"

Ezra snickered. "That, my boy, was Miss Honey, warning you that Homer had better *not* be your early Thanksgiving dinner."

"Homer?"

Ezra looked at Millie, who shrugged. "Homer," she said.

"Well, I'll be dam-…danged," Blake said, watching Honey, who was obviously showing her new beau around. "Where'd *Homer* come from?"

He listened while Ezra explained about finding the wounded gander, then slapped the old cowboy on the back. "Oats, the next town we come to, I owe you a drink. Hell, if this keeps that damned *duck* off my back, I'll buy you the whole bottle!"

Millie handed Ezra a cup of coffee, then turned her face into the wind and took a deep breath. It was like breathing in pure snow. She drew her shawl closer about her shoulders. "Mr. Oats, do you think it will snow before we get to the valley?"

Ezra shook his shaggy head. "Don't know, Missy. It could. Smells like it might. This high up and far north, it snows early. But maybe it won't. We're nearly there. John Eagle says it's only about two more weeks, if the weather holds."

"That close?" Millie grinned. "I'll pass the word."

****

Blake noticed the buzz of excitement among the women. He stopped Thunder beside Ben. "What's going on back there?"

"Don't know, but we haven't made such good time in several days. Maybe they can smell the snow in the air."

"Maybe." Blake looked upward and took a deep breath. He could almost touch the snow, its smell was so strong. "Sure hope it holds off for a week or so." He looked back at the women again. Naw, they looked too happy to be expecting snow.

He turned Thunder around. "Better find out."

He'd dismounted by the group of women before he realized one of them was Millie. He nodded to Emily, but though his gaze lingered a moment on Millie, he addressed the older woman in the group. "Good afternoon, Miss Hannah. What's all the excitement about?"

"Mr. Donovan, is it true we're within two weeks of our destination?"

He shook his head. It never ceased to amaze him how fast word traveled. "Yes, and no, ma'am. Under normal weather conditions, yes. But it looks like we might be having snow any day now. If that happens, it could be a week before we can travel on. So far, we've made good time. Let's keep it up and get as far along as possible. There's a good chance the storm will pass us by." He didn't believe that for a minute, but no use worrying the ladies until necessary.

Miss Hannah tugged her coat closer, then glanced heavenward. "I certainly hope you're right. Would you care to join us for supper?"

He glanced at Millie. She didn't look too pleased at the invite. He certainly wasn't going to force his attention on the woman. "No, thank you, ma'am. Reb is cooking something special for us guys tonight." He leaned close and grinned. "I certainly hope I don't live to regret turning down your kind invitation, though."

"So do I, Mr. Donovan."

Blake tipped his hat, gazed a moment more at Millie, then mounted and rode on. Damn. More and more every day he regretted the death of Otto Watts. He'd like to kill the man himself, for the way he'd treated Millie. Because of that bastard, she was afraid to let a man get close.

Millie watched Blake ride off. What was wrong with her? Why did she suddenly feel so depressed at his leaving? Men were nothing but trouble. Women were possessions to them, and she was never going to be a possession again.

"Millie? Millie Watts, what's the matter with you?" Miss Hannah demanded.

Millie started. "What? Oh, I'm sorry. I guess my mind was wandering. What did you say?"

"I said we need to double our efforts and pray that this storm passes."

She nodded. "Yes, ma'am. I think you're right." Millie's teeth chattered as she hurriedly climbed into the back of her wagon and exchanged her shawl for a real coat. It was amazing, even frightening, how quickly the weather changed in this country. At home it usually worked up to being this cold. She folded her discarded wrap and put it neatly in her trunk, then jumped from the wagon and took her turn at driving.

Cindy came breathlessly abreast of Millie. "What are you so out of breath for?" Millie asked.

As soon as she could speak, Cindy pointed to the west. "I just saw a herd of something that looked like deer. But I don't think that's what they were. Anyway, they had antlers. I thought maybe you'd get us one."

Millie grinned. "You wouldn't by any chance be hoping to go along, would you?"

The girl's eyes widened in mock surprise. "No, of course not. But if you think you'll need some help, I guess I could lend a hand."

Millie snapped the reins. She could just taste one of Emily's pot roasts. And Cindy was a pretty good hunting partner. She was a better than average shot and could skin the kill as quickly as Millie could. She'd be even better if her mother would allow her to practice more often. Ever since the girl's near brush with being an Indian's wife, Angie seemed reluctant to let Cindy out of her sight. "Well, I would, but that herd will probably be gone by the time we manage to get horses—"

Cindy grinned. "Strange you should mention that. There seem to be a pair of saddled horses and two pack animals tied to the back of your wagon."

Millie looked toward the back. "Well, imagine that. And I do believe one of them is the mare I always ride. I wonder how they got there."

"It would be a shame to let someone's thoughtfulness go to waste."

Millie struggled to keep a straight face. She snapped her whip over the head of the far ox. "It surely would, but someone has to drive these lazy beasts. I guess we'll have to make it another time."

From the corner of her eye, Millie saw Cindy motion to someone from behind them. "Hi, y'all. Isn't it a beautiful morning?" Emily said as she winked at Cindy. "On chilly days like this, I start dreaming about cooking all sorts of tasty treats. Wouldn't a hot vegetable beef soup taste good tonight?"

"It sure would," Millie agreed. "But where would one get the beef?"

"Well, it wouldn't have to be beef. Deer, antelope, or any type of meat would do as well."

Millie grinned. These two had been conspiring behind her back, as if they needed to. She loved to hunt. "You know, that does sound good. I could use some soup to warm me up about now. Let me know when it's ready."

Millie could hardly contain her mirth. Emily and Cindy exchanged looks, and then Emily reached over and snatched the reins from Millie's hands. "Give me those. Now you get on that horse and get me a piece of meat for my soup, or I just might use jerky."

"No!" Millie gasped in horror. "Not jerky soup!" She snatched her rifle and hurried for the horses. "I've got to save us all from that fate."

Millie and Cindy, each leading a pack animal, had just topped a hill and ridden out of sight of the wagons when they heard the pounding of hoofs coming from the north. They both swung their horses around and held their rifles at the ready while waiting to see who was trying to intercept them.

They didn't have long to wait. The rider topped the hill, pulled his horse to a slow walk, and raised his hands.

"Mr. Donovan," Cindy exclaimed as both women lowered their weapons. "What are you doing out here?"

He lowered his hands, giving Millie a cautious glance. "That's exactly what I came to ask you two." He spoke to Cindy, but glowered at Millie.

"We came to get some fresh meat," the girl answered. "If it snows, we might need it."

Millie grasped the saddle horn to keep her hands from trembling. Her heart raced like a herd of frightened antelopes. This man made her feel like this every time he came near lately. She couldn't understand it. She did know, though, that if he stayed with them, she probably wouldn't be able to hit a thing.

He nodded. "Yeah, we thought the same thing. Guess we should combine our forces and see what we can do."

"We?" Millie managed to ask.

"Yeah, John Eagle is scouting a herd of antelope just over that ridge. I take it that's where you two were headed."

Millie nodded. That's what she was afraid of. Now they'd have this man watching their every move. The way her whole body shook, her shots wouldn't come within a country mile of any game.

Cindy seemed totally enchanted with the prospect. As they topped another rise, John Eagle was kneeling behind a group of boulders. They rode as quietly as possible and dismounted beside him as he gave them his count of about twenty animals in the herd. After a quick conference, each selected their prey and, on signal, fired. When the smoke cleared, they'd gotten seven.

Cindy was beside herself. It didn't bother her that everyone got two to her one. "John Eagle, will you teach me to cure the hide?"

"Sure, but what do you plan to do with it?"

"I…I don't know. I just want to keep it."

He ran his hand through the coat. "It's already nice and thick. Tell you what. I'll not only teach you to cure it, I'll also teach you how to make something useful from it."

"Hey, Johnny," Blake said in a low voice, "we've got company."

Millie turned and saw three mounted Indians not ten yards from them. Her heart jumped into her throat several times. "What do you suppose they want?" she whispered.

Blake shook his head. "Us, the kill, both maybe. Don't move, ladies."

John Eagle was already heading toward the

uninvited visitors. He made the sign of peace, but the Indians weren't inclined to be friendly. Their tone was angry as they conversed with John Eagle.

Millie, with Cindy close at her side, eased closer to Blake Donovan. "Can you understand what they're saying?"

He shook his head. "I don't speak their lingo. We'll have to wait for Johnny."

After several minutes, John Eagle returned. He squatted down beside his cousin. Blake calmly plucked a blade of grass and nibbled on the end. "What's the problem?"

"They're madder'n hell. Seems our 'firesticks' chased off the herd before they could make a kill. Now their children will go to bed hungry tonight."

Millie and Cindy kept an eye on the Indians. "What do they want?" Cindy asked when John Eagle and Blake stood up.

"I'm not sure. Each one seems to have his eye on something different. The big one on the paint pony was looking at the kill. The one in the middle was nearly drooling over you ladies, and the smaller one seems to like our mounts."

"Oh, no," Cindy exclaimed in alarm. "I'll...I'll kill 'em before I let them take me."

"Quiet, girl," Blake ordered. "Remember what I told you last time. Don't let them see you're scared. We're four against three. That's pretty good odds to start with. Now, what d'you say we offer them three of our kill? We probably can't use all seven before the meat goes bad."

John Eagle nodded. "You ladies agree?"

Millie nodded. "All right," Cindy agreed reluctantly, "but..."

"But what?" Blake prompted.

Cindy glanced over her shoulder at her downed antelope. "Nothing," she whispered, hanging her head.

Millie put her arm around the girl. "Surely they don't have to have any particular ones. Yours is rather small compared to several of the others."

John Eagle got up. "It's agreed, then. I'll offer them three and…" he smiled at Cindy, "…steer them toward the ones over yonder." The girl grinned back.

When John Eagle returned, the Indians walked behind him. The one with the paint pony went straight to Cindy's kill. She hurried over beside the dead animal. "No." When the Indian looked hard at her, she bit her lip and stood silently. He picked up the animal's head by the horns, then ran his fingers through the thick fur. He looked at her and nodded his approval.

He said something to her, but when Cindy shook her head and shrugged, indicating she didn't understand, he put his foot forward. Pointing to his moccasins, showed her the fur lining on the inside of the footwear.

John Eagle placed a hand on her shoulder. "He says it was a nice kill. And that the fur is already getting thick. It would make warm boots for the winter."

Cindy grinned and nodded her thanks. Then the Indian walked to the next downed animal. This he picked up and slung over his horse. His companions followed his example. Their leader nodded to John Eagle and the three Indians left. Blake whistled. "That was close. Let's get out of here before someone else wants to horn in on our meat."

They loaded up and headed back to the wagon train. Angie hurried up to Cindy before the horses were even stopped.

"Where have you been?" she demanded. "I've been worried sick."

"Ah, Ma, I just went hunting with Millie. Look, we got fresh meat. I shot this one myself. Isn't it pretty?"

Angie opened her mouth to berate her daughter further, but Miss Hannah laid a restraining hand on the woman's arm. "May I see you a minute, please, Angie?"

She led the agitated mother away from the others. "Angie, you're going to have to allow the girl to breathe. I know things out here are frightening sometimes, but we all have to learn to survive, and if you expect Cindy to live a full and happy life, you have to allow her to learn. She's the pet of the whole train. No one's going to let anything happen to her."

Angie started to protest, then evidently thought better of it. "I know. But she's all I have left. I nearly have heart failure every time she gets out of my sight."

Miss Hannah petted the woman's hand. "I know you do, dear, but we'll have to work on that."

Ben rode in and pulled up beside the small group. "Hey, looks like good camping about a mile or so ahead. There are caves where we can wait out the coming snowstorm."

Blake nodded. "Sounds good. Mount up, ladies, and let's see how fast we can get there."

****

Millie lifted the lid on the dutch oven and sniffed. The soup smelled wonderful. They'd camped early, skinned the meat, and distributed it among the wagons. The caves weren't very deep, but with a wagon surrounded with extra canvas as a windbreak in front of each of the two larger ones, they would do in case of snow. Ezra insisted the storm could still miss them, but everyone was prepared in the event he was wrong.

The largest cave wasn't big enough for all of them for any length of time, but it made a nice kitchen. She looked around at the thick walls. It was really rather warm and cozy. The organ sat in the back of the cavern, out of the weather, and the little orchestra was holding its nightly practice session. Millie envied them their talents. Oh, she could play the piano a little, but her talent was by no means near the measure of theirs.

Millie dropped the kettle's top and stared as Reb stumbled toward the fire. His jacket was filthy and his pants were torn. "Reb! What in the world happened to you?"

He set a half-full milk pail down beside her. "This here's the last time I milk that wild cow for you, Miss Millie. It just ain't worth riskin' life and limb for half a pail of milk."

Millie smiled. "Maybe not, but I certainly appreciate it, Reb. In fact, you get the first and biggest helping of dessert tonight."

He tipped his hat. "Thank you, ma'am…I think," he added as he left. She laughed and turned back to her supper preparations. Using the fire not only for warmth but for cooking, the ladies cooked stews and soups, and grilled steaks. Millie sautéed wild onions and chunks of antelope, then added diced potatoes and dried peas she had put on earlier to soak. This was served with a rich cream gravy. Several delicious desserts with thick cream sauce were served to top off the evening. The night continued to get colder. What was left over would definitely be in no danger of spoiling, Millie thought as she covered a pan of peach cobbler.

****

Millie shivered and reached to pull up the quilt. *Where is it?* She opened one eye. Then she opened both eyes. *It's already pulled up and still I'm shivering?* She rolled over, shivered again, then peeked from under the wagon canvas. At first, she thought she was seeing Honey's feathers, but they were a dirty white, at best. This was so white it hurt her eyes. "I don't believe it!"

"Believe what?" Emily mumbled.

"Wake up and look out there," Millie exclaimed holding up the canvas a little more.

"Huh?" Emily finally rose up and looked over Millie's shoulder. "What is that?"

"Snow! I've never seen so much at one time. Come on, let's go out and see how deep it is."

Both women scrambled out of bed and into their clothes. By the time they climbed from the wagon, the others were doing the same. They laughed and chattered. Someone hit Millie in the shoulder with a snowball. She scooped up a large handful and threw it just as Blake Donovan rounded the back of the supply wagon.

He swiped the snow from his face and looked around for the culprit. His gaze fell on Millie. Her gloved hands covered her mouth and most of her face, but he could see her eyes, still wide with horror.

"I'm so sorry, Mr. Donovan. I didn't see you coming," she apologized.

Blake stared at her while pulling on his gloves. "Oh, that's quite all right, Mrs. Watts," he answered as he reached down and scooped up a very large handful of the cold powder.

"Oh, my," Emily whispered. "That's such a wicked gleam in Mr. Donovan's eye."

Millie began backing up, one step at a time. "Now,

Mr. Donovan, I said I was sorry. It was purely an accident, really."

"I'm sure it was, Mrs. Watts." He'd waited a long time for just such a moment as this. Accident or no, he wasn't going to let it pass. He heaved his snowball at her.

Millie squealed and turned to run, only to trip on something just below the snowy surface, and fall. The snowball sailed past her, coming to a stop in the middle of Miss Hannah's chin.

"Ohhh!" The woman wiped the cold snow away and glared at the equally shocked wagon master. She scooped up a handful of snow and slowly molded it into a round firm ball. "Attack a poor old lady, will you!" She advanced upon him as fast as she could under the circumstances.

Blake backed up with each step she advanced. Damn, how could things have turned out so badly? The one chance he had to avenge all the humiliations *Mrs. Jinx* had heaped on him, and look what happened. He just couldn't win.

But he wasn't going to lie down and take it. "Ma'am, if you let that fly, I'll…" A mouthful of snow stopped his threat. Suddenly, the air was thick with white missiles. At first most of them seemed to be aimed at him, but very shortly it seemed to be the women against the men. Finally, it turned into a free-for-all.

Blake ducked and dodged until he was in position to bombard Miss Millie. He was going to get his revenge no matter what. He hit her in the middle of the forehead with his first try and in the front of the neck with the next. She squealed, turned her back, and began frantically wiping the cold stuff from inside her collar.

Blake spent the next several minutes dodging. When

he finally had a new supply of snowballs, he couldn't find his target. Where did she get off to? She didn't seem to be the type who'd run and hide.

Millie dashed around the wagon and came up on the wagon master's blind side. *Now I've got you, Blake Donovan. You've been picking on me for months. Your time has come.* She tapped him on the shoulder. She had intended to taunt him some, but when he turned, he loomed so close, she lost her nerve. The snowball never left her hand as it hit him in the face.

Millie gasped. *Oh, my gosh, that wasn't supposed to happen.* The best thing for her to do was to disappear like she had done when Pa came home drunk. She turned and fled toward her wagon.

She'd run past about six wagons before she realized she was going the wrong direction. The squeals of the others seemed a long way off. She turned to retrace her steps. The carpet of snow muffled her steps, but also those of her pursuer. She dashed right into Blake Donovan's arms. Her gloved fists shoved against his massive chest.

"Running away is very cowardly, Mrs. Watts," he said as he backed her against a wagon. "Not at all what I'd expect from you."

Millie froze in his grasp. There was that wicked gleam in his eye again. She looked around for help. Not a soul was in sight. "Mr. Donovan, release me at once, or I'll scream."

"Oh, really?"

His tone, coupled with the wicked gleam in his eyes, was more than she could bear. Millie opened her mouth to scream, but his lips effectively muffled her cries. Her eyes crossed as she looked at his closed ones. She pushed on his chest as best she could with her arms pinned between them. How dare he take such liberties...

In spite of herself, a warmth spread through her. Instead of pushing against him, her fists opened of their own accord. Her fingers curled around his coat lapels, pulling him closer. The tingle in her toes had nothing to do with the ankle-deep snow they stood in. She closed her eyes and strained to move even closer. She'd never been kissed with such gentleness, nor held so firmly yet with such tenderness. Her whole body trembled as she returned his kiss.

"Well, 'scuse me!"

Blake and Millie jumped apart. Scalding water wouldn't have affected them more than Ezra Oats' voice.

Millie's hand flew to her mouth. She looked from Blake to Ezra, and back to Blake. With a stifled sob, she fled toward her wagon.

Oats spit a stream of tobacco juice into the snow. "Well, at least this was more pri-vate, young feller. Sorry I spoiled it fer ya."

Blake braced himself against the wagon and watched Millie flee. "So am I, old man. So am I." He was breathing hard. His lower clothing was uncomfortably tight. How could *Mrs. Jinx* affect him like that? As soon as she was out of sight, his unseeing gaze moved to the old cowboy beside him.

The knowing look on the old codger's face rubbed him the wrong way immediately. "Listen, Oats, you say anything about this, and I'll leave you staked out over an ant hill somewhere," he threatened. "You got that?"

Ezra grinned and rubbed the spot on his chest where Blake had been punching with his finger. "Yeah, I got it, son, I shore do."

Blake stomped off. "Damned old coot'll keep his mouth shut just as long as it takes him to find someone to tell," he mumbled. How had he let this happen? He scooped up a handful of snow and rubbed it over his own face. He'd better find Miss Millie and set things right—unless, of course, she didn't shoot him on sight.

Chapter Twenty-Five

Millie ran blindly, tears of humiliation and confusion clouding her vision. She passed the wagons, where the snowball fight was still in progress. The last thing she needed was to encounter Emily or, heaven forbid, Miss Hannah. All she wanted was to be alone, but how could she do that on a wagon train of fifty women?

Finally, out of breath, she stopped at the face of the cliffs. Before her was one of the smaller unused caves. She ducked her head and hurried in. It wasn't big but was large enough to sit in without being seen.

Millie dropped to the floor and rested her head on her knees. The tears came in torrents. How could he have done that to her? Why would he kiss her so intimately when he didn't care for her? Did he think she had no feelings? Or maybe, because she'd been married, he thought she'd be one of those loose hussies?

She wiped her cheeks angrily. Well, he could just think again. The more she thought about it, the madder she got. How *dare* he kiss her like that! How dare he kiss her at all?

He'd probably defend his reprehensible conduct by pointing out that she'd kissed him back. She certainly wouldn't have if he hadn't... Kissed him back? Oh, Lord, did she ever kiss him back! Who could blame him for thinking her a hussy? She'd never kissed a man like that in her life! She'd never been *kissed* like that in her life, for that matter.

"Ohhh," she moaned. Her body trembled and ached at the mere thought of that kiss. If Emily wanted to throw them an engagement party after his friendly peck on the cheek, she'd have them wedded and bedded for this one. The tears cascaded down her cheeks again. What was she going to do? There was no way to avoid the man. They saw each other every day. He was the wagon master. And she was the appointed captain, for heaven's sake.

Millie didn't know how long she sat there crying. She had no tears left by the time she realized she was shivering from the cold. Her legs ached as she got up, and she wasn't certain she still had any toes. Pulling her coat close, she slowly left the cave.

After finally making her way back to her wagon, she climbed inside. Most of the women were about their regular chores. She rummaged through her trunk until she found some dry woolen socks. She'd just have to avoid Blake Donovan whenever possible, and otherwise she'd act as if nothing had happened. They were nearly to their destination. Once there, it should be relatively easy to have nothing to do with the man.

She pulled on her socks, then froze as voices from outside the wagon reached her.

"Good morning, Mr. Donovan."

"Good morning, Miss Emily. Have you seen Miss Millie?"

"No, not for a while. Maybe she's in the wagon."

"Would you check, please? I need to speak to her."

As soon as Emily climbed in, Millie met her with a finger over her lips. "Don't tell him I'm here," she whispered. The expression on Emily's face left no doubt what she thought of Millie's sanity. Emily started to protest, but Millie shook her head. "Please," she mouthed.

Finally, Emily nodded and poked her head back out. "I'm sorry, Mr. Donovan. Can I give her a message when I see her?"

"No. No, I'll find her myself. Thanks."

As soon as he'd left, Emily pulled her head back inside and glared at Millie. "I can't believe you had me lie like that. What in the world is the matter with you? Are you ill?"

Didn't she just wish. Millie shook her head. "No, but I have a lot of things to do and just don't have time to socialize." She pulled on her boots, grabbed her coat, and made a hasty exit before Emily could ask any more questions.

****

Blake watched as Millie dished up second helpings of her peach cobbler. For the last two days, she'd managed to keep herself surrounded by a gaggle of chattering females. He hadn't managed to say a word to her in private. From the glare she gave him when he held out his plate for seconds, he wouldn't get to speak to her now either.

It was almost dark when Emily refilled Blake's coffee cup. It had been a long, cold day, any way he looked at it. The weather was clearing outside, at least. They'd be on their way in the morning. Maybe things would thaw between him and Miss Millie in a day or two.

He'd dreamed about that kiss for the last two nights and didn't have any reason to believe tonight would be any different. When he'd chased her during the snow war, he'd only intended to pelt her with a few snowballs. He never intended to get so personal. And personal it was. Lordy, how that woman could kiss! He still ached.

He watched Millie chatting with her friends. There didn't seem to be anything she couldn't do. She got along with everyone, was an excellent shot, a wonderful cook, a hard worker, and promised to be an excellent bed partner, if that kiss was any indication. Yes, more and more, he was rethinking his reluctance to take a wife. This woman had overcome all his objections to her coming on this trip, and proved to be quite an asset…most of the time. Well, they still had a couple of weeks' travel ahead of them. She couldn't stay chaperoned forever.

****

Millie stepped from the wagon and stretched. It was a beautiful morning. They'd been camped for six days while the snow melted and the ground dried. Hopefully, they'd be on their way this morning. At the sound of a saddle creaking, she turned.

"Good morning, Miss Millie."

Millie stiffened. She returned his greeting as curtly as possible. "Good morning, Mr. Donovan." At least it was.

"Brr, it's cold out," he muttered.

"I beg your pardon? Did you say something?"

"Yes, ma'am, I said it was a beautiful morning. Seems pretty dry. We'll pull out as soon after breakfast as you ladies can be ready."

"Thank you. I'll pass the word." She turned and headed toward the woods in the opposite direction from him. Surely there would be less time for the man to bother her if they were traveling. And the sooner they reached the valley, the sooner she could get on with her life.

She and Emily had spent the last six days finalizing their plans to open a restaurant once they were settled in the valley. They'd collected as many recipes from the other women as they thought they could use. There was absolutely no time in her life for a man.

****

Horace shoved back his dirty, battered hat and squinted against the rising sun. "Well, I'll be!" He watched for several minutes as the camp below came alive with women. "Gus! Gus, wake up. Ye gotta see this." He poked at his sleeping partner with his boot. Gus snored loud enough to wake a hibernating bear. "Come on, Gus. It's mornin'. This ain't no time to sleep."

Gus snorted loudly a couple more times before opening one eye. His head ached and his mouth felt dry as a desert after a sandstorm. He grabbed the offending foot and yanked its owner off the rock he was perched on. With a yelp, Horace hit the ground.

"Goldarnit, Gus. What'd ye go an' do that fer? They mighta heared us."

"Horace, the next time you poke me with them dirty boots, I jest might go an' shoot yer foot off." He cocked his head, looking at Horace through one eye. Suddenly he opened both eyes. "They? They who?"

Horace scrambled back up on his perch and peeked down the other side. "They didn't hear us. Come on, ye gotta see this."

Grumbling, Gus climbed up beside his companion to take a look-see. "Well, I'll be damned. Look at all them purty-colored wagons. And women!" He looked closer. "Why, they's honest to gawd white women."

"That's what I was a-tryin' to tell ya. Looks like old Moose wasn't a-funnin' us after all. He said they's going to some valley up here to be wives. And to men they's never even seed afore."

They'd been so drunk when they camped the night before, they hadn't looked to see if anyone else was in the area. Gus closed his eyes, shook his head to clear his drink-fogged vision, then looked again. After watching a while, they both slid down to sit with their backs to the rock and grinned. "Well, iffen it's men they wants, I don't see why we can't oblige a couple of 'em."

Horace nodded and grinned, showing all three of his remaining front teeth. "See? Didn't I tell ya our luck would change'?"

"Yeah, yeah. Now shut up an' let me think." Gus popped the cork from a jug and took a long pull, then set it on his thigh, not bothering to share with Horace. He scratched his tangled red beard, then scratched his personals. "Maybe we otta ride in there about suppertime tonight and—"

"No, no, 'member Moose saying they wouldn't share? Even run him and his two pards off. We'll hev ta think of another way." He picked up his own jug and the men spent the next hour drinking and watching the activity below.

Gus rose up and peeked at the wagon camp. "Hey, they's pulling out. Come on, Horace, we can't let 'em get away. One a them purty little things is my future woman."

****

Blake mounted Thunder, then looked over his shoulder. Everyone seemed ready. He waved his hat in a circle over his head and signaled to pull out.

Millie snapped the reins against her oxen's rumps and led the others toward their future home. She was as excited as everyone else about being so close. However, as she walked beside the wagon, she began to realize what she'd done. Her apprehension grew as she thought of all the things that could go wrong. Suppose her cafe wasn't a success. What if they insisted she take a husband? What if she just plain didn't like it there? She was alone out here, halfway across the world from any known civilization. She rubbed her throbbing temples. Whatever had possessed her to do this thing? Or any of them, for that matter?

Millie didn't hear Mr. Donovan until he was right at her elbow. "Good morning, Miss Millie."

She squealed and jumped. She would have fallen if he hadn't caught her arm. "Thank you," she said curtly as she disengaged herself from his grasp. His touch did strange things to her insides. "I…I didn't hear you come up."

He smiled. "No, I guess you didn't. I've been walking beside you for several minutes."

They walked silently onward. Millie adjusted the reins, snapped them against one ox's rump and then another. She looked around. Where were all the women when she needed them? Why didn't the man go away? Surely he could tell she wasn't interested in talking to him.

Blake cleared his throat. "Miss Millie, about that kiss in the snow the other day."

"I don't care to discuss it, Mr. Donovan. Please leave me to my work."

"I can't do that." He quickened his step to keep up with her when she tried to move away. "I'm truly sorry—"

"What!" She stopped in her tracks.

"No, no. Not about the kiss. No man could be sorry about that. It was about the best kiss I've ever had," he hastened to explain.

"Then exactly what are you sorry about?" she demanded. Suddenly the moving wagon took up the slack in the reins and jerked her forward.

Blake heaved a sigh of relief and hurried to catch up with her. "What I was trying to say is that…well, we spent most of this trip snapping at each other and were just beginning to become friends. That's what I'm sorry about."

"Oh, I see. You're sorry that we were just beginning to be friends. I must say you certainly found a unique way to stop it."

Blake flung his arms up and let them fall, slapping his hands against his legs in exasperation. This was not going the way it was supposed to. She twisted everything he'd rehearsed. "No, I'm sorry this all happened to spoil our budding friendship. I don't want to spend the rest of my life snapping at you. And the valley isn't so large that we can avoid seeing each other most every day." He reached down, plucked a blade of grass, and worried with it as they walked. "What I'm trying to say," he said softly, "is that I'd like us to start over."

After a rather long silence, Millie nodded. "We'll see."

Blake nodded. That was better than a flat-out no. They walked for several minutes without speaking, until Blake noticed her worried frown. "Is something wrong, Miss Millie?"

"No, not really. Well, it's just that…" She took a deep breath and began again. "I suddenly realized… I mean… We don't know anything about any of the men we're expected to marry. Or very much about this valley we're to spend the rest of our lives in."

"Ah, getting jittery. Well, what would you like to know?"

What? Nothing. Everything. What she really wanted was a guarantee that she hadn't made a mistake. That she'd be happy way out here. But of course that was impossible. "Will there be a place for us to live when we get there?"

He pulled his hat low over his eyes to block out the sun. "It's customary for a woman to live with her husband."

"I know that," she snapped, then took a deep breath. "What I mean is, they *will* give us time to get to know them before they insist we choose, won't they? Surely they aren't expecting us to travel clear across the world and then just…just jump into bed with the first one who steps up?"

"No, ma'am."

She stopped and gasped. "No! No what? No, they won't allow us time…?"

He placed his hand on her arm. "Easy, Miss Millie. You're working yourself into a snit when there's no need."

Millie bit her bottom lip to keep it from trembling. What was wrong with her? She'd faced Indians, outlaws, even faced down her drunken pa. Now she was ready to fall apart at the mere prospect of reaching her destination. "I'm sorry. It's just that I was so intent on getting away from Pa that…I guess I'm just beginning to realize what lengths I've gone to, to gain my freedom."

"I think I understand…"

"No, you don't," Millie snapped, brushing a stray

tear from her cheek. "In all my life I've never known but one man who wasn't abusive. Now all of a sudden I'm expected to meekly allow a strange man to take over my very life. Well, I won't do it! I can't."

Blake watched the tears roll down her cheeks. She was frightened out of her wits over a maybe. "What makes you think the man you marry won't be like that one good man you knew?"

She wiped the tears on her jacket sleeve. "Because he was only one out of many bad ones. There just aren't many like Uncle James."

Blake bit back a curse. He might not be a saint like this Uncle James, but he sure as hell wasn't the wife-beating bastard Otto Watts was. It would take time, but he'd prove it to her. "Well, let's take a look at some of the men in the valley. There's Ed Hogan, but of course Miss Hannah already knows how to handle him." He grinned, and was encouraged to see the twitch of a smile on her face. "The men have a little side bet going as to who will finally pair off with whom."

Millie jerked her head around to glare at him. "You're joking! How could you?"

He shrugged. "We know the men, and as we got to know you ladies, it was only natural to wonder who'd end up with whom. We didn't mean any disrespect."

Millie sniffled and shook her head. "Of course not. I'm sorry, I don't know what's gotten into me today." She took a deep breath. They walked quietly again for a while. Finally, she glanced at him and sighed. "All right, you win. Who have you paired off so far?"

He'd wondered how long it'd take for curiosity to get the better of her. "Well, there's Miss Cora. Ben swears she'll be perfect for Reverend McCoy."

Millie nodded. "She'd be good to him, I'm sure." She'd overheard Cora tell Ben about her past and her former intention to marry a preacher. "Who else?"

Blake chuckled. "I don't guess it's a surprise to anyone that Oats is rather sweet on Miss Elsa. Then there's…"

She began to relax as he named each woman on the wagon train and explained who they'd chosen as her mate and why. They all sounded like fine men. Maybe she was being silly.

"And what about me? Have you chosen someone for me, too?" Millie couldn't believe she'd asked such a thing. She wanted to know and yet she didn't.

Blake stopped dead in his tracks. *Lord, if she was mad over one little kiss, I'd hate to think what her humor would be if she knew the men and a good many of the ladies have staked a claim on her as my woman.*

He shook his head. "I don't think I'd better answer that. I expect you to keep what I've said just between you and me until we see what happens. As for telling you about yourself, I think we'd best just let nature take its course, so to speak."

Chapter Twenty-Six

Millie glanced over her shoulder as Blake mounted Thunder, who'd been dutifully following behind his master, and made a hasty escape.

Just like a man, always running off when there's work to be done…or questions they don't want to answer. Well, she'd most certainly not let a group of cowboys pick her next husband just so they could win a bet. This time, *if* there was a "this time," she fully intended to do the selecting herself.

****

Horace and Gus sat on their horses, watching from the woods as the wagons prepared for the night. "How ye figger we otta do this, Gus?"

"I don't know. Maybe we otta go down and ask the man fer a couple of 'em first."

Horace shook his head. "Moose said he tried that. Them men wouldn't share."

Gus scratched under his beard thoughtfully. "Yeah, ye might be right. Guess I wouldn't share iffen they was mine, neither. How-some-ever, I think we otta give it a try. That-a-way we can get a good look at them womens and take our pick. Then, if we has to, we can wait 'til they's all asleep and jest go down there and he'p ourselves."

"Yeah, I think I like that idee," Horace agreed.

They rode toward the camp shortly before supper.

"Hello the camp. We's friendly. Can we warm ourselves at yer far?"

Blake glanced at John Eagle, who shrugged, then stood and looked in the direction the call came from. "Yeah, just keep your hands away from your guns."

Two men rode in slowly, hands resting on their saddle horns. "Howdy. We seen ye earlier from the ridge. Hoped ye'd have a spare cup o' coffee. We been out for nigh on to a week now."

"Sure," Blake said. "Step down. We just made a fresh pot."

The men dismounted, then pulled their cups from their possibles bags before heading for the large black coffeepot. After Ezra filled each cup, they took seats near Blake.

Whew, Blake thought as they sat upwind of him. It was obvious these men were complete strangers to soap and water—all summer and last winter too, from the smell of them.

"I'm Gus Scruggs. This here's Horace. You be Donovan?"

Blake raised a brow in surprise, but nodded. "How'd you know?"

"Oh jest 'bout ever'body in these here parts knows about you bringing these here purty-colored wagons full of womens all the way from back east to be brides." He shook his head. "Boy, some men has all the luck. All those months alone with all that many womens. How many ye got, all tol'?"

Blake wasn't too pleased to hear word of their coming was being heralded throughout the territory. They'd have every scruffy varmint within a thousand miles overrunning their valley. "Oh, about fifty," he answered. "But I'm not the only man on the train."

"Well, 'course not. Them little things couldn't make this trip without a man's he'p. Horace and me, we ain't got no womens to tend us, and we thought we'd see about gettin' a couple of yourn. We'uns 're plum hungry fer a good white woman."

Blake shook his head. "Sorry, can't oblige. These women are all spoken for. Besides, we promised they'd get to do the choosing."

"Well, that's fine with us. Just trot 'em out and let 'em see what fine specimens we is."

Blake shook his head. "Can't do that. The men we work for paid us to bring these women out here, and they have the right to first pick."

Gus squinted at Blake. "Ye mean yer selling these here little things?"

"No, of course not."

"Then bring 'em on. They's a right to see their choices."

John Eagle squatted down and whispered in Blake's ear. "Play along with them. This oughta be good."

Blake nodded just as Cindy walked by on her way back to her own wagon. "Hey, missy," Gus called. "Tell some of them purdy little ladies to come up here. They's two mighty fine prospects wantin' wives."

Cindy's eyes widened in obvious horror. She backed away, swallowed, and hurried toward the other wagons. In a few minutes several women, armed with rifles stepped into the firelight.

"I hear there are some fine prospects looking for wives," Miss Hannah said.

Gus stood. He scratched his belly and eyed Miss Hannah for a long minute. "Yes, ma'am, that's us, but we warn't lookin' for anyone so long in the tooth as ye are, meanin' no disrespect, ma'am."

Miss Hannah glanced at Blake, who shrugged, then back to the men. "Oh? Just what did you have in mind?"

Gus looked at each of the ladies gathered around Miss Hannah, then pointed at Millie. "Well, that there little yeller-haired gal will do nicely fer me."

"Now just a minute." Blake started to get up, but John Eagle placed a restraining hand on his shoulder.

"Hold on, Blake," he muttered. "These men expect some poor helpless little things. Give them time to see their mistake. Miss Millie will sure put him in his place." Then he stepped over and whispered in Miss Hannah's ear.

She nodded, then turned back to the visitors. "Excuse us just a minute, please." The ladies gathered together for a quick conference, then several giggled before turning their attention back to the men.

Blake sipped his coffee. *Who knows, maybe I'll get lucky for a change. Haven't I wished a hundred times during this trip to be rid of Mrs. Jinx? And here's a dumb bastard willing to take her off my hands.*

He wasn't sure whether to feel sorry for Miss Millie or for this poor boob who thought she was some helpless little twit. If ever there was a woman who wouldn't take kindly to being looked after, it was Millicent Watts. He sat back. Johnny was right, this should be a good show.

"An' I's kinda partial to blue eyes, so that one right there will do me jest fine," Horace said, pointing to Emily.

Millie and Emily looked at each other. "How'd we get so lucky?" Millie whispered under her breath. Emily shrugged. They both moved forward, looking the two men over as if they were bugs under a glass.

Emily tapped her cheek with her finger thoughtfully. "Well, I, for one, insist that my husband take a bath every night."

"Me, too," Millie agreed. "And I simply cannot abide liquor of any kind. My man would have to faithfully promise never to touch the stuff again."

"Oh, yes," Emily chimed in. "Under no circumstances will spirits be allowed anywhere near any man I take to wed."

Both men gasped.

Gus turned almost white, in spite of all the dirt and grime that clung to him. "A bath? *Ever' day*?"

"No *whiskey*?" Horace screeched in horror.

Gus turned to Blake. "Now, see here. Everyone knows womens is notional. They needs to be tol' what's good fer 'em." He pointed to Millie and Emily. "We'll take them two and won't hear no more about baths and no whiskey."

Over my dead body, thought Millie. She stepped closer, then wished she hadn't as a gust of wind blew past. "Let's get something straight from the beginning. No one tells me what to do, ever. I didn't come halfway across the continent to marry some social outcast and live from one campfire to another. If you want that kind of a wife, you certainly won't find her on this wagon train."

"Don't you backtalk me, bitch." He raised his hand to strike her. When next he opened his eyes, he was lying on the ground, flat on his back.

He shook his head. "What…what happened?"

"She done it," Horace whined. "She jest grabbed yer arm and pushed ye over like you was a rotten tree."

Millie stepped up and pressed the barrel of her rifle against Gus's bulbus nose. "I wouldn't have you if you were the only man on earth," she said.

Though the wind was cold, beads of perspiration dotted Gus's forehead. "Donovan, git her offen me."

Blake stepped to where the man could see him and shrugged. "Not me, man. You see, we sorta created our own monsters. In teaching these women to take care of themselves on this trip, they became very self-reliant. There isn't a woman among them who can't shoot a fly at fifty paces."

"You did *what*?" Gus squealed.

"And you, being much bigger than a fly, would be an easy target," Millie assured him as she stepped back. "Now, get out of here. We don't want the likes of you."

Emily poked Horace hard in the stomach with the barrel of her rifle. "You, too. Git!"

Both men scrambled to their feet, grabbed their cups from the ground where they'd dropped them, mounted, and rode away as fast as they could.

As soon as they could no longer be heard, everyone burst out laughing.

****

Gus took a pull on his last jug of whiskey. He and Horace had been nursing their wounded pride for the last two days while keeping the wagons in sight. "They ain't gettin' away with runnin' us off. I took a shine to that little yeller-haired gal, an' I'm damn well gonna 'ave her."

Horace took a long pull from his jug as he squinted at the women in the distance. "I shore 'nough wanna teach that red-haired one a thing or two my ownself. We kin sneak up after they's all asleep, grab 'em both, and no one'll never know. Looks like that there yeller wagon is their'n."

"Yeah, then we'll learn them womens to keep to their place."

****

Gus, along with Horace, crawled closer to the wagons. They'd been watching for several hours, trying to decide where their two women were. Suddenly, Gus grabbed his partner's arm. "Would you look at that," he whispered as Millie poured herself and Emily a cup of tea. "Jest like they's a-waitin' fer us," Horace snickered. "Let's go get 'em."

Gus tightened his hold. "No. Let's give them other womens time to get to sleep. And we gots to do this quiet-like. They's too many gun-totin' females in this camp to suit me."

Horace nodded as Millie and Emily both started walking in opposite directions.

Emily met Millie halfway around the circle. "All's quiet, as far as I can tell. Do you really think those men will come back?"

Millie shook her head. "I hope not. Any more delays and I'll scream. I'm ready to get to that valley and start establishing a life."

"Me too. Be careful when you get to Allyson's wagon. I thought I heard a noise."

Millie nodded. "Probably a night creature prowling around for a free handout." She walked slowly on around the ring of wagons. When she passed her own wagon, a hand clamped over her mouth just as an arm caught her around the waist, pinning her arms to her sides.

Her screams were stifled by the hand. The thick carpet of grass muffled the thud as she dropped her rifle.

Millie clawed at the arm that lifted her off her feet. She kicked as hard as she could. Though she couldn't see her attacker, one whiff of his disgusting odor left little doubt who he was.

She kicked again, this time landing a hard blow to his knee on one leg and one to the shin on his other. He grunted and loosened his hold on her mouth. She bit his hand as hard as she could.

When Gus yelped and released her mouth, Millie screamed as loud as she could. Renewing her struggles, she managed to free one arm, reach behind her, and rake her nails down his face.

Millie heard Emily screaming on the other side of the camp. At least both men wouldn't gang up on one of them. She also heard a welcome honking and hissing from behind her attacker. Gus yelped again as the bird nipped the backs of his legs. Millie jerked free, grabbed the man's hand and arm, and threw him to the ground. Honey rushed forward, wings spread, honking and nipping at her owner's attacker. Homer, though not as aggressive, hissed and honked at his mate's side.

Blake ran up as Gus Scruggs struggled to get to his feet. "Wouldn't take no for an answer, huh?" The angry wagon master grabbed Gus by the shirt front and planted his fist firmly into the man's jaw. Honey flew at the fighting pair. She bit Blake's leg.

"Ouch! Dammit, Duck, get him, not me!" Blake yelled. Honey honked. It could have been an apology, but Blake was willing to bet it was more like telling him to get out of her way.

Gus took advantage of Blake's momentary distraction to jab the wagon master in the gut, then the jaw. Blake staggered backward.

Millie picked up her rifle, swinging at Gus' head. He ducked. Blake, regaining his breath, rushed back into the fight just as Millie swung again. He caught the stock across the shoulder blades, sending him face first into the dust. "Oh, no!" Millie dropped the rifle. She dropped to Donovan's side. "Blake, Blake! I'm so sorry! Are you hurt?"

He shoved her aside and struggled to his feet. "Lady, sometimes it's hard to tell which side you and that damn *duck* are on," he snapped.

Honey, evidently not willing to let the fight end, flew at Gus. He caught the bird around the neck. "Iffen I can't have her, I'll take you," he told the bird as he started to run.

"He's got Honey," someone screamed. Blake whirled, drew his gun, and shoved Cindy out of his line of fire. "Oh, no, you don't. That's my Thanksgiving supper, damn you!" He fired, hitting Gus in the arm. The man screamed and dropped the goose. Blake started forward, but Horace struck him from behind, sending him sprawling to the ground, his head hitting something hard.

"Blake," Millie cried as she dropped to the ground, rolled him over, and gently pulled his head onto her lap. She tapped his face several times. "Blake! Blake, speak to me!"

He opened his eyes. A sea of feminine faces hovered over him. He looked around groggily. His head rested in *Millicent the Jinx*'s lap. Blake? Had she actually called him by his name? It was almost worth a whoop. Then he remembered Honey.

He quickly sat up, grabbing the nearest arm when his head seemed to be spinning on his shoulders. "Where are they?"

"You and Honey chased them off," Millie answered.

He tried to shove the women aside. "Did he get her?"

"No," Miss Hannah said. "Both Emily and Millie are right here, safe and sound."

"Good. Fine," said Blake hurriedly trying to see past them. "What about *the duck*? Did he get her?"

In answer to his question, Honey waddled through a forest of pantlegs, past the women, even past Millie, and gently nibbled at his cheek.

The universe seemed to stand still. No one breathed as Honey squatted in Blake's lap and rubbed the top of her head against the underside of his chin. Hardly daring to believe what was happening, Blake looked up at the equally astonished Millie. Slowly he brought his hand up to lightly stroke the large bird's neck. "Are you all right, Duck?"

Honey honked and closed her eyes.

After several minutes of astonished silence, Blake swallowed a lump from his throat. "She likes me," he whispered. "I think she finally likes me."

"Why, you traitor," Millie said as she playfully tugged on her pet's bill.

****

Each night for the next two weeks, the women worked feverishly on their clothes. And every night the men sat around their own campfire eating Ezra's cooking.

Blake stared across the wagon circle at the women huddled around their campfires, eating and talking. He turned and joined the other four men at Ezra's fire. "What do you suppose they're plotting over there?" he asked no one in particular.

John Eagle made room on the log for Blake to sit down. "Don't know, but you'd think, after all we've been through, they'd at least feed us. We might as well not be here."

"Yeah," Ben agreed. I'm starving, but do you think they care?"

"Starving, my ass," snorted Ezra. "Ye big galoots jest et a whole pot o' stew."

Ben laughed and shook his head. "It's not food we're starving for, you ol' coot, it's their company."

Ezra tossed his spoon in the empty stew pot. "Yeah, Me, too. Why, Miss Elsa tol' me she wouldn't have time to cook for me no more. That I should do my own from now on."

After the men dropped their dishes in the wash pot, they sat around talking and sipping their coffee. Finally, Blake turned to John Eagle. "Have you seen any sign of anyone following us, or lurking around the camp at night?"

"No, looks like—at least I hope, we won't be having any more trouble between here and the valley."

"Well then," Blake said as he stood and adjusted his hat, "let's take a stroll around camp, and I'll call it a night. First thing in the morning, I plan to hit the trail. Wanna be sure they're ready for us on the other end. Think you can handle things from here on, Johnny?"

"Sure, cousin."

Millie looked up to see all five men heading their way. "We're about to have company, ladies. Better put your unmentionables away."

Several of the women folded and put away things they were mending. With nothing else to do, they got up and loaded five plates with dessert.

"Good evening, gentlemen. Could we interest you in some dessert?" Miss Hannah asked.

The men looked at each other, then smiled and nodded.

Miss Elsa smiled shyly and handed Ezra a plate of apple strudel. "I vas hoping you vould come by, Ezra. I haff miss you."

Speechless, Ezra accepted the offering. "I…I missed ye too, Miss Elsa." He looked at his plate. "Did ye cook this?"

She nodded. "Ja."

"'Course ye did. I can tell jest by smelling it. This here's a mighty big helpin'. Would ye share it with me?"

Blake watched them walk off to the darker side of the camp before he cleared his throat. "Ladies, are you about ready to see your new homes?"

Everyone began talking at once. "Are we really that close?" someone asked. "When will we get there?" someone else wanted to know.

Blake raised his hand for silence. "Ladies! Ladies, please, hear me out." When they became quiet, Blake continued. "Yes, we're pretty close. I figure, with no more trouble or delays, we should be there in a week, more or less. I'll be leaving in the morning to alert the men in the valley that we're near and to get everything ready. Also, to make new arrangements for your living quarters. When we started this, the men expected you to be married as soon as you got there. However, since you've insisted on being courted first, we have to change a few things."

Winifred stepped forward with her hands on her hips. "By your tone, Mr. Donovan, I take it you don't approve of our wanting to get to know the men we're to spend the rest of our lives with, before we marry?"

"No, Miss Winifred, I'll admit I didn't at first, but after getting to know you ladies, I think it's a good idea. So unless you want to be sleeping under a tree somewhere, I need to get to town ahead of you to make a few changes."

Millie stared at Mr. Donovan with mixed feelings. She was as excited as all the others about getting to her new home. However, it also meant the prospect of taking a husband was close at hand. If she refused to do so, would they force her to leave the valley?

"Millie? Millie?"

"Wha...what?" Millie was pulled out of her deep thoughts by Emily. "I'm sorry, Emily. What did you say?"

"My word, Millie, where were you? I've been trying to get your attention for the last several minutes."

"I'm sorry. I was just...just thinking about what the future holds for us. It was all so exciting when we started, but now that it's really here...well..."

"I know what you mean," Emily said. "All the plans we've been discussing day after day are about to come true. It's both excitin' and frightenin'."

****

Dawn was creeping across the sky as Blake finished saddling Thunder. He was about to mount when a cup of hot coffee was shoved under his nose. "Thanks, Ez...Miss Hannah? What are you doing up at this hour?"

Hannah, in her nightgown and robe, handed him an envelope. "I'd like you to give this to my husband when you get to the valley, if you please. Among other things, I've tried to explain how these women feel about waiting to marry." She grinned at him. "Maybe it'll keep the men from lynching you."

He drained his cup, then smiled ruefully as he handed it back to her and took her letter. "Thanks. I just might need all the help I can get."

He mounted, then tipped his hat and rode off.

Chapter Twenty-Seven

Cowboys raced across the valley from all directions as Blake rode into town. How in hell did they know he was here? If they'd had this kind of warning system during the last war, the South might have won. He waved and nodded as he rode into town. There were some strange faces here and there, but most were the men he'd ridden with for the last several years.

Blake looked around. Since he'd gone back East for the brides, the men had built a real town. There was a row of buildings on each side of the street. All appeared to be empty except for a feed store, a mercantile, and a freight office. There was also a church and a schoolhouse being built at one end of town.

He pulled up in front of a jailhouse, which appeared to be finished except for the bars, where a group of men were waiting for him. Before he could dismount, he was mobbed with questions.

"Where are the women? Why didn't you bring them with you? They are coming, aren't they?"

A man pushed through the crowd. "Hold it. At least let the man get off his horse, for heaven's sake."

Blake stepped down. "Thanks, Ed. Everything seems to be going all right here."

"Yeah, but you'd better explain your being here without the women. These men have been driving me crazy for the last several weeks."

Blake pulled a letter out of his saddlebag. "Miss Hannah sent this. Said it'd explain everything to you."

"Quiet down, men," Ed said. "Give me a chance to read this letter from my wife. As soon as I know what's going on, I'll tell you."

The cowboys grumbled, but little by little, they stood silently while their boss read.

Blake looked around the town. It was a whole town, the row of buildings on each side of the street complete with boardwalks. He noticed how the church and schoolhouse were at one end of town and the sheriff's office at the other. Right in the middle of town was the frame of what looked like a two-story building, probably a hotel. It was a nice layout. He could imagine all the stores in full operation, with men, women—couples— strolling up and down the boardwalks, taking care of business.

Couples. Would he be one of those couples? Did he want to be part of a couple? He was going to be the law in this new town. Being sheriff was at best an iffy occupation. Until now, he'd felt it was wrong to subject a wife and maybe a couple of kids to that kind of uncertainty. But he'd thought of the women as helpless, clinging little things who couldn't take care of themselves if their lives depended on it. However, he'd never met anyone like...

"Okay, men. Here's what my wife says. The women are camped at the oasis just outside the valley. They want to get cleaned up before they meet us. We can expect them tomorrow afternoon."

Everyone began talking at once.

"I can't wait. Let's go meet 'em," one of the cowboys yelled.

As the men ran for their mounts, Blake fired his pistol in the air. "I wouldn't do that. The women said they'd shoot anyone they caught within rifle range, and believe me, they won't miss. Every one of those women are crack shots." Then he turned to Ed. "You'd better tell them the rest, Ed."

"What do you mean, 'tell us the rest'?" someone shouted.

Ed rubbed the back of his neck. "Well, seems the women have changed the rules a bit."

"You mean they ain't gonna marry us after all?" another cowboy asked.

"No, yes, well, not exactly. Seems they don't intend to marry a stranger. They want to get to know their men, have a say in who they marry. In other words, they want to be courted."

There were angry murmurs through the group, and Blake heard comments like, "You're joshing." "That ain't part of the deal." "Well, we'll see about that."

He stepped up onto the boardwalk beside Ed and held up his hand for quiet. "Hold on, men. If you were in a town back East and met a pretty girl, wouldn't you expect to court her before standing before a preacher? Well, these women are no different. When they marry, it's for life. But there's no one they know to introduce you, no parents to check your background or your folks, no one to be sure you're good, decent men. They have to do it all themselves. It's scary for them. They want to be sure it's a good match. Think about it. Isn't having a good match worth a bit of courting?"

The men muttered among themselves. "Yeah, it's worth it to me," one young cowboy said. "My folks were happily married for over forty good years before they died. That's what I want, too."

Ed grinned. "You men can do as you think best, but I haven't seen my wife in three years. If I don't smell better than I do now, I might not see her for another three. I need a bath."

Blake watched as the men laughed and began to scatter for their own ablutions. "Hey, we have one more problem to solve." When they turned to look at him, he shoved his hat back on his head and grinned. "Might be nice if we had somewhere to bed down fifty beautiful little gals."

"Forty-nine," Ed said. "I already know where one of them is going to bed down."

Everyone laughed. "Well," the preacher said, "we could turn two or three of the empty stores into bunkhouses for them."

"Yeah, we have all them beds waiting for the hotel to be finished. Might as well put them to use."

"Great idea," Ed said. "We have until tomorrow afternoon to get it done. If we all work together, it shouldn't take that long."

"Yeah," said a dark-haired man from the back of the crowd. "By then, we really will need that there bath."

****

Blake stood in front of the jailhouse, watching the wagons roll in, Miss Millie's in the lead. "Of course," he muttered. The men waited, hats in hand, as the wagons pulled to a stop. Cowboys stood staring at the women, all of whom looked back.

Miss Hannah finally stood up in the second wagon. "Well, we've come a long way. Isn't anyone going to invite us to step down?"

As if someone shouted, "Go!" the race began. Men

rushed the wagons nearest them, introducing themselves and helping the women down. One cowboy reached up for Miss Millie and Honey flew at the hapless man.

Blake resettled his hat and rushed to the cowboy's aid. "Man, you have to get on the good side of that goose before you can get near Miss Millie. Better let me help her down." *If I can win over a hardened watch goose, how much harder can it be to win this skinny little jinx?*

Thank you for purchasing
this publication of The Wild Rose Press, Inc.

For questions or more information
contact us at
info@thewildrosepress.com.

The Wild Rose Press, Inc.
www.thewildrosepress.com